Implied Consent: A Maureen Gould Legal Thriller

Keenan Powell

Three Hooligans Press

Praise for Maureen Gould Legal Thrillers

Praise for *Implied Consent*, winner of the Ippy Gold Medal

Powell has written a book that dares to be legal thriller, family drama, and polemic. Remarkably, she succeeds at all three. – Booklife Reviews, Editor's Pick

Keenan Powell has penned her most memorable heroine to date. Powerful and authentic. *Implied Consent* is a must read! — Bruce Robert Coffin, award-winning author of the Detective Byron Mysteries

Sharp-witted, big-hearted and authentic, *Implied Consent* is a knock-out of a novel from a writer who knows both the letter of the law and the messiness of real life. Treat yourself - you won't regret it. — Catriona McPherson multi-award-winning author of *In Place of Fear*

Praise for *The Millionaire*

Book two in the Maureen Gould legal thriller series will keep you up into the wee smalls! The author, a lawyer herself, invests private attorney Gould, her prosecutor husband Jake, and daughter Quinn (an attorney wannabe) with such authenticity that I feel they are family. I even adore their kitty Germaine Greer. The court scenes explode as Gould defends Tony Paredes, accused of murdering his former coach Oscar, who raped him at school. Oscar's wife contends Tony is guilty. Senior Prosecutor Vivian Thandie, who has never lost a case, agrees. Gould fights for justice, all the while contending with her own scars as an abuse victim. I was so gripped as the taut story unspooled that I skipped meals and virtually ignored my husband (sorry, babe). If you love legal thrillers that are smart, jet-paced, and ring with such truth that you can't put them down, THE MILLIONAIRE is for you. Highly recommended! — Char Jones, Reviewer

Powell's second Maureen Gould thriller (after *Implied Consent*) packs a wallop. Trial lawyer Gould now represents Tony Paredes, a young man accused of murdering his abusive childhood chess coach, Oscar Wenderholm. Despite a successful prior trial against his coach, Tony and Maureen faced an overturned verdict due to a technicality; now under arrest on suspicion of Oscar's murder, Tony is imprisoned and brutally beaten, giving Maureen added incentive to save him. Meanwhile, Maureen's own difficult childhood rears its ugly head, making the case exponentially more taxing. -Booklife Review

To: HK

Thou findest not one that could equal his splendour, his fame and his voice, his shape and his power, his form and his speech, his strength and his feats and his valour.

Contents

Chapter One

I LOVE THE LAW. The law is my life.

When I stepped out of the courthouse, microphones were thrust in my face. Television cameras jockeyed for a better angle while besuited young women and men gazed up at me, cell phones cradled in hand, poised to thumb my words to the masses.

Woe befalls she who misspeaks on a hot mic. I rehearsed soundbites silently.

An old glory-hound once said to me, "Maureen, if you want to get on-camera, give reporters short phrases that can be cut up into soundbites. And if you don't, talk in long-winded, Latin-laced nonsense."

I wanted on camera.

I set my briefcase down on the cement landing, a cue to senior reporter Mickey Wong. She raised a hand. "Ms. Gould, what is your reaction to the verdict?"

"On behalf of my client, I thank the jury." Little red camera lights began to glow. "Today's verdict affirms that sexual harassment will not be tolerated."

Mickey's hand was still up. "Does your client have a statement?"

"He's happy to be vindicated, but no amount of money will compensate him for what he's endured." It's never about the money. But when criminal justice fails, money is the only way society manifests its judgment.

Anthony Paredes—"Tony," to his friends—had been a chubby-faced twelve-year-old when he enrolled in the Lafayette Academy. Tony's parents had chosen Lafayette for the chess club, tutored by a former champion who hadn't quite made it. Tony loved the game and was good at it. His parents hoped that they had another Bobby Fischer on their hands.

The chess coach, Oscar Wenderholm, took a special interest in Tony. Appealing to the parents' ambition, he easily talked them into private lessons.

Young and confused, Tony never told anyone what really went on. He was sixteen years old when the assistant principal found them together. Rather than report the crime,

Lafayette Academy gave Wenderholm a severance package and recommended that Tony be transferred to another school.

After years of therapy, Tony realized what had happened was not his fault. He reported the crime to the police. They took his statement, opened a file, and swiftly concluded they had insufficient evidence to prosecute. Too much time had passed. Evidence disappeared. Memories faded. Case closed.

So he'd called me, the hotshot former prosecutor, now champion for the abused.

A delivery truck rumbled by, earning frustrated glances from the reporters. One young man shouted, "Is it true that Lifetime is planning a movie about your case?"

Lifetime? Good God, no. This wasn't a romance. Netflix, maybe. By the time I got back to my office, I should have messages from *Dateline*, *60 Minutes*, and prospective clients. Splashy wins always lit up my phone lines. I gave the boy reporter a frown and scanned the crowd for another question.

Another reporter raised her hand. "The jury awarded a little over fifty million dollars, the second largest verdict of its kind. Are large awards the trend in alleged sexual harassment cases?"

Here was the trap. Something I said could be cut into a soundbite that made me sound greedy.

"Not alleged. Proven." I was shouting, ostensibly to be heard over the truck's clamor, but, in truth, infuriated by the word "alleged." Juries decided what the truth was.

"Our case was proven. We—meaning the judge, opposing counsel, and I—carefully selected a jury that was committed to fairness to both sides. The jurors worked diligently, and we have complete faith in their verdict."

With that, I hiked my briefcase onto my shoulder and pushed my way through the reporters. Yolanda Martinez, my secretary/paralegal/office mom, was waiting for me on the sidewalk, a red patent leather tote hanging in the crook of her arm. We headed across the street to the parking lot where I had left my BMW. When I saw the yellow fender peeking out from behind a sedan, I pushed the remote start button. She rumbled to life.

"That's my girl," I said, patting my Beemer on the hood.

In the privacy of the coupe, we pulled out our cell phones. A text popped up from my soon-to-be ex-husband. "Answer your goddam calls!" I deleted the message and tossed the phone back into my briefcase.

"Have you heard from Jake?" Yolanda asked.

I spiked her a look.

"He's a good man, and you deserve to be happy. That's all I'm saying."

I jammed Sunny into gear and pulled out onto the street.

"You won, girlfriend."

The case had dragged on for two and one-half years. Reams of motions. Countless hearings. At trial, psychologists explained how a child's mind works, that Tony was not capable of consent, and that his delicate mental state was not pre-existing or faked. It was real, caused by repeated rapes.

Today's verdict was the largest, the most significant case anyone in my family had litigated, earning my place in the Gould mythology alongside my venerated grandfather, the Supreme Court Justice, and my father, the senior partner in the most respected law firm in the state.

I reached for the pearl necklace I always wore to court for luck, checking that it was still there. It had belonged to my maternal great grandmother, Elizabeth Shaughnessy. "You're as smart as any of them and smarter than most," Granny Shaughnessy used to say. She would have been proud of me. The Goulds? Not so much. To them, I was damaged goods. Just like Tony Paredes.

Yolanda took a hard look at me. "So how are *you*?"

Before I could answer, a Gene Krupa drum solo erupted from the cell phone in her hand. A man's voice rumbled from the other side—that of my investigator, Eli Conroy.

"It's for you," she said.

"Put it on speaker."

Eli shouted over my engine roar. "Chief, when are you coming back to the office? We have a situation."

"Tony?" My throat tightened. He had seemed stronger in the past few weeks, but he was still a fragile young man.

"Nah. I dropped him off at his place. Hold on." He spoke to someone, assuring that he would be back in a moment. A door closed. "New client. Found her standing in the hallway outside the office when I got back. Been waiting a couple hours. Has a suitcase. Looks like she's been crying."

"What's her story?"

"Won't tell me. She'll only talk to you. Says Mickey Wong sent her, says you're the only one who can help."

Chapter Two

ELI WAS ON THE couch, fishing magazine in hand. Beyond the glass wall, a young Black woman with braids arranged in a chignon was sitting at the conference table. Yolanda stashed her purse in her desk while I stopped in front of Eli. He dropped the magazine on the side table, stood, and snapped the crease of his pressed jeans.

"Josephine Navarre. She's pretty upset. Her boss fired her this morning. They were staying at the Mark Hopkins on a business trip. Security escorted her to the street at dawn. That's all I got out of her."

I laid my briefcase on Yolanda's desk and led my team into the conference room. "Good afternoon. My name is Maureen Gould. This is my paralegal, Yolanda Martinez. You've already met Eli Conroy, my investigator. Sorry to have made you wait."

The young woman attempted a smile. "Josephine Navarre."

I slid into the chair opposite her. Yolanda and Eli took seats on either side of me. I folded my hands in imitation of my favorite nun in boarding school. "How can I help you?"

Josephine peeked over my shoulder at the open conference room door. Eli got up and closed it.

"I was fired from my job this morning."

Yolanda started taking notes.

"Who was your employer?" I asked.

"The Duke. I mean, Reginald Cleville, the movie producer. Everyone calls him The Duke. We're in town scouting locations for the movie he's shooting next year, *Golden Gate*. Girl tech genius meets boy street artist." She took in our polite smiles. "I know. It's stupid, but I have to start somewhere."

"Tell me what led up to your firing."

Josephine glanced at Eli. "It's hard to talk about. You understand."

I did. "Hey, Eli. We missed lunch. I'm starved. Run down the street and get a round of coffee, will you? Pick up some cookies too, the giant ones."

"You got it, Chief. What kind of cookies?"

"All of them. See you in a bit."

After he left, I turned back to Josephine. "You said Mickey Wong referred you?"

"She said this was your specialty, that you would know how to handle it."

"When did you speak with her?"

"This morning, right after it happened. I don't know anyone in San Francisco. She was on the TV news last night, talking about this big case you have. So I thought she'd know who I could talk to. I didn't know who else to call. I'm not the kind of person who goes running to a lawyer."

I get that a lot. With periodic yammer about frivolous lawsuits, prospective clients need to show me that while other people might be gold diggers, they are not. They were *really* hurt.

"No problem. I'm not sure if I can help you. I might not be the right fit, or maybe you just need advice. I need to hear your story before we can decide what kind of assistance you need."

"But Mickey Wong said you were the only one who could help. I have nowhere else to go." She touched her suitcase. "I can't go back to L.A. like this. My career is ruined."

"Something must have set Mr. Cleville off."

"Last night, we met some bigwigs for a late dinner. The Duke kept calling for more champagne. So there I was, sitting between him and another old guy when The Duke slipped his hand between my legs and started groping my thigh. I have bruises. Do you need to take pictures?"

I wasn't sure I wanted the case yet. "Maybe later. Tell me what happened next."

"Then the old guy on my other side started leering at me. I felt like I was on the dessert menu. So I told them I had to go to the ladies'. But I went back to my room instead. I was kind of hoping The Duke was so drunk, he'd forget about me."

"Did he?"

"I wish. My phone rang around midnight. I had to answer. He's my boss. He sounded normal. He said the bigwigs had given him some ideas we needed to talk about, so I had to come to his suite."

"In the middle of the night?"

"Day and night don't mean a lot in the movie business. So I went. When he opened the door, he was wearing a bathrobe."

Yolanda looked up from her notes and gave me a side glance. Josephine caught her expression. "Seriously, it's no big deal. I'd seen him prance around in the buck before. Exhibitionist, whatever. I sat at the dining table where we usually worked. He said, 'No, over there,' and pointed to the couch. So I moved. He sat down next to me. Opened his robe. Then he grabbed me by the back of the neck and shoved my head down. Do I have to say it out loud?" She covered her mouth with one hand.

"Did he want you to perform oral sex?"

"He made me. But I started gagging. Next thing I know, I'm on the floor and he's coming at me. So I kicked him. Maybe I shouldn't have done that, but it stopped him long enough so I could get the hell out of there. That's when I heard some giggling behind the bedroom door. It sounded like a couple of young girls. I went back to my room. Laid awake trying to figure out how to go home without making him mad. I could come up with a story, like my mother was in an accident.

"Then the landline rings. It was security, telling me they were in the hall and I had to let them in. One of them blocked the doorway, like I was going to run away, while the other guy watched me pack. Did they think I was going to steal the towels? As if. They steered me through the hotel, one on each side, like I was a prisoner. Then, when we got to the sidewalk, they told me I would be arrested for trespassing if I tried to come back in."

Hell, yes, I wanted this case. "Yolanda will print our fee agreement. Do you need to take a quick break?"

Josephine shook her head. Yolanda left the conference room. A few moments later, I heard the printer grinding out paper.

"I don't know anything about lawyers," Josephine said. "I mean, I know you go to court, but what exactly happens?"

"We can file a lawsuit for damages, that means an award of money, to compensate you for your lost income, your mental anguish, and to punish the wrongdoer."

"But I don't have any money to pay you."

"No worries, most folks don't. I can represent you on a contingency fee basis, where I receive a percentage of the recovery. It's all set out in the fee agreement."

"And how long does it take?"

"It could be over next week, if they settle, or go on for years. It depends on how the defendants want to proceed."

"Okay, fine, but I want this over fast as possible. And I don't want anyone hearing about this. Is there some way to keep it secret?"

Sexual abuse victims drown in shame. The only escape is to confront what happened, but that would put the spotlight on them. Like Tony Paredes, they're afraid of being blamed. So they're trapped with their secret. Abusers count on it.

The scars on my arm began to itch. I rubbed my sleeve, trying to satisfy the urge to scratch. Josephine's eyes followed my movement.

"Bug bites," I said. "Look, I've been working on sexual harassment cases a long time. I used to prosecute them. And as satisfying as it was to put bad guys away, I felt like I wasn't helping the victims. That's why I opened my own practice. Nothing is going to erase what happened to you. But I'll try help you start a new life."

"I just want it all to go away."

"The quickest way through is to make a settlement offer. Is that what you want?" It might work. Hardly ever does, but it makes the clients feel better for having tried.

"And then I can go back home and go back to work?"

"I don't see why not."

"And you promise not to file suit unless I say it's okay?"

"It's your life and your case. I work for you. Nothing will be filed unless you say so."

"Great, let's do that."

Yolanda returned to the conference room and slipped the fee agreement in front of Josephine.

"Where do I sign?"

"Hold on," I said. "You need to read the agreement, be sure you understand it, and ask me any questions you have. I'll give you a few minutes to look it over."

YOLANDA FOLLOWED ME OUT. As she settled behind her desk, I grabbed my briefcase and wandered down the hall to my office. Eli was seated in my chair, curled up in front of my computer. His bear paw-sized hands danced across the keyboard.

He moved to get up. "I dropped the food in the kitchen."

"Stay where you are. I only have a few minutes." I wanted to enjoy the view. An antique partners desk, bookcases, and oxblood-colored leather chairs and couches were crammed into the space. The corner windows overlooked brick buildings and rooftops, with Coit Tower in the distance.

Against my father's advice, I had used part of the Granny Shaughnessy inheritance to buy the office condo. He'd said it would be smarter to invest the money and rent an office, so I could move more easily. But I wanted roots. I found this small unit, just big enough for me and a paralegal, in a historic Jackson Square building and filled it with furniture that was too heavy to carry. There wasn't an office for Eli so he used whatever desk was available.

"Find anything?" I asked Eli.

"The Honorable Reginald Cleville likes to get his picture taken." He rolled his chair aside so I could see the monitor: a portly, balding man in a tuxedo jacket and a kilt. His arm was wrapped around the waist of a deeply-tanned, dark-haired woman whose dress "barely covered her assets," as Granny would have said.

"Who's the woman?"

"No name given." Eli swiped through similar pictures depicting the same man, gaining weight and losing hair, posing with never the same woman twice but all of whom resembled the first. As he aged, the women remained preternaturally young.

"He goes for a certain type," I said.

Eli grunted in agreement.

Chances were this was not the first time Cleville had assaulted a young woman. "Strange he should cycle through women so quickly. Do you think you could track some of them down?"

"Absolutely."

"What have you found so far?"

Eli pulled out a steno pad from his shirt pocket and read his notes. "Reginald Louis Phillip Cleville, the ninth Marquess of Haverfordwest. Parents sent him to school at Eton, then he spent a year plus at University of St. Andrews in Scotland. Next thing you know, he's in London, carrying some financier's briefcase by day and lighting up the clubs at night. Drops out of sight, then turns up in New York. Started Crown Productions. Released his first film, *The Seven Sorrows of Merlin*, to 'modest critical reviews.' Then he started cranking out movies, about one a year. Each new picture had a bigger budget and more revenue."

"You got all that in just a few minutes?"

"It was on his Wikipedia page."

"Did Wiki tell you how he gets financing? I read somewhere he was broke. All he inherited was his title."

"Must have investors, right? Don't they all?"

"Right. Tonight can you go by the Mark Hopkins, see if you can talk to these two security guys, find out what they have to say?"

"Most likely they won't talk."

"Try anyway, okay?"

Yolanda walked in. "Josephine's ready for you."

WHEN I SETTLED BACK into the chair opposite my new client, the fee agreement was lying on the table between us next to a plate of cookies. I spun the document around, saw that she'd initialed every page and signed the last.

"Any questions before we get started?"

"So how does this work? Do you call him?"

"I'll send him a short letter. I won't discuss what happened, merely offer to enter into a settlement. If he knows what details we think are important, he'll start conjuring evidence to dispute your story."

"But it's all true. Seriously. How could he come up with evidence to dispute it?"

"People lie for their friends, Josephine. Honest people don't expect them to, but they do. Especially in work environments. Former coworkers' jobs are on the line if they support you. So we won't show them our evidence. We'll just go straight to the negotiations. How much money do you want?"

"Whatever's fair, I guess."

"How about a year's salary and a ticket back to LA? I imagine jobs like yours aren't easy to get. It may take you a while to line something up."

Her entire body stiffened. "That's not much for what I've been through. And you're taking, what, one-third?" She waggled her cellphone. "While you were gone, I saw you got a huge verdict this morning. So what about this guy, Anthony Paredes? Isn't my case worth as much as his?"

To the untrained ear, Josephine would sound greedy, but it's not about money. It is about validation. Clients feel they have been wounded and they need reparation so they can heal. The problem is translating their emotional injury into a mathematical calculation. What is shame worth? One dollar per day? Ten? One hundred? There is no amount. The exercise is absurd. So they pick a symbolic number, meant to represent how aggrieved they feel: the more zeros, the better.

"The facts of every case are different, Josephine. That was a jury verdict. You said you wanted a quick settlement. If you want it over fast, you're going to have to take less than a jury might award."

"I want a million dollars for myself, after you're paid. That's a whole lot less than you got this morning."

I grabbed a chocolate chip cookie and broke off a piece, then pushed back in my chair. "Okay, no problem. We'll ask for two million dollars."

She leaned into the space I had vacated. "You think they'll give it to us?"

"No way." I took a bite, chewed slowly, and washed it down with coffee. "It's not an amount he could write a check for. After he receives our letter, he'll call his attorneys and tell them he has no idea what you're talking about. The lawyers, who don't care he's lying because they have a job to do, will interview your coworkers. They'll look for anyone who will say nothing happened, you made it up. Presto, you're headed for court."

"Seriously? How can you be so sure?"

"Because that is what defense attorneys do. It's their training. Our problem is, once they get to a witness—especially one who needs her job more than she needs to stand up for the truth—they will mold her testimony in his favor and lock her into it."

"I'd be surprised if anyone gets involved. That's the thing about Hollywood. When stuff flies, no one wants it sticking to them."

"Know-nothings are fine. They're better than coached witnesses. Meanwhile, the money guys get involved. At some point they come up with a magic figure for what this case is going to cost them and what they're willing to pay to get out of it."

"When do we find out how much that is?"

"Never. It's their little secret. So honestly, opening with an amount that large—if you want to settle quickly—makes no sense. But if you're ready to commit to the long haul, we should file the case and discuss settlement offers later."

Chapter Three

"I don't know what the right choice is. Seriously, I want it over, but I don't want to walk away with nothing. I need money. I just got out of school and have all these student loans coming due. What would you do?"

Every client asks that question: if something like that happened to me, what action would I take? It sounded like a hypothetical on a college philosophy exam, a simple exercise in logic. Life wasn't that straightforward.

"Hard to say. Going into a legal battle is an intensely personal decision. It involves who you are, where you are in your life, where you're going, and how much you're willing to take on. Make no mistake, starting a lawsuit will be time-consuming and stressful. If you want to give The Duke an opportunity to settle fast, your only choice is to ask for a figure that is easy for him to come up with on short notice."

"I don't know. It's all so new." I had overwhelmed her with too much information. She was approaching mental paralysis.

"How about this? We don't ask for a specific sum. I'll just say we are interested in settling your claim for a fair amount."

"I like that."

"Great. Yolanda's going to settle you in a hotel close by while I get to work. The letter will be delivered this afternoon. I'll give you a call as soon as I know something. Meanwhile don't talk to anyone, most especially the press."

"Not even Mickey Wong?"

Mickey was one of the good guys, but she was still a reporter. We had to lay ground rules before interviews in each and every case.

"Not now. Maybe later."

Yolanda reserved a room for Josephine in a boutique hotel and put it on my credit card, then gave her a lift over there while I drafted the settlement demand.

When Yolanda came back, I sent her up to the Mark Hopkins, telling her she could take the rest of the day off after she delivered our letter. I still had time to make my appointment.

▼

I PARKED SUNNY IN front of the Pacific Heights Victorian, after cruising around the block to make sure my father's Jaguar wasn't nearby. This was my mother's home, inherited from Granny Shaughnessy. When my parents were married, she refused to leave, so my father had been forced to move into his wife's house.

The door was opened before I rang the bell. "Good afternoon, Miss Maureen," the housekeeper said. She was new, meaning she'd been hired sometime after I had gone to boarding school, twenty years before. I had met her a few times, but could not remember her name.

I stepped into the shadowy vestibule, several degrees cooler than the outside temperature.

"She's expecting you," the housekeeper said. She led the way up the sweeping staircase to the second floor, as if I were a guest in the house I had grown up in. I suppose I was. Poor little rich girl. Right, that's me.

She led me to the master bedroom my mother occupied, separately from my father. He had moved down the hall sometime after I left home.

"Thank you, Emily," my mother's voice creaked from somewhere in the gloom.

"Thanks, Emily," I said to the housekeeper, as if I had remembered her name the whole time.

My mother had been born in the four-poster bed, now silhouetted by light streaming through the windows. Dazzled, I couldn't find her but I knew where she would be, sitting up on one side of the bed.

"Come closer," she said. "I can't see you."

My foot caught on an oriental rug. In an obvious attempt to find something to blame my clumsiness on, I searched the vicinity. There was nothing. My childhood, all posture and etiquette instructions and feelings of inadequacy, came flooding back. I hoped she hadn't seen.

"Lift your feet, dear."

She had. My face prickled with sweat. "Honestly, Mother, you should have this thing secured. It's an insurance nightmare."

"As you wish. Now come over here, sit down."

I managed to maneuver around the foot of the bed without ramming into it.

A nurse was sitting in a wingback chair, a paperback in her lap. She slotted a bookmark in place. "Shall I take a break, Mrs. Gould?"

"That will be fine," my mother said, ever the indulgent regent.

My mother wasn't sitting up as I had expected. She was lying on her back, her head plopped on a soft pillow, her dyed auburn hair loose about her face. She raised an arm a few inches and pointed at a chair. "Over there, dear, where I can see you."

Her skin was ashen.

"Are you okay?" I asked.

"Just having a bad day. Good days, bad days. That's how these things go."

I hadn't visited as often as I should, but I had the feeling there were no good days, just worse days. I didn't need to ask what the doctors had said. I already knew. They had made their final pronouncement weeks ago: make her comfortable.

"I understand congratulations are in order."

I had forgotten about this morning's verdict. "Oh, right. Thank you."

"Is your client happy?"

"Stunned, to be honest. When the jury comes back, it's like getting off a rollercoaster ride. The good news is that I have more time to visit. Is there anything I can bring you? I drove by the Ferry Building this morning. The vendors have tulips." I caught myself prattling and stopped before I was told.

"I would like that. Yes, please, next time bring tulips." Her voice was so creaky it was difficult to hear her.

"Do you need a drink of water?"

She made a slight movement. It could have been a nod.

Plastic bottles cluttered her marble-topped nightstand. I found a cup with a straw piercing its lid. As I sat on her bedside, she groaned.

I jumped to my feet. "Sorry, am I hurting you?"

She shook her head. "I need some help sitting up, if you don't mind."

I slipped a hand beneath her shoulders and slowly lifted, then brought the straw to her lips. She weighed less than a pile of law books. The bones of her spine crackled as she tried to curl her neck. She took a small sip and swallowed with all the concentration she could muster. After that had gone down, she whispered, "Enough."

I lowered her onto the pillow. She stared up at the copper-coffered ceiling, struggling for breath. "The nurse gave me some pills just before you came. It will be all right soon."

The four-poster bed had been the pride of the home, imported from England and ferried on a boat around Cape Horn. It was a rickety old pile of lumber now, long past its value as an antique, but still strong enough to support the weight of one old woman dwindling away.

When I was little, it had looked like a castle with its ornately carved posters. I had played hide-and-seek with the maid, me wiggling around under the sheets while she pretended she couldn't find me. It was so tall, pirates could bury their treasures underneath, safe in the knowledge their hoard was hidden, until that treasure, a forgotten half-eaten bologna sandwich, made its presence known.

My eyes swept over the room. Upon the fireplace mantle were two silver candelabras, one with a small dent at its base. When I was little, I had stretched up to lift it. I wanted to look at the design. It was heavier than I expected, and I dropped it on the hearth. It bounced and clattered until it landed on a rug. I started to cry, worried that I would get into trouble. The maid comforted me by saying that no one would notice. Later, when my mother discovered the damage, the maid said she had knocked it over when dusting. My father had wanted to fire her, but my mother refused. I think she knew the maid had taken the blame to protect me.

Something was amiss, but I couldn't put my finger on it. The room in all aspects seemed identical to how it had appeared in my youth. Silver gleamed and crystal sparkled, even if the rugs and drapes were starting to fray. Then I noticed a ghost on the wallpaper, a place where a picture had once hung.

Growing up, I had been fascinated by the small Diego Rivera landscape over the bedside table. The story went that Rivera had been painting murals in San Francisco in the early 1930s, before the Golden Gate Bridge was built. One day, The City was enjoying atypical sunny weather. Granny, sensitive to his south-of-the-border need for light and warmth, rescued Rivera from his drudgery with her chauffeured Bentley, a picnic basket, and a bottle of Italian wine.

They drove around San Francisco with the top down until he commanded the driver to stop. He clambered out, field easel in tow, and began a picture of the pre-bridge Golden Gate. The painting showed where the two peninsulas pointed to each other, with the brown hills of Marin County rolling away from blue bay waters. Thus they spent the afternoon, supping upon cheeses and wine, while he daubed oils upon a small board and she witnessed his genius bring forth creation.

After the light had faded, the chauffeur drove them back to his hotel. There, in the back of the Bentley sitting next to Granny, Rivera presented her with the painting. "A small picture *para una bella dama*—for a beautiful lady." Or so the story went. As a child, I wondered if the truth was more prosaic. As an adult, I toyed with the idea that the real story might have been more salacious.

Granny had hung that small painting over her bedside table so she could see it the first thing in the morning and the last thing at night, and the strength of her personality was such that her descendants did not dare to move it. Now, in that place where the painting should have been, was a small oyster-colored rectangle.

"Where did the Rivera go?"

My mother's breathing had become regular. "Your father took it out for cleaning."

"How nice of Frank."

One side of her mouth tightened. It was the gesture she made when she said, *Don't be like that, dear.* "For the life of me, I don't know why you use his first name. He is still your father."

"It started when you sent me away."

A light breeze lifted the curtains, carrying in children's laughter from a nearby playground.

She said, "You used to be daddy's little girl."

"A long time ago."

"So it was." A few moments later, her body arched with pain.

"What is it? Should I call someone?"

"No. It will pass." She squeezed her eyes shut. "Before you go, there's something in the drawer for you." She nodded almost imperceptibly towards the bedside table.

When I opened it, I found a manilla envelope with my name written on it. "What's this?"

"Don't open it now. Later, when the time comes."

It had to be her will. I had assumed she appointed Frank as her personal representative. There was no need for me to have a copy. "But –"

She grimaced as she adjusted her position. "I'm so very tired, Maureen. So very tired."

Should I hold her hand? I didn't know. We were never a demonstrative family, even in the best of times. I folded my hands in my lap. Sunlight glided across the floor in skewed shapes until only shadow filled the room.

The door opened. A switch was flicked and the chandelier began to glow. The nurse crossed the room and stood beside my mother, taking her pulse. "She's resting comfortably."

I heard quiet snoring. My mother's face had softened. The tension from pain, physical and otherwise, had drained away, and I could see why so many had remarked upon her beauty. Even like this, drugged and emaciated, she had a grace about her.

"She'll sleep for a few hours," the nurse said.

It was time for me to go. "I'll be back tomorrow."

"I'm certain she will enjoy that."

When I stood, the nurse said, "Don't forget the envelope. She said it's important."

Chapter Four

My feet ached. All I wanted to do was kick off my heels and feel the cool concrete floor of my loft. As I slipped the key into the lock, the door drifted open. I was sure I had locked it that morning, both the knob and deadbolt. Not crossing the threshold, lest an intruder leapt out at me, I nudged the door open with my shoe.

Germaine Greer, the Siamese my ex had given me, wandered across my view, flicking her tail, and sauntered down the hall. The sound of gliding metal reached me as an unseen closet door moved across its rails. Footsteps echoed. A man's low voice cooed. The cat purred.

Jacob Kuhn, my soon-to-be ex, was in my home.

I stepped inside and slammed the door shut. The cat hissed, thumped to the floor, and skittered away. I hoped she'd scratched him.

He stepped into view. Six foot. Athletic. Black hair. Square jaw. Lightning-white teeth. He wore faded blue jeans, and, on the broadest shoulders I'd ever seen, a San Francisco Police Department t-shirt, a memento of his time on the force before law school. I felt a tingle in the bottom of my stomach.

"So, you're home," he said.

"So, you're breaking and entering."

"Technically, Red, *no*." He drew out the last word. "I have a key."

Sparring with another lawyer was not what I had imagined for my evening but arguing was who I was. He'd known that when he married me. "Technically, Jake, *yes*. Your name is not on the title, since I bought it before we were married."

"The judge said we were to set up a mutually agreeable time so I could get my stuff, but you don't return my calls."

"I was in court."

"Congratulations are in order, I hear." Jake rubbed the hand Germaine Greer had scratched. That was what he got for coddling the cat that was supposed to be mine. He flopped on the couch and threw his feet on top of the coffee table, furniture we had picked out together.

I dropped my briefcase on the floor, peeled off the blazer that was sticking to me, and dropped it on the granite counter of the combination kitchen-living-dining room. The open concept design was one big airy box with artistically swirled concrete floors and urban chic pipes overhead. I wasn't sure whether the pipes functioned or they were just a twentieth-century version of crown molding.

I kicked off my heels and sent them flying across the room.

"Missed," he said.

"Wasn't trying. Wine?"

"If you're buying."

"You pour while I change." I started unbuttoning my shirt before I walked out of the room.

"Need any help?"

I slammed the bedroom door. To say I was conflicted would be an understatement.

The man still made my heart patter. But I had felt trapped by our marriage. It wasn't anything he did. By the time the wedding afterglow had burned off, he was just a normal man going about his business, hanging his clothes in my closet, taking showers in my bathroom, eating over my kitchen sink. Normal stuff. Whatever was wrong was inside of me.

I stripped, hung my bra on a doorknob, then shimmied into an old, thin t-shirt and running shorts. Mixed signals, I knew. Wrong of me, without a doubt. But I yearned for the intimacy I had with Jake. It had been a long time.

As I padded out in my bare feet, he followed my entrance, a wineglass held to his lips. I picked up the goblet he'd left on the coffee table for me and sat just within arm's reach.

"Hello, beautiful lady. Come here often?"

I took a sip of the Chablis. "Just on weekends."

"It's Wednesday." He reached down, gripped my feet, and pulled them into his lap. I lay back on the couch while he massaged.

"Tell me about your day." I wanted to hear every monotonous, mind-boggling ridiculous bureaucratic protocol and umbrage-taking that came with working in the District Attorney's office. We had met there when we were both prosecuting.

"Just your basic dragon-slaying stuff," Jake said. "Combing through spreadsheets, looking for assets buried in money laundering schemes, hunting for secret investors."

I snorted.

"Someone's got to do it."

"I know. It's important work but sounds funny the way you talk about it." I propped myself up on an elbow. "Hey, what do you know about this movie *Golden Gate*, how it's getting financed?"

"Never heard of it. Do you know who is involved?"

"Reginald Cleville. I was just wondering where he got the money."

"Looking for deep pockets? Got a new case?"

"If I did, I couldn't tell you."

He squeezed my toe. I squealed and pulled myself to a sit. When he reached to brush my hair away from my face, I caught sight of his wedding band. Mine was in a jewelry box on top of my dresser.

"Could you take that off, please?" I asked.

"It's just a ring."

We'd had this discussion before. Many times.

"It means something special to you, I get that. And I cherish how you feel about me. You're the only person who ever made sense in my life. But the ring makes me uncomfortable. It's like if we're married, we're not us anymore. We're something else. Can't we just be us tonight?"

"Us is all I ever wanted to be, Red." He pulled the ring off and slipped it into his pocket. Then he took both my hands in his own and kissed my palms.

Chapter Five

THE NEXT MORNING, JAKE was still asleep when I woke. I felt a tickle deep inside. Last night had been a new beginning. I wanted him to hold me again. I tugged on the sheet, most of which was wrapped around him.

He twisted to look at me over his shoulder. "Hello, you," he said, sleepily.

"Hello yourself."

He rolled onto his back and made room for me to snuggle. That's when I saw it. He had put his wedding ring back on during the night.

I couldn't breathe. I pushed myself up and sat on the edge of the bed. I was dizzy.

"It's just a ring," he said.

I gawked at the bedside clock. "Oh my God, will you look at the time?"

"It's six A.M." He ran a finger down my spine.

I shrugged his hand away. "Late for my jog."

"Since when do you run?" he asked as I dived into the walk-in closet.

I rummaged for trainers and found a pair on a shelf, brand new. I bit the tags off and tossed them onto the floor. I found some workout clothes in the bottom drawer of the built-in bureau and dressed. When I stepped out, he was pulling on his jeans.

"Got a long day," I said. "Have to hit the office early. You know how it is when you've been in court for weeks. Lots of fires to put out."

"I can take a hint."

"Don't be that way."

"*Me*?"

"It's just—" I started. I would always love him, but the depth of intimacy he expected terrified me. I couldn't tell him why. "I'm sorry."

He whisked past me on his way out. "Me too."

▼

Jake left so quickly, I didn't need to fake the entire jog. I settled for a brisk walk to the coffee pot. After I had showered and dressed, I lingered in front of the hallway closet, wondering whether I should bring a raincoat. I opened the sliding door to see Jake's banker box still on the shelf, with his high school athletic trophies poking out the top.

He'd be back.

When I passed the Ferry Building, the flower vendors had not opened yet. I made a mental note to send Yolanda at lunch to pick out a bouquet for my mother. I parked Sunny in a garage near my building, ran by a café and grabbed a raspberry mocha and the world's largest cinnamon roll, then went up to my office.

After kicking off my heels, the first order of business was clearing the hundreds of e-mails and dozens of messages that had come in while I was in trial. When I got up from my desk to refill my coffee cup, Eli called.

"Went by the Mark last night."

"And?"

"And the security guys say there's company policy against talking about guests, sort of what happens here, stays here. And they don't want to get fired."

"So you got nothing."

"Nada. Sorry, Chief."

I was still standing in the middle of my office, empty coffee cup in hand, computing our next step when Yolanda came in with a messengered envelope. Inside was a letter printed on engraved stationery that bore the standard of Gould and Napier, Attorneys at Law. Only two Goulds practiced in San Francisco. I was one. The other was my father.

Dear Ms. Gould,

Please be advised that our firm represents Reginald Cleville and Crown Productions in respect to your recent demand letter. Your client does not have a valid cause of action. Additionally, as you will see from the enclosed contract, Ms. Navarre is bound by a nondisclosure agreement and arbitration clause. If she files suit, the court would no doubt immediately dismiss it.

Sincerely,

Ian Napier

My father had never entered into a case against me. Ian Napier was his partner, but the use of a minion didn't mean anything. Frank did not know the first thing about harassment cases. When I began prosecuting, he made it clear that sexual abuse law was distasteful. What happened in the privacy of one's own home, or hotel room, or back of a car, or broom closet was not a matter for the courts. The state could not legislate what went on between two people privately.

So how was it that Reginald Cleville had my father's firm on such a short leash that some poor secretary was made to drop everything to get this letter out by lunch time? Someone had stayed up all night, interviewed The Duke, negotiated a fee agreement, discussed strategy, obtained copies of the employment agreement from Crown Productions corporate office, collected the retainer, and wrote this letter.

I tossed the correspondence on my desk and read the enclosure entitled "Employment Agreement." On the last two pages were the two clauses I dreaded: nondisclosure and arbitration. Case killers. I flipped to the last page. It bore the elegant signature of one Josephine Navarre.

"Yolanda!"

She appeared at my door.

"Does this look like Josephine's signature to you?"

She took the letter. "Looks like. I'll get the fee agreement." A few minutes later she handed me the contract Josephine had signed the day before. The signatures were identical.

Josephine hadn't mentioned a nondisclosure agreement. Then again, I hadn't asked—I was too excited. Still pumped from the Paredes verdict, I had plotted the fastest way to another win instead of thinking about possible barriers. The Navarre case would be the biggest and splashiest victory of my career. Hollywood rags to riches story. Real-life royalty. And deep, deep pockets.

A nondisclosure agreement and an arbitration clause could kill the case. Without the looming threat of a public jury verdict, I had no leverage to force negotiations. The quick settlement Josephine had hoped for was not going to happen. A sour taste rose in my throat. I reached for the antacids in my drawer, pried two out of the package, and washed them down with cold coffee.

I pulled my heels back on. "Call Josephine. Tell her you're coming to pick her up."

"When?"

"Now would be good."

▼

JOSEPHINE ARRIVED LOOKING LIKE the lead character in a television legal drama. She wore a short black blazer, white tank, pencil skirt, and three-inch black patent leather heels, and carried a slender briefcase over her shoulder.

After she settled into a visitor's chair, I offered her a copy of the letter and contract. "This came in an hour ago. Did you sign it?"

She flipped through the agreement. "Maybe, but I can't be sure. I signed some papers when I was hired."

"Did you read them first?"

"What was the point? I wanted the job. They said it was no big deal—you know, industry standard."

If she testified honestly that she hadn't read the agreement, she would be painted as a "weasel," someone who would sign anything to sneak her way into Crown Productions. The defense would chant "personal responsibility" through the trial, arguing that when things hadn't gone as she hoped, it was everyone else's fault but her own. Juries love that stuff.

"What the contract says is you promised not to file suit if a disagreement arose. Instead, you promised to arbitrate. That means an arbitrator will decide if you have a case, and if you do, how much you're entitled to. It's binding arbitration which means if you lose, there's no appeal and the case is over."

"So no quick settlement, that's what you're saying."

"Exactly. Besides that, there is an NDA, a nondisclosure clause. You agreed not to discuss your employment with anyone."

Josephine twined her fingers so hard her joints blanched. "Am I in trouble because I came to you?"

"Lawyers are okay. But from the defense point of view, you already violated the agreement when you talked to Mickey Wong."

"Then I'm screwed. Is that what you're saying?"

"Not at all. The right judge could find that this agreement is not enforceable. But to get a decision like that, I have to file suit."

"Can't we make a settlement offer?"

"We tried. They're not interested in settling quick. For all I know, the attorneys don't understand what happened between you and The Duke. He could be telling them anything, hoping you're too ashamed to tell the whole story. Or they do know the truth and they don't care, they're just taking marching orders."

"Why would they do that? How could an attorney defend someone who is guilty?"

"Because that's what they're getting paid to do."

"So it's over."

"Not yet. Listen to me. I can file a lawsuit together with a motion asking the judge to find that both clauses are unenforceable."

"I'm confused. Why would they put something in the contract if it wasn't legal?"

"Those clauses might be enforceable if this was a routine wrongful termination case, but it isn't. It's sexual harassment. You didn't bargain to have someone put his hands on you. It wasn't part of your job. We can arbitrate if that's what you want, but I'm worried about the NDA. If you don't challenge it in court, and they ever think you told anyone, they would come after you for damages."

"You mean he could get money from me? Even if I win? Seriously?"

"That's exactly what I mean."

"How much?"

"The agreement says you will pay him two million dollars."

"So he shoves my head into his whatever. Then he fires me and throws me out in the middle of the night. And I end up paying *him* two million dollars?"

"Galling, isn't it? Look, Josephine, I'm a fighter. If it were me, I'd take this to court, challenge the contract, and ask for a jury trial."

"Or I can go home with my tail between my legs."

"That is your third alternative."

"It isn't right."

"No, it is not right." Clients need time to come to a decision. Ten minutes was plenty. "Can I get you anything?" I grabbed my coffee mug.

She shook her head. I walked down the hall and told Yolanda to clear my calendar for the rest of the day, anticipating I would spend the afternoon drafting Josephine's court documents. I dropped my cup in the kitchen. When I came back, Josephine was composed.

"If the judge does what you said and he lets us sue, then The Duke might agree to a settlement."

"It could happen. But here's the thing. Hoping for a settlement is getting ahead of ourselves. Let's just get this thing filed. Do you agree?"

"I agree. File the lawsuit."

She remained in her chair.

"Is there anything else?"

"Like, what am I supposed to do? I can't just stay in a hotel for however long this'll take."

"We have a lot of work to do and I need you for a few days more. Then you can go back to L.A."

"And what do I tell my mom?"

"That your lawyer said you a brave young woman and she is honored to represent you."

Chapter Six

AFTER YOLANDA TOOK JOSEPHINE back to the hotel, I spent the rest of the day and well into the night drafting the complaint and motion to set aside the NDA and arbitration clauses. I wanted it filed and handed to opposing counsel first thing the next morning. I'd show Cleville and Frank that for every swing they took at me, I'd hit them back harder.

By the time the documents were assembled in neat piles on Yolanda's desk, my eyes burned so much, I couldn't see well enough to drive home. So I dug out the pillow and blanket stashed in the supply closet and lay down on my couch for a few hours of sleep.

The next thing I knew, Yolanda was standing over me. "Ready for company?"

Disoriented and jittery, I pushed myself up. A take-out bag and a large paper cup were waiting for me on my desk. Inside was a cold breakfast croissant, half of which I ate in two bites and washed down with the lukewarm mocha.

I stashed the bag in a desk drawer. "Wait! Where are my shoes?"

"Under your desk."

I tried to slide into my heels, but my feet were too swollen from being up most the night. I had to pound them on.

"How do I look?"

"Like you were run over by a truck."

"Nevertheless she persisted."

Yolanda gave me a wicked grin, then retreated down the hall. A few moments later, she escorted Josephine into my office.

After we settled into our chairs, Yolanda slid a copy of the documents to my client.

"The case was filed this morning," I said. "It will be assigned to a judge today and the file will be routed to his office. Opposing counsel will have the opportunity to respond in writing to our motion and then there will be a hearing. Any questions so far?"

Josephine shook her head.

"Great. Between now and then, I'd like to dive into your background and find out anything you know that could help us develop the case."

"Like what?"

"Your life story. Start at the beginning."

Yolanda took notes while my client spoke. Josephine Isabelle Navarre was born twenty-three years prior in southern California, the oldest of two daughters, to a Hollywood lighting technician and an elementary school teacher. Visiting her father on set, she had become obsessed with behind-the-camera movie making. She had acted in high school productions but didn't enjoy that as much as being backstage, pulling ropes and throwing light toggles.

Her dream was to become an independent film producer. She received scholarships to the University of Southern California. While there, she found an internship with one of the big studios, basically a gofer job, but she worked hard and was noticed. Soon after she graduated, the same studio had hired her as a production assistant, but the threat of layoff was constant due to problems with financing. The Duke came to her workplace one day for a meeting, was impressed, and told her to apply at Crown Productions.

"So tell me about relationships. Romantic. Boyfriend. Girlfriend."

"My personal life shouldn't have anything to do with it. Just saying."

"If you were involved with someone intimately during your employment at Crown, you may have said something to him or her about your job. Or that person may have seen something if they had contact with your coworkers, say at a social event. A disgruntled ex-lover or former best friend can be treacherous. You can bet Cleville's investigators are already looking for these people at this very minute. I'd really like to talk to them first."

"No serious relationships. I dated, but nothing long term. No best friends."

"So tell me about Cleville. Was he friendly?"

"Friendly but we weren't friends, if that's what you mean. He's my boss."

"Any prior come-ons?"

"Like what?"

"Like did he proposition you? Touch you inappropriately? Make suggestive jokes? You said he walked around naked."

"Sure, all the time. But it was no big deal. Like when he got out of the shower or was changing clothes."

"Didn't that make you feel uncomfortable?"

"That's the industry. Artists are a different kind of people. If you don't adapt, you will never make it." She thought for a moment, uncrossed, and recrossed her legs. "There was one thing, one time. It was weird so it stuck out in my mind."

"When did this happen?"

"We were in a pre-production breakfast meeting with the director. There was a buffet set up, coffee and pastries. At some point, he slid an empty cup at me and asked me to refill it. That's when he said it."

"What was that?"

"I like it hot and black."

Yolanda stopped writing. Silence filled the room. A low-flying gull swooped past the window. The constant whine of passing tires on pavement seemed loud. Far in the distance, a cable car bell clanged.

"What did you do?" I asked.

"I got him the coffee."

"Did you say anything in response?"

"I pretended I didn't hear it. I mean, it could have been nothing. It wasn't so much what he said but how he said it that was weird."

It could have been nothing. Or a test, to see if she would object. And it could have been grooming, the first step to normalizing sexual intimacy in their relationship.

"And after that?"

"Nothing."

"When did this happen?"

"Months ago."

I pulled the stack of screen grabs Eli had printed for me out of a file folder. "Tell me about these women. Do you know them?"

Josephine bent over the stack, examined each picture, then set it aside. She paused on the most recent one, a leggy young woman with long dark tresses in a skin-tight sapphire blue gown. "This is Amber LeRoux. She had a supporting role in the picture Duke released last year, *A Summer in Paradise*. She played one of the sisters. She was supposed to play the female lead in *Golden Gate*, but it didn't happen."

"What is she doing now?"

"No idea. I'd heard she took some time off, jetting around with a rich boyfriend in Europe."

"How would we contact her?"

"Through her agent or manager. I could probably dig that up somewhere if you need it."

"That'd be great. Do you recognize anyone else?"

"Sophia Lamar. She was the talk of the town a couple of years ago. She was up for a part in *A Summer in Paradise* but didn't get it. I heard she had gone to London for acting school."

"Why didn't she get the part?"

"Again, no idea. I wasn't involved in the project. You could probably contact her through her agent or manager, or maybe even the school."

My cell rang. The caller ID said Mickey Wong. I swept a thumb across the screen, declining the call. When I looked back at Josephine, she was holding one of the photographs.

"The only other one I recognize is Valerie Vann," she said. "Actually, I had heard they had a thing back in the day."

"Do you know where she is now?"

"I think she quit the business, went back to college to get a degree."

Josephine slid the photographs across the desk to me. The women appeared strikingly similar. Dark skinned. Big eyes. Full lips. Long dark hair. Dressed in elegant gowns so tight I wondered how they could sit down, much less eat.

"Anything else you can tell us?"

"There was talk about the casting couch. But you hear rumors all the time. I never heard anything specific, just warnings from the other girls not to get caught alone with The Duke."

"That should do it for now." I stood. "Thanks for coming in Josephine. I want you to sit tight at the hotel for a few days until we get our hearing date. Then you can go back to LA and fly up again if we need you."

"What am I supposed to do?"

"If you think of anything else, make a note of it and give me a call. If I'm not in the office, you can talk to Yolanda. Otherwise, chill. Watch TV. Read a book."

After Josephine left, I had just enough time to pull the paper bag out of my drawer and gobble down the rest of the breakfast croissant. Then I put in a call to Mickey Wong.

She answered with, "Gould, you filed Josephine's case against Reginald Cleville. No warning. Not feeling the love."

"That was just this morning. I haven't had time to call. How did you find out?"

"We watch for new filings. It's running on the evening news."

"You'll use her initials, right? You won't name her."

"Give me a break, Gould, I know my job."

On the way out, I ran by the kitchen to grab the pink tulips Yolanda had waiting for me on the counter, then stopped by her desk. "Give Josephine a call and let her know the press found out about the case. Mickey's running an item tonight. Let her know there's nothing I can do about the story, but she won't be identified by name."

"She isn't going to like it."

"It's the best I can do. Just let her know."

When I cruised by the mansion, Frank's Jaguar was parked on the street. I kept going.

Chapter Seven

Saturday morning, I cruised the block looking for Frank's Jaguar and didn't see it. I knocked on the door.

Emily the maid greeted me, her face tight. "The missus is resting. She just took her medication."

"I promised her these flowers." I took a step toward the stairs. "I'll just go up and stick my head in, say hello."

Emily made the slightest movement, not blocking my way so much as drawing my attention toward her. "Now isn't a good time. She had a rough night. Maybe later this afternoon, you could drop by?"

I felt the air pressure change. A door somewhere deep in the house had opened.

A slow and steady tapping of shoes came from the direction of my father's den.

Emily's expression became more urgent.

"I didn't see his car," I said.

"It's in the shop, having the oil changed."

I had forgotten about Frank's militaristic schedule of Jaguar maintenance. Someone from his mechanic's shop would have called for the vehicle the first thing that morning and would return it by the end of the day. The work was always performed on a Saturday so he could drive the Jag to work during the week.

Emily gave me a quick, apologetic smile.

It was too late. He knew I was there. If I left before he greeted me, it would look like I was running away. "It's not your fault," I said. "I should have known."

He would appear in a few seconds, wearing slacks, a dress shirt without a tie, a sweater, and wingtips. It wasn't until I met Jake that I learned professional men wore jeans or sweatpants around the house.

As the slap of his leather soles grew closer, the scars on my arm burned. I wanted to scratch them furiously. Instead I tightened my grip on the bouquet.

"Your mother had a difficult night," he said as he stepped out of the hallway gloom into the vestibule. "The doctor came by this morning and gave her an injection. She can't take visitors at the moment. You can leave the flowers with Emily."

The maid gave me a pleading look. I handed her the bouquet.

"Thank you, Emily," my father said.

"Yes sir." She dipped. Was that a curtsy? Did anyone do that anymore? She disappeared toward the kitchen, leaving me alone in the foyer with my father staring at me.

I spun to face him. "I wasn't expecting to see you."

"Put away your hostility for a moment. Do you think you can do that, Maureen? As luck would have it, I'm glad we ran into each other. There's something we need to talk about. This Josephine Navarre case of yours. You should consider a quick settlement, get it over. It would be best for everyone concerned."

Now he wanted to talk? "We made an offer and you demanded arbitration."

"Come now, that's just posturing. You should know that. I'll have a word. We can have this wrapped up by Monday. How much money are you looking for?"

"How much are you offering?"

He gave me his indulgent smile. "Have a word with your client. Come up with something reasonable. I'm sure we can work it out." He turned to walk away.

"How about we let the jury decide, Frank. That's how it's supposed to work."

He stopped. Speaking from the shadows of the hallway, he said, "You don't know who you're dealing with, Maureen. It should have never gotten this far. This movie project is important to San Francisco. If you push too hard, the production could fall through. Millions would be lost."

"That's ridiculous. The City is thriving. Real estate is so expensive, most people are driven out of the market. You have to fight for a parking place. One movie isn't going to make a difference in our economy."

"I'm warning you, Maureen. You do not know what you started."

Reginald Cleville was an impoverished British aristocrat who had refashioned himself into Hollywood royalty. Frank's diatribe smacked of the old English law, The King Could Do No Wrong. Nothing angered me more than the suggestion that abusers should be excused because of their power.

"Is that some kind of threat, Frank?"

He didn't answer. Instead, he disappeared down the hall. Blood rushed in my ears. Dizzy, I touched the wall to steady myself.

▼

I NEEDED TO MEET with Josephine, but I was too tired to go home and switch out of my jeans into something more businesslike. I drove back to the office and let myself in.

I often came into work on the weekend to catch up. I liked having the place to myself. The phone didn't ring. No deliveries. No Yolanda tapping at my door with yet another emergency. As much as I depended upon and loved her, having a few uninterrupted hours to concentrate on files was bliss.

I dialed Josephine's number. When she answered, she sounded groggy.

"We need to talk. Can you grab a cab and come down to the office right away? I just ran into Cleville's lawyer. They want you to make a settlement offer."

"I thought we already did that."

"Not quite. We offered to enter into negotiations. Now they say they want a number."

"Seriously? What's different?"

"They claim they were just posturing, but they would prefer to wind this up by Monday."

"I'll be there in half an hour."

When I greeted her at the door, she said, "Sorry, I was in a hurry. Just pulled on whatever I could find." She was wearing leggings with a tweed jacket and cute little high-heeled boots. A slender briefcase was slung over a shoulder.

I was keenly aware of my wrinkled jeans, t-shirt, and runners. At least they weren't torn or stained. "It's Saturday. No big deal."

I showed her into the conference room and recounted my conversation with Frank, identifying him only as The Duke's attorney. My relationship with Josephine needed to remain professional, so my family problems were out of bounds. I made it sound like he had called the office that morning. She didn't need to know that we were verbally sparring in my mother's home as she lay dying upstairs.

"That's fabulous," she said. "I want this over with. I'm sorry I let you talk me into filing suit. It's going to get blown up all out of proportion. My life will be turned into a circus."

Buyer's remorse was common. In the early days of a case, before the defendant responds and the court schedules hearings, plaintiffs feel like nothing is happening and wonder if they did the right thing.

"When you agreed to file suit, you were concerned about the nondisclosure clause and that you would have to pay them two million dollars if you told your story. Have you reconsidered?"

"I don't want this stuff getting out any more than they do."

"We can get a gag order, Josephine. It's pretty standard in these types of cases. The press would be prohibited from mentioning your name or showing your face."

"But once the case is over, the press can do anything they like? Is that what you're saying? Seriously. I don't want what happened to me getting spread around. Not in court. Not online."

Mickey Wong was not going to be happy if she didn't get an interview, an exclusive one at that. I'd have to make it up to her somehow.

Josephine went on. "I get that this is an everyday thing for you, Maureen. But it isn't for me. This is my *life*. I want my life back. I've been cooped up in this hotel for days. I want this all to go away and I want to go home."

"But what about the penalties clause? The two million dollars if you tell anyone and they find out about it."

"That's just noise. I'm not worried about it. I'm not going to tell anyone—ever."

"Okay, Josephine, okay. It's your case and I work for you. I'll handle it any way you want. How much money do you want me to ask for?"

"I told you. Weren't you listening? I want a million dollars in my pocket after you're paid. You get a third, so ask them for one million, five hundred thousand."

"That doesn't leave you any room to move if they counteroffer."

"Okay, fine. Then two million."

"I understand where you're coming from, but as your attorney it's my job to consider the long game if we don't settle now. Here's the problem with sending a number that high this early in the case. They aren't going to agree to it. They want out cheap."

"My case is not *cheap*. I am not *cheap*. You just got the huge verdict against that school for that Tony Paredes guy. Everyone knows. Two million dollars is a deal by comparison." She reached for her briefcase. "Do you need me to sign something, or can I go?"

After she left, I sent an email to Ian Napier, Cleville's attorney of record, and copied Frank, setting out Josephine's settlement offer of two million dollars.

Josephine called my office twice a day for news. And twice a day, I told her that I'd call her if I heard something. They never responded.

The hearing was inevitable.

Chapter Eight

A FEW WEEKS LATER, I was seated at plaintiff's table with Josephine beside me, Eli in the pew behind us. Josephine had decided to fly home after our last meeting, and he had picked her up at the airport earlier that morning. A thick file waited on the judge's bench.

At the defendant's table sat Reginald Cleville. Beside him, Ian Napier flipped through papers. In the first pew behind them were two men wearing conservative, but expensive dark suits. One looked familiar. He was movie-star handsome with square jaw, broad shoulders, and styled hair. The other was older, doughy, with a combover and thick glasses. LA lawyers, I figured. While we waited for the judge, Cleville leaned across the bar, deep in conversation with the two men.

Otherwise the courtroom was empty. The defense had convinced the judge to seal the proceeding. The nondisclosure agreement would be worthless if the hearing was public and everyone found out about the lawsuit. Until the judge ruled the NDA was unenforceable, if she did, it would be honored. For that reason, the case appeared on the docket identified by initials, so as not to alert the press. The court clerk locked the door after we arrived.

Beside me, Josephine sat erect in her chair, her breath shallow and fast.

I whispered, "Before court, I massage my hands. It helps you to relax." I demonstrated, first massaging the palm and working my way up each finger to the pad. Josephine hid her hands beneath the table and worked them as I had shown her.

Judge Denice Han entered the courtroom through her private door, crossed to the bench, and settled into her chair. She was slender, with black hair pulled into a bun at the nape of her neck. A pair of reading glasses hung on a chain around her neck.

She called for the case to go on record, then addressed Cleville's attorney.

"Mr. Napier, I've reviewed the filings of both parties. At this point, I would like you to explain why I should not grant Ms. Gould's motion for a ruling that the nondisclosure and arbitration clauses are unenforceable."

Napier took the lectern and read from typed notes. "Your Honor, firstly, it's about the sanctity of contract. Parties are entitled to the utmost liberty to arrange their affairs according to their own judgment. Secondly, it's about personal responsibility. Ms. Navarre entered into the contract volitionally. Where would this society be if everyone were allowed to back out of their promises? We couldn't operate. Finally, my client detrimentally relied upon Ms. Navarre's promise to abide by these clauses when he hired her."

Napier turned to the two attorneys in the gallery. They both gave him short nods. He went on. "Movie production is a highly competitive industry, Your Honor. If the particulars of a production are leaked, such as the script, an unscrupulous company could rush a similar story to the theatre, thus capitalizing on Crown Productions' pre-release publicity and usurping ticket sales. By example, Your Honor, when a moviegoer has already seen one space opera, he is unlikely to spend his valuable time and money to watch another one any time soon.

"Thus the monetary value of the project hinges upon secrecy. Ms. Navarre's employment agreement is identical to all of those entered into by Crown Productions. The goal of the contract with Ms. Navarre is to protect the value of Crown's investment."

"Thank you, Mr. Napier. Now the court will hear from Ms. Gould."

As Napier sat down, Cleville greeted him with a pat on the back.

I touched Elizabeth Shaughnessy's pearl necklace, remembering her words: "You're as smart as any of them and smarter than most." I stepped into place at the lectern. "Your Honor, this is not about the validity of the employment contract. The issue is whether the employment contract, even if valid, applies to these facts."

Cleville snorted. Napier stood. "Your Honor, if plaintiff concedes the employment agreement is valid, then I am at a loss. Why are we here? Josephine Navarre was the employee of Crown Productions. She sued Crown Productions and Reginald Cleville. But for her employment, we would not be in court."

The judge said, "That's an interesting point, Mr. Napier. Is it your position that Crown Productions is an alter ego of Reginald Cleville?"

The attorneys behind Cleville inched forward, preparing to stand. This was dangerous territory. If the court found Crown Productions was merely a front for Reginald Cleville, then the company was responsible for anything he did even without proving that its Board of Directors knew or should have known he assaulted his employee.

"Not at all, Your Honor," Napier said. "Crown Productions is a separate entity with an independent Board of Directors who oversees its operations. While Mr. Cleville is a member of the Board and the chief executive officer, every aspect of the business is ultimately decided by the Board. In most respects, he is merely another employee."

"Very well. We have established that Mr. Cleville is Crown Productions' employee. Ms. Gould, please address counsel's point."

Napier sat down. The attorneys settled back into their pew but remained tense.

"Your Honor," I said. "Regardless of how the parties met, the employment contract does not govern all interactions between them. Consider a hypothetical. Let's say Ms. Navarre went to dinner with another production assistant. We will call her Mary Smith. Before the meal is ordered, there is no discussion as to who will pay for the meal. It is Mary Smith's unspoken belief that Ms. Navarre would pay because she suggested dinner. However, Ms. Navarre believes that each will be responsible for their own tab because she did not explicitly offer to purchase Mary Smith's meal. Does the employment contract determine who will pay for the dinner?"

Cleville's entourage snickered.

I answered my own question. "No, of course not. The employment agreement does not control this transaction. Now, say a disagreement arises between Mary Smith and Josephine Navarre about payment of this dinner tab. Mary Smith, who has drunk a considerable amount of wine, becomes agitated. She pushes the table, which then falls over, crushing Ms. Navarre's foot. All parties agree that she intended to push the table, but she did not intend to injure Ms. Navarre. Does the employment agreement determine the extent of Mary Smith's liability for the resulting injury?"

The two lawyers in the front pew leaned across the railing. The doughy one tapped Ian Napier's shoulder. There was a whispered conversation as Napier rose to his feet. "Your Honor, I must object. As amusing as Ms. Gould's hypotheticals are, they are merely fiction. These are not our facts. I don't see the relevance. What does this have to do with our case?"

The judge slowly pivoted her head in Napier's direction. "I will allow you to respond to Ms. Gould's arguments when she has finished. Sit down, sir."

"Yes, ma'am." Napier lowered himself into his chair.

I went on. "Now assume that instead of pushing over the table, Mary Smith strikes Ms. Navarre across the face with the intent of causing her harm. Ms. Navarre falls out of her chair, strikes her head, suffers a subdural hematoma and a fractured jaw. Does the employment agreement govern these acts?"

Napier was on his feet. "Again, Your Honor, I must object. These hypotheticals are pure fantasy."

The attorneys behind him were on their feet as well. The doughy one raised his hand, "Your Honor, if I may be heard."

"State your name for the record," Judge Han said.

"Grant Houssier. I'm in-house counsel for Crown Productions, and beside me is Kenneth Vincent, our general counsel." He gestured in the direction of the movie star. In-house meant Houssier had an office in the same building as Cleville and worked exclusively for him. Vincent, however, would have other clients.

Now I recognized him. Ken Vincent had been my father's associate when I was in college. My mother had invited me to dinner once when he was there. It felt like a set-up. He was pleasant enough, but I felt no electricity.

Eventually, he had moved back home to Los Angeles to work in the entertainment industry. No wife. No children. A confirmed bachelor who traveled extensively. Ken Vincent must have been the reason Cleville had hired Frank's firm.

"Have you entered appearances in this case?" Judge Han asked.

"We have not," Houssier said.

"Then you may not be heard. Sit down, sirs."

"Respectfully, I can have the entries filed later today," Houssier said, still on his feet.

"On behalf of whom?"

"We represent Crown Productions. Mr. Napier would continue to represent Mr. Cleville personally." It appeared a rift had developed between Crown Productions and Reginald Cleville. The movie company didn't trust Cleville or his attorney to protect them, and wanted their own lawyers involved.

"Ms. Gould, what is your response?"

"Justice delayed is justice denied" is not a cliché. Clients' stress is surreal. Josephine's commitment to her case had already fluctuated. From the corner of my eye, I saw my client picking at her cuticles.

"Let them be heard," I said.

"Very well. At the conclusion of Ms. Gould's statement, gentlemen, you may make your argument. Now you shall all remain seated. I will not tolerate another disruption. You may proceed, Ms. Gould."

"Ms. Navarre was hired as a production assistant."

The judge held up a hand. "Did the employment agreement reference or attach a job description for this position?"

The in-house counsel rifled in his briefcase and produced a sheet of paper. He stood, passed through the gate, and tried to shoulder his way to the microphone. I refused to move, which forced him to stand to the side. "For the record, Grant Houssier representing Crown Productions. I have the job description that is included in the employment package. The job titles match. If I may approach?"

"Show it to Ms. Gould," the judge said.

Houssier handed me the piece of paper. The job duties included capturing footage, managing equipment, scheduling meetings, collaborating with others, and tasks as assigned. I handed the paper back to him.

"Do you object to the introduction of this document, Ms. Gould?"

I couldn't see how the job description could hurt us. "No, Your Honor."

Judge Han beckoned. "You may approach."

Houssier crossed the well and placed the document in the judge's outstretched hand.

"You may return to the gallery, Mr. Houssier."

He walked past the defendant's table without making eye contact with Reginald Cleville.

Judge Han slipped on her reading glasses and studied the paper. Then she peered over her lenses at Houssier. "I note that one of the job duties includes 'tasks as assigned.'"

"Yes, Your Honor," he said.

"Is it your client's position that when Ms. Navarre executed this contract, she agreed to provide Mr. Cleville with sexual favors?"

Cleville launched out of his seat. "Never! Look at me. Do I look like someone who has to pay for women?"

Napier grabbed Cleville's forearm. The Duke jerked away.

Both LA lawyers were on their feet, whispering Cleville's name and pointing to his chair. He spun around and jabbed a thick finger into Grant Houssier's chest.

The judge waited for silence before she spoke, like a teacher with an unruly class. The attorneys quickly gave her their full attention. Cleville, with no one engaging with him, faced her as well.

"Take a seat, Mr. Cleville. You have an attorney speaking for you. I now put the question to all three defense counsel. Did the contract contemplate that Ms. Navarre would provide Mr. Cleville with sexual favors?"

Napier half-stood. "On behalf of Reginald Cleville, the employment contract did not include sexual favors, Your Honor."

"And counsel for Crown Productions, what is your response?"

Houssier stood. "Prostitution is illegal in the State of California. Crown Productions did not agree to provide sex to Mr. Cleville."

"Very well," Judge Han said. "You may be seated. You too, Ms. Gould."

The judge folded her hands. "It is the decision of this court that the cause of action pled by Ms. Navarre, sexual harassment and sexual assault, allege facts which if assumed to be true are beyond the scope of her employment agreement with Crown Productions. Accordingly, the employment agreement, and specifically the nondisclosure and arbitration clauses, do not apply to this cause of action. Ms. Navarre's motion is granted. The parties shall meet to schedule a trial date."

Game on.

The defense team exited the courtroom swiftly. When I had a chance to look at Josephine, she stared ahead.

"Are you okay?" I asked. Eli was on his feet, twirling car keys around a finger, ready to take Josephine back to the airport.

"This is all your fault. I just wanted this over with." She picked up her briefcase and stalked from the room. Eli fell in behind her, giving me a reassuring look as he held the door open for our client.

I pulled out my cell phone and turned it back on. Notifications of texts and calls buzzed, one after another. Jake had called, left no message, then texted to call him back. Yolanda had left several voicemails and texted that I needed to call the office as soon as I got out of court. I'd missed a call from a landline with a San Francisco number I immediately recognized, the Shaughnessy mansion.

Chapter Nine

It was raining on the day of her funeral. Jake kept a lookout for the limousine from my living room window while I lingered in front of the bathroom mirror, arguing with myself about the appropriate amount of makeup. My eyelids were too tender to touch. Puffy and red, they made my eyes look bright green. My complexion was so pale, I would look like a circus clown if I put on blush. I slathered on lip gloss and called it good.

I found myself standing next to the bed, unable to remember how to put on clothes. My one dress, a black knee-length sheath, suitable for banquets as well as funerals, was laid out on the bed. Next to it was a red velvet case containing the Shaughnessy pearls.

Jake appeared at the door. He leaned against the jamb and glanced at the Rolex I had given him our first Christmas together.

"I can't do this," I said.

He handed me a highball glass with two fingers of whiskey sloshing around the bottom. I took a sip and handed it back. He set the glass down on the bureau, then lifted the dress and held it open before me.

I put a hand on his shoulder for balance and stepped into the dress. As he pulled it up, I slipped my arms into the sleeves. He stepped behind me and closed the zipper.

I retrieved my drink and took a long sip.

The cell phone in Jake's pocket buzzed. He checked the screen. "They're here."

I knocked back the rest of the whiskey.

"Shoes," he said.

I slipped into a pair of low heels I had positioned at the foot of the bed.

"Are you good to go, Red?" He reached an arm out to guide me from the room. We had taken two steps when I noticed my neck was bare. "Wait," I said. "The pearls."

He retrieved the red velvet case and offered it to me.

My hands were shaking. "I can't."

He flipped the case open, removed the necklace, and set the case back on the bed. I held my hair up while he draped the string around my neck and worked the fastener. When I heard the catch lock, I lowered my hair. He rested both hands on my shoulders. "I'm right behind you."

I reached up and squeezed his hand. "I know." It came out in a hoarse whisper.

THE LIMOUSINE RIDE WAS torture. My father had insisted that the family ride together. I had wanted Jake to drive me, but didn't have the energy to argue.

The passenger compartment was mercifully large. Frank sat opposite us, looking sharp in his black suit with his silver hair recently trimmed. I avoided eye contact by looking out the window. San Francisco was gray. As we drove up the Embarcadero, the slate-colored bay waters churned. Beneath the Bay Bridge, I felt a sudden chill and shivered. Jake rested his hand on top of mine. I was warm again.

St. Patrick's—the church where all the Shaughnessys had been baptized, took their first communion, were confirmed, married, and eulogized—was full. Those gathered watched my father as he led the way up the aisle. The mourners included my mother's girlhood friends and my father's business acquaintances. Ken Vincent sat with Ian Napier. Yolanda and Eli, my only allies, sat together.

When we arrived at the front pew, I stepped in with Jake behind me. My father was forced to sit on Jake's other side.

Mass lasted precisely one hour. A soprano performed "*Ave Maria*." Frank read Corinthians 13, suggested by the priest. Ironic.

On the ride to the graveyard, Frank was flicking his fingernails, a thing he did if he wanted to be elsewhere. When I was a child, this habit would be followed by a declaration that he needed to return to the office, even if it was a weekend.

Standing at the graveside, I thought about the upcoming Mother's Day. Last Christmas, I had lunch with my mother in a darkened restaurant to exchange our presents. It was a secret from Frank. She didn't want him to know we were meeting. During dessert, she suggested we celebrate Mother's Day with afternoon tea at the Palace Hotel. Maybe we were building a bridge. I had hoped so at the time. Even then, she seemed tired. Later I learned that the cancer had been diagnosed weeks before. She had kept it a secret for as long as she could.

▼

AFTER THE BURIAL, THE limo took us to the mansion, now filled with black-clad guests wandering about, drinks in hand, like a gothic cocktail party. As Jake escorted me through the crowd, hands reached out to touch my arm or shoulder. Faces snapped into focus, each person offering their condolences. I thanked them, then moved on to the next.

The parlor was in the back of the house. In the adjacent dining room, caterers silently replenished platters of food. Guests shuffled down the buffet line, filling their small plates. A bartender served drinks to the three-deep crowd.

I stopped before the window overlooking the rose garden.

"Hungry?" Jake asked.

I shook my head.

"A drink?"

I nodded.

He shouldered his way through clusters of people and disappeared.

Beyond the window, rain puddled along the cobble path. Granny Shaughnessy had originally planted the garden. Over time, her descendants replanted the rose beds. My mother's contribution was the John F. Kennedy rose, an ivory hybrid tea. She had a thing about the Kennedy Camelot. Rain and mist drained the garden of color. The sky, the shrubs, and the ground appeared in varying shades of gray.

A hand touched my back lightly, then slid beneath my hair. A finger drifted across the bare skin of my neck. I felt moist breath on my ear.

"I see you're wearing the Shaughnessy pearls. That would have made your mother happy."

In the window's reflection, I met Frank's gaze. I was almost as tall as he was. He lowered his eyelids halfway. Something deep inside me, in the place where I imagined my womb would be, slithered.

"She hated you, you know. She knew you were fooling around."

"Nothing of the sort. She understood me. And my needs." He lifted his drink to his lips and as he did so, a reflection of light flared on his wedding band. "Your mother was a good woman. She stood by me for better—and for worse."

From the moment they announced the decision to send me to boarding school, I had resented her.

I didn't see my father the day I was sent away. The maid came into my room that morning with a tray of dry toast and a message from my mother. I was to get up and get dressed. In the cab ride to the airport, my mother faced away from me, ostensibly observing the scenery just as I had on the way to her funeral mass. She led me through the airport without looking at me. I felt like baggage, as if I was not a living human being anymore. After the plane lifted off, I tried to curl up against her. I wanted comfort, warmth. She pulled away. It was then I saw she was vibrating with anger.

By the time we reached the school, I was exhausted. We met with Mother Superior in her office. She called a novice to show me to my room. When we left the office, I didn't realize that was the last time I would see my mother, so I had not said goodbye. I assumed we would have a farewell before she left for the airport. But she made her getaway while I was being distracted with a tour of the school.

That night was the first time I cut myself. I used the end of a bobby pin pulled open. The first couple times I tried, I could only bring up welts. On my third attempt, I dug deeper. The tip penetrated my skin. A few seconds passed while I was mesmerized, waiting for something to happen. Would it hurt?

During that moment, my fear vanished, so intent was I on the desire to witness every millisecond of the event unfolding. As glistening red beads oozed to the surface, a searing pain rushed up my arm and I passed out. One of the other girls found me in the bathroom and shook me awake. She handed me a wad of toilet paper to mop up the blood and told me to go back to bed before the nuns found me.

Later, it was hard to find anything suitably sharp because the sisters kept searching my room. If I hadn't managed to steal a knife from the kitchen or a pen from a teacher's desk, my fingernails would do.

I found myself back in the present, in the mansion, pressing my forehead to the cold, damp window overlooking the rose garden. I touched my forearm, feeling the ridge of an old scar. At times I had cherished its bumps and grooves like badges of honor. Now I felt shame and disgust. With myself. With Frank. My mother. The nuns. All of them.

"Join me in the library," Frank said. "We have business to discuss." He said it matter-of-factly, then drifted across the room and down the hall, confident that I would follow.

I fell into step like an obedient puppy.

In the den, he stood before a sideboard, pouring brandy into two snifters. "Close the door."

The room had been the sanctuary of generations of men who had married into the Shaughnessy family. It was masculine: dark wood paneling and bookcases filled with fat leather-bound books. The fireplace, blackened from use, was unlit. The open flue pulled up a current of air, making the room feel colder than the rest of the mansion.

An antique desk was near the far wall. Above it was a large landscape oil painting, one of the Hudson River school, with dark trees and leaves framing the foreground, pastoral scene beyond, and in the far distance a tiny bead of light representing the sun. The room smelled of leather, furniture polish, and faintly of the cigars my long dead grandfather had smoked.

I pulled the door shut.

He crossed the room and handed me a snifter. "Have a seat." He gestured to the couch where, as a child, I had read fairytales while he worked. Sometimes, he would step away from his desk and sit next to me. Then he would pull me onto his lap, promising to tell me a story.

"I think I'll stand," I said.

"As you wish." He leaned against the desk. "It's about the house."

"The Shaughnessy mansion." That was how it was always referred to. It was part of my mother's inheritance. On the occasion of Granny Shaughnessy's funeral, I was brought home for a two-day visit. The last night's dinner included a discussion regarding my parents' wills. They informed me that since Granny had left me so much money, they had revised their wills, naming each other as their sole survivor. When both of them were gone, I would inherit whatever was left.

That meant the house would go to Frank. It had not felt right to me. He had always felt like an interloper, perhaps because Granny did not like him. Regardless, my mother had the right to dispose of her property as she saw fit, and I would not argue with a dead woman's wishes.

Frank spoke. "When Betty Shaughnessy died, she left you funds in a trust, as you know. What you don't know is your inheritance was the bulk of her estate. She left your mother this house, but not in fee simple."

"Fee simple" meant outright. If my mother had received the title to the mansion in fee simple, it was hers to sell, donate, give away, or will to my father.

"Betty Shaughnessy saw fit to leave your mother a life estate and a small amount of money to maintain the property. Unfortunately, Betty's advisors failed to consider inflation and the inevitable age-related deterioration of the structure when fixing that number. The money was soon spent."

If my mother had received only a life estate in the house, then upon her death, it would pass to someone else named in Granny Shaughnessy's will. I could see only one reason Frank thought I needed to be told.

He sipped his brandy, then rolled his lips before speaking. "The problem is I have put quite a bit of money into restoring and maintaining this grand old lady. It doesn't seem equitable that my contributions should vanish upon your mother's demise."

"You're telling me this because?"

"The house goes to you under your great grandmother's will." He clinked his glass against mine. "That makes us housemates."

The mansion was mine. We weren't housemates in any sense of the word, but he could make a claim against the title—if he proved he had spent money on it.

"If that wasn't enough, your mother revised her will a few weeks ago. She appointed her personal representative. Having the last word, as she was so fond of. I only just found out when *her* attorney delivered the document to my office. She didn't have the courtesy of telling me personally. So, not only am I now a tenant in my own home, I have no authority in the disposal of her estate."

That manilla envelope she had given me on the last day I saw her. I had dropped it on my desk in my home office and forgotten about it. It must have been her will.

"I find myself at your mercy, madam." One of his hands reached for my hip and he pulled me close. I had to take half a step to keep from losing my balance. As his hand floated upwards, he grazed my breast. It wasn't an accident. Then he ran his fingers under the pearl necklace, brushing my bare skin. He was so close, I could smell the brandy on his breath and see where his morning shave had left a scratch near his ear.

He cocked his head to one side, examining me. "I hate to see you so unhappy, Maureen. This vendetta of yours. Give it up. Let's be friends again, shall we?"

A blade of light cut across the carpet as the library door opened.

"Maureen?" It was Jake's voice.

There was a bemused expression on Frank's face, the naughty little boy caught, but accustomed to having his way.

It was then I remembered the brandy in my hand. I swirled the snifter. The golden liquid rolled like a tiny ocean—silvery waves slid across the surface and vanished.

I tossed the brandy in Frank's face. "I'll see you in hell first."

I walked past Jake and said, "We're leaving."

Chapter Ten

JAKE SPENT THE NIGHT. I hadn't invited him. He didn't ask. There was never a right time for him to leave.

Soon after we returned to my loft, he went out to pick up dinner while I took a hot bath. The scars on my left arm reddened as I soaked. They began to prickle. I wanted to dig at the largest one—it itched the most—but resisted. Instead I scrubbed my arm with a loofa until blood seeped from the scar. When I dunked my arm into the hot water, an exquisite sear of pain radiated up to my chest. Bloody tendrils snaked and curled from the wound into the bath. They were beautiful.

After the water had gone cold, I got out and pulled on a long-sleeved t-shirt and sweats, found an old Jack Nicholson movie on the TV, and crawled into bed. I heard Jake let himself in and walk down the hall. He came into the bedroom with two bags of food.

I wasn't hungry, but felt I should acknowledge his foraging for his woman. "What did you get?"

"Chinese," he said. "What are you watching?" He viewed the screen for a few minutes, then said. "Kind of grim, don't you think?"

"I wasn't paying attention."

He flopped down on top of the covers, pulled the containers from the paper bag, and handed me a carton and a set of chopsticks. "Eat! I'm famished. You should be too. You haven't eaten all day."

"Yes, mom." I gave him a fake smile as I prodded at noodles. My stomach lurched.

He elbowed me gently. "Hey, babe, are you okay?"

"It's not like we were that close."

"But she was your mother. You only get the one."

"Right," I said. I pinched a piece of celery with my chopsticks, thought better of it, and let it drop. "Have you ever thought about having children?"

He had been about to insert a clump of rice into his mouth. He put it back into the carton. "Where's this coming from?"

"I was just thinking. We never talked about it."

"We weren't married that long. You divorced me, remember?"

Actually, he had left me after another one of my withdrawn periods—but in a fit of hurt and anger, I was the first to file papers.

"Sorry, you're right." I spun the chopsticks, wrapping a noodle around them. A savory whiff rose from the carton. I felt sick. Nothing new, I'd had stomach problems all my life.

"No, it's me who's sorry. I shouldn't have snapped at you like that. Not today of all days. So, kids—yeah, I've thought about them. A boy for me and a girl for you. Just like in the song."

"I never told you this before, and it doesn't seem fair. You should know. I don't think I want kids. In theory, it sounds nice. But can you imagine sitting up all night with a colicky baby, then going to court? Toys all over the floors? Emergency room visits? Pink eye or whatever disgusting diseases they get. And the spew? To hear Yolanda tell it, they vomit continuously until they're teenagers. And then teenagers! God help me. Besides, I'm too old."

He moved the food aside and scooted closer. "Hey, babe, you're barely thirty-five. Look at those movie stars. They're having babies in their forties. There's still time." He stroked my hair, then stopped. I felt his body tense. He was looking at the red stain that had bloomed across my sleeve.

"Oh, that. Cut myself shaving."

"You shave your arms?"

"No, silly—not that there's anything wrong with that. I dropped the razor in the bath. No big deal. It's just a scratch."

"Babe, I've seen the scars."

I should have told him. He had probably guessed already. When we were working at the DA's office together, we had both seen cases of self-harm. He would have suspected the truth, not the details, but he would have the broad outlines. I groped for words, knowing that the first revelation would lead to question after question until he dug so deep I didn't want to answer anymore. He was a lawyer, after all.

When we did talk about it, he was entitled to the whole story. I wanted to feel safe enough to share it with him or not care about the consequences anymore.

"Not now, okay? Let's just be us tonight."

He put an arm around me. "As you wish, my lady love. Take as much time as you need." He took off his wedding ring without being asked.

THE FOLLOWING MONDAY, I was back in the conference room, seated at the head of the table with Yolanda and Eli on either side. We each had a paper cup in front of us. I slathered cream cheese on half a bagel, took a bite, and put it back on a plate. I wasn't hungry, but they wouldn't eat until I had. They both reached for bagels. While they were eating, I chased my food with coffee.

Frank's ambush at the funeral had unnerved me. I had spent the rest of the weekend in bed, flicking through television channels, not settling on anything. The Shaughnessy mansion was mine, but he was in it and he wasn't leaving without a fight. That battle would wait.

"First off, I want to thank both of you for coming to the funeral. Sorry I didn't get a chance to say hello."

"We're here for you, girlfriend," Yolanda said, dusting crumbs from her blouse. "Whatever you need."

"Let's get to work. Where are we on the Navarre case?"

Eli consulted his notes. "I've tracked down those three actresses Josephine identified from the online photos: Amber LeRoux, Sophia Lamar, and Valerie Vann. The first one, Amber LeRoux, is in the British tabloids a lot. She's the girlfriend of some rich European guy. Lots of photos of naked sunbathing on yachts, going to glitzy parties, that kind of thing."

"Did you contact her?"

"Found her agent easy enough. He said he couldn't help me, but gave me the phone number for her manager. I left a message for him. So far, no return call. Had better luck with Sophia Lamar. She's the one in acting school in London. That's an eight-hour time difference, did you know that? I had to get up at three in the morning to call over there."

"My hero," Yolanda said. Yolanda had been the mother of four active children. She once told me that when they were little, she hadn't slept through the night for ten years.

"Whatever," Eli said. "So I got this Sophia Lamar on the phone. She admitted she had auditioned for a part in Cleville's last movie, *A Summer in Paradise,* but that's all I got out of her. Said she couldn't talk about it, said she was sorry, and hung up on me."

I said, "Another nondisclosure agreement."

"Could be. If you want, I can give it a couple of weeks and try again."

"Or maybe Eli's the wrong woman for the job," Yolanda said.

"What?" He craned his head around to look at her—a little dramatically, I thought.

Yolanda leaned toward him. "Cleville attacked, or tried to molest, Josephine, right? We think these other two actresses saw something, know something, or were assaulted too. They won't trust men after that. If that happened to me, and if I was minding my own business an ocean away, and some strange man called up and started asking me questions, I wouldn't talk to him either. For all she knows, you were a spy for Cleville."

"Yolanda's right," I said. "We need to find an introduction to Sophia through someone she trusts. Eli, give what you have to Yolanda. Yolanda, you dig around the internet and see if you can build a path through mutual friends to get us in with Sophia. Woman to woman."

Eli threw himself back into his chair. "What about me?"

"What do you know about the third actress?"

"Valerie Vann. Quit the business. Went to college, got a degree in early learning. Got married and took her husband's name. We got lucky here, Chief. She's living down the road in Saratoga."

"Great work, Eli. You're with me."

He stood. "To where?"

"Saratoga."

IN LIGHT TRAFFIC, SARATOGA was just an hour south of San Francisco. I took I-280, opening Sunny up as we launched from the onramp. Zero to sixty in 3.9 seconds. As I shifted through the gears, Eli braced his legs against the firewall.

"Are you okay?" I asked.

"Going a little fast, don't you think?"

"I'm going as fast as everyone else. I just got up to speed quicker." With that, I downshifted and slipped into the left lane to pass a minivan. A dark sedan had tried to close the gap I was moving into. I floored it and we pulled away, even as the driver tried in vain to keep up.

Eli gripped the dashboard. "I can't look."

"Then don't."

Saratoga's downtown was charming, with tree-lined streets bordered by nineteenth century brick buildings. We made our way into a neighborhood of vintage Craftsman-style houses. Sunny's GPS led us to a porched bungalow with weathered shake siding.

I knocked on the door and stepped back. A little dog barked inside the house. Eli stood behind me, watching the windows. "A curtain moved. Someone's home."

I waited a few minutes, then pushed the doorbell that buzzed inside the house. The dog became frantic. It scampered away and back again, alerting the occupant with its yapping.

A few more minutes passed before the door opened a few inches. A woman's face appeared in the crack. "Shush, Bella," she said as she blocked the door with her foot. A little mixed-breed squeezed in between the woman and the door and bared her tiny fangs as she locked eyes with me.

"Good morning," I said. "Are you Valerie Vann?"

"Who wants to know?"

"My name is Maureen Gould." I handed her my business card. "And this is my investigator, Eli Conroy."

"What do you want?"

"We'd like to talk to you about Reginald Cleville."

"Who?"

She knew full well who. "Reginald Cleville, the movie producer, who escorted you to the Critics' Choice. Your picture was on several magazine covers. I represent a young woman who recently worked for him."

"Oh, that's who you meant. I didn't hear you at first. Right, I know who he is. How did you find me?"

"The internet. No privacy these days, I'm afraid. Can we talk to you for a little bit?"

"What about?"

"We'd like to ask you a few questions about your experience with Mr. Cleville."

"Sorry, I can't. You need to leave." She nudged the dog inside with her foot as she pulled away.

"If you reconsider, please give me a call."

The door shut. She was gone.

"At least she didn't slam it," Eli said.

Back in the car, I hesitated before starting the engine.

Eli asked, "What's up, chief?"

"The thing is, I don't have any corroborating evidence. We don't have any witnesses to the assault on Josephine. No rape kit or semen-stained dress proving there was an exchange of bodily fluids. No one to say they saw Cleville grooming her. There's no way she was the first; he was way too confident. He knew exactly what to say to get her into his suite and how to get close enough to grab her. If we could find someone who is willing to testify they too had been assaulted, then we can show a pattern. Otherwise it's Josephine's word against his."

Chapter Eleven

SEVERAL WEEKS LATER, JOSEPHINE and I arrived at the Law Office of Gould & Napier for her deposition. She had flown up two days before so we could prepare. Located in a mirror-sided office tower overlooking the Embarcadero, the reception area had a view of the Bay Bridge and Treasure Island through floor-to-ceiling tinted windows. Mid-century-modern seating was arranged beneath an oversized painting of the Golden Gate Bridge. The air had a metallic odor so strong I could taste it.

My heels echoed on marble tiles as I approached the reception desk. I searched the room to see whether Frank would pop out at me. He wasn't the attorney in this case, but it was his office.

The receptionist, an expressionless young woman in a tight dress and stilettos, showed Josephine and me to a conference room where a court reporter was setting up her equipment. Tiny microphones had been placed before three chairs, from which a videographer draped electrical cords back to a recording deck.

I showed Josephine to her chair at the head of the table, then dropped my briefcase in the adjacent chair with my back to the view. We had arrived early so I could stake out my territory. One of the dirty tricks big law firms play is to post opposing counsel—me, in this case—facing the window so that he, or she, would become distracted by the view while defense counsel grilled the witness. The big law firms think the little solo practitioners don't know what they're doing. We know.

"Water, coffee, tea?" I asked Josephine.

"Water, please."

I strolled the length of the conference room to a cabinet behind the court reporter, poured water for Josephine and brought it to her. Then I went back to the cabinet to pour coffee into a tall black mug with the Gould & Napier logo written, of course, in gold. On the third trip, I grabbed a box of tissues and placed that at Josephine's elbow. During depo preparation, Josephine had hidden her hands beneath the table and picked at her cuticles until they bled. The solution I devised was to give her a tissue she could shred instead.

Just as I was unloading a legal pad and pens from my briefcase, men filed into the room: Ian Napier first, followed by the two LA lawyers. Last was Reginald Cleville.

Napier froze. The three other men clustered against the wall, waiting for a resolution of the present crisis. I had taken Ian's chair.

"Good morning, gentlemen," I said cheerily. I clipped the microphone onto my blazer lapel. The men moved down the table, each taking a chair, with Cleville the farthest away. They all had legal pads and pens. If Cleville wanted to communicate with Ian during the deposition, he would have to write a note and pass it up the chain.

The seat across from me was empty. The clock on the wall said 9:58. The deposition was scheduled to begin at 10:00 A.M. I raised my eyebrows at Ian in question.

That was when Frank walked in, dapper in a double-breasted blue pinstripe suit. He greeted "Madam Court Reporter," said hello to his team as if they hadn't just spent the morning huddled together in the next room, then smiled at me with his shark-dead gray eyes.

"Frank," I said. "I wasn't expecting to see you here."

"Maureen." He smiled indulgently. "It *is* my office. I'm taking over as lead counsel in Mr. Cleville's case. Mr. Napier will stay in the case—as my assistant."

It appeared the defense team had suffered a crisis of faith. Having lost the NDA hearing, Cleville wanted the big dog barking for him instead. Why my father's firm had taken the case was a mystery, when its specialty was business law.

Frank reached his hand across the table to my client. "Good morning, Ms. Navarre. My name is Francis E. Gould. I will be taking your deposition this morning."

Josephine placed her long fingers in Frank's hand. "Gould? You mean like Maureen's last name?"

"The very same," Frank said. "You'll be happy to learn that your fine counsel is my daughter."

Josephine's head whipped around. I hadn't told her that Cleville's law firm was helmed by my father. It wasn't relevant to her case. I ignored her. We'd talk about it later.

Frank sat down, clipped his microphone to his tie, and set his shoulders. "On record," he said, cueing the court reporter to begin.

The court reporter pushed a lever on the tape deck. "On record."

He opened with the usual: background questions trying to warm up the witness and accustom her to the question and answer format. With some clients it worked. I had warned Josephine about this, and Eli had asked similar questions. But today she grew increasingly nervous as Frank delayed discussion of why we were there: that night when Cleville had called her to his suite.

Her hands were beneath the table, where she was already picking at her cuticles, when he asked, "Do recall signing your employment agreement?"

"Yes."

"Did you read it before you signed it?"

"No."

"So you were unaware of the clause that prohibits you from discussing your employment? For ease of discussion, we will refer to it as the 'NDA' clause."

"I was told that it didn't matter in my case."

"That's not the question, Ms. Navarre. The question is, were you aware that you had signed a nondisclosure agreement?"

"No."

Frank set a document aside, then turned back to Josephine. "Do you have friends at Crown Productions?"

She grew still. "What do you mean by 'friends?'"

"As distinguished from people with whom you only interacted for work purposes." Josephine eyed me. I nodded.

"Some of us would meet at a bar. Just about everyone went one time or another. I can't remember who. What are you trying to get at?"

I had warned Josephine that it was routine for the defense to dig around for people who might testify against her. Cleville's attorneys were entitled to know who she might have talked to about her employment. If she didn't name her confidants, they would find out anyway. They probably knew already and were only trying to find out what she would lie about.

Frank folded his hands. "Why don't you tell me what the term 'friends' means to you? How about that?"

Josephine reached for me. "Can we take a break?"

Frank spoke before I could. "I would prefer you answer the question on the table first."

"I don't know how to answer your question," she said. "That's my answer."

I stood and Josephine stood too. I led her from the conference room through reception to the elevator that opened onto Gould & Napier's office. I pushed the button. When the doors opened, a woman with a briefcase took a step back to allow us to enter. I pushed for the ground floor and the doors closed.

"What happened back there?" Josephine asked.

I shook my head. The numbered lights ticked off the floors as we descended. After we stepped out into the lobby, I led her to the sidewalk. She pulled an e-cigarette out of her purse and started puffing on it.

"We can't talk about the case in the building," I said. "For all we know, that woman on the elevator was a friend of Frank's."

"Frank, your father. You call your father by his first name? Why didn't you tell me he was The Duke's attorney?"

I had taken to calling Frank by his first name when they sent me away. He didn't feel like a father to me anymore. That was none of Josephine's business. "I didn't tell you because he wasn't Cleville's attorney when we started this case. His partner was."

"Isn't that like unethical or something, for two attorneys from the same family to work on the same case?"

"It would be a problem if I had discussed the case with him, but I haven't. So the answer to your question is no."

"You talk about me to people?"

"Only my team. Anything I say to them is confidential."

"Okay, fine. I get that, but why does he need all this personal stuff about me?"

"They're looking for evidence they can use against you. Is there something you don't want them finding out about? Because if there is, I might be able to head it off beforehand. But once it's out in the open, there isn't much I can do. Is there anyone at Crown Productions you're worried about?"

"Worried, like how?"

"Who might say something damaging to the case."

"What, like I'm a slut or something?"

"Or a liar, a gold digger, a schemer, a thief, a fraud."

Josephine took a deep drag on the cigarette, then blew the smoke out overhead.

"No, nothing like that."

"Great!" I said, not feeling great at all. Something was out there I didn't know about. I could feel it. She was afraid Frank was about to surprise me with it. I reached up to stroke my pearls and found that I wasn't wearing them. "You know anything you say to me is confidential."

"Right, you said that." Her eyelids fluttered while she thought. "But do I have to answer all these personal questions?"

"I can't object unless I have a reason. The only time I can instruct you not to answer the question is if you need to take the Fifth Amendment."

She barked a laugh. "Like a criminal or something?"

"You have the right to remain silent if anything you say could lead to criminal prosecution."

"That's the only rights I have? I'm not a gangster, but I don't want my life spread around. It's no one's business."

"Then you need to answer his questions."

"Okay, fine," she said, stashing the e-cig in her purse. "Can we get this thing over with?"

In the deposition room, everyone was where we had left them. We took our seats.

"On record," Frank said.

"On record," repeated the court reporter.

"Ms. Navarre, before you took a break and spoke to your attorney, I had asked if you have any friends at Crown Productions. Would you please answer the question?"

"I thought I answered it." Josephine wasn't glancing at me anymore. She was completely engaged with Frank, not necessarily a good sign if that meant she had excised me from the conversation.

"You did not. Please answer the question."

"There were people I hung out with, but not like bosom buddies or anything."

"See, that wasn't so hard, was it?" Frank tracked his finger across his typed notes. "Now, tell me about your relationship with Cameron Aguilar."

"What about him?"

"What was his position at Crown Productions?"

"He was an assistant cinematographer. Still is, for all I know."

"Were you friends?"

She shrugged. "Again, I don't know what you mean by 'friends.'"

Frank slid a file folder out from under his legal pad. He tilted it so I couldn't see the contents, selected an 8" by 12" photo, and passed it down the line of seated men. "Madam Court Reporter, please mark this as Exhibit A."

"Exhibit A marked," the court reporter said as she placed a blue sticker on the lower right hand corner, then handed it back to Cleville. Before he passed it back up the chain, he turned to me, eyes glinting.

"Ms. Navarre, for the record, would you please identify this picture?" Frank asked, as he handed it to her.

"You son of a bitch." Josephine sailed the photograph down the table, then stood so fast her chair banged into the wall. Purse under her arm, she strode out the conference room.

It was then I got my first glimpse of the photograph. Josephine was nude and sprawled across a bed with a come-hither look in her eye.

By the time I reached the elevator, she had disappeared. I found her outside, pacing on the sidewalk, puffing on the e-cigarette.

"What the hell was that?" Josephine asked.

"Maybe you should tell me."

"It's none of their damned business, that's what it is. It's private, personal."

"That much is obvious. Where did it come from?"

"My cell phone. How the hell did they get photos off my cell? Did someone steal it and download them? Can someone, I don't know, get on Wi-Fi and hack into my phone?"

"Or maybe you sent it to a friend?"

She stopped pacing. "And so what if I did? It's still personal."

"But not quite as private as if you hadn't. Who did you send it to? That cameraman Frank asked about?"

"He's a cinematographer. He asked for a selfie. It's no big deal."

"I don't get this. Why would you send a picture like that to some man you hardly knew?"

She took another drag, cupping her elbow in her other hand. She gave me a withering look. "How bourgeois can you be?"

"Did you have a sexual relationship with this man?"

She flicked away an imaginary ash. I waited for an answer.

"A sexual relationship," she said mockingly. "Okay, fine. We had *a sexual relationship*. One time, that was it. I thought it was going to turn into something, but I was wrong. Like I said, it's no big deal. I don't see what that has to do with The Duke sticking his thing in my face."

"It doesn't, I agree with you. The thing is, the courts won't. Evidence of a plaintiff's sexual history is admissible in a harassment case. Especially if the defendant was aware of it. It goes to the issue of consent."

"How many times do I have to tell you? I did not consent."

"To what The Duke did, I get that. But he might have thought you would consent if he knew that you were engaged in sexual activity with your coworkers. And that's admissible evidence."

"Come on, seriously? Whose side are you on? You're supposed to be working for me. You don't believe me, do you? You think I'm just some tramp that gives blow jobs so I can get ahead in the industry."

"I didn't say that."

"No, but that's what you're thinking." She squinted into the sunlight. "My career is ruined. Everyone's talking about me. I can't find work. And now I find out my own attorney thinks I'm a whore."

"Josephine," I dropped my voice to a conciliatory tone.

She held up one finger. "Don't talk to me. Not one word. I need space." She waved to a passing cab. It pulled over and she climbed inside. The taxi pulled into traffic, then disappeared.

THE , I STEPPED into my reception area and found an arrangement of lilies on Yolanda's desk, purchased at a grocery store by the look of them.

"What's this?" I asked.

"It's from Josephine. She left a note."

Yolanda handed the card to me. "She says she's sorry and she'll behave from now on and she hopes you'll keep working on her case. She flew back to L.A. right after she dropped them off."

Jake had predicted as much the night before while we sat up in bed, watching a late night talk show. "Quick to anger, quick to regret. She'll be back in the morning, all hearts and flowers."

I had not been so certain. And I wasn't sure I wanted her back. I knew I was a glory hound, but I was fine with that as long as I earned the acclaim. I had a noble cause, empowering victims, but what really sparked my bloodlust was when I found an evil wrongdoer who I could expose and humiliate in court. The mightier, the better. Reginald Cleville was the most powerful man I had taken on. When Josephine brought the case to me, I'd been too quick to assume there would be no problems.

I should have known about the selfies and the boyfriend. Either I had not communicated my need for this information—which would be my failing, because I was the professional communicator—or she, knowing what I wanted, had withheld it. Whatever the reason, I had a problem: I didn't know the whole story.

"Put the flowers in the conference room and give Josephine a call. I'd like to see her right after lunch, say one P.M. Then call Eli for a team meeting."

"When do you want him?"

"Now would be good. Make copies of those photos I forwarded to you last night, one set for everyone."

"She never mentioned them. Where'd they come from?"

"Frank. He's taken over the Cleville case. He sent them over after we walked out of the depo." Afterwards, I had gone straight home. Feeling guilty about taking the day off, I had checked my office email late in the afternoon. He'd had more than just the one picture. The additional photos were even more graphic.

"So now what?"

"Get Eli in and we'll talk about it."

When I walked into the conference room for the team meeting, the flowers were on the console. Stacks of thick files were lined up neatly on the table. The photographs, discreetly covered by a blue title page bearing the case name and "CONFIDENTIAL" written in bold, were arranged in front of our chairs. Eli was flipping through the photos with his eyebrows raised when Yolanda followed me in with a pot of coffee.

On the wall behind my chair was a whiteboard. I'd had cabinet doors installed to conceal it when visitors were in the office. Today, the doors were open to show the *Navarre vs. Cleville* story map: centered at the top, a photo of Reginald Cleville. A photo of Josephine was on his left. On the right were photos of the three actresses who had disappeared from Cleville's circle: Sophia Lamar, with "London" written under her name; Valerie Vann, "Saratoga. Uncoop;" and Amber LeRoux, "Whereabouts unknown."

I slid into my chair. "So, as you know, Josephine walked out of her depo yesterday. She was upset when they handed her one of these photos. She's coming in this afternoon. We need to discuss how we're going to handle this new evidence and where we're going from here."

"Why didn't we get this stuff sooner?" Eli asked.

Both parties were required to exchange evidence early in the case, but the defense's disclosures had not included these photos. Nor had it listed Cameron Aguilar as a witness.

"It was a ruse to fix their evidentiary problems."

Eli gave a huff. "I hate it when you use those two-bit words."

"A ruse, a trick. However they got their hands on these selfies, they can't prove or won't admit where they came from. So they couldn't get them into evidence at trial unless Josephine verified they are authentic. They withheld them from our exchange because I would have gone to the judge to ask for an order excluding them before the deposition, thereby stopping them from fixing their problem. But the big payoff was humiliating Josephine with a dirty little secret."

"Bastards," Eli said.

"And there's another thing. Frank's taken over the case."

"You guys don't get along, do you?" Eli asked.

"What does my relationship with my father have to do with it?"

"It's not like you ever said anything, but I can tell by the way you talk about him. You hate his guts. So how's this going to play out, Chief?"

"Business as usual," I said. "Last night after the deposition, the defense sent me a revised witness list with the name of this guy Josephine sent the photos to."

"The new witness list is at the bottom of the packet," Yolanda said.

I flipped through to the document and read fifteen names we hadn't seen before. Cameron Aguilar's name was buried in the list. "This guy, Cameron Aguilar. Eli, I want you to find out everything there is to know about him. Then you need to start calling these witnesses and see if they'll talk to us. What do they know about Josephine's sexual history? Have they heard or observed anything about Cleville's interactions with other females: employees, actresses, anyone in that circle?"

"You got it, Chief. You want me to call this Aguilar guy?"

"After you've talked to everyone else. I want the calls started today. The word will get back to defense counsel that we are working the case. Let them worry about that. On second thought, don't call Aguilar at all. By the time you get around to him, he'll refuse to talk anyway. Save him for me."

"Gotcha," Eli said.

"Yolanda, now you. Did you get through to anyone who knows Sophia? Is she willing to talk to us?"

"Her manager took my call yesterday when you were at the deposition. After I told her about what happened to Josephine, she called Sophia and then called me right back. Sophia will talk to you, but there are conditions. First, it has to be in person. Second, no video or audio recording. Third, you have to promise not to tell anyone what she said. It's totally off the record, confidential, and non-attributable."

"Well, what good does that do us?" Eli asked.

"We'll get insight into his pattern so I'll know where to find more evidence," I said. "When does she want to meet?"

"Friday."

"Yolanda, book the trip for you and me."

"So what am I supposed to do while you're gone?" Eli asked.

He had been my investigator since I started the firm. Talking to witnesses had been exclusively his purview, because he had been a cop. I had met him through Jake, who had been on the San Francisco police force before he went to law school. Eli didn't drink to excess, was responsible and intelligent, so I took him on. Young men found his oversized masculine presence calming. But he had the wrong effect on women. This wasn't the right case for him. He had to feel left out and insecure about his role when I assigned work to Yolanda that should have gone to him.

"I want you calling all those witnesses Cleville named and get everything you can on Cameron Aguilar. See if he has had any recent unexplained influx of cash. Shiny new car, recent move to a better neighborhood, stuff like that. Also look into Crown Productions, the board of directors, their backgrounds."

I stood and wrote Eli's name on the whiteboard. Under that I listed "Cameron Aguilar, witness list, investigate potential witnesses." Under my name, I wrote "Sophia with Yolanda." I made sure Eli's list was longer than ours, hoping to assure him that his contribution was vital.

"Everyone clear on what we're doing?"

"Sure thing, Chief," Eli said.

Chapter Twelve

Yolanda and I left for London Wednesday night. She showered me with safety tips as we walked through San Francisco International Airport: *Don't flash your money. Bad guys will see where you keep it and pick your pocket. Carry your credit cards in a scan-proof wallet. Don't hang your purse on your shoulder; thieves can slip it off your arm and run away before you know what happened. Wear a crossbody instead. Secure your smaller bag on top of your wheelie case, again to thwart grab-and-run thieves.*

Yolanda had booked us into a grand old hotel near Buckingham Palace. I would have been fine near the airport, but she wanted to see the sights. By the time we registered, it was Thursday afternoon. I went straight to my room, called Jake and told him we had landed safely, ordered a club sandwich for dinner, and slept until morning.

Over a breakfast of scones and tea delivered to my room, I reviewed notes for the interview with Sophia. I had promised Yolanda a sightseeing tour before we went to our appointment.

When we met in the lobby, Yolanda was sporting a new purple faux-crocodile tote.

"I went shopping last night," she said when I noticed the bag. "And I found a real British pub where we can eat, just down the street." She pulled out a tourist map. "But first I want to see the Tower of London. That's where Anne Boleyn lost her head, you know."

I knew. I had spent a summer in London during law school while attending a course on international law. I hit the streets every day, soaking up history, much of which had been built upon the bones of discarded women. Anne Boleyn, Catherine of Aragon, Mary Queen of Scots, Jane Grey, and Diana Spencer, just to name a few. I was firmly convinced the only reason Elizabeth I lasted so long was that she had never married.

Yolanda led me down to the Thames. She stopped near the water's edge, dug around in her purse, and handed me her phone. "Here, take a picture of me with that giant Ferris wheel in the background."

"It's the London Eye."

"No way! I heard about that. Did you know people make reservations weeks in advance to ride on that thing?"

She posed and smiled. I took a few pictures, then handed the cell back to her. She aimed her phone at me next and took several photos while she backed up and circled.

"What are you doing?" I asked.

"We're being followed." She dropped the phone back into her purple tote.

I wondered if I had made a mistake asking her to assist in the investigation. Yolanda had always been wary, but letting her out of the office seemed to unleash her suspiciousness to the brink of paranoia. Witness interviews were hardly spy craft. "Why would anyone follow us?"

"I don't know why. I just know they are," she said, then began walking along the river. "Two big blond thugs with crewcuts. They look like the Russian guy in that Rocky movie. Don't look now. I've seen them before. They were at the airport in San Francisco."

I had to take several long strides to catch up to her. "So? They were probably on the same flight. There must have been three hundred people on that plane."

"And now they're following us."

"To popular attractions like tourists from all over the world are doing." During our short walk, I had already heard at least three different languages spoken.

After several minutes, she stopped and consulted her map. "The Tower of London is this way."

We arrived just as they opened. As we stood in line, she whipped around with her phone and snapped another photo of me. "At least warn me before you do that," I said.

"I'm not taking a picture of you. It's those two guys."

I turned to look.

"They're gone now."

"Where? There's no place to hide."

"They must have gotten into the end of the line."

"I'll be right back. I want to get a look at them."

"No. Don't let them know we're on to them. They'll just get sneakier." She pulled me inside.

We saw the ravens with their clipped wings that made them captives. I imagined the prisoners as they marched from dank cells to the chopping block in the yard. Their first exposure to light, warmth, and fresh air in months, if not years, would have felt surreal, if it weren't for the jeering crowds. It was not ironic that royals hoarded their prisoners and their jewels in the same castle. A better metaphor for power coupled with exploitation could not exist.

Yolanda was sullen as we drifted back onto the street. She had been particularly bothered by the story of the two little princes who had been locked up and then murdered. How frightened they must have been, she said over and over. When they had died, they were younger than her children were now.

"Where to next?" I said cheerfully, trying to pull her out of her funk.

"St. Paul's Cathedral, where Lady Di got married."

We found the church. As we were waiting for traffic to pass, she whipped around and took more photos. "You think I'm nuts, but I'm not. Those two thugs are behind us again."

I twisted around to see who she was talking about. She grabbed my arm and steered me across the street. "Don't look now. They'll see you. They weren't in the Tower. They must have waited for us to come out."

After taking the requisite photos with the church in the background, we found a gift shop selling Lady Di souvenirs. Yolanda bought two commemorative china plates, one for herself and one for her daughter.

On the way back to the hotel, we found the pub she had wanted to visit. We huddled over fish and chips while she thumbed through her phone.

"There!" she said. "These two guys!" I saw a picture of my shoulder with a gaggle of tourists in the background. The screen was so small, everyone in the picture was blurred. Then she flicked through more images, stopping on photos she'd taken in front of the Tower and the cathedral. A similar crowd lined the street. "There they are." She pointed. "There and there!"

"Sorry, Yolanda, not seeing it."

"When we get home, I'll print the pictures and then you'll see."

After lunch, we went back to the hotel, checked out, and called a taxi. Our flight left early that evening, so the plan was we'd go straight to Heathrow after interviewing Sophia. When we arrived at her flat, police cars were parked helter-skelter along the street.

A uniformed officer directed the cab to keep going. As we passed, I saw several officers clustered around the entry.

I asked the driver to pull over and wait.

We walked back to the building and were stopped by a young, uniformed woman. "The building is closed," she said.

"I'm here to see someone. We have an appointment. I just flew in from San Francisco. Is there a way we can get a message to her?"

"Who are you meeting?" she asked.

"Sophia Lamar."

"Please wait right here." She walked to the cluster of suits and uniforms by the door and spoke to them. They each peered over her shoulder at us. One of the suits broke away from the group and approached.

"My name is Detective Ahmed," he said. "I'm told you're here to meet with Sophia Lamar."

"We have an appointment," I said.

"And you are?"

"Maureen Gould and this is my assistant, Yolanda Martinez."

"What is the nature of your business?"

"I'm an attorney from San Francisco. Ms. Lamar is a witness in one of my cases. I'm afraid I can't say more than that."

"All the way from San Francisco to interview one person? She must be a fairly important witness." He paused, the cop-pause that is meant to sweat out the interviewee with oppressive silence. Jake, who had been a cop, used it on me early in our marriage. I didn't fall for it anymore.

Instead, I used the time to consider our itinerary. If we couldn't get in to see Sophia this afternoon, we could call her and reschedule the appointment. Depending on her availability, we might have to stay in London another day, or even longer. We would need to reschedule our flight home and find hotel rooms.

I'd almost forgotten Detective Ahmed when he spoke again. "I'm sorry to inform you that Ms. Lamar can't meet with you."

"Yolanda just talked to her yesterday to confirm the interview. Is she around? Perhaps we can reschedule?"

He turned to Yolanda. "How did she sound when you spoke to her, Miss Martinez?"

"Mrs. Martinez," Yolanda said. "She was nervous. She made us promise not to tell anyone we were coming and not to record the interview."

"Look, sorry to have bothered you," I said. "It's obviously a bad time. We'll call her and reschedule." I jerked my head for Yolanda to follow me to the waiting cab.

"Just a minute," Detective Ahmed said. Then he lowered his voice. "I'm what you would call a homicide detective, Ms. Gould."

Yolanda grabbed my forearm firmly enough to feel the scar ridges beneath my clothes. She frowned, looked at my arm, then up at me. I patted her hand. "Are you okay?" I asked.

A third-floor window had its drapery drawn back. I could see several people milling around inside.

"You're here about Sophia?" I asked. "Was she murdered?"

"So it appears."

"When?"

Another suit broke from the gathering at the door and tapped Detective Ahmed on the shoulder. "Excuse me," he said. They stepped away and spoke quietly. Afterwards, the other man went back to the group while the detective came back to us. "I must apologize. We're very busy right now, but I need to talk to you. Where are you staying?"

"We were on our way to the airport right after the interview," I said. "Our bags are in the cab."

"Tell you what. We'll bring you back to the station, have a chat, then you can be on your way."

"We'll miss our plane," Yolanda said. She had never been away from her children for twenty-four hours before. "The flight leaves at ten."

"No worries," he said. He lifted a hand, beckoning the young woman who we first met. "Mills, collect these ladies' bags and take them down to the station." Then he turned and joined the group huddled by the door.

We were shown into an interview room, given tea and cookies. I texted Jake to give him an update. Yolanda paced the room, peaking out the door's small window every few minutes. Officer Mills came back after an hour to tell us Detective Ahmed was on his way.

"We're going to miss our flight if we don't leave soon," Yolanda said. "How bad is London traffic this time of day? Our check-in is at seven."

"Look," I said. "We'd be happy to give a statement. Is there anyone else around we could talk to?"

Mills shrugged and left the room, closing the door behind her.

"My kids," Yolanda said. She was starting to cry.

"Nuts," I said. "Grab your stuff. We can do the interview on the phone." I took my wheelie in hand and started out the door. It was unlocked. I don't know why I hadn't tried to leave before.

"But won't we get into trouble?"

"We're not under arrest. We haven't done anything wrong. Now, come on. You want to get home to your kids, don't you?"

I led her the way we came, down a hall, past a squad room, to a set of elevators. When the doors opened, Detective Ahmed stepped off. "Ladies, where are you going? We haven't had that chat yet."

"We'll miss our flight," I said.

"Your flight is at ten."

"Check in is three hours ahead of departure," Yolanda added.

"Tosh. That's a suggestion only. We'll get you there in plenty of time." He steered us back to the interview room, then just before he closed the door on us, he said. "I'll be along in a moment."

"When's the next plane?" Yolanda asked.

I opened my phone's browser. The next departure was early in the morning. The only tickets left were in economy class. Fifteen hours bent like a pretzel would be brutal. Our only choices were a flight later the next day that had seats in premium class but with two long layovers, making for a twenty-hour trip, or take the fifteen-hour evening flight, which meant another day in London, without a hotel room. I booked the early morning flight. The sooner Yolanda got home to her kids, the better.

She called her sister who had been babysitting to tell her what was going on. A furious conversation in Spanish was taking place when Detective Ahmed walked into the room. She spiked him a look, spoke a few more sentences, then dropped her phone into her purse.

"I know you're worried about missing the flight, and I promise to have an officer take you directly to the airport once we have finished." The door opened and another officer joined us, who was not introduced.

Ahmed asked me, "Why did you come all the way to London to meet with Ms. Lamar? Wouldn't a telephone call do?"

"She insisted on meeting in person. That's the only way she'd speak to us. We hoped she would have information useful in our investigation."

Ahmed took what looked like a calming breath. "It would be helpful to our inquiries if we knew what this case was about."

"Something that happened back in America." By now he would have had someone look at my website and would know that I specialized in sexual harassment cases. "It had to do with an employer she used to work for."

"Does this employer have a name?"

He wouldn't have to look very hard online to find Mickey's story about the lawsuit I had filed against Cleville. The less I talked about the case to strangers, the less chance of The Duke's attorney finding out that I came here to meet with Sophia. Although they might assume that I was investigating his past, knowing who I was talking to would direct them to any potential witnesses and then they would beat me to them. The problem was, some people can be easily molded by the person asking questions and once they're locked into a story, they are unlikely to correct themselves.

"Here's the thing, Detective. It's a sensitive matter."

"Let's get to the point," Ahmed said. "Ms. Lamar was an actress. You recently filed a lawsuit against Reginald Cleville, the movie producer. So what did you suppose she was going to tell you?"

"Sophia Lamar had worked with him a while ago and then left Hollywood. I represent a young woman, an employee of his, who he accosted. We believe this was an ongoing pattern with Mr. Cleville so we're checking with women who had been associated with him in the past."

"So you're looking for proof of prior misconduct. Isn't that character evidence? Can you get that admitted in the States?"

"It depends on who the defendant is," I said. "I'm suing Cleville but I'm also suing Crown Productions, which he is employed by. Prior misconduct would prove that Crown Productions knew Cleville had a pattern of sexually assaulting his employees."

"Who knew you were coming to London?"

"Just my team."

"And who would that be?" Ahmed asked.

"Yolanda and my investigator, Eli Conroy," I said.

"Do you have a number for Mr. Conroy?"

I recited it for him, then said, "But he isn't answering right now. I tried yesterday and just before we met you."

"Is it unusual for Mr. Conroy to be unavailable?"

"He's working right now. Until he has something to show me, he'll avoid my calls. He'll turn up sooner or later."

"Now, if you would, please give us an accounting of your actions from the time you arrived in London."

Yolanda slapped the table with both hands. "What? You're accusing us of murdering her? How stupid would that be, for us to come back to her apartment?"

"It would have been suspicious if you hadn't arrived for the appointment. I need to rule you out of the inquiry. Then you can be on your way."

I gave them the flight number we arrived on, the hotel we stayed at, the time we checked in, and the time we left for sightseeing. At that point, Yolanda pulled out her phone and began reciting exact times we were at each location, reviewing the pictures she had taken. Ahmed asked for a copy of the photos and gave us an email address. Yolanda tapped her screen a few times and announced they had been sent. Ahmed nodded at the unnamed detective, who left the room.

"I need to check on a matter and then I can let you go." Ahmed stood.

"You said you'd give us a ride to the airport," Yolanda said.

"And we shall." With that, he left.

My internal clock was disoriented from travel, but I knew that it had been a long time since I had eaten. "Got anything edible in that bag of yours?"

Yolanda was sifting through her photos again. "Just the Mars bars I picked up for the kids."

"I'll pay you back."

"Promise?"

I crossed my heart. She pulled out the candy and we each ate two. My pulse immediately began racing in response to the sugar. I hoped I could find some protein soon. I checked the time. If Ahmed was right, we might still make the flight.

An hour later, during which time Yolanda had several conversations with her kids and sister in Spanish and Jake and I had exchanged texts, Ahmed rolled in with Officer Mills behind him.

"Very well, ladies. I'll need your contact information and then I'll have everything I need for the time being. We've checked our surveillance cameras and you're free to go. Mills here will drive you to Heathrow."

We made it to the airport and were standing in security in time to hear the first call for our flight.

"All I want is to go home," Yolanda said. "This trip has been horrible. Do you think it's our fault Sophia was . . ." She broke off and looked around to see if anyone was listening. "Maybe he, you know who, found out we were coming here. And then he sent those two guys to follow us around. They knew we were going to meet her. And they got to her first. But they kept following us around, thinking maybe we were going to talk to someone else they didn't know about. Did you ever think about that?"

Chapter Thirteen

AFTER CLEARING SECURITY, WE went to the ladies' room. I wanted to call Jake to tell him we were waiting to board and to make sure he would pick us up. When I pulled out my phone, I saw that it was dead.

"Can I borrow your cell?"

"Sure," Yolanda said. She handed the phone over, then went into a stall.

Jake's number rolled over to voicemail. I left a short message.

"Say 'hi' for me," Yolanda called.

"Yolanda says hi. See you soon." With that, I hung up and dropped the phone into my purse.

On our way to the Virgin Air lounge, Yolanda dragged me into yet another gift shop. We were both pulling wheeled carry-ons with our purses stacked on top. I was scanning the paperbacks as Yolanda stood in line to buy replacement Mars Bars for her kids when I heard her voice raised. "Where's my bag?"

A group of people stared at her.

"My bag is gone!" She searched the floor around her. "Has anyone seen my bag? It's purple."

The new tote was gone.

"I just put it down for a minute," she called over to me. "So I could pay for these." She was holding her open wallet in one hand and a clutch of candy bars in the other.

The onlookers, obviously anxious for her to complete her transaction, said they hadn't seen anything. I gave the cashier my credit card to complete the sale.

A horrible thought struck me. "Where is your boarding pass?"

"In the pocket of my suitcase with my passport." The wheelie was on the floor next to her. "But my phone! With all my pictures!"

"I have it." I rummaged in my purse. "I accidentally kept it."

Yolanda grabbed my sleeve and leaned in. "It's them. They took my bag. I just know it."

"Who?"

"Those guys who followed us all over London."

If there were two thugs, it was highly unlikely they'd wait while we were in the police station, then follow us to the airport. "You would have recognized them if they got close enough to steal your purse."

"Maybe there was a third one I didn't notice. Or they paid some kid to do it."

I'd tried to be gentle, but that was not my natural mode and I was out of patience. "Assuming for purposes of argument that two big blond men flew with us from San Francisco, followed us around London, and were involved in murdering Sophia Lamar, why would these guys want your purple purse?"

"Because they thought I had taken pictures of them on my phone and it was in the purse. They didn't know you had it."

That made sense. "Maybe you're right."

"I know I am. You'll see."

We arrived at San Francisco International in the late morning. Jake met us at the airport, driving his old brown Jeep. He had cleaned out the debris from various fishing, camping, and ski trips, but it still smelled like the outdoors. I rode in front beside Jake with Yolanda in the back seat.

As soon as he pulled away from the curb, he said, "Did the cops tell you anything about Sophia?"

"Murdered, that's all I know. They didn't give us the exact time other than the evening before our appointment. Nothing about who, how, or why."

"But they don't suspect you, right?"

I waited to answer while he negotiated the freeway onramp and lined up for the junction so we could drop Yolanda off in Daly City.

"No way. London is covered in wall-to-wall surveillance. They checked it before they let us go. We went to our rooms after we arrived and stayed there until the following morning, all during the time period they said she was killed."

He visibly relaxed. "Who do you think did it?"

"Cleville," Yolanda said before I could answer.

"It couldn't have been him," Jake said. "He was at a political fundraiser hosted by your father at the mansion Friday night. It's all over the net."

"You're keeping an eye on Reginald Cleville?" I asked.

He gave me a meaningful look. "I couldn't tell you if I was." He was serious this time, not like that night in my loft. He was investigating Cleville.

"Did you tell him about the goons?" Yolanda asked.

Jake risked a glance at me. "What goons?"

"Yolanda thinks we were followed in London." Her head was between ours now. "And my brand-new purple tote got stolen in the airport."

"Why would someone steal your bag?"

Yolanda poked me in the shoulder. "Because that's where my cell phone should have been, the one I used to take photos of the goons following us. But I gave it to Maureen and she dropped it in her purse." She poked Jake's shoulder. "We got 'em."

BACK AT THE LOFT, I spread the Sophia Lamar witness file across the dining table. My laptop was open, humming away. Germaine Greer leapt up and sprawled across my keyboard. I shuffled to the next chair and left her to it.

I wasn't certain that Cleville had Sophia murdered to prevent our interview. But it was the easiest theory to rule out, so I grabbed a legal pad and wrote out a list of everyone who knew we were going to London.

I had announced it to Eli and Yolanda in our Monday morning staff meeting. That afternoon, Yolanda had called Phillipa, Sophia's assistant, to tie down the day and time of our appointment. Jake knew, of course. I assumed Yolanda's family knew. She still had two teenagers at home. It was unlikely that anyone in her circle had ties to Cleville and would have tipped him off.

"What if Sophia called Cleville?" I wondered aloud. "What if she wanted permission to talk to us first?"

Jake handed me a glass of beer, then headed back into the kitchen to check on his bouillabaisse. He gave the pot a stir, then said. "Give it a break, Red. There's nothing you can do. You don't have the resources the police have."

"Don't you think it's a strange coincidence that she agreed to talk to us and then she's murdered the night before our appointment? I don't care if Cleville has an alibi. Come to think of it, his having an alibi is suspicious. Since I filed suit, the only real time reporting on his whereabouts was the very night she was murdered."

"So you think he had an actress who used to work for him murdered because of a movie he's planning to make now."

"Because of a multimillion-dollar venture that might collapse if Josephine's case goes forward. That's what Ian Napier said in our last hearing." The cat rose from my keyboard and casually walked across my notes, scattering them. I picked her up and gingerly set her on the floor. "And then there's Josephine. I called her with an update just before we left. If someone hacked into her phone to get the selfies, they could have bugged it. Maybe she told her family and Cleville's guys listened to the conversation."

"You don't have any proof her phone was hacked. For all you know, her boyfriend gave the photos to Cleville. Or he gave it to a dozen of his best friends who sent them all around the world. Or he could have posted them online. Revenge porn."

"If he had posted the selfies, Eli would have picked it up."

"Did you ask him to research her before you took the case?"

"Dammit." I rested my head in my hands. I should have had Eli do a deep background check on Josephine, just like the defense would do. Investigating the client was standard operating procedure for plaintiffs' lawyers. It's better to find the unsavory stuff before the defense attorney does.

Social media destroys cases. The whiplash victim snowboarding days after the accident. The client too depressed to get out of bed strolling on the boardwalk, eating junk food and getting a tattoo. The back-injured worker golfing. Before social media, defense firms had to hire private investigators to follow the clients around to collect damning evidence. Now plaintiffs post the photos themselves. All the investigators have to do is surf the net.

I had been so excited about the case—Hollywood, deep pockets, tons of publicity—that I had skipped the basics. How much of my faith in Josephine's case was fueled by hubris, having just won the Paredes verdict? Was I beginning to believe I had the magic touch, that my advocacy gifts could overcome any problem? Was I that arrogant?

Jake said. "Another thing: if they bugged her phone, they would have known your strategy sooner and would have done something to stop you."

"Valerie Vann refused to talk to us."

"She probably has an NDA. Besides, you decided to visit Saratoga Monday morning right before you left. There was no time for Cleville to find out and send someone ahead of you to threaten her." He pulled two fresh beers from the fridge. "You've been in the business a while, Red. Things don't always shake out the way you want. That doesn't mean there's a conspiracy to sabotage you. This guy isn't as powerful as you think he is. Who's going to risk getting caught for murder on his account?"

"A hitman. Life's cheap. Cleville can afford it," I said. Maybe he was right. "Do you think I'm paranoid?"

"I think you're exhausted, overworked, and over-invested in this case. You need to take a break."

"I just spent thirty hours sitting on planes doing next to nothing. How many Julia Roberts movies can you watch?"

"You are such a lawyer," he said. He came back into the dining area, stood behind my chair, and massaged my shoulders. I hadn't realized how tight they were until he worked his hands into them.

I let my head drop back. Jake was a good man. He deserved children. He deserved a wife whose darkest secrets would not disgust him. My neck tightened.

He quit massaging. "Look, I talked to one of the IT guys in my office. He said Josephine's phone could have been hacked. It's easy enough to do. The hacker could have sent her an email with a link and when she opened it, an app downloaded that monitored her device. Or he could have gotten into her cloud account."

"See!"

"Or the boyfriend passed around the photos."

"I'll find out when I go to see him."

"Or she could have sent the photos to Cleville herself. Ever think about that?"

The case crumbled before me. What if Josephine had sent the selfies to Cleville? What if she was a willing participant in his sex games? Then something went wrong between them, something she hadn't told me about, so he fired her; and she called me in revenge. It was the standard defense trotted out by abusers. From their point of view, it might be true. They conveniently omit from their analysis the inherently oppressive nature of the employer-employee relationship. With her job on the line, was it even possible for an employee to willingly consent to sex with her boss?

Having doubts about a case was healthy. Thinking like a defendant's lawyer allowed me to predict the defense's strategy. Every case had times when I wasn't sure if I'd win, but as long as I had enough evidence to pursue the claim, I plowed ahead. My commitment to victim advocacy spurred me on. When all the evidence was in, and the whole story was told, the jury would decide.

WHEN ELI ROLLED IN for our staff meeting the following Monday morning, Yolanda and I were already sitting at the conference table.

"Why haven't you returned my calls?" I asked.

"Good morning to you too, Chief." He wandered to the console, poured coffee, dumped a little pot of creamer and three packets of sugar into the mug, and stirred. "No doughnuts. Man, I could really use a doughnut. How was the London trip?"

"Total bust," I said. "Sophia was murdered the night before our appointment."

Eli stared into his cup. "Murdered?"

"You would have known that if you answered your phone," Yolanda said.

Eli gave her a quick frown. "Who says it was murder?"

"The homicide detective we met," I said.

"How do they know it wasn't an accident or suicide?"

"He wouldn't say. So where were you?"

He didn't answer my question. "Why did the cops talk to you?"

"They were at her flat when we arrived. Focus, please. What the hell happened to you? I called and left messages all weekend."

"I was tracking down stuff on Josephine's boyfriend, Cameron Aguilar. My phone died and I didn't notice. Didn't even see that you called until this morning."

"What about the witnesses on Cleville's list? Did you get anything on them?"

"No time. I'm just one man, Chief. If that's what you wanted me to do instead, you should have said."

I had. Twice. And written it on the whiteboard that was on the wall behind me. "And Crown Productions, did you get the players' names?"

"No time, like I said."

Yolanda picked up her pen, poised to take notes. "Where do we go from here?"

"Josephine's deposition will be rescheduled," I said. "Before I agree to the date, I want to see if we have grounds to get a protective order against using the selfies. To do that, I need to talk to Cameron Aguilar to make sure he didn't give them to Cleville. If he didn't, there's a chance they were stolen from her phone."

Eli snorted. "High level espionage for a he said-she said case. More like, she sent them to Cleville herself."

Yolanda threw her pen down. "You can't believe that."

"Don't get your panties in a bunch. I'm just playing devil's advocate."

I went on as if I hadn't heard them. "If we can establish the boyfriend didn't share them with anyone, her phone must have been hacked. I can file a motion for protective order against Cleville using stolen evidence before we resume Josephine's deposition. I need the deep background on this Aguilar guy before I go down there to talk to him. Eli, you think you can get that to me by end of Tuesday? I'll fly down Wednesday."

▼

ELI LEFT THE OFFICE promising to have the research on my desk no later than close of business, a day early. I went back to my office and began surfing through the hundreds of emails that had come in while we were in London.

I ran across a message with the subject all in caps and five exclamation points: "WARN-ING!!!!!" I was about to delete it when my eye caught the word "Cleville" in the body of the email. It read, "Drop the case against Reginold Cleville if you know what's good for you. Signed, A Friend."

Crank mail. And whoever the "friend" was, they'd misspelled "Reginald." The case had hit the news and was drawing out every opinionated person with a Wi-Fi connection. I had just moved it into my junk folder when Yolanda appeared in the doorway, a sheet of paper in hand. She had that stern look on her face.

"What?" I asked.

She dropped the document on the desk and came around to read over my shoulder.

Dear Lawyer Lady,

You been talking to the wrong people. You don't know what your (misspelled) getting yourself into. Drop the case against Reginold Cleville before bad things happen.

-A Friend.

At least the misspelling was consistent. "Where's the envelope?"

Yolanda handed it to me. It had no return address, no postmark. The address was typed, as had been the letter. Someone must have slipped it through the mail slot while we were in London.

"Who sent it?" Yolanda asked.

"Cranks," I said. I didn't tell her about the email. She was upset enough. "It could be anyone."

"How can you be so sure that Cleville didn't send it?"

"He would have spelled his own name correctly. Think about it. It's got to be someone in San Francisco who's mad that the production was stopped."

"You didn't stop the production."

"What is true doesn't matter. What matters is what people think is true. Cleville is telling everyone he can't make his movie here now because the lawsuit means that investors are withdrawing. He might move it to Vancouver or even make it in a Hollywood backlot. From the public's point-of-view, it all comes back to Josephine's case. The tradespeople are counting on the work. Locals were hoping to get cast as extras. The hotels and restaurants expected that the Hollywood people would spend lots of money. Not to mention the free tourism advertising."

"And you know this, how?"

"Mickey Wong has been doing a series of stories about the case. Here's the thing about justice, Yolanda. People are exploited because of money and power. The first thing bad guys do when you try to right a wrong is threaten. If I'm going to be afraid of the rich and powerful, then I can't fight for victims. We've had unpopular cases before. What would you have me do?"

"Just be careful. First Sophia was murdered, now this. That's all I'm saying."

Chapter Fourteen

I KEPT LOOKING OVER my shoulder during the trip to southern California, unnerved by Yolanda's warning. The other passengers were tired business travelers, some preoccupied with devices, while others slumped in their chairs as they spoke into Bluetooth headsets. The men hauled leather bags, the women stylish totes.

Much of the same group accompanied me on the shuttle to the rental car companies. While I stood in line, Yolanda texted me wanting to know if I saw anyone suspicious. I truthfully reported not a big blond thug in sight. Any one of my fellow travelers could have been a private investigator—I wouldn't know—but I didn't mention that to Yolanda. One by one, we pulled out of the parking lot in bland midsized sedans and fanned across the interstate to our various destinations. I checked my rearview mirror several times to see if I was being followed. I didn't notice anyone.

I found the café after just one wrong turn, so I was still early for the appointment. The place had a Hollywood sign logo etched onto a brushed steel marquee over the front door. Inside, oversized photographs of bygone movie stars hung on gray walls. Humphrey Bogart clutched Ingrid Bergman. Rita Hayworth smoldered in a close-up, Hedy Lamar smoldered in another. Gene Tierney, too. A lot of smoldering going on in those early days of Tinseltown.

I had settled with my raspberry mocha into a back corner table and was scrolling through my messages when a young man coasted into view on a bicycle. With the grace of a gymnast, he dismounted while still in motion. He took off his helmet and shook out his shoulder-length thick black hair. He could have been a shampoo model.

His jeans hung loosely from his hips. His t-shirt was fashionably faded. When he caught me staring at him, I waved. He jerked his head upwards in acknowledgment, then went to the counter and ordered. A lithe, very tan, bleached blonde with her dark roots showing lowered her chin when he spoke. The appearance she strove for was repressed delight, for discretion's sake, yet unable to control herself in the beam of his animal magnetism. It was a difficult look to manage, but she seemed practiced.

He rewarded her with a slow smile. She slinked to the fridge, retrieved his water, then slinked back to the register. Her eyes followed him as he wove through the tables to my corner. When she saw me, her face dropped. I smiled, then took a sip of my raspberry mocha. The drink was bitter. I was certain I had ordered a double shot of syrup. I swished the drink and took another sip. Still bitter.

After he hung his helmet on the seat post, I extended my hand. "Maureen Gould."

He reached across the table. His hand was large, warm, and dry. My palm began to perspire.

"Cool," he said. "I'm Cam. But you already knew that." Then he gave me that same slow grin he had given the barista. His teeth were very white. He could have been a toothpaste model, too.

"I had guessed." I hadn't. I knew who he was when he rolled up on the bike.

Eli hadn't shown up with his report, so I had surfed the web. Josephine had said Cameron graduated from USC film school shortly before she did. On the university website, I found mentions of him associated with independent productions but no photographs. An article in a small southern California newspaper discussed this bright young high school student with big Hollywood dreams. The photo was dated, but it was the same boy. His thick hair was chin-length then. He had the same heavy dark eyebrows, same fringe of black curly lashes on both upper and lower eyelids. It was doubtful that he had ever heard the word "no" from a female of any age, regardless of the question posed.

I cleared my throat, preparing to dive into the interview.

"How's Josephine?" he asked. When I had called him to set up this appointment, I had given him a thumbnail sketch of who I was and my reason for calling. He'd already heard about the lawsuit, through the grapevine. When I asked who was talking about it, he claimed he couldn't remember. He said he wasn't sure he could help her case, but he agreed to meet with me anyway.

"Good, good," I said. I needed to be circumspect. I didn't know whose side he was on, but I did know he was talking about the case. "And she sends her regards."

"Cool." He unscrewed the cap of his water bottle and drank it half down. "So there was something you wanted to talk about?"

"Can I get some background on you first? Are you currently working?"

He shook his head. "There are some projects coming up. Hey, have Josephine give me a call. Maybe she could get in on them." He set the water bottle down, then nudged it a few inches to the side by sliding his fingertips along the table surface, leaving a trail of condensation.

I felt an urge to mop it up with a napkin, but I wasn't his mother. I took another sip of my bitter, now lukewarm, coffee. "When was the last time you worked for Reginald Cleville?"

He dipped a forefinger into the condensation puddle, then lifted it slowly, head tilted, as he studied the water's adhesion to his skin. When it broke, he dropped the finger into the liquid again. This he did twice more before he wiped his hand on his jeans. "I had a gig with him last year. It's still in post-production. I'm not sure what they're calling it now. Josephine was on it, too. You could ask her. That's where we met."

"So you work for Cleville regularly?"

"Right now, I work for whoever calls me. It takes years to establish relationships and earn a reputation that can lead to steady work. So, if he called me, sure, I'd take a job."

"If you were to support Josephine in her case against Cleville, are you concerned that it would hurt your job opportunities?"

He spun his chair away from the table and perched an elbow across the seatback. "What do you mean by support? It's not like I saw something. I was never in the same room with Josephine and The Duke. If I did see him, he was passing through during a shoot and I was busy working. I'd be surprised if he even knows who I am. Not sure how I can help you."

"Even if you didn't see anything between them, you could fill in some background for me."

He casually flipped his hand into the air. "That's cool, I guess. Whatever."

"For instance, had you heard rumors about The Duke?"

"Like what rumors?"

"Have you heard Reginald Cleville harassed his staff, sexually or otherwise?"

"Nope."

"You sound certain."

"I'm not much into gossip. I go to the job, do my work, and go home."

He claimed he wasn't into gossip, but he had heard about a lawsuit filed in San Francisco a few weeks earlier from a source he either couldn't remember, because everyone was talking about it, or refused to name.

"But you socialize with people from the company."

"Well, I mean, it depends on what you call 'socializing.' We go out for beer once in a while, sure."

"So you would know some of your coworkers pretty well." It was a safe bet.

"Again, not sure what you mean by that." He wasn't going to name names. He was setting himself up as the gatekeeper against my further contact with Crown Productions employees. Whether he was volunteering for the job to ingratiate himself with Cleville, or it was on direct orders, remained to be seen, but whatever I would get from him would have to come in the next few minutes.

"Let's talk about Josephine, then. You two had a relationship."

"Yeah, well, sure, we were friends." He began tapping his now-empty water bottle on the edge of the table.

"You were close friends."

"What are you getting at?"

"She texted you some pictures of herself."

He began to color. Red splotches spread across his throat.

"So what? Women send me pictures all the time. It doesn't mean we're doing anything."

I'd never sent a nude selfie to anyone in my life. Either there was a lot I didn't understand about the contemporary courting rituals of young adults, or Cameron Aguilar was lying.

"Women send you unsolicited nude selfies?"

"Yeah, sure, all the time." He wasn't looking at me anymore. He was staring at a smoldering Marlene Dietrich hanging on the opposite wall.

"Did Josephine send you these photographs unsolicited?"

"Hey, maybe you should ask her." He began to push himself to a stand. "You know what? I've got somewhere to be."

"Wait," I placed a hand on his arm to stop him. "I just have one more question."

That lecherous smile spread across his face, and he sat back down.

"Did you share these photos with anyone?"

"Yeah, right, like that's going to happen. What do you think I do, sit around the steam room with a bunch of Neanderthals, drooling over pictures of naked girls? You got me mistaken for someone else. That's not who I am."

"Then who are you?"

He shrugged. "Someone girls can trust."

This time when he stood, he tossed the water bottle across the room in a perfect arc, sinking it into a plastic recycle can.

"One more question," I said.

"That's what you said a minute ago."

"I lied. Are you willing to sign a statement that you never shared these photos?"

He gave me an indulgent look. "Leave me out of this, okay? I don't want to get involved. Tell Josephine good luck."

STACKS OF PAPER TOWERED on my mother's bedroom floor: bills, letters, contracts, warranties, and receipts, the detritus of her life I had unearthed during my search of the mansion.

I had arrived mid-morning the following day, hoping Frank would have left for work already. When I stepped into the vestibule, the air was musty. It felt empty. No Frank. No Emily the maid. No other staff. If a mouse had scampered across the floor, I would have heard it.

I didn't know what to do with the house now that it was mine. The place was filled with memories of the sad girl who only wanted to be seen. Yet it was all that was left of Granny Shaughnessy. Frank had no right to squat in my inheritance.

He had refused to leave. A series of letters had passed between Ian Napier, acting as his attorney, and myself, regarding Frank's claim that he was owed money for maintaining the premises. He insisted that the mansion should be sold and the proceeds divided "equitably," whatever that meant, arguing that he was entitled to at least half. Figuring my response would one day be filed as an exhibit in a lawsuit and read by a judge, I was circumspect: I would be happy to entertain his offer once he provided the documents supporting his claim.

In the next letter, Frank offered to vacate if I paid him an unspecified sum of money. He had once told me the first party to call out a number always lost; the trick was to force the other party to commit to an amount that would become his floor or ceiling, depending on whether he was receiving the money or paying it. I wasn't falling for it. Again I responded that I would be happy to review his evidence.

In the third volley, Frank promised to move out once I paid him half a million dollars. It was a fire sale, he claimed. I laughed out loud and tossed the letter into the "to be filed" pile. I wanted Frank out of the house, but apparently not as badly as he wanted money, lots of it, without proving his claim. Time was on my side.

That morning, as I wandered through the house collecting documents, forgotten memories came to mind. I saw grooves in the hallway floors where I had roller skated. In my father's den was the couch where I had read fairy tales while he worked. I found myself standing in the parlor corner to which I was banished while my mother painstakingly decorated the Christmas tree.

I flopped on the couch and put my shoes on the table. No one was left to tell me I couldn't.

I wandered into the kitchen, opened the fridge, and found a quart of milk long past its best-buy date. Crusty dishes were in the sink. In the cabinet underneath, a rank smell rose from a garbage can so full, the lid couldn't shut. Frank was fending for himself.

It was then I noticed dust had settled throughout the house. A soft gray layer blurred the tables and the bookcases, the picture frames and the windowsills. In a corner of the French doors that led into the garden hung an elaborate spider web. The grass was shaggy.

The now-dim dining room table reminded me of my last night in the mansion. I had not eaten with the family for some time, because I had been sick. That evening, I was in bed, dozing, when the maid knocked on the door. I knew it was around dinner time because I had smelled food cooking earlier.

"Come in," I called.

She softly opened the door and closed it behind her again. "I've been sent to bring you downstairs."

"I'm not hungry," I said.

She shook her head. "Dinner was cleared away an hour ago. They want to speak with you."

I pushed myself up. "What about?"

Without answering, she pulled a robe from the closet and held it up for me.

When the maid led me into the dining room, my mother was sitting at her end of the table. Frank was facing the liquor decanters on the buffet, his back to me. He was pouring himself a drink. The maid disappeared.

My mother pointed at a chair. I sat.

Her hands were folded on the dining room table, the surface so shiny that an image of her was reflected on the surface. "A decision has been made. You're going to boarding school."

The news thrilled me. Boarding school, like in the movies. Switzerland, perhaps, where I would learn how to ski downhill and jump horses. On holiday, I would visit my new friends' British estates. There would be parties where I would giggle and twitter in flawless French with the other girls about their handsome, aristocratic brothers.

"When do I leave?"

"Tomorrow."

"But—" I said. I had clothes to buy. And I needed a passport. And I wanted to say good-bye to my teachers.

It was then she faced me. Her expression, filled with emotions I could not identify, told me she would brook no further discussion. Later I imagined she had felt anger and sadness. As an adult, I tried to convince myself she must have also felt guilt.

During the entire audience, Frank never turned around. He never looked at me.

I stood now inside the doorway of my mother's room, surveying the paper towers. Where to start? I needed to know whether any bills or taxes were due, the state of the household finances, and where the bank accounts were kept. I needed the homeowner's policy to make sure the structure and contents were adequately insured. Most importantly, I needed to find the paper trail that would show who had paid for the upkeep, in order to see if indeed Frank had a claim.

The documents were so numerous that my sorting system was useless. It didn't matter where I started. I needed coffee. I made my way back to the door.

"I wasn't expecting to find you here," Frank said. I hadn't heard him come in.

"It *is* my house."

He moved into the doorway, blocking my exit, and scanned the chaos. Any lawyer would see that I was looking for evidence.

"Perhaps this is a task best left to an accountant. I could have my staff box up this mess and we'll send it out to someone. Someone mutually agreeable, of course."

"I'm the personal representative. I'll handle it."

"It was unfair of her to saddle you with that responsibility. I've handled the household accounts since we were married. It simply makes sense that I should wind up the estate."

"She wanted me to do it. And that's how it's going to be, Frank."

He took another step toward me. "What happened, Maureen? Why are you being this way?" He studied me, first my hair, then my ears, chin, and settled on my mouth. "When you were little, you were Daddy's little girl." He slipped his hands into his pockets. "You're grown now, I know that. Married or divorced, is it? Nothing needs to change between us. You will always be my little girl."

Bourbon was on his breath. He weaved subtly as he looked down upon me. I didn't remember Frank being a morning drinker, but would I have noticed? I was a child when I last lived in the house.

Children miss so much.

My parents had often hosted cocktail parties. The guests arrived in the early evening, ladies in cocktail dresses, men in suits. Long before the party started, I would have been sent to my room, having been told that "children were seen but not heard."

When I was bored, I would sneak to the top of the stairs to watch the grownups, hoping to be seen by one of my mother's nicer friends. Sooner or later, I would be spotted, and a kindly matron would call me down to join the party. I would skip down the stairs and curtsey when introduced, as I had been taught, invoking praise from the ladies.

One night, a man asked me what I wanted to be when I grew up.

Quickly, I answered, "A judge, just like my grandfather."

I can still remember the laughter. "Come on, little girl," one man said. "Don't you want to do commercial transactions like your daddy? The pay is much better."

"It's not about money," I said. "It's about justice."

I was fourteen years old. When I wasn't reading Nancy Drew, I read books about court cases. My heroes were Atticus Finch, Clarence Darrow, and Thurgood Marshall. I believed that judges held real power. I imagined that my grandfather had been a fair and kind judge, and had made positive impacts on people's lives. I wanted to be like my image of him.

Drunk by then, the men guffawed. I knew I had said something wrong, but I didn't understand the joke. Heat rose to my cheeks. I was certain they could see me blushing.

"Better keep an eye on that one, Frank. She might put you in jail!"

I remember my father's face, stiff muscles twitching as he tried to smile. He clamped a hand on my shoulder so hard it hurt. "To bed. Now."

A long time passed while I lay in the dark listening to waves of laughter from downstairs. I must have drifted to sleep because I was suddenly aware the door was open. My father stood on the threshold, silhouetted in gauzy light.

He closed the door. "I came up to say good night."

Chapter Fifteen

"Where's the Diego Rivera?" I asked, not giving ground, cramped as we were in the bedroom entry.

"What are you talking about?"

"The little painting Diego Rivera gave to Lizzy Shaughnessy. It goes with the house. The house and all its contents are mine, you said so yourself. It hung beside Mother's bed and now it's gone. She said you had sent it out for cleaning. That was weeks ago. It should be back by now."

"Oh, that." He waved a hand in dismissal. "There were condition issues and repairs had to be made, so it took longer than expected. With the sudden decline in your mother's health, then the funeral, I lost track. I'm sure you understand." He walked away.

"Tell me where it is. I'll go pick it up."

He reeled back around. "Is that all you care about? That little painting? The house is in shambles. It's falling apart. Rotten lumber, antiquated boiler, copper plumbing, leaky roof and windows, all these things need to be replaced. A complete renovation would cost millions. You can't afford it. Neither can I. You need to sell this place and everything in it. Let some tech billionaire take over this money pit. When the sales proceeds come in, I'd be happy to accept a return on my investment."

"After living here rent free for forty-odd years."

"And there you have it! It *is* the money. When it comes down to it, the only thing the high-minded Maureen Eugenia Gould cares about is wealth." A fine spray made me blink when he spit out the last word. He wiped saliva from his face with the back of his hand. "I gave you a name you could be proud of. The Goulds are a long line of respected lawyers and jurists."

"And philanderers?"

"Nonsense. Your mother was lucky to have me. I legitimized her and that shanty Irish family of hers. They got rich exploiting immigrant labor. Proud of that, are you? How many coolies suffered to fill the Shaughnessy coffers? And that tramp Lizzy Shaughnessy, what a nightmare! My family told me not to marry your mother. Begged me, but I was blinded by—"

"Her money."

He slapped me. The momentum pulled him off balance, and he threw a hand up against the door jamb to steady himself.

I didn't move. My face burned where it had been struck. I felt tears well. I didn't want him to see me cry, even if they were tears of anger instead of pain, but I would not hide my feelings anymore.

"Show some respect, Maureen." He walked away stiffly. The front door slammed. His Jaguar roared.

I was still standing in the same place as his Jag faded into traffic.

▼

YOLANDA AND I FERRIED eight full bankers boxes back to my loft. We arranged the collection in the great room, two stacks against a wall, leaving the dining room table surface clear for sorting.

I grabbed a box, flipped off its lid, dumped the contents out, and started sorting. Piles for bills, warranties, and tax records. And a pile for letters and greeting cards saved in their envelopes. My mother had pen pals throughout her life, mostly distant cousins and girlhood friends who had moved away. Some postmarks had faded with age, but the stamps had cost four cents. More recent letters were tied up with a pink ribbon, the envelopes written in a neat longhand, return address "Q. Brennan." They had been postmarked within the last year.

I argued with myself about reading my mother's personal correspondence. I had yearned for closeness to her, to know what she regarded as important, what she thought and felt. Although she had not penned these letters, they were sent in response to something she had written. I decided to set the mail aside and let the dilemma work itself out in the back of my mind while I attended to more pressing matters.

Invoices recorded work on the house since it had been built: receipts from plumbers, bricklayers, glass companies, electricians, and landscapers. I even found the garden plans that had been drawn and redrawn through the decades, including the one my mother had commissioned.

I searched for the bank accounts. My mother had inherited a pile of money along with the house. She was fortunate, she had often said, that she married a lawyer to handle all the paperwork. And apparently he had, as those papers were gone. He must have kept them at his office. Those records would prove whose money had supported the mansion.

I opened the hallway closet and stacked my boxes on the floor. As I straightened, Germaine Greer slithered past me on her way to the great room. I heard the front door open.

"There you are, cat," Jake said. Loud purring ensued.

I walked out of the hall and found Jake squatting, petting the cat. He had dropped his briefcase on the floor.

"Hi," I said.

"Hey, Red, didn't expect to see you here."

"I've been getting a lot of that lately."

He frowned in response.

"Frank showed up while I was at the mansion."

"And?"

"And words were exchanged, as they say."

He stepped closer. "What's that? Looks like you got some dirt on your face." He lifted a hand to brush away the imaginary smudge and I flinched. I imagined a hand-shaped bruise was now darkening on my cheek.

"It's nothing." I made my way around the kitchen island on the way to the fridge. "Want a beer?"

He settled onto a bar stool at the breakfast counter. With my back to him, I pulled two bottles of Anchor Steam from the fridge and two pilsner glasses from the cabinet, then filled each glass. I was stalling. I didn't want Jake asking questions about the bruise. I didn't want to answer, but I didn't know why. I hadn't done anything wrong.

When I turned around to serve him, he took a hard look at my face. His voice was low when he spoke. "Did he do that to you?"

I couldn't answer. I had lost my voice.

"Has he done something like this to you before?"

Had he? Was it the same?

"I can't talk about this."

"Someone needs to kick that bastard's ass."

"Jake, you're an officer of the court. You can't go around beating up people."

"Fine. We'll file charges. A man never strikes a woman. I don't care how pissed off he is. I don't care what she did."

I knew how criminal law worked. If Jake called the police, they would interview Frank and he would deny he had slapped me. Charges would or would not be filed, depending on the caprice of the deputy prosecutor who reviewed the case. Regardless, the story would be out. If the case went the distance, I would have to testify at trial where a jury would decide who was telling the truth, me or my father. Without witnesses, it would be my word against his.

"I can't."

"You can't what? Press charges? What he did was wrong, Maureen. You can't let him get away with it. What are you afraid of? I've seen the scars on your arms. I know what they mean. The most common reason kids hurt themselves—"

"Don't recite journal papers to me, Jacob Kuhn. I'm not your juror."

Prosecutors were trained in psychology so they could understand why victims sometimes refused to testify or recanted. Training inoculated them against the "she had it coming" mindset and taught them how to approach victims in a sensitive manner so as to better shepherd them through the system.

I took my beer, walked down the hall to the master suite, and began the shower.

He followed a few minutes later, stopping on the other side of the bedroom wall. "We're still married."

"I'm not the one who moved out."

"I was wrong and I'm sorry. I want to be your husband for the rest of my life. Love, honor, and support. That's what we wrote into our vows."

I stepped into the shower.

"Maureen, I'm not an idiot. You're different when you're around him, did you know that? It's like I lose you every time you see him, and it takes days for you to come back to me. I want to make everything all right for you. I want you to trust me, but you keep throwing up these walls. You've locked me out of your life."

I couldn't tell him. The barrier that had built up between us was more bearable than admitting Jake into the secret. If he knew, there would be three people in our marriage: Jake, Frank, and me.

When I was a child, I had craved oneness with Frank. I didn't know why the time we spent together was not to be spoken of, but I understood that my mother was shut out of our relationship. I was glad she was. I wanted him to myself.

After the rape, I believed it was my fault. What had I done that made Frank do that to me? Intellectually I knew that this was the source of my shame. I also knew that I had been groomed and had no way of knowing what to expect. Still, I couldn't forgive myself. And I couldn't share the secret with Jake—I was too afraid of what I would see in his eyes once he knew.

Through the shower door, I could see a blurred image of Jake. Facing away from me, he reached for my cosmetic jars one at a time, examined them, and then replaced them in the exact spots where they had been. Mist curled up around me, the glass door sweated, and his image was gone.

I stayed in the shower until the water ran cold. When I stepped into the empty bathroom, I heard him putter in the kitchen. The fridge door opened and closed. Pans rattled on the stovetop.

That night, we ate dinner in silence.

▼

OVER THE NEXT SEVERAL days, I sorted my mother's papers on the dining room table, creating separate piles for household expenses, insurance appraisals, and property taxes. Her personal correspondence I put back into a box. Someday I might want to read them, but now it was too soon.

I had thought all the banking records were missing but I was wrong. Old-style ledger books from decades ago had been saved, showing my mother had inherited two million dollars along with the house. Payments were made, yet the amount kept growing with accrued interest. The entries abruptly stopped a few years after my parents' marriage. She had also saved the bank statements which corresponded precisely to the ledger.

I suspected that the monies had been moved to another account. I called the bank, identified myself as the personal representative of her estate and was eventually put through to Mr. Walsh, an old friend of my parents.

"I didn't have a chance to speak to you after the funeral, but I wanted to tell you how sorry all of us at the bank are to hear of your mother's passing."

It would have been years since my mother had visited the bank personally and I suspected that anyone she had known had already died, but I thanked him.

"To what do I owe the pleasure of this call?"

"My mother appointed me her personal representative and I need to pull together an accounting for the courts."

"I understand. We deal with this from time to time."

"So I need to have access to the household accounts. I found a ledger and statements from years ago but nothing from the past twenty years plus."

"Yes, yes, I see."

"I assumed the accounts were with your bank."

"They were."

"Were?"

"Several years ago your father decided to invest those funds. He felt that simple passbook interest rates weren't yielding a sufficient return so he moved the money to an investment firm." He paused. "Or so I was told."

"When was that?"

"Back in the roaring 80's. He was quite right. The stock market was performing above expectations."

My father's first Jaguar was a maroon 1986 Daimler. He had a photograph of it on the wall of his den. That was also about the same time he moved his law firm to one of the top floors of a Financial District high rise.

"Do you know the name of the firm?"

"I'm sorry, Maureen. I do not. Oh, it appears I have a call coming in on another line. Again, allow me to extend my condolences."

The line went down before I could say goodbye.

I was staring at the blank screen of my cell phone when Jake walked in. "Find anything interesting?"

"My father took all my mother's money."

"Slow down, Red. What are you talking about?"

"All of her Shaughnessy inheritance. He closed out her bank account years ago and told Mr. Walsh he was going to invest it."

"He probably did just that. Why don't you give him a call and ask for the accounts? You need it for the court, right?"

"Right."

I punched in my father's office number and was put through.

"If this is about your motion to exclude your client's pornographic photos, my response will be timely filed."

"It's not about that. It's about the Shaughnessy money."

He sniffed. "What about it?"

"You took all the money out of the bank years ago."

"That's right. It wasn't earning enough interest so I moved it into stocks and bonds."

"I need to provide an accounting to probate court."

"Of course. There's a problem with that, Maureen. The money was used up years ago, as I told you."

"She had over three million dollars when you closed out the bank account."

"Between supporting that aging monstrosity of a house and unfortunate reversals in the market, the money was gone years ago. In fact, I don't have the accounts anymore."

"Then tell me where you invested the money and I'll get the records from your stock-broker."

He sniffed again. "He passed away several years ago. I expect his records were destroyed long ago."

Chapter Sixteen

THE TRIAL WAS EIGHT weeks away. Josephine arrived at the courtroom ten minutes early for the pretrial hearing. She had driven up for the hearing, arriving late the night before. She slid a thumb drive across the table to me. "I forgot to give you this."

"What is it?"

"Videos from Cleville's investor parties. You wanted to know where the money came from, right?"

The court clerk entered from a backdoor and settled into her station.

"Do I have enough time to go to the ladies' room?" Josephine asked.

I checked my watch. It was 1:50 P.M. Frank and Cleville hadn't arrived yet. The hearing would start precisely at two. "If you hurry."

I tossed the thumb drive into the bottom of my bag, then organized my papers: a copy of my motions, Frank's opposition briefs, and my replies. I scribbled on a legal pad to check three pens had ink. I was digging around in my briefcase for my highlighter when Josephine's stilettos tapped back into the courtroom. She was blinking rapidly.

Right behind her was Frank, an amused look on his face. He appeared to be sober, although it was well past noon. Cleville trailed behind him.

Josephine slipped into the chair beside me and asked, "Is he allowed to talk to me?"

"No, he is not. Did he try to?"

The clerk struck her gavel. "All rise!"

"We'll talk about this later," I whispered.

Judge Han entered from her private door and sat at the bench. As she took a slow look around the room, a frown flickered across her face. She slid on her reading glasses and flipped open the file on her desk. "We're here in the matter of *J.N. v. Cleville and Crown Productions*. This hearing was set upon the plaintiff's motion to exclude certain photographs and motion for discovery of the corporate defendant's financial records.

First, I would like plaintiff's counsel to address why the court should find the 'selfie' photographs are inadmissible."

I moved to the lectern. "Thank you, Your Honor. There are two reasons why this evidence should be excluded. The first is my client's privacy interest. These photographs are personal. The photographs were taken by her to be distributed to only one person, Mr. Aguilar. When she sent the photos, it was with the understanding that he would not show or give them to anyone else."

The judge thumbed through her file. "I see you attached an affidavit from your client. However, I do not see an affidavit from the photograph recipient, Mr. Aguilar."

They say if you don't have the facts, argue the law. "Yes, Your Honor. His affidavit would be immaterial to these proceedings, as it is not our burden to prove these photographs were stolen. Rather, the defendant has the burden to prove they were obtained lawfully. It will be the defendant who seeks to introduce these photographs into evidence. To date, he has given no explanation for how he obtained them." It was the only argument I had.

The judge wrote a few notes, then lifted her head. "Anything else?"

In my peripheral vision, I saw Josephine staring at me, her arms wrapped tightly around her waist.

"My second argument for excluding the photographs from evidence is that, regardless of their provenance, the photos did not come into the possession of the defendant Reginald Cleville until after this case was filed. If he had these photographs before he sexually assaulted—"

"Objection!" Frank was on his feet.

Judge Han took her glasses off and rubbed the bridge of her nose. "Mr. Gould, as an experienced attorney, you should be aware that anything said in oral argument is not evidence. Moreover, I am an experienced jurist. I am perfectly capable of discerning evidence from argument. Objection denied." She then addressed me. "However, Ms. Gould, I wish to note that we are not before the jury. We could do without the hyperbole, if you please."

"Certainly, Your Honor." I waited for Frank to sit down. His interruption of my argument was meant to flex muscle for his client's admiration. A flamboyant gesture and nothing more. If it were any other attorney, I would have started speaking again while he realized how ridiculous he was standing there. But it was my turn to flex. I had the floor, and I wasn't going to resume until he sat down. Cleville was paying Frank by the minute to stand silently with the last thing on his lips—a flaccid, and failed, objection.

Judge Han spiked Frank a look. He sat.

"As I was saying, there is no evidence that Mr. Cleville was in possession of these photographs before he assaulted my client." Cleville clutched Frank's sleeve. Frank ignored him. "So if the defendant argues at trial that he believed that she would welcome his advances, a defense he suggested in his brief, he cannot support that belief claiming he had seen these photos before the night in question. He didn't have them. That makes the photographs irrelevant to his defense."

"Very well, Ms. Gould. Mr. Gould, would you like to argue?"

"Indeed I would, Your Honor."

As I settled into my chair, he took the lectern. "First, I wish to address the provenance of the photographs. I strenuously object to the plaintiff's accusation that we stole the selfies. I have never been accused of stealing evidence in my entire career. I am insulted that such an outrageous allegation would be made against me or my office. We ask the court to find this argument is meritless and scurrilous, and we request the court to enter sanctions against plaintiff's counsel for making them."

"Mr. Gould," Judge Han said, "As I instructed plaintiff's counsel, we could do without the hyperbole. Every attorney has a duty of good faith, meaning their motions must be supported in law and fact. Ms. Gould provided an affidavit supporting her motion. She satisfied her duty. There will be no sanctions. Continue."

"Yes, but the plaintiff has no proof these photographs are stolen. Your Honor wisely noted that there is no affidavit from the friend, Mr. Aguilar, supporting their argument. This lack of evidence is telling. There is nothing stopping plaintiff's counsel from flying down to Los Angeles, meeting with Mr. Aguilar and obtaining an affidavit from him, if these allegations are true."

He knew I had met Aguilar. I could tell by the way his voice shifted. Either he had someone following me, or Aguilar talked. The latter was more likely. Or maybe I was paranoid. Maybe some friend of his had spotted me in the airport, here or in LA, and he surmised the rest.

He went on. "As for the relevancy argument, Your Honor, under the law of the State of California, any and all of the plaintiff's behavior at the workplace or amongst her coworkers is admissible on the issue of whether she consented to intimate advances."

Cleville leaned across Frank's empty chair and plucked at his blazer. Cleville shook his head, mouthing, "No, no." He then pushed Frank's chair aside and rolled his closer to the lectern. Frank bent over for a whispered conference.

The judge spoke. "Is there something you would like to add, Mr. Gould?"

Frank patted Cleville's shoulder and resumed position behind the lectern. "For the record, we are not conceding there was any kind of advance, sexual or otherwise, by Mr. Cleville to Ms. Navarre. The plaintiff must prove it occurred. However, for the purposes of argument, if Mr. Cleville had made intimate advances to Ms. Navarre, her behavior in and around the workplace would be evidence that he had a reasonable expectation she was amenable to the alleged advances."

The judge's posture hardened. "Your 'implied consent' defense."

"Exactly, Your Honor. If my client made such an advance, the evidence will show that by her acts and statements, Ms. Navarre impliedly consented to sex with him."

Frank continued, "As to the provenance of the photographs, as an officer of the court I represent they came into my possession via an anonymous delivery. A messenger dropped them at my office in a brown paper envelope with no return address. I have no idea who delivered them to me."

It could have been true. More importantly, I had no way to prove otherwise.

"Are you finished, Mr. Gould?"

"Yes, Your Honor."

"Don't sit down quite yet, Mr. Gould." Judge Han stood. "The attorneys will report to chambers."

"What's going on?" Josephine whispered.

"No idea," I whispered back. "I'll let you know as soon as I get back."

"Can I come?"

"She said just the attorneys."

"You're going to leave me in here with *him*?" She pointed at Cleville with a look.

"Go back to the ladies' room. I'll find you when the judge is done with us." I escorted Josephine to the courtroom doors. By the time she was safely away, Frank was hovering by the back door. The clerk was on her feet, looking at her desk, eyebrows raised. No one kept a judge waiting.

JUDGE HAN WAS SEATED at her desk. "Close the door behind you."

Frank did.

There were two empty visitors' chairs, but she did not invite us to sit.

Judge Han said, "Before we discuss the case, I want to extend my deepest condolences upon the passing of Mrs. Gould."

"Very kind of you," Frank said.

I gave her a grateful smile before I looked away. Since the funeral, grief had washed over me in waves. Some days, I thought of my mother's death as just another event, like taking on a case or buying a car, as a result of which I had more paperwork. On other days, I was overwhelmed with the sense that the world was emptier. Even though we had not been close, every time I asked myself how my mother would react or what she would have thought, I remembered that she was gone.

Judge Han took a deep breath, signaling a new topic. "Now, what am I going to do with you two?"

I declined to answer but Frank jumped in. "This is a case that should have never been filed."

Judge Han held up her hand yet again. "It was a rhetorical question, Frank. I don't require a response."

On the ledge outside the window, a pigeon sat on her nest, oblivious to the office occupants. Sun glinted from the windows of the facing building. Street traffic rattled below.

"Very well." She pulled herself closer to her desk. "I've read your briefing. I will rule on the motion regarding disclosure of financial records without oral argument. However, I wanted to bring the two of you in here to talk about where this case is going. There are a few matters at the forefront, the first of which is a trial date."

"My client wishes to proceed as early as possible," I said.

Frank scoffed. "Her client hasn't completed her deposition, and we intend to file for dismissal if she does not. If and when that deposition is complete, we anticipate there will be additional discovery. It's premature to set a trial date and we ask that you defer doing so until later in the year."

"We'll return to that," Judge Han said. "As for your motions, I am prepared to make rulings on both the 'selfie' photographs and the financial records. I can assure both of you that neither party will like my rulings. So this is what we're going to do. I'm going to put the two of you in a jury room and close the door. Work it out. It's in the best interests of your clients."

She pushed a button on her phone. "Madam clerk, report to chambers, please."

A few minutes passed while we waited.

"One more thing," Judge Han said. "I hesitate to comment, but there is something about this case that I find deeply disturbing. I've never had related attorneys oppose one another in my courtroom before. Related parties are common, but not attorneys. When family members become involved on opposite sides, acrimony is escalated. What I see passing between the two of you is troublesome. I would suggest that your own conflicts may be overshadowing your clients' interests. I'm speaking to you as someone who has known you both professionally. Frank, Maureen, work it out."

Frank spoke. "On behalf of my client, Your Honor—"

"Enough, Frank," she said. "Save it for the courtroom."

The door opened and the clerk appeared.

"Show counsel to jury room A."

The clerk led us to the jury room, unlocked the door, and stepped aside so we could enter. When the door clicked shut, I wondered if she had locked us in.

I squeezed around the table to see if I could spot the pigeon, but an edifice was in the way. This view was even more bleak than that from Judge Han's chambers. All was in shadow, an alley below and the building opposite.

"Let's cut to the chase, shall we?" Frank said. "You can't win this case. You and I both know that you don't have enough evidence. No one saw this *attack*. If that isn't bad enough, your client has engaged in, shall we say, salacious behavior, all of which is admissible. Your case has all the hallmarks of a disgruntled former employee trying to exact revenge for her well-deserved discharge. I can't imagine what your motivation is for pursuing it. Glory seeking, perhaps? Did you ever stop to think it's a bit unfair to your client to get her hopes up?"

I spun around to face him. "Why was Josephine fired in the middle of the night, then? Have you come up with an explanation for that?"

"You're suffering from two incorrect suppositions, counselor. First off, your client wasn't terminated in the middle of the night. She was given her notice the morning after she disappeared from a work meeting. Second, it's your job, as plaintiff, to convince the jury that her discharge was wrongful."

"That's your defense? You're going to hide behind the burden of proof? The difference between you and me, Frank, is that I believe in justice. The jury will see your machinations for what they are: nothing but sleight-of-hand. You can't hide the truth forever. Your client could be a better man if he acknowledged his wrongdoing and made amends."

"Amends?" Frank barked a laugh. "You mean 'pay my client a pile of money.' Filthy money. For you and your client." Rich for someone who was demanding to be paid before he would move out of my house.

"Justice means outing the abuser, Frank. Sexual exploitation will not end until it's brought into the light and the wrongdoers are exposed. Cleville needs to bear the consequence of his actions."

"Oh, get off your soapbox, Maureen." He came around the table, trapping me against the window. "The real difference between you and me is that I understand the true nature of men. And women. You can't change nature, Maureen. You can't legislate it out of existence. Once you strip away culture, we are nothing but feral animals, no more evolved than dogs rutting in the streets. I understand this. I accept it."

"You don't scare me anymore, Frank."

"It was not me you feared, Maureen. It was your own nature."

I planted a hand in his chest, forcing him aside. "I'm out of here."

"I have a settlement offer," he called out.

My hand on the doorknob, I spun around. "Make it."

"My client is willing to pay one year salary, expunge the personnel files of references to her dismissal, and provide a letter of recommendation, your fees to be negotiated."

There was a condition. I could feel it. "If?"

"If she signs a new nondisclosure agreement. And there will be no admission of wrongdoing. This is what you wanted, Maureen, a settlement. That's what you asked for in the beginning. You never meant to take this to trial. You were in it for a quick win. So here it is, on a silver platter. Take it. Let's get this over with."

"I'll convey your offer."

Chapter Seventeen

JOSEPHINE WAS SEATED ON a ladies' room bench, scrolling through her phone. "What took you so long?"

"The judge ordered us to talk to each other, see if we could settle the case."

She lowered the phone. "You didn't, did you?"

"I can't without your agreement. But they did make an offer."

"Which is?"

"One year salary, your personnel records expunged, a letter of recommendation. But—and it's a big 'but'—you must sign a new nondisclosure agreement. And Cleville will not admit that he attacked you."

"So I'm back where I started. What's all this been for, then? I didn't do anything wrong. He did."

"He's never going to confess. Not in a settlement agreement. Not when he takes the stand in trial, not afterwards."

"So, you're on his side now?"

"No, Josephine, I'm on your side. But I am ethically obligated to convey any and all settlement offers to you. Also, I'm ethically obligated to advise you regarding the strengths and weaknesses of your case."

"Weaknesses? Seriously, now you say we have weaknesses?"

"I have to be honest with you. The selfies are a problem. If we don't settle the case, today, the judge will decide our motions. She didn't hint how she would rule, but she did say that neither party would be happy. The pictures might come into evidence. I can't predict how the jury will react. And we have other problems. I suspect Frank knows Aguilar refused to support your case. Sophia's dead. Valerie Vann is scared to talk to us. And Amber is hiding. All of which means, the only evidence we have is your testimony. It's your word against his."

"I told the truth."

I sat down beside her. "I know you did."

"Before long, everyone in the business will know that I sued The Duke. If he doesn't admit he did something wrong, then they're all going to think I was lying."

"I get that. I just need you to understand that you could have money now and get on with your life, or risk losing the case and paying Cleville's attorneys' fees."

"You never mentioned that."

"It's in the fee agreement. I gave you time to read it and ask me any questions you had before you signed."

"Pfft. I didn't read it. I just signed because you wouldn't help me if I didn't."

"And that's what you said about the nondisclosure agreement. You will have to testify about that and if you testify truthfully, the fact that you didn't read the agreement plays right into their theme that you are out to get what you can, that you're not an honest person."

"So now my own attorney thinks I'm a liar?"

"That's not what I said. Like I said, it's my job to explain the weaknesses of the case to you. If I didn't, I would be committing malpractice. You don't want a lawyer who can't or won't give you an honest assessment, do you? The only way to prepare for trial is to think like the other guy, anticipate what he will do and say, and cut him off before he makes those arguments. That's all I'm saying, Josephine. We have to deal with why you signed the NDA."

"Whatever." She took one last swipe at her phone, then tossed it into her bag. "Look, Maureen, do you feel you're up to the job? I mean, the other attorney is your dad and all. Am I just playing into some family drama? I need you to be honest with me. This is my whole life on the line."

Fair question. "Josephine, I have devoted my career to protecting sexual assault victims. The only way for victims to be free of their shame, and to prevent more tragedies, is to haul the abusers into the light. Until they are exposed, abusers own a piece of the victim. They took that piece when they convinced the victim to keep this dirty, dark secret. Take away the secret, take away the shame. This is what I live for."

I felt like a hypocrite. I couldn't give up my own secret, yet I advocated that it was the only path to freedom.

She considered me for a long time. "I believe you."

"Excellent. So, we have to talk about the settlement offer."

"What do *you* think?"

"He won't settle unless you keep his secret."

"You can just tell them to kiss my ass."

"I'd love to, but that would show up in an affidavit. So how about I tell them we decline their offer and we'll take our chances in court?"

"Works for me," Josephine stood and slung her bag over her shoulder. "I feel good about this."

"Me too."

And then she hugged me. I didn't have time to protest.

I remembered the scene just before court. "Just as the judge walked in, you asked me if Frank was allowed to talk to you. You seemed upset. Did something happen?"

"When I came back from the ladies' room, he and The Duke were getting off the elevator. He got to the door before I did and pulled it open. Just as I walked past him, he kind of leaned over me and said 'good afternoon' in a dirty way, like he's seen me with my clothes off. I guess he has. The selfies."

She crossed her arms tightly. The young woman who first showed up at my office all those weeks ago, so elegant and dignified, cowered when she spoke of my father. That was his game. Intimidate his way into someone's head and then consume her sanity from inside her mind, like a parasite.

"I am so sorry, Josephine. I promise not to leave you alone again."

"WE'RE READY TO GO back on record," I said as we entered the courtroom.

Cleville fell back in his chair, a victorious grin on his face. He assumed we had accepted the offer.

Judge Han appeared at the bench a few moments later. "Would one of the attorneys advise the court as to the status of this case?"

I stood while she was still talking, edging out Frank. "There has been no resolution. We wish to proceed, ask the court to rule on our motions, and further to set trial for the earliest date available."

Cleville's head whipped around. "But I thought—"

Judge Han's hand was up. "Are you certain?"

"We are, Your Honor." I took my seat.

"Very well. The court determines that it would be most expeditious to bifurcate the trial into two proceedings. First, the jury will hear evidence regarding the events in question. If the jury finds that the defendants are liable, then a second trial will be scheduled to determine punitive damages. Thus, as to the motion for disclosure of financial records, the court reserves its ruling. In the event the jury finds for the plaintiff in the first trial, then the court will order the release of the defendants' records."

Cleville spoke *sotto voce*. "This can't be happening."

Judge Han spiked him a look over her reading glasses. "And as to the motion to exclude certain photographs, I hereby rule that the so-called 'selfies' are likely to lead to the discovery of admissible evidence and as such are fair game for continued discovery. The plaintiff is ordered to answer questions about these photos in her next deposition."

Cleville slapped the table. "Yes!"

"As for admissibility, I will delay ruling upon whether the photographs will be admitted into evidence at trial until discovery has closed." She took a hard look at me. It was a warning. If a jury saw those photos, I could lose the case.

What Judge Han and Frank and Cleville didn't understand was that fighting a case is not about the big win at the end, or the risk of losing. The fight itself, the pursuit of justice, was reason enough to go into battle. I was fully committed to this war regardless of the outcome.

I picked up a bottle of cabernet on my way home to celebrate. I couldn't wait to tell Jake about my day in court. Although I had technically lost both motions, I felt like the victor. The judge had reserved ruling on whether she would admit the photographs. She might exclude them from the jury later. And she would give us the financial records after we won the first trial.

The best part was that Josephine had recommitted to the case. She finally understood why I fought for her.

When I opened the door, the loft felt abandoned. I dropped my briefcase, pulled off my raincoat, and wandered into the great room. It was empty and pristine. The plates and coffee cups Jake and I had left next to the sink that morning had been washed and were upended on the drainboard. The cat's dishes were full.

Since the day my father slapped me, Jake had been distant. He still cooked every night or brought home take-out, but we worked through dinner to avoid conversation, me at the table while he was in the home office. By the time I got to bed, he was already asleep.

There had been no real argument, so could not make our way back with a simple apology. Neither of us had been in the wrong—unless it was me for not being able to break through the barrier that I had brought into our marriage. But he had married me for better or for worse. That was the oath we took. He had seen the scars on my arms before our wedding. He should have suspected something so shameful in my past, I couldn't speak of it. Still, I yearned for a connection with him. A smile, a hug. Maybe today's court news would get us talking again.

"Jake?"

I opened the hallway closet to put my raincoat away. The boxes containing my mother's effects were stacked on the floor where I had left them. The shelf where Jake's box and trophies had been was vacant.

In a flash of beige fur, Germaine Greer dashed to the great room where she began a plaintive cry. I followed her. That's when I saw the note on the counter.

"My Dearest Maureen,

You are in a dark place where I cannot reach you. I tried. You always said that you wanted our marriage to be just us, but it's like you're gone and I'm the only one here. There is no 'us' anymore. Maybe it's for the best. I won't stand in the way of the divorce any longer. But please remember, that you will always share my soul.

All my love, Jake"

I skipped dinner, uncorked the cabernet, and took the bottle and a wineglass to my bedroom for a night of old movies.

Chapter Eighteen

A WEEK AFTER THE hearing, Yolanda, Eli, and I stood in the conference room gazing at the mountain of paper in disbelief.

Eli shoved a wad of tobacco into his cheek. "Holy sh—"

Yolanda interrupted, "Holy tamole."

The conference table was covered with stacks of paper, three reams high. Frank had delivered a new deluge of evidence. Piles of paper it would take days to comb through, discern what was there, what was important, and what was missing. There was one thing I could count on: the information I wanted, where Cleville got his funding, wouldn't be in that heap.

"Holy something, that's for sure," I said. "Eli, did you do the background on Crown Productions?" I had asked him weeks ago to pull together information on the corporate directors.

He shifted the wad of tobacco around in his mouth. "Didn't get around to that."

He hadn't done the research on Cameron Aguilar either.

"Have you been busy working for someone else?"

"Got a drug case."

"With anyone I know?"

"Best if I don't say."

"I'll do the backgrounds," Yolanda said.

"While you're at it, I have a thumb drive from Josephine. Take a look at that and see who turns up."

"There's video?" Eli asked.

"Josephine took footage at parties."

"You seen it yet?"

"No, or I would know who was on it, wouldn't I?"

"Right," Eli said. "I can handle that for you."

He hadn't been invested in the case since the day I decided to take Yolanda to London. He hadn't done the research assigned to him. He didn't answer his phone. He disappeared for days at a time. I knew he worked for other lawyers, and that was all right with me—I didn't have enough investigation work to keep him busy—but I expected him to be reliable.

"That's okay. I know you're busy. Come to think of it, combing through documents isn't the best use of your talents, Eli. Thanks for stopping in. I'll give you a call if something comes up."

"You're firing me in the middle of a case? That's the thanks I get?"

I wasn't sure what thanks he expected. He was paid every time he billed. "It's not like that, Eli. It's just that I don't have anything for you to do right now. When something comes up, I'll give you a call. Promise."

"Right." Eli launched a glob of spit into a wastebasket.

After the door slammed shut behind him, Yolanda gripped my arm. "I didn't want to say anything around Eli, but if you touch any of these documents before I get them indexed, I'll break both your hands."

Yolanda's apprehension was justified. I may have occasionally become flustered shortly before a hearing when I couldn't find an exhibit. It would always turn out to be my fault. I would have put it down somewhere bizarre, like on top of the office fridge, or in another casefile. And then she would scurry around, find the document, and put everything right again. The cases might be ours, but the files were hers.

"How about I do the background checks?" I suggested.

"Sounds good."

Back at my desk, I swirled the computer mouse and began my search. Crown Productions was a corporation organized in the state of New York. I didn't bother researching Ken Vincent, Crown Productions' corporate counsel who had appeared at the first hearing, and Frank's former associate. I already knew that he was a confirmed bachelor who was swooned over by women and who vacationed in Thailand for yoga holidays.

The Board of Directors of Crown Productions included Reginald Cleville; Grant Houssier, the in-house counsel who had appeared at the first hearing with Ken; and three names I didn't recognize: Ellis Richard, Trevor Anderson, and Crispin Cleville.

Grant Houssier was licensed to practice in California and New York. He'd graduated from UCLA law school in 1998. According to his alumni biography, he had worked at a firm specializing in business, much like Frank's, before Cleville hired him. He had homes in Brentwood and Malibu and drove a Jaguar. His wife drove a Mercedes.

Trevor Anderson was a British national. He had a home in London, England, and a condo in Los Angeles. A Corvette was registered to him in California.

Crispin Cleville was The Duke's younger brother. Unlike Reginald, his photo was not splashed across British gossip sites. His Hollywood Hills home was featured in *Architecture Digest* for its lavish Old World furnishings and art I'd read in the dentist office. According to his biography, he had served in Her Majesty's diplomatic service until his brother lured him to Hollywood. Crispin was the Chief Financial Officer for Crown Productions.

By the time I completed my online research, I had worked through lunch. It was mid-afternoon and I was starved. I decided to go home early. I grabbed my briefcase and stopped by Yolanda's desk on my way out.

Yolanda peered at me over the monitor, her fingers hovering over her keyboard. "Gone for the day?"

"You don't mind?" I don't know why I felt like I had to apologize to staff for leaving early.

"I like having you out of my hair when I'm doing stuff like this," she said, as she rested a protective hand on the pile of documents to her left. "I should have this done in a day or two and then we can start looking through them."

"Yolanda, you have no idea how much I value you."

"Go on with you, girlfriend. See you tomorrow."

IN MY KITCHEN, I found a forgotten lunchbox-sized bag of stale pretzels. I polished that off and a microwaved dinner of chicken and green beans in an unidentifiable sauce, then tried to fill the hours of my new life without Jake. I had not realized how much of the housekeeping he had done, not that I had performed any chores more than occasionally. The loft was always spotless, so I had not given it much thought, but now cat hair was floating across the cement floor. I set the robotic vacuum to its patrol and began cleaning. With earbuds, I listened to 1950s and 60s rock music to boost my enthusiasm.

I was on a stepstool, wiping the overhead pipe fixtures with a long-arm dustmop when the doorbell rang. My watch said it was 10:12 P.M. The bell rang again and again as I picked up speed. I pushed the intercom button and looked into the grainy camera image. "Yolanda?"

"Thank God, you're all right. Let me in."

I pressed the button to open the building's entry door, then stepped out into the hall to greet her. When she hustled into view, she was wearing blue jeans, an oversized sweatshirt, and sneakers. No makeup.

"There was a break-in at the office," she said. "The security company tried calling you and there was no answer, so they called me. We need to meet them at the office ASAP."

"Give me a few minutes to change." I was wearing yoga pants and one of Jake's old t-shirts. I was barefoot.

"Just put on a coat. No one will notice."

I slipped on a pair of flipflops and grabbed an old zip jacket from the closet. We piled into her VW hatchback, parked in a loading zone, and she sped through the streets, as fast as one can speed through San Francisco.

When we pulled up to the building, a safety-green compact car with a flashing yellow light was parked in front. Standing at the door was a young man in a baggy brown uniform with an elfin-like face. His badge said "Klinkhart." He introduced himself as "Tim." He asked to see our identification before he would let us by. Yolanda jangled her building keys at him to show that she had a right to go inside. I thanked him for his thoroughness. Once we produced identification, he led us upstairs to my office.

The door hung open, with no damage to the casing. The lock must have been picked.

"Stay here," Tim said. He gestured with an open hand, the way a dog trainer signals his animal. His flashlight beam played through the dark as he moved out of our sight toward the conference room, back again into reception, then to the kitchen, and down the hall.

A few minutes later, the overhead light in my office came on.

"It's all right," he called. "There's no one here."

When I flipped on the light switch, Yolanda whispered, "Oh my God."

Her computer was on the floor, smashed, the monitor shattered. The couch and chairs were overturned, and the underside netting had been cut away. File drawers stood open and empty, the floor covered with their contents. Through the conference room glass wall, we could see the reams of Crown Productions discovery tossed about as if by a windstorm.

Tim joined us in reception. "The back office looks about the same. You should make a list of everything that is missing or damaged for the insurance company. And you need to make a police report."

"Who would do this?" Yolanda asked.

"Kids high on something. Or maybe you got an angry client. You're a lawyer, right?"

"Let's check the video surveillance." I pointed at the ceiling camera.

"Oh, yeah, right," Tim said. "Let me call HQ and get them to email that to you."

"On what computer?" Yolanda gestured to her broken tower.

I edged around Tim on the way to my office. Paper tossed around. The couch and visitors chairs up-ended, netting cut away. Bits of the computer tower scattered across the carpet. Monitor smashed. I joined the others in reception.

I wrote my email address on a piece of paper and handed it to him. "Send the surveillance video here. I'll log on from my home laptop."

Tim pulled out his cell phone and called his dispatch. He gave them my email and asked to have the video sent there. When he hung up, he said, "HQ says it might not be until tomorrow, but they'll get it to you." He cleared his throat. "Look, I'm sorry but I have to go, I got rounds to do. I don't think you ladies should stay here alone."

"There's so much to do," I said.

Yolanda said, "You have that deposition tomorrow. I'll come in early and start cleaning up. Don't worry about it."

I MET JOSEPHINE IN the lobby of Frank's office building. "Do you have any questions before we go upstairs?"

"Did you check out the thumb drive I gave you?"

With the truckload of paper Frank dumped on me and the break-in, I had forgotten. "Sorry, not yet. Is there something I should look out for?"

"Just wondered if you recognized anyone."

"I'll take a look at it tonight and let you know." I glanced at my watch. "Ready to go upstairs? It's almost time."

Frank and his entourage were already seated in the conference room. He had taken the chair I liked, with his back to the window. Reginald Cleville was beside him and Ian

Napier in the third chair. Cleville smiled when we walked in. He was a man who fed on the anger of others, sucking it out of them to stoke his own fire.

Ian gave me a polite nod. I didn't make eye contact with Frank. The videographer and court reporter fiddled with their equipment as we took our chairs and attached microphones to our blazers.

"On record," Frank said. The video camera's little red light began to glow.

The court reporter pushed a button and read from her notes. "This is the deposition of Josephine Navarre in the matter of *J.N. versus Reginald Cleville and Crown Productions*. Do the parties have anything to put on record before we begin?"

Frank spoke. "I wish to note this is a continued deposition, made necessary after Ms. Navarre departed unexpectedly when we last convened."

Josephine flinched. I gave her a small shake of my head. Frank's snarky comment was meant to flex muscle for the benefit of his client and to put her on the defensive. The best way to handle it was not to react.

"Ms. Navarre," Frank said. "Do you recall walking out of our last deposition?"

Josephine fixed on him. "I do."

"What was the reason you left?"

"I was upset."

"Was there something in particular that I said or did which upset you?"

"It was the photographs. I didn't expect to see them."

Frank rested a hand on a file folder on the table in front of him. "And why is that?"

"Because I only sent them to one person, and I don't believe he shared them."

"Your attorney alleged in court that the photographs were stolen."

"They must have been. I see no other way you could have gotten them."

Cleville made a small phlegmy sound.

Frank continued. "Please explain to us how these photographs came into being."

"I took them."

"Were you alone at the time?"

She paused. "Yes."

"For what purpose did you take these pictures?"

"To send to my friend."

Ian Napier was staring at a blank legal pad, his face reddening.

"Did you spontaneously send them to him?"

"I don't understand the question."

"I'll rephrase. Did he request you to send these selfies to him?"

"He did."

"And if he testified otherwise, how would you respond?"

"I'm telling the truth. I don't know what he would say. You would have to ask him."

"Let's talk about your friendship with this man. His name is Cameron Aguilar, is that correct?"

She pushed back in her chair a little. "Yes, that's his name."

"Tell me how you met."

"At work."

"Both of you were employed by Crown Productions when you met?"

"Yes. What are you getting at?"

"I'm asking the questions, Ms. Navarre. To summarize, you claim you sent sexually explicit photos of yourself to Carmen Aguilar, a coworker at Crown Productions, at his request."

She folded her hands in her lap, an instinctual protective move. Cleville snorted. Ian Napier closed his eyes. I leaned back in my chair tapping my pen as if to say, "When you're done playing games, let's get to work."

"Do you need a break, Ms. Navarre?" Frank asked.

"No, I'm fine."

"Would you answer the question, please?"

"What question?"

"Are you claiming that you sent sexually explicit photos of yourself to Carmen Aguilar at a time when you both worked at Crown Productions and who you met through your employment at his request?"

"I'm not *claiming* it. I'm telling the truth. That's what happened."

"Did you have a sexual relationship with him?"

"I don't see how that's any of your business."

Cleville choked down a laugh.

"Let's take a break." Frank stood. "Counsel, I suggest you have a word with your client." As they left, Cleville leered at Josephine then at me. I gave him a cold look in return. People like him couldn't stand to have their behavior questioned. His turn would come. His grin faded.

"We'll be in reception if you need us," the court reporter said. She and the videographer stepped out. The door closed behind them.

We were alone, but in a goldfish bowl for all to see. The wall that divided the conference room from the hall was glass. A secretary strutted by and Josephine shielded her face as she spoke. "What's he getting at?"

"We talked about this. Remember? The nature of your sexual activity at work will be used to show that Reginald Cleville believed you would be receptive to his advances."

"And so they can just ask me questions about what we did? You know, like intimate things?"

"If he asks something like that, you can refuse to answer his question. He could go to the judge and try to get an order forcing you to answer. I doubt she'll give it to him."

"Okay, fine."

I signaled the court reporter we were ready. She came back with the videographer. Frank, Cleville, and Ian Napier filed in and took their seats.

"We're back on record," the court reporter said as she pushed a button on her tape machine.

Frank spoke. "Before we took a break, I had asked you if you were in a sexual relationship with Mr. Aguilar."

"The answer is: yes."

Frank raised his eyebrows in surprise. Apparently he hadn't expected her to answer truthfully. "I think we have enough. Thank you for coming in, Ms. Navarre, Counsel." The men stood again and filed out.

Exactly one hour had passed from the time we arrived. Someone—Cleville, or perhaps his chief financial officer—had put Frank on a budget.

Josephine and I needed privacy. "Let's grab a cup of coffee."

There was a café around the corner. We bought a raspberry mocha for me, a skinny decaf latte for her, and took them to a back table.

"What was that all about?" Josephine asked.

"Flexing. He just wanted to prove to you and to Cleville that he could make you show up. He's training you to answer and trying to intimidate you with the questions he asks. He's hoping by the time you take the stand at trial, you will be so afraid of him, you will look guilty. But it wasn't working. He didn't scare you."

"Well, it feels like I was used. He's an attorney and I'm not, so I had to sit there and take his abuse. Because he has all the power."

"And that's how Frank wants us to feel." I paused to collect my thoughts. She needed a pep talk. "But trust me, Josephine, we are not powerless. We have one thing on our side that Frank and Cleville are terrified of."

"What's that?"

"The truth."

Chapter Nineteen

WHEN I WALKED INTO the office, Yolanda was typing on a pink laptop, the cover of which was decorated with Disney princess stickers.

"Where did you get that?" I asked.

"I borrowed it from Juanita."

Juanita was one of her kids. "Thank her for me. Would you order a couple new computers, monitors, and all the other stuff when you get a chance?"

"Already done. Delivery is tomorrow." She leaned back in her chair. "As for the paper files, there's one missing."

"And that is?"

"The attorney notes from the Navarre case."

"What about notes from other cases?"

She shook her head.

"No other files at all?"

"Not even the external hard drives." She tapped her finger on the block attached to Juanita's computer by cable. "We're up and running."

"Damn. My notes."

"They're scanned. We have an electronic copy."

"But someone has them." The attorney notes file is where my scribbles are kept. Anything I had committed to writing, my strategy, weaknesses of the case, names of potential witnesses, and what yet had to be done.

I dropped onto the couch. If the reason for the break-in was to steal my attorney notes in the Navarre file, someone in Cleville's camp had to be responsible for it.

"How did the depo go?"

"Josephine was awesome. Spoke her truth. Didn't back down. Got a little nervous once, but she recovered. She's going to be brilliant on the stand."

Only one person would want my notes: Cleville's attorney, Francis E. Gould.

Yolanda was talking. "I made a list of everything that was damaged or stolen and called the insurance company. They said we had to file a police report. So I called SFPD and they're sending someone over."

Would Frank steal my attorney notes? Was he that desperate? I pushed myself off the couch and made my way into my office. Heading for the chair, my thigh struck the desk corner. A sharp, but remote, pain registered. I laid a hand on the desktop to measure a safe distance and eased around. When I lowered myself, the chair began to roll away. I fumbled for the armrests and gripped them to steady it. Gauzy light enveloped me. I heard buzzing in my ears.

Frank had sent someone to break into my office.

When Yolanda appeared at the door, I was piecing together the progression of *Navarre vs. Cleville*, my way of creating order. A pattern developed, one that I did not want to accept. I kept challenging it with "buts" and "what-ifs" yet every time it reformed, it was more solid than before.

"The police are here."

"Send them in."

A uniformed officer stepped into my office, hat tucked under one arm. Mid-thirties, dark hair in a buzzcut. His starched shirt strained with gym rat bulk. The badge over his right shirt pocket said "Tucker."

Right behind him was my soon-to-be ex-husband, Jake Kuhn, wearing a charcoal pinstripe suit and diagonal striped tie, both of which I had picked out for him when we updated his wardrobe about a year ago. His hair had been trimmed. How was it he remembered to go to the barber when he always needed me to remind him before? No, it wasn't trimmed, it had been styled. That was new. I wondered who she was.

I stood. "To what do I owe this honor?"

"When the report came in, a friend of mine was on the desk," Jake said. "You should have called. Are you okay?"

"Assistant District Attorney Kuhn wanted to sit in on the interview, ma'am," Tucker said. "Is that all right with you?"

"That's fine, Officer. Thank you for asking. Have a seat."

Tucker and Jake took seats in the visitor chairs. Yolanda perched on the couch arm and I settled in behind my desk. I gave the cop my complete attention, all the while feeling the side of my face warm as Jake stared at me.

"I understand you had a break-in last night," Tucker said. He pulled out a tiny steno pad, just like the one Eli used.

"Around ten o'clock. They tripped the alarm. The security company should have the exact time."

Jake stiffened. "Did anyone come to the loft?" Not *our* loft, not *your* loft. *The* loft.

I parroted his neutral language. "Why would someone come to the loft?"

Tucker put down his notepad. "Excuse me, ma'am, sir. Can we focus on the office burglary for the time being? Was anything stolen?"

"Just one file," Yolanda said.

Jake twisted in his seat to look at her. "Which file?"

She dropped her voice and looked him in the eye. "The attorney notes in *Navarre vs Cleville.*"

He whirled around to face me. He knew as well as I did that only one person would be interested in that particular file.

"But how are you going to prove it?" I asked. I was reticent to accuse Frank in front of a police officer. The next thing that would happen was Tucker would interview him. He would deny it, then file something in court saying I had made a false police report. Nothing would come of it, except that Judge Han would be even more irritated and might haul us in for another heart-to-heart talk.

"What about the external hard drives?" Jake asked.

"Weren't touched," I said.

Tucker shifted in his chair in an attempt to close the gap between me and him. "Ma'am? I'm a little lost here. Maybe you could help me out. What do you need to prove?"

I didn't respond. To Jake, I said, "To answer your earlier question, no one came to the loft except Yolanda, to tell me the office alarm had been tripped."

"Why didn't she call?" Jake asked.

"I couldn't hear the phone. I was cleaning."

"You were what?"

Tucker extended his arm across the desk, now physically inserting himself between Jake and me. "Excuse me, ma'am, sir. Let's set some ground rules, if you don't mind. I was sent to take down information relating to a burglary that occurred here last night. I need to fill in the squares on my form and then I can be on my way. After that, you two can discuss whatever you want. Does that work for all of us?" He craned his head toward Jake.

My husband sat back in his chair. "Sure, officer. Go ahead."

"Thank you." Tucker leaned toward me. "Now, what is it that you need to prove? Is there something going on in this Navarre versus someone case?"

"Cleville," Yolanda said, then spelled it out for him. "C-l-e-v-i-l-l-e."

I gave Yolanda a look. She ignored me. She knew as well as Jake and I did that Frank was the only person who would be interested in the missing file. I shook my head at her and mouthed the word "no." Tucker didn't notice; he was busy writing. When he was done, he directed his attention to Yolanda, apparently sensing she wanted to share information more than I did. "Is there something special about this case?"

She opened her mouth to answer when I jumped in. "It's just a lawsuit. The notes could be misfiled. We're not even sure they're missing."

Yolanda huffed, outraged. Not only had I failed to acknowledge she took meticulous care of her files, but I had invoked the "blame the paralegal defense," a ploy invoked by unscrupulous attorneys to cover up for their own mistakes.

"Let's move on, then." Tucker pointedly looked around the office. A faint scowl crossed his face when he saw my gold-framed degrees. This was a cop who didn't like lawyers, although truth be told, I'd yet to meet one who did. "Was anything damaged in the break-in?"

Yolanda crossed the room and handed him a list. "Our computers, the monitors, and keyboards. The furniture was upside down and the fabric underneath was cut away. I straightened up when I got in this morning."

Tucker wrote notes in his pad. "Did you get pictures before you cleaned up?"

"I did." She pulled her cell phone out of her skirt pocket. "I can email them to you."

"Do you have any idea who might have done this, ma'am?" Tucker asked. "A client with a grudge, maybe?"

"Officer Tucker," Jake said. "Ms. Gould is a highly respected and successful attorney."

Tucker gave Jake a cold look. When they had met outside my office, Jake would have introduced himself and Tucker would have recognized his name as the prosecutor who used to be a cop. To some police, Jake was the ultimate enemy—he had betrayed the brotherhood when he went to law school. It didn't matter that he was a prosecutor and they were on the same side. "Sorry if you took offense, sir. I just thought, you know, clients, lawyers ..."

"Know what?" I asked.

"Arguments." Tucker appeared to search for words. "The kind of people you work for. They can be hard to handle sometimes. I mean, that's why they're in trouble in the first place, right?"

"What about the surveillance video?" Yolanda asked.

"What video is that, ma'am?" Tucker seemed relieved at the change of subject.

"We have a camera in reception," I said.

"I saw," Tucker said. "Wasn't sure if it was working. Some people install those for show and don't bother to keep the videos."

"The security company promised to email the footage. I was in a deposition this morning and haven't had a chance to check."

"Now would be good," Jake said.

Tucker glared at Jake. "Can we see this video?"

I pulled my laptop out of my briefcase and entered my password, *JacobK<3*. Silly now. I had programmed it right after he proposed and never got around to changing it. A password, like marriage, can be nothing more than a habit, maybe one that had grown obsolete with time.

The computer booted up and new emails downloaded, including one from the security company. I opened it and spun the laptop around so everyone could watch the video. It began with darkness. The camera was temporarily blinded by light, then refocused. Two beefy, blond men were standing in my office reception. One of them put something back in his pocket.

"He had a key," Jake said.

"Seems like," Tucker said. "I took a look at the door when we came in. The lock is pretty generic. Wouldn't be hard to find a key that fits."

"Agreed," Jake said. He had warned me before: I should install a coded mechanism.

Yolanda, pressed against my desk, reached across and paused the video. "That's them! It's the two guys that were following us around in London."

Jacob lifted an eyebrow in my direction.

"I know you don't believe me, but I'll show you," she said. She produced her cell phone, swiped a few times, and laid it down on my desktop. "Them! I took this in front of St. Paul's Cathedral. They were on our flight. They followed us around all of London. And then Sophia was murdered."

"She was murdered the night before these pictures were taken," I said.

"That's what I'm saying. She was murdered after we landed, before we went to see her. And these guys were on the same plane. They had something to do with it. I just know it."

We huddled around the desk, each of us examining the frozen video on my laptop, then Yolanda's cell phone, then the monitor again.

"And then there's the threats," Yolanda said.

Jake broke away from the video. "What threats?"

"No big deal," I said. "Some crank."

"Can I get a copy of these threats?" Tucker asked.

"You bet." Yolanda scurried out of the room.

A vein in Jake's temple began to throb. "You didn't tell me."

"I forgot. You know how people are. All bark, no bite."

On the street below, a car horn screeched. Another blared in response. The room suddenly felt cold. We could hear the copier spitting out paper.

Yolanda came back with four copies of the letter, one for each of us.

Dear Lawyer Lady,

You been talking to the wrong people. You don't know what your getting yourself into. Drop the case against Reginold Cleville before more bad things happen.

-A Friend.

Jake said, "So one of the Cleville witnesses is killed, you get a threatening letter, some thugs follow you and Yolanda around London, then your office is broken into by the same guys and the only thing taken is the attorney notes from the Cleville matter. What else are you not telling me?"

I couldn't get into any more trouble than I already was, not that it mattered since Jake had left me, so I told him. "And there was an email."

"What email?" Yolanda asked. "You didn't tell me about an email."

"Yeah, what email?" Jake was halfway out of his chair.

Tucker folded the letter and put it into his pocket. "Could we see this email, ma'am?"

I spun the laptop back around. "Like I said, I figured it was a crank." I found the message and ordered the computer to print. Yolanda left and brought back four copies. The subject line said, "WARNING!!!!!"

Drop the case against Reginold Cleville if you know what's good for you.

Signed, A Friend.

Jake read the letter. "'Reginald' is misspelled in both messages. It was written by the same person."

"When did the letter come in?" Tucker asked.

"The same day as this email."

"You never told me." Yolanda looked hurt.

"I forgot about it. Honestly. I figured it was some crank."

"Where's Eli?" Jake asked. "Why isn't he here?"

More and more, I had begun to suspect Eli's loyalty. In Saratoga, Valerie Vann had refused to talk to me and Eli. She was nervous and kept looking down the street. Eli was the only person who knew Yolanda and I were going to London to interview Sophia. Eli hadn't done the background checks I'd asked for. He had been argumentative and remote. He had a key to the office. And his spelling was terrible. "He hasn't been around lately."

Jake frowned at me. I hadn't told him about my employee problems. Yet another secret, from his point of view.

Tucker put his folded copy of the email in the same pocket he had put the letter. "Who is this Eli, ma'am?"

"My investigator. He works part-time for me and picks up work from other attorneys too. He used to be with the force."

"I want him here," Jake said. "There's something going on and I don't like it. Someone needs to be here in case they come back."

Yolanda folded her arms in an "I told you so" stance.

I didn't want to talk about Eli in front of Officer Tucker. He'd question Eli. Whether my suspicions were right or wrong, Eli would blow up and quit. Then I would never be able to confirm or rule out that he was a spy. On the other hand, I was not immune to group paranoia. With the break-in, Yolanda upset, Jake worried, and Officer Tucker showing up, I might not be thinking clearly.

"Look, Jake, no one is coming back during the day. They're burglars. They skulk around under the cloak of darkness. And I'm not in any danger. I never was. If they wanted to physically hurt me, they would have come to the loft instead."

Tucker pulled a business card out of his pocket, scrawled on the back, and slid it across the desk to me. "This has my cell number, email, and the police case number. If anything else comes up, please give me a call."

Jake hung behind for a moment after Tucker left. "We'll talk about it tonight over dinner."

"Fine," I said. "Pick up Chinese."

Chapter Twenty

An hour after Jake and Tucker left, Eli appeared at my door without warning.

"Well, this is a surprise, stranger," I said. "Where's Yolanda?"

"In the conference room, files everywhere. What the hell happened? Jake called me. Says there was a break-in last night." He dropped onto the couch.

"He's overreacting."

"He says he wants someone here all day, make sure you're safe."

I shook my head. "Honestly, Eli. I'm not in any danger. The bad guys just made a mess of the office and smashed up the computers."

"They take anything?"

If Eli was a spy for Frank and had given the thugs his office key, he would know they had the Navarre attorney notes. If I lied, he would know that I didn't trust him. If I told the truth, then he would follow up with questions I did not want to answer. "Nothing we don't have backed up. Honestly, there's no reason for you to babysit me."

"Here's the thing, Chief. Jake's my buddy. And you're my friend. I don't want to see anything bad happen to you. So I'm just going to hang out here for a few days until this blows over. As a favor. Off the clock, don't worry about it."

"Okay, fine, if you insist. While you're taking up room, maybe you can help me kick around some ideas."

I rocked back in my chair and twiddled a pen in the air for a few moments. "I don't quite have a grip on the theme of the Navarre case. I need a phrase, something that will resonate with the jurors, lock into their minds. Something unique, but common sense. The rape culture has been around since the dawn of time. It's a primal thing. Why do you suppose that is, Eli?"

"That's just how men are, Chief."

"Not very catchy. Also not true. Not all men are rapists. Jake's isn't. You aren't."

Eli tugged on a pantleg as he repositioned. "So she's saying he raped her now?"

"Her story hasn't changed. I'm saying if she hadn't run out of his suite, I have no doubt he would have. As it is, he assaulted her."

"But she was there. I mean, they were partying. Drinking champagne. Middle of the night. She had to know he wanted something. That's how a jury's going to see it."

"That's what I'm worried about. The jurors need to understand that because he was her boss and her job was 24/7, when he called her to his room, she believed it was for work. And because he was her boss, she had to do what he asked. Work was just a ruse, the way he got her to come."

"A ruse? A trick, right?"

I had a specific reason for using that word. "Right. He used her job to lure her to his room. If she had known he wanted sex, she wouldn't have gone."

"Chief, you're going to have a hard time convincing a jury she didn't know. Like I said. Booze. Hotel bedrooms."

"A jury of men perhaps. But women would understand."

"How do you mean?"

"Sexual exploitation is ubiquitous."

"Oh, man, you and your lawyer talk. Ubiqui-what?"

"The power dynamic. It's everywhere, all the time. Male bosses ask female employees to do personal errands for them, pick up the dry cleaning, order flowers for the wife, make the coffee. Next thing you know, they're standing too close or patting their lap when she walks into the room. And then there's the complete strangers in public, men who come up to women and demand a smile. Like we came into this world to decorate theirs? Women get it. We don't talk about it to men, but trust me, every woman you know has experienced it in one way or another over and over again. We learn to live with it."

"So what does dry cleaning have to do with rape?"

"It's the same dynamic. Men think they have a right to control women. They test us in innocent ways, like the dry cleaning. Sure, sometimes it goes nowhere but sometimes it's the groundwork for the next level violation."

Eli scoffed. "The dry cleaning. A violation."

I pointed the pen at him. "And that's why this discussion is so valuable. You're showing me the weakness in my theme. The truth is there. I just have to figure out a way of burrowing down to its most common sense expression. The very idea that Cleville can claim implied consent is part and parcel of the rape culture. No decent man would contemplate that he was allowed to touch a woman without her permission."

"No problem. Just get a jury full of women."

"Right." Eli knew that jury selection wasn't picking the jurors you liked, it was deselecting those who couldn't be fair to your client. Whoever was left was who you got. "I need something evocative for both men and women."

"Well, good luck to you. That's all I can say. You're the brains of the operation. You'll figure it out."

That was my plan. "Thanks, Eli. I appreciate your confidence."

THE AROMA OF CHINESE food hit me as soon as I closed the loft's front door. The dining table was set with two white linen placemats and matching napkins that had been a wedding gift. Jake was in the kitchen heaping food from cartons onto our good china plates, another wedding gift. Germaine Greer was on the floor eating canned cat food—salmon, by the smell of it.

"Looks nice," I said.

"You deserve something special."

"To commemorate my office break-in?"

He brought the plates into the dining room and set them on the table. "Look, Red, I owe you an apology. I was an ass. You're going through a hard time. I know that. My feelings were hurt because I felt like you had shut me out. I should have known that sometimes you need me to be there, maybe not for talking, but just a presence."

I pushed myself up on my tiptoes and kissed him. "Accepted." I fluffed his hair. "Who's the new stylist?"

"The secretary's daughter is in hair school and needed the practice. Does it look okay?"

"How old is this daughter?"

"You're joking, right?"

I wasn't, but I had made my point. "Enough of this mushy stuff, I'm hungry."

Jake pulled my chair out for me. "Got plans for tonight?"

I smoothed my skirt in a prim motion as I sat. "Reviewing video."

Jake lifted my napkin, snapped it open, and draped it across my lap. "No problem. I have some things to look at, too. By the way, did Eli show up?"

"He did. And I want to thank you for your thoughtfulness." This was the post-argument phase where we would be meticulously polite. It felt artificial but it must be another one of those primal things, a stage that had to be passed through before a couple settled in again. When he was locked into his chivalry mode, it was the best time to drop sensitive information on him. "But there might be a problem. I think Eli is Frank's spy."

Normally his response would be "you're shitting me" but he didn't say that. Instead, he sat down. "That's a pretty big suspicion. What makes you think that?"

"A lot of little things. The actress in Saratoga wouldn't talk to me while I was down there with him. In London, the witness was murdered. He was the only one who knew we were going to interview her. Then, there's those thugs that Yolanda caught following us. They were the guys who broke into my office. They had a key. You saw it on the video. Eli could have given it to them."

"Should I call him off?"

I shook my head. "If I'm right and he figures out I'm suspicious, it'll get back to Frank. The less Frank knows, the better."

"I forgot the beer," Jake said. He left the table, came back with two filled glasses, and set one down for me. "That's a pretty drastic thing for Frank to do, enlist a spy. He could lose his license. If he did do this, then it's much more than just a case to him. Do you think it has something to do with you?"

I was so close to telling Jake the truth. But our relationship was fragile, and far too precious to let my father in.

"I'm starving," I said. I leaned over, kissed him again, then picked up my fork. "Let's eat before this gets cold."

AFTER DINNER, JAKE AND I fell into our old routines: me on one side of the dining table, hunched over my laptop, and him on the other side with his. The home office was abandoned in favor of working together in companionable silence.

I inserted Josephine's thumb drive into my laptop and watched a short video of a glamorous party in a hotel ballroom. A long table was set with appetizers, seafood mainly, which no one seemed to be eating. Bottles of Anchor Steam beer and Napa wines lined another table. A slide show of iconic San Francisco scenes flashed across one wall: The Golden Gate bridge, Alcatraz, Coit Tower, Lombard Street, Victorian homes, and some of the best kept secrets—statues, mosaic stairways, neighborhood parks. A crooner backed by a small band sang, "I Left My Heart in San Francisco."

I recognized the mayor and the heads of San Francisco's tourism and film bureaus, then Cleville and his brother Crispin, whose picture had been in the *Architectural Digest* article. The crowd parted. That was when the tall silver-haired man talking to Cleville turned his face to the camera. My father, Francis E. Gould. Beside him was his former associate, the movie-star handsome Ken Vincent.

Frank handed a small present to The Duke, who passed his drink to his brother, then tore off the wrapping. Frank said something into his ear while Cleville's head bobbed enthusiastically. He held the gift up for the camera operator, Josephine I presumed, to record. She moved in for a close-up.

It was the Diego Rivera painting, the one that had hung on my mother's bedroom wall.

"Oh my God!"

"What?" Jake said, looking up.

"The sonofabitch. I don't believe it."

"What?" he asked again and came around to my side of the table.

I rewound the video and ran it for Jake to see the presentation and the close-up.

"That's your father," Jake said. "When did this happen?"

"Josephine took it. Sometime before she was fired and came to me."

"What's Frank doing at the party? I thought they didn't know each other until he took the case."

"That's what I thought. You see what Cleville's holding up?"

"A painting."

"The painting that was hanging in my mother's room. Diego Rivera gave it to Lizzy Shaughnessy. Frank told my mother he had taken it out for cleaning. After she was gone, I asked him where it was, and he claimed it needed repairs and he would get it for me. The sonofabitch gave it to The Duke long before I noticed the painting was missing. He lied about it."

"Why would he do that?"

"That's what I'm going to find out. Back in an hour."

"Hold on, Red. You're not going anywhere without me."

"Fine, but I'm driving."

I called Josephine on our way out the door and we agreed to meet in the bar of her hotel. Halfway out of my building, I went back for my laptop and the thumb drive.

The bar was decorated in rococo, curvy guilt carvings, and plush jewel-tone velvet upholstery. When we arrived, Josephine was sitting alone at a table with a view of the door. The bar was about half full of people dressed in tourist garb: chinos, raincoats, and comfortable shoes. We made our way to her table, and I introduced Jake.

Josephine already had a glass of white wine. I decided to stick with beer, as did Jake.

"I want to talk to you about this video you gave me." I pulled out my laptop, fired it up, and inserted the thumb drive. "What am I seeing?"

"The party was at the Mark Hopkins. The Duke hosted it for his investors. The idea was to get them drunk, make them happy, and squeeze more money out of them."

I cued the video up to the photo of Frank, Cleville, and the painting, and spun the laptop around for her to see the screen. "That's my father."

"He's one of the backers."

"How can he afford to put money into a movie?"

"Got me. He's your dad, not mine. But what I do know is that he's with some investment group. And he was given an extra piece of the movie because of that painting."

"Why didn't you tell me he was there?"

She took a delicate sip of wine. When she started speaking, her unfocused gaze was aimed over my head. "First off, I didn't know your father was The Duke's attorney until the deposition. So how was I supposed to know the man in that video was your father when I first met you? There was nothing for me to tell. Then, after the deposition, I wasn't sure it was him. I mean, all old guys kind of look alike. And when I started to think maybe he was your father, I didn't know if you would believe me. So that's why I gave you the video. I figured if it was him, you'd know. And you did. So here you are." Her eyes fell upon me.

When the waiter came with our drinks, I snapped the laptop closed. Jake dropped money on his tray and the waiter went to the next table.

"It explains how Frank got on to this case so fast," I said. "The minute Cleville got my letter, he called Frank."

I turned to Josephine. "That last party you were at the night you got fired, was Frank there too?"

"He was in the bar."

"Was he in the hotel suite when Cleville accosted you?"

"I don't know. All I know is that there were a bunch of people in his bedroom, and they sounded like they were having a good time. The doors from the living area to the bedroom were closed. He could have been in there."

"I can't picture Frank in an orgy with a bunch of old men. You think those guys were partying with each other?"

"No way," Josephine said. "I heard giggles. Girls. They sounded young. Real young."

▼

I WAS SO DISTRACTED I forgot where Sunny was parked, so I let Jake drive us back to the loft. When we arrived home, I flopped on the couch. He brought me another beer and one for himself, then sat down beside me. "It's a lot to take in."

"He stole the Rivera from my mother."

"It's his word against hers." What he didn't say was, "and she isn't around to testify about it." I could sue Frank, but the painting was gone. I'd never get it back. With my mother not around to testify, the chances were I wouldn't win. If I won, I'd have to hound Frank for the money equivalent. Or I could file a police report. But then we'd be back to the same problem as before. He would deny it and claim I had filed a false report. Without my mother's testimony, it was unlikely the DA's office would file charges.

"The break-in. It had to be him, you know it. No one else would be interested in my attorney notes. But was that the only thing they were looking for? Why turn the furniture upside down and cut away the netting? My notes were in a folder in the cabinet. They could have slipped in and took the file, and we might not have noticed it was missing for days. And even then, we would have thought it was just misfiled.

"I assumed they trashed the place to cover up for stealing my file. What if they were really looking for that thumb drive? Eli knew I had it. Frank stole the Rivera and lied about it to cover up the theft. Then Sophia is murdered. I can't honestly believe my father would have someone murdered just so he could win a case. Frank Gould? Wheeler-dealer, maybe. Betrayal and greed, sure. But murder?"

"Red, don't let yourself spin out of control. All that stuff happened, but that doesn't mean they're connected."

And there were girls at The Duke's party, Josephine had said. Young girls. My scars began to itch. I scrubbed my arm with the palm of my hand until it was numb.

For the second time that day, I didn't know what I should do next. We finished our beer in silence and went to bed. When he put his arm around me, I pulled away. "Sorry, not tonight."

"Nothing to be sorry about." He kissed me on the top of my head. "Sweet dreams." With that, he rolled over.

I listened to his breathing as it slowed. When I was sure he was asleep, I got up, pulled on his bathrobe, grabbed an extra blanket from the closet, and walked to the great room. Germaine Greer was curled up on one end of the couch. When I sat down, she lifted her head long enough to give me a nasty look, then went back to sleep. I curled up on the opposite side and wrapped the blanket around me.

Frank had stolen the Rivera from my mother. When he told my mother he'd sent it out for cleaning, she believed him. I did too, because she had. But by the time I had asked him about it, he had already given it to Cleville. And he lied about it to me, too.

Frank had broken into my office. It had to have been Frank. No one else would want my attorney notes files.

Frank had jerked us around at Josephine's last deposition, just hauling us there to prove that he could. Josephine said it felt like being used.

There were young girls at the party.

The buried memory erupted into my mind on an endless loop. It started with me spying at my parents' cocktail party from my perch at the top of the stairs. One of the matrons called me down. A man asked me what I wanted to be when I grew up. "A judge," I said, "just like my grandfather." The men laughed at Frank. The cold look on his face. How hard he squeezed my shoulder when he sent me to bed. Me waking up to him in the doorway. "I came to say good night."

He'd closed the door and crossed the room. Vertical slats of light from streetlamps shimmered on the ceiling and walls. As he approached, he stepped into one bar of light, then faded into the dark, then reappeared in the next bar of light. He sat on my bed. His weight made the pulpy mattress sink, and I rolled against him. He stroked my hair. Then he climbed on top of the bed, spooning me from behind. He had done that countless times before when he told me bedtime stories. I waited for the sound of his deep soothing voice and had already drifted half-way back to sleep when I felt his cold hand slip beneath my nightgown.

I must have made a sound. The next thing I knew, his free hand covered my mouth, clamped down so hard that his wedding ring dug into my lips. "You're Daddy's little girl," he said. "Always remember that."

His fingernails dug into my flesh as he groped for my panties.

When the pain between my legs first registered, I saw a red explosion. Then I tumbled into darkness, falling away like Alice in Wonderland.

And then he was gone. I had passed out. Or maybe I had blocked out the rest. I'll never know.

The next morning, the maid asked me why my lips were bruised and bloody. I told her that I had run into the door. No one else asked. Not my mother. Surely not Frank.

No one would see the angry scrapes across my hip where he'd clawed at me.

I drifted to sleep with the one thought on my mind: I was chained to the monster that was my father. He lived in my head. And I had made a place for him there because I was too ashamed to tell anyone what had happened.

Chapter Twenty-One

I WOKE TO THE sounds of my own screams. My arms were flailing as I tried to fight free of the blanket tangled around me.

When I dragged myself into wakefulness, Jake was standing a few feet away. I remembered his hand on my shoulder, his voice in my ear. That was what had frightened me.

"Whoa, Red, it's just me," he said. He was dressed in a fresh suit, ready for work. He placed a mug on the coffee table. "Made you this. There's more in the pot. Careful, it's hot."

"What time is it?"

"0700. You slept in. You were yelling in your sleep, sounded like you were having bad dreams."

I pushed myself up and unwound the blanket. I could feel a crust of dried tears on my face. I wrapped both hands around the mug. Heat sank into my palms.

I searched my mind for images from the nightmares. A man was there. It could have been Frank. I was afraid, a little girl again, lost in a big, dilapidated house. It was supposed to be the Shaughnessy mansion, but it was transformed into something out of a horror movie—one dark hallway after another, empty rooms, locked doors. I was trying to run away.

I gulped for air, then coughed. "Right. Nightmares."

"I'll give Yolanda a call and let her know you're coming in late. You just take it easy, all right? If you need anything, call. Promise."

"I promise I'll call."

I couldn't sleep after he left. I drank the coffee while Germaine Greer prowled across the room. I wished that cat didn't hate me. I would have liked to pick her up and hold her on my lap, feel her warmth, pet her silky fur. That wasn't going to happen. Instead, I went into the kitchen and poured more coffee, then made my way to the bathroom for a shower and to dress for work.

It was just before 10:00 A.M. when I arrived. Yolanda stopped typing when she saw me. "Are you okay?"

"Yeah, sure, I'm fine."

"There's someone in your office waiting for you."

"Eli?"

"No, I called him, said you were coming in late. He didn't answer, but I left a message."

I cocked my head in a gesture to convey the question, "Who?" Yolanda had never left a client in my office alone before.

She raised her eyebrows as if to say, "Go see for yourself."

I quietly approached my open door to see if I could get a look at the mystery man before he saw me. As the office came into view, the visitors' chairs were vacant. When I stepped across the threshold, I saw that the stranger was not a man, but a woman. She had her back to me as she examined my diplomas.

"Good morning," I said. "I'm Maureen Gould. How can I help you?"

She spun around to face me, startled. She was wearing a turtleneck and a rain jacket over hiking pants. I had the same pair of pants in my dresser at home.

"Sorry," I began, "I didn't mean . . ."

She was young, twentyish. My size. My build. My red hair, shoulder-length like mine. My face. The only difference between us was the color of her eyes. Mine were green. Hers were grey, the color of Frank's eyes. She was our daughter.

I fainted.

I CAME TO ON the floor, with Yolanda fanning me.

"Stop that, please," I said.

"What happened to you?"

"I passed out. No big deal. Low blood sugar, I guess. I forgot to eat." I was telling the truth.

"Are you sure?" She put a hand against my forehead.

I mugged a patient smile, not feeling patient at all. "Cross my heart and hope to die. Now, if you don't mind, I'd like to get up off the floor."

She squinted at me, then pushed herself to a stand. "I'll run down to the café and bring back something."

I reached for her hand and she pulled me up. "That would be great."

She looked at my daughter. "What will you have? Latte? Mocha?"

"Raspberry mocha, please."

Yolanda cast a meaningful look my way as she left. Raspberry mocha was my favorite drink. She already suspected who this young woman was. She would expect an explanation later. "I'll bring one for each of you. And something to eat." To my daughter, she said, "I bet you like chocolate chip cookies."

"Doesn't everyone?" she said. Her smile was my smile.

Unsure of the proper etiquette when meeting the baby one gave up for adoption, I decided against hiding behind my desk and instead gestured toward the couch. "Have a seat."

She took one end of the couch, angled toward me. I mirrored her posture.

"Do you know who I am?" she asked.

"How could I not?"

"Is it okay that I came to see you?"

She deserved an honest answer. I took a moment to sift through my emotions. I had never expected to see her again, yet I had thought about her—constantly at first, still often now. Every time I saw a baby or a baby advertisement, I thought about her. Every time Jake brought up having kids. Every time I went to the grocery store to buy tampons and I was forced to walk down the infant products aisle because for some bizarre reason, someone thought they belonged together. After rushing through the self-pay line, I would hide in my parked car until I had finished crying.

"Very okay," I said.

For a long time we were silent. From the street below came the sound of rubber tires wearing on asphalt, squeaky brakes, honked horns. In the distance, a cable car clanged. Outside my window, Coit Tower was stark against a pale blue sky. The office building's front door opened with a whoosh and shut with a bang, followed by a muffled conversation as people walked through the halls.

The light caught by her stray hairs sparkled.

"What did they name you?" I asked.

"Quinn. Quinn Brennan."

"There's a fine Irish name," I said. In those days, the philosophy was to place a child with a family it could blend into so that no one would ever know the child had been adopted. My baby was predominately Irish. Irish nuns had run the girls' school. It made sense they had placed her with an Irish-American family.

"Where are they now, the people who raised you?" I couldn't bring myself to refer to someone else as her parents.

"Gone," she said. "My mother. Oh, sorry. This is so awkward. I mean, the lady who adopted me died when I was twelve. She'd had brain cancer. And her husband passed away last year. He had a heart attack. They were teachers. I grew up in New York state."

"Brothers? Sisters?"

"Only child."

"Were they good to you?"

"Very."

"I'm glad." I meant it.

She had a tiny nose piercing.

"How did you find me?"

"DNA," she said. "I had always wondered who my natural parents were, so after my father passed away, I signed up on a website. That's how I connected with your mother."

"My mother? My mother signed up on a DNA website?" She had kept it a secret. A feeling of regret washed over me that I had not known her better. But whose fault was that? She was the one who dumped me in a boarding school when she realized I was pregnant.

"She was looking for me," Quinn said.

"Okay, totally blown away here. Let me get this straight. My mother signed up on a DNA website so she could find you, her long-lost granddaughter."

"That's right. She seemed like a nice lady."

My mother, a nice lady? I suppose she was well-mannered. She knew which fork to use. Even at the best of times, she was remote and cold with me. Even that last day together, after I won the Paredes verdict, our visit was awkward.

"I'm sorry, by the way, I never got to meet her. After we connected, we started writing letters and she invited me to come to San Francisco for Mother's Day so I could meet you. And then when I hadn't heard from her in a long time and one of my letters came back, marked 'deceased,' I found her obituary online."

When my mother suggested the Mother's Day tea at Christmas, it had struck me as an odd thing for her to do. She had to have known even then that she was dying. Apparently, one of the last things she wanted to do was bring us together: her, my daughter, and me.

A sob moved up from my chest. I took a deep breath, smothering it with air. The person whose loss had made me feel inadequate and incomplete was sitting right in front of me. And my mother had made it happen.

"I was going to name you Betsy," I said. Before she was born, I would lie on my back, my swollen belly even larger than the day before. To the tune of "Itsy Bitsy Spider," I would sing "Itsy Bitsy Betsy," in a whisper so no one would hear, while my fingers crawled spider-like across my middle. Then, I'd feel a squirm deep inside and a little foot or elbow would press out, distorting our shape. I had not thought about that for a long time.

"Elizabeth, actually—after my great-grandmother, Elizabeth Shaughnessy—but I was going to call you Betsy. It's silly now when I think about it." I wiped my face, trying to refashion a less fragile expression. "I was fifteen when you were born. There was no way they would let me keep you. I don't even think I signed the papers. My parents must have."

"They did," she said, fishing in the backpack at her feet. She unfolded a document and handed it to me. They had both executed the consent for adoption, my mother and Frank. He had given away his own daughter so no one would know what he had done.

"I hope this isn't too soon to ask," she started.

"Ask away."

"On my birth certificate and on the adoption papers, the box for the name of the birth father is blank."

Oh, dear God in heaven.

"Did my birth father know about me?"

"READY FOR COMPANY?" YOLANDA called from reception. Look who was hollering in the office now.

"Sure, come on back," I yelled.

"Jake's with me." Her voice was closer now.

I stood. Quinn saw panic on my face. She stood too.

Yolanda stepped in and placed a coffee carrier on my desk together with a grease-stained bag. Jake followed her in.

"I just wanted to—" he started, then stopped when he saw Quinn. An embarrassed smile flashed across his face. He didn't know what to do. He had assumed my visitor was someone he knew. "I'm sorry, I didn't realize you were with a someone."

I scanned the room, looking for a legal pad and paper. I could pretend she was a client, but he wouldn't buy that if I wasn't taking notes. But I wasn't fast enough, and he saw the resemblance.

"Family!" Jake said.

"This is Quinn Brennan. She's visiting from out of state. Quinn, this is my husband, Jake Kuhn."

"That's great. Welcome to Baghdad by the Bay, Quinn Brennan. Will you be staying long?"

Yolanda passed between us, her head low, and handed Quinn her mocha. "I'll get plates," she said and left the room.

Quinn said, "I haven't decided."

"Have a seat." Jake gestured to the couch while he swung a visitor's chair around for himself. I took the armchair beside Quinn. He glanced at me, then asked, "So what does Quinn Brennan do other than visit family?"

"I'm going to school. I have a semester left on my degree."

"What's your major?"

"Political science. I'm thinking about law school after that."

"Law? Just like Maureen. That's fabulous."

I wanted him to go away. "To what do I owe this honor?" I asked with excessive cheerfulness.

"We need to talk," he said. "Privately."

To Quinn, I said, "Stay right there. I'll be back."

He stood and I followed him out of my office, past Yolanda seated at her desk, and into the conference room.

"You never mentioned having family from out of state," he said.

"Can we talk about this later? You had something you wanted to tell me."

"Those two guys who broke into your office. The cops identified them from fingerprints. Roman Ajeti and Aleksander Doda. They were printed when they got their green cards. They're originally from Albania. They work for a private security firm called Alpha Inc. It's one of those elite outfits that hires ex-military and former MI-6. SFPD sent the photos to the Met in London, and they confirmed those two had been spotted on street surveillance near Sophia Lamar's house the night she died."

Yolanda was right. They had followed us to London. They had been in the airport with us, gotten on the plane with us, followed us from our hotel to the London Tower to the

St. Paul's Cathedral. They had seen her take their photos, and they had probably stolen her bag at Heathrow so they could get the cellphone those pictures were on.

"I don't want you alone. Where's Eli?"

"Yolanda called him to let him know I was coming in late. He hasn't shown up yet. You don't think Frank hired these thugs? That's just not his style. He's a commercial transactions lawyer, for chrissake. Murder, I can't believe it."

"Maybe not him, but someone he's involved with. It all comes back down to this case of yours. Speaking of which, who is with Josephine? If Sophia was a problem for the Duke, you would think Josephine would be next."

I reached for the phone. He clamped his hand down on mine, preventing me from lifting the receiver. "Not the landline. It could be bugged."

HE PULLED OUT HIS cellphone and handed it to me. I dialed Josephine's number.

Josephine answered tentatively, not recognizing the number. "Hello?"

"This is Maureen. I borrowed Jake's phone. Where are you?"

"On my way back to the airport. Sorry, I thought I told you last night I'm going home today. Thanks for sending Eli over. He's giving me a lift."

She hadn't told me she was leaving today, and I had not sent over Eli.

"Eli's with you now?"

"All morning. We went out for breakfast. In a diner, a real diner. Very cool. It'd make a great movie set."

"Can you put him on the phone?"

A pause.

Josephine again. "He says he can't talk while he's driving."

"Great. Well, I need you to sign something," I lied. I didn't want to tell her about Ajeti and Doda on the phone. Eli would overhear, or she would tell him. I didn't trust him anymore. "Sorry, I forgot about it. I'll just dash down to the airport and meet you. What terminal?"

"Alaska Airlines."

"So tell Eli he can just drop you off. I should be there in about twenty minutes, got that?"

She repeated the information to Eli.

I jogged down to my office. Quinn jumped up when I came in. "Look, I don't mean to run out on you. I have to run a quick errand. Please wait for me. Yolanda will order in some lunch. I should be back in an hour. Is that okay?"

"What's going on?"

I grabbed her hand. "I wouldn't leave if this wasn't important. There's so much for us to talk about. I don't know where to start. Please wait for me."

"But if you're busy, maybe I should come back later."

"Please stay. Please." I hung out my doorway. "Hey, Yolanda, grab the takeout menus and come on back here."

When she arrived moments later with a fistful of menus, I said, "Jake and I are going out for a bit. We'll be back soon. Order lunch for everyone. Whatever you want."

I hovered for a moment, wondering if I could hug my daughter, and then settled on waving a hand. She waved back. I grabbed my purse.

Yolanda followed me to reception. "But what about?" she jerked her head in the direction of my office.

"Quinn is staying here with you."

Jake was in the conference room. He finished a call and put his cell in his pocket. "Yolanda, lock the door behind us and don't let in anyone you don't know."

We ran to the parking garage. On the way, I pulled my remote starter out and clicked the button. By the time we piled into Sunny, she was humming and ready to go. We didn't need to discuss who would drive.

"Did you catch where Josephine thanked me for sending Eli over this morning?" I asked as I slammed the car through its gears. Jake was used to my driving. He didn't brace himself the way Eli did. Instead he faced out the window as San Francisco went by. We were both quiet as we passed the church where my mother's burial mass had been held, then he said, "He must have told her that."

"What is that guy up to?"

"It could be nothing. Maybe she misunderstood."

"Right." I launched the car from the highway on-ramp and darted through traffic. After I had pulled into a long empty stretch, I called Josephine using the car's Bluetooth.

"Where are you now?" I asked.

"We just took the off-ramp for the airport." The rumbling of Eli's voice came through. "He said he'll give you a call this afternoon."

"Where should I meet you?" I asked, stalling for time.

"Where they take your luggage, does that work?"

"Perfect."

"I don't have a lot of time."

"No problem. It's just a quick signature."

I took the off-ramp and got stuck in a clog of cars cruising for a place to pull over at the departure gates. When we found Alaska Airlines, I angled into the loading zone and leapt from the car. Jake stayed behind. If needed, he could show his badge to the airport cop to keep them from impounding the car.

Josephine was waiting for me by the baggage drop-off.

"Where's Eli?" I asked.

"He's gone, like I said. I need to get into the security line. Where's that thing you needed me to sign?"

"I lied. The police have confirmed that the two guys who broke into my office the other night are the same two guys who followed Yolanda and me around London."

"Seriously? I don't get it."

"And when they stole my attorney notes file, they got your home address in LA."

"No way! That's my mother's house."

"So you and your mother and whoever else lives there should clear out and go somewhere safe."

"Oh, hell no, that's not going to happen. I'll call my cousin. He'll get his friends to come over. As long as my mom's cooking, they'll hang."

"Is he a cop or military?"

"He's a football player. Running over big guys is what he does."

"I'm really worried about you. I'd feel so much better if you went somewhere they couldn't find you."

"What about you?"

"Jake's a retired cop. We'll be fine. I'm much more worried about you."

"My mother won't leave her home. And I'm not leaving my mother. I'll call my cousin, and that's the end of it." The conviction in her voice told me argument was useless.

As we walked toward security, I flipped through my texts to show Josephine a still of the two thugs standing in my office and the photo of them in London.

"These are the guys," I said. "If you see them, call the cops. And call me when you get through security and after you boarded the plane and when you get home. I want to be sure you're okay. I'm sending you the photos." I texted the photos to Josephine's phone.

"If anything happens, I'll call you. Otherwise, the next time I'll see you is the week before trial. All right?"

"I'm fine. Don't you worry about me."

I hung back while Josephine went through security. She stopped to wave from the other side. I waved in return, then jogged back through the airport.

Chapter Twenty-Two

QUINN STAYED IN THE spare bedroom we used for a home office. I was treating this as a temporary visit, not sure if I wanted her to stay. After all we didn't know each other. She seemed tentative as well. I hadn't told Jake who she was, other than a long-lost relative, but he graciously made dinner and disappeared into the master bedroom after we finished eating.

She and I sat in the great room with mugs of hot chocolate I had made myself, dazzling Jake with my hitherto unknown kitchen mastery. Mothers should make cocoa for their children, a belief I must have picked up from old TV shows. Before we left the office, I had secretly Googled a recipe, and made an excuse to go by the grocery to pick up odds and ends—like milk, cocoa powder, and sugar.

Germaine Greer, curled up in Quinn's lap, purred while we sat shoulder to shoulder on the couch and paged through my mother's albums. We looked at sepia studio portraits of my ancestors, fading pictures from the silver mines showing tired workmen and debris, society page clippings including that of my parents' engagement and their wedding photos.

"Why aren't there any pictures of you?"

I hadn't noticed before. No portraits of me were hanging in the mansion, no albums of my growing up years. Didn't most parents memorialize their children's first steps, Easter Egg hunts in little white gloves and bonnets, birthdays and Christmases? "I guess she got too busy after I was born."

I flipped another page. There was a photo of the mansion with cherry trees in bloom along the street. "I'll take you over there tomorrow so you can see the place."

"Won't your father mind?"

"The mansion belongs to me now. He's living there until it's sold, kind of a caretaker." He still wouldn't leave. Through correspondence with his attorney, I had continued to refuse to pay him a settlement unless he proved he had spent his own money on the house, and he had continued to refuse to produce the evidence. "But we'll go during the day so we won't run into him. We don't get along. You might have guessed that."

"Can I ask you a question?"

I had not answered her previous question about her biological father and had dominated the evening so she wouldn't have the opportunity to ask again. She had the grace to let me. "You can certainly ask."

"Did you want to keep me?"

I didn't have to think about it. "More than anything in the world. I had these dreams of you and me living in the mansion ballroom. It's one giant room on the third floor. I would paint it pale yellow. My bed and your crib would be on one end, separated from the rest of the room by a gauzy curtain. We would have our own little kitchen table and a kitchenette. The floor would be filled with gigantic teddy bears and toys and playhouses. And we would have a big old rocking chair where I would sing to you and read to you every night until you fell asleep."

After Mother Superior had told me what was happening inside my body, I daydreamed about my daughter and me crawling around together, playing hide and seek, going to the park, baking cookies, and doing all the things I had seen mothers and babies do on television. Like drinking hot cocoa.

"Did you ask your parents if you could keep me?"

"I didn't see them again for a long time. When Mother Superior told me I was pregnant, she also said the decision had been made to put you up for adoption. One did not argue with my parents' decisions."

I closed the photo album. "In those days, they didn't let the mother see the baby. They just whisked it away. But there was a really nice nurse who brought you in when no one was looking, the day after you were born. I had been sobbing constantly, and they gave me sedatives. Still every time I woke up, I started crying again. So she brought you in and let me hold you for a few minutes. She said you had been crying too, that you were inconsolable. I'm not sure that was true or if she said that to be nice."

I pictured the scene. Me, in a flimsy hospital gown, shell-shocked by the violence of childbirth, in a room to myself on the maternity floor. On the walls were murals of children's toys, teddy bears and building blocks, the icons of a promised happy future for those other mothers who would go home with their babies.

I felt like my heart had been torn out when my womb was emptied, leaving a hollowness inside me. Sometime later that day, the young nurse opened the door, carrying a bundle.

"When she laid you in my arms, you looked up at me with those big eyes of yours. You had the curliest black eyelashes I had ever seen. You were so tiny. I was afraid you'd float up into the air, so I put my hand on top of you to hold you down. I told you that I was your mother and that I loved you very much, and you smiled at me. The nurse said you did, although I've read babies don't smile when they're that little. And I kissed you on the forehead, just there"—I touched the spot on my own head where I had kissed her—"and then she took you away."

We sat like that for a long time as the din from the city streets faded. I heard Jake take a shower, his nighttime ritual, then flip on the television, volume low, to watch a talk show. When Germaine Greer leapt down from Quinn's lap and took her corner on the couch, I noticed my daughter had fallen asleep. I couldn't see her face as her head rested on my shoulder, but I could tell by how relaxed she was.

"Quinn," I whispered. "It's time for bed, young lady."

She stirred, groggily got her bearings, and then looked up into my face with those black curly eyelashes framing her gray eyes. "I must have fallen asleep."

"Up you go, sleepy head," I stood and pulled her up. "Do you need me to tuck you in?" That was stupid. I had gone too far with the mother thing.

She smiled. "Thanks, no. I got it from here."

We parted in the hallway. As she opened the door to her room, she caught me watching her. She came back, kissed me on the cheek, and said, "Good night, Mom."

Mom. Thought I'd never hear that.

JAKE WAS STILL AWAKE when I went into our bedroom.

"Did you have a good talk?" he asked.

"Absolutely." I went into the bathroom and changed into the t-shirt and yoga pants I slept in, then sat down on his side of the bed. "I need to tell you something."

He muted the television and pulled himself to a sit. "I'm listening."

"I hope you don't hate me. I couldn't tell you before. If she hadn't shown up, I don't know if I ever would have." I took a deep breath. "Okay, here it goes. Quinn Brennan is my daughter."

Jake let a moment go by before he said, "I had figured that out for myself."

"Don't be that way."

"Sorry." He took my hand. "Do you want to tell me about it?"

I told him the story of being abandoned in boarding school at fourteen years old when my parents realized I was pregnant, that I was fifteen when the baby came and they took her from me, and that I hadn't known where she was all this time.

"And that's why I didn't want children. I felt unworthy to be a parent. I was afraid that if we tried to have a family, something horrible would go wrong and I would lose you."

"No chance of that, babe." Jake pulled me into his arms. We laid down, spooning with me on the inside. A few tears slid out of my eyes. We were quiet for a long time. I could feel him thinking. "Is she staying?"

"We haven't talked about it."

"Yet," he said.

"Yet."

As I was drifting to sleep, I realized that Jake never asked who the father was.

THE NEXT MORNING, WE began our tour of San Francisco with coffee and bagels at the Ferry Building. Jake took the day off to keep an eye on us. After breakfast, we wandered through the bookshop and then the myriad of specialty stores, cheese, wine, bread, flowers, and we purchased the makings for spaghetti Bolognese. When we were loading our bags into Sunny's trunk, my cell phone rang. It was Yolanda.

"Morning," I said. "I'm taking the day off. Sorry, forgot to tell you."

"No problem. Just thought you'd want to know. Mr. Gould called here a moment ago. He said you should call him back. It's urgent."

Frank didn't have my cell phone number. I gave Jake the keys to my car and asked him to give Quinn the grand tour of San Francisco after they dropped me at the office. It would take them at least two hours to do the loop, more if they stopped for a walk around the sights.

I loped up the stairs with a bundle of flowers and handed them off to Yolanda.

"What are these for?" she asked.

"Just felt like it."

I grabbed my messages and went down to my office, closed the door, and settled behind the desk.

My call to Frank was put through after an unnecessarily long wait.

"Late for you to come into the office," was his greeting.

"We have out-of-town company. Is there something you needed?"

"My clients authorized me to make an offer."

This juncture in a case, if it came, was painful. When negotiations had previously broken down, the chances the case would settle were unlikely as one or both of the parties would have to shirk some pride to make it happen.

I pulled a legal pad close so I could write down the terms. "I'm listening."

"Your client suffers from the misapprehension that the jury will be sympathetic to her claims. Her claim that my client called her to his room in the middle of the night was not witnessed by anyone, even by her own admission. She can't prove that it happened. Nor can she prove that if he called her to his room, he used work as a ruse to lure her there."

Ruse. That was one of the words I had planted with Eli. I had given him two unique words so that if I heard them again from someone else, I would know that he was the source. With two unusual words, there was no possibility of a coincidence. If Frank used the second word, then I would be certain Eli was a spy.

"Anything else?" I asked.

"This new 'wokeness,' the #metoo movement, is predicated upon a myth of ubiquitous male exploitation. You can't sell that to a jury. The world is full of people who understand and appreciate the differences between the sexes. That doesn't make one superior to the other. It means they understand their roles. You'll have a hard time convincing an entire jury that women are downtrodden. If anything, they've been exalted and pampered. Every man on that jury who was subject to draft will remember that women were excused from military service."

Ubiquitous. That was the second word. Eli had leaked information to Frank. He had betrayed me and my client. I had to fire him.

"You're joking, right?"

"Nothing of the sort," Frank said. "I've been authorized to double our offer. Your client will receive the equivalent of two years' salary plus her personnel file will be expunged. And, of course, she needs to sign a new NDA."

"I'll convey it. By the way, I'm coming to the mansion this afternoon. I would prefer that you not be there."

"I have every right to be in my home at any time I please. I believe my attorney sent you a letter informing you that you needed to coordinate visits with me so I can attend. We don't want any accusations of missing property, do we?"

"Very well. Be there if you wish. I'm bringing my out-of-town guest to visit this afternoon."

"And who would that be?"

"My daughter."

A long moment passed with only the sound of phone's electronic noise in my ear.

"You don't have a daughter."

"Oh, but I do. And she's looking forward to meeting her family."

As it turned out, we didn't make it to the mansion that afternoon.

I HAD JUST PICKED up the phone to call Josephine when Yolanda buzzed me. "You have a visitor."

When I walked into reception, I found Valerie Vann, sitting on the couch, a purse clutched in her lap.

"What brings you from Saratoga?" I asked.

"Can we talk?"

I showed her into the conference room, closed the door, and we sat at the table.

"What's up?"

"I heard about Sophia. They said she was murdered."

I should have called her, warned her that life might be in danger. "That's right."

"This has all gotten so far out of control. I can't believe it." She rocked back and forth with the purse clasped to her chest.

"You seemed afraid to talk to me when I came to your house."

"I was. I still am. Two scary-looking guys had been sitting in a car outside my house a few days before you came. They show up all hours of the day and night, just sit there and then drive off. I thought maybe they were cops watching a house down the street for drug dealing, but then I got a letter warning me to keep my mouth shut about The Duke."

"Do you have the letter?"

She opened the purse and pulled out a document. It was written on the letterhead of Gould and Napier, signed by Ian Napier, and dated the Monday after I had filed suit. It reminded Valerie that she had signed a nondisclosure agreement and that if she violated it, she would have to pay Reginald Cleville two million dollars. I blew out a whistle.

"Two million dollars!" she said. "I don't have that kind of money."

"Did you sign a nondisclosure agreement?"

"Yes."

"Were you paid for signing it?"

"Seventy-five thousand dollars. It was enough to keep me alive while I finished my degree, but I had to take out student loans, too."

"Did you have an attorney?"

"No. I should have. That was stupid." Her arms were wrapped around the purse again. "I'm so afraid. Did they kill Sophia so she wouldn't talk?"

"We don't know yet. But what I can tell you is that there were two scary-looking guys who followed my paralegal and me to London to meet with her and she was murdered the night before our appointment. And the same two guys broke into my office a few days ago." I pulled my cell out of my blazer pocket and thumbed through the photos. "These guys."

When she saw the photo, the color drained from her face. "Oh my God, that's them—the guys that were parked outside my house. I am so scared. I don't know who to trust."

"You have choices. You can go to the police. Or you can hire a lawyer, me or someone else. Do you want me to recommend some names?"

"I don't want to sue him. I'm just here to help Josephine. You believe me, right?"

"You haven't told me what happened yet, what led up to you signing the nondisclosure agreement."

"But you believe Josephine or you wouldn't have taken her case, right?"

"Right. So tell me what happened to you."

"I auditioned for a part in one of The Duke's movies. He said he liked me, that I had talent. He took me to industry events. Free publicity, he said. He had a new portfolio taken of me, wearing practically nothing. I was so embarrassed, but he said he needed pictures to show to his production team and then they could pair me with the right leading man. There were dinners with investors. It went on and on for months like that. Then one night, he invited me up to his suite to read a new script. And that's when it happened." She was hyperventilating.

"Do you need a glass of water?"

She waved me off. "No, I'll be fine. Just give me a minute." She put the purse aside and covered her face with her hands. Her breathing slowed. When she lowered her hands, her face was wet with tears.

"We read through a few lines. He talked about the movie he was going to make and how he wanted me to play the lead in it, but he still had to convince the investors I was right for the part. Then he said he had to go to the bathroom. We had been drinking a lot of champagne, so I didn't think anything of it. I heard the toilet flush and when he came out again, he was wearing just a robe."

"That had to be weird."

I exchanged glances with Yolanda, who was keeping an eye on us from her desk.

Valerie continued. "That's when I started thinking this wasn't right. But he didn't do anything right away. He poured another glass of champagne for each of us and then sat down on the couch beside me. I was trying to think of an excuse to get out of there and that's when it happened."

I waited.

"He opened the bathrobe and shoved my face in his lap. He held my head down. I had no idea he was that strong. I tried to get away, but I couldn't. It was hard to breathe. I was afraid he was going to smother me. So I did what he wanted me to do. And when it was over, I got the hell out of there."

It was exactly what had happened to Josephine. With Valerie's testimony, I could prove that long before Josephine Navarre had been hired, Crown Productions knew Reginald Cleville was a predator who targeted women under his control.

Behind Valerie, I noticed the reception door open. Eli stepped in, spotted me with a client whose back was to him, and sat on the couch.

"What are you looking for?" I asked.

"I want the truth out. No one is safe until it is. He's just going to keep doing this to other women, forcing them, and then he's going to ruin their careers. And I don't want those thugs sitting outside my house anymore. I have kids. I have a husband. I hadn't told him what happened. Last night, I read about Sophia and I couldn't take it anymore. So I told him, and he said I should come to you. You'd know what to do."

If Eli spotted Valerie, he would tell Frank and his thugs before she made it back to her car. I motioned a writing gesture to Yolanda and for her to join us. When Yolanda arrived with a legal pad and pen in hand, I stood and gave my chair to her. "Valerie, tell Yolanda what you told me. She's going to type up your statement for an affidavit. We'll keep it under wraps until the trial in Josephine's case. And then I'll need you to testify."

"Will he be there?"

"He will. Are you willing to tell your story in front of him?"

"Does he have to be there?"

"I'm sorry. That's how court works. He's entitled to see you testify and his attorney is entitled to ask you questions. I'll be there through the whole thing and so will Yolanda. It's the only way to get the truth out."

"Can he sue me for libel?"

"He can't sue you for defamation for anything you say in court. It's privileged. As for the NDA, we'll have to deal with it later."

"Fine," she said. "I can't take it anymore. I'll do whatever I have to do to get it over with."

I pulled the curtain closed across the glass wall so Eli couldn't see Valerie, and joined him in reception.

"What's going on in there?" he asked.

"Not to worry," I said. "What brings you in?"

The conference door room opened. Valerie came out.

"Excuse me," she said as she passed between Eli and me, then left the office.

Yolanda mouthed "ladies' room" to me.

"I got to go," Eli said.

"Wait," I called, but the door was already closing behind him. I followed, taking the stairs as fast as I dared.

On the street, I caught up to him and grabbed his arm, stopping him. His cell was in his hand. "Who are you calling?"

"No one."

"Bullshit. You're a spy. You've been feeding information to Frank and you're about to call him to let him know Valerie's cooperating with us."

He guffawed. "You have no proof of that."

"I know it was you. Sophia's murder. You were the only one who knew we were meeting her and when. Come to think about it, what about Josephine's sexting? You're the IT expert. You know how to bug someone's phone. Not only did you jeopardize my case, I could lose my license over this. You do understand that, don't you? Jesus, Eli. I thought we were friends."

"Friends? Right." He took a step toward me. "I'm nothing but a grunt to you, doing all your dirty work, and look what I get paid. You talk all high and mighty about fighting the good fight, but it's all about money and glory to you. Your money. Your glory."

I held my ground. "So that's what this is about? Money? Frank paid you to spy on me?"

"Not Frank," he said.

"If it wasn't Frank, who was it?"

"People you don't want to know. You need to drop this case, Maureen. You don't know what you've started. These are not nice people. They don't play by the rules. I tried to warn you."

"You warned me. How?"

"The letter. The email."

"You sent those?"

"I was looking out for you."

I stepped toward him. "You need to make this right. I want your statement. Recorded and written."

"No way," he said, pulling away from me. "I'd be a dead man." He pocketed the phone and began striding down the street.

I jogged to keep up.

Something caught Eli's attention. He seemed to hang in the air for a moment, one foot aloft, his attention locked on an object in the distance. I looked down the street to see what it was. We were halfway down the block from an intersection. The street was lined with parked cars. A dark sedan was double-parked down the street. I had first noticed it when we began arguing. It was not uncommon for a driver to idle while waiting for his passenger to come out of an office.

The sedan was rolling forward. Its movement was what had caught Eli's eye. It picked up speed as it approached us. Eli swung a long arm around, clotheslining me across the chest. I staggered a step backward to keep my balance, all the while thinking about how much I wanted to hit him back even though I'd lose the brawl as soon as he swung at me again.

Out of the corner of my eye, I saw a glint, a reflection off something metallic.

Eli lunged toward the approaching car. His hand was splayed in front of me.

I never saw the passenger's face. The sound was more like a sneeze than a blast.

The car's tires squealed as it sped off. It was nothing but a dark streak in my mind, just a memory, even before Eli staggered. He braced himself against the building, a hand to his chest. He looked down at his shirt, trying to assess the damage, as he slid to the sidewalk. Blood began to seep out from beneath the hand.

I found myself on my knees, pressing my hands on top of his own. His face was pale. I prayed for the bleeding to stop. One tear slid from his eye. He grimaced in pain. He tried to speak, but he made no sound. His eyes focused on me for a second. And then his pupils fixed.

Chapter Twenty-Three

THAT EVENING, I WAS on the couch wrapped up in a blanket, trying to get warm. Jake was sitting on the coffee table, wearing his shoulder holster with a pistol, taking a call on his cell. Quinn was in the kitchen grilling cheese sandwiches and warming tomato soup. I kept telling them I wasn't hungry, but they both insisted I eat.

Jake snapped his cell shut. "They got witness statements. Someone wrote down the license plate. They were about to call the police because the car had them blocked in. The license plate was stolen. So was the car. They found it in a parking garage. Looks wiped clean, but we'll know more tomorrow when forensics takes a look at it. Vague descriptions of the perps. Two white men, both wearing stocking caps."

I shivered. He swung around to sit next to me and pulled me into him. "The working theory is that you were the intended victim and Eli got in the way."

Eli had been a spy, betrayed me, yet he had given his life to save my own. "Why would he do that?"

"Jump between you and a gun?"

"Spy on me. He said it wasn't Frank, it was someone else, but they're all the same team. He sold me out for money. Why would he do that?"

"Look, I am so sorry. This is my fault. I knew he left SFPD under a cloud. There were questions about gambling debts. I shouldn't have recommended him to you in the first place. I had wanted to believe him when he said it was blown out of proportion and a political thing to get rid of him. It made sense, he wasn't good at ass-kissing. I thought he deserved a second chance."

"It's not your fault. Eli made his own choices. I feel like such an idiot. I should have figured it out sooner. He had to be the one who hacked into Josephine's phone and got the selfies. Oh, geez, I just remembered. Where's my phone?"

"Who are you calling?"

"Frank called me with a settlement offer right before Valerie came in. I have to convey it."

"Tomorrow's soon enough," Jake said.

Quinn came into the great room carrying a tray of sandwiches and mugs of soup. "Is there anything else I can get for you?"

I shook my head. She sat in the adjacent chair.

I took a small bite of a sandwich, not tasting it. But things were so new between us, I didn't want to inadvertently hurt her feelings. "My kid sure can cook."

Quinn tilted her head toward Jake. With everything that had happened, I hadn't a chance to tell her that he knew.

Jake reached for her hand. "Welcome to the family, Quinn. I mean it." And he did.

She relaxed.

Jake stood. "Anyone for a beer?" He went into the kitchen and puttered around in there while Quinn moved into the spot he had just vacated. I put an arm around her. We sat like that for a long time.

I had never imagined I'd see my baby again. She might not have returned if her adopted parents were still alive. From time to time, I'd thought about registering with an agency to find her, but I always chickened out because I was afraid. Afraid she'd hate me for giving her up. Afraid the truth would come out.

I WAS BACK IN my chair the next day. Yolanda was out in reception, the door locked. An off-duty cop friend of Jake's was on the reception-room couch with an Elmore Leonard paperback. His name was Gerry, and he was big—tall as Eli had been and twice as heavy. All muscle. As if his size wasn't intimidating enough, he wore a gun in a shoulder holster.

Quinn was in the conference room with a stack of paper. Yolanda had put her to work going through the piles of discovery Frank had delivered before the break-in.

My phone call with Josephine was brief. I conveyed the offer. The increase in money was better, but the nondisclosure clause was still a deal-breaker.

As I was putting down the receiver, Yolanda came into the office with the day's mail. On top was an order in *Navarre v Cleville, et al.* Judge Han's entire caseload had been transferred to Judge Wilbur St. James, the most conservative judge on the bench.

I hit the speed-dial for Jake's office.

"Is everything okay?" he asked.

"Judge Han's cases have been reassigned to Wilbur St. James. Have you heard anything about it?"

"Her husband had a heart attack a few nights ago. Was touch-and-go at first. She's out on personal leave until further notice."

"Damn it all anyway," I said. "I mean, I hope he's all right."

"Sorry, Red. But you know what to do." What he meant was that I would make sure the record was stuffed full of arguments and evidence so that when Judge St. James ruled against me, I might have a chance on appeal.

"I'd rather win."

"Wouldn't we all. Other than that, all quiet?"

He was asking if I had been attacked. "All quiet. Any news on Ajeti and Doda?"

"They've gone to ground."

"Has anyone figured out Alpha Inc's connection? Who hired them? And what about who Eli was talking to? He said he wasn't working for Frank, he was talking to someone else—but it had to be someone close to Frank, because he knew exactly what I had said to Eli."

"Someone's on that. Look, I'm about to go into a meeting. If anything comes up, call me on my cell. Love you."

"Love you too."

The next document in the pile on my desk was an order on my motion to exclude the selfie photographs in the Navarre case. Judge Han had promised to reserve judgment until we got closer to the trial. If I could prove the pictures were stolen and that Cleville hadn't known about them before he assaulted Josephine, I expected her to exclude them from evidence.

I flipped to the last page. Typed in all bold letters was the word "denied." It was signed by Judge Wilbur St. James.

"Figures," I said. "The way things were going, I would lose Judge Han. She would have kept the photos out." I handed the order to Yolanda.

"Can't you appeal?"

"Not until after the trial. The photos are coming in, and we have to deal with it."

"Hey, Mom?" Quinn was standing at my office door, a single sheet of paper in hand.

"Hey, you. What's up?"

That morning, I had sat her down in the conference with the piles of Frank's evidence and asked her to look for Alpha Inc.

"Bingo!" she waved a paper in the air. "I found a year-old visitors list, people who security had permitted to go into the Crown Productions building. Two visitors from Alpha Inc named Roman Ajeti and Aleksander Doda were signed in a bunch of times."

She handed me the page. Sure enough, they had signed in to see Crispin Cleville three times. "You have a knack for this, my girl. Go back and see if you can find more visits."

I sent Jake a text: The Duke had contact with Alpha Inc last year.

A few seconds later, he texted back: Roger that.

▼

THE POLICE TRACKED DOWN Eli's next-of-kin, an estranged sister who lived in Oregon. Her name was Susannah Conroy. She came into the office to pick up his final paycheck, pulling a old carry-on suitcase. She must have been older than him. Her salt and pepper hair was pulled back into a thick ponytail. The skin of unmade-up face was loose with age. She wore faded jeans, Birkenstocks, and a lumpy sweater. She had been a hippy chick. He was a cop. No small wonder they were estranged.

After Yolanda sat her in my visitor's chair, she got straight to the point. "You were there when my brother died."

"I was." How much did she want to know? Planting images of death in someone else's mind without permission is not a kindness.

"He was shot." Her eyes cut to the window. "Just out there, in front of your building."

I nodded.

"Did he suffer?"

I couldn't say how painful a gunshot wound to the torso was, but I imagined it was horrific. "He was gone in a few seconds."

"Have they found who did it?"

I shook my head.

"We didn't get along. Hadn't spoken in years. But I wouldn't have wished that on him."

Yolanda returned with a cup of tea for Susannah, then slipped out of the room.

I should have documentation of work in my cases, but I wondered if there was a letter or note that would prove who killed him.

"Is there anything you need?" I asked. "Can we help clear out his apartment for you?"

"All done."

"What about the case files?"

She shrugged. "All the paper went to recycling."

"Did the police take anything before you cleaned out the apartment?"

"They said they didn't need anything." She took a sip of tea. "Well, that's it, I suppose. Did you have a check for me?"

"Certainly." I pulled an envelope out of my pencil drawer, addressed to "Estate of Eli Conroy" and slid it across the desktop to her. "Will there be a memorial? I'd like to go. I'm sure his old friends at SFPD would as well."

"There's no reason for that. I'm on my way to the airport now. When I get home, I'll spread his ashes in the woods. He loved the woods when we were kids."

I pointed to the suitcase.

"Yes," she said. "His ashes." She stood. "I have a cab waiting and I'm sure your busy, Ms. Gould. I'll show myself out."

The last I saw of Eli Conroy was a beaten-up two-wheeled suitcase as it was dragged out of my office.

ONE WEEK BEFORE THE trial, I was in my office, staring out the window, tapping a pen against my tooth. It was a Monday morning. The skies sparkled with light. When Quinn and I came in, Jake's cop friend Gerry was already settled on the couch with a new Elmore Leonard book, a tall mug of coffee, and a piece of coffee cake at his elbow. Ajeti and Doda were still at large.

Gerry was wearing aftershave. That was new. I faced Yolanda so only she would see my curious expression.

She avoided meeting my eyes. "There's more in the kitchen. Help yourselves." Yolanda had been divorced long before I had met her and hadn't dated in the time she had worked for me. Nor had she baked for the office before.

"Thank you," I said.

"You're welcome." She bent to her task, blushing.

Quinn grabbed a slice of coffee cake for herself, then went into the conference room to continue her work analyzing Frank's evidence. She had already discovered a number of visits to Crown Productions by Roman Ajeti and Aleksander Doda that coincided with industry events attended by Reginald Cleville. Online, she had found photographs of the two hovering around him, earpieces in place.

As I sat at my desk, I still struggled with the theme of the case, that one short phrase that would resonate with the jury. I had to seize them from the first words I spoke.

Yolanda appeared at my door with a fresh mug of coffee. She placed it on my desk. "You have a visitor."

I wasn't sure I could handle another surprise.

"I don't have any appointments today." I put the pen down on my blank legal pad.

"She didn't make one."

"New client?"

"I don't know, maybe. She says she has information about your case against Cleville. Her name is Abigail Lawrence."

There hadn't been an Abigail Lawrence in any of our investigation results or in the evidence from Frank.

"Okay, show her in."

Yolanda left and returned with a young woman and a cup of tea which she set in front of the visitor's chair, then softly closed the door as she left.

Abigail Lawrence had a dark olive complexion. She could have been in her early thirties, but was gaunt from excessive weight loss and had dark circles around her eyes, which made her look older. I motioned for her to sit down.

"Good morning," I said, extending my hand. "I'm Maureen Gould. How can I help you?"

"I'm not sure," she said in a flat Midwestern accent.

"Yolanda said you have something to share about Reginald Cleville?"

She looked at her hands. She took a deep breath, then sighed, allowing her eyes to lift to the window. She stared out it for what seemed a long time, then a frown crinkled the thin tissue across her brow.

"He raped me."

That had to be a difficult thing for her to say. Given her demeanor, she had not said it often or to very many people. Her pain was raw.

I lifted my pen and clicked the cap to expose the nib. I put pen to paper. "Can I get your full name, please?"

"Abigail Ethel Lawrence is my real name, but you might know me as Amber LeRoux."

▼

AFTER YOLANDA AND I took her statement and made sure we had her contact information, she went back to the East Bay home of a childhood friend, where she was staying. As long as The Duke didn't know she was in town, she wouldn't be in danger. As far as he or anyone else knew, she was still partying in the south of France.

Jake called that afternoon. When I answered, he said, "Got them."

"The thugs?"

"Ajeti and Doda. Caught them trying to cross the border into Baja."

"Have they said anything?"

"The first words out of their mouth were 'diplomatic immunity.'"

"Fuck."

"Don't worry, Red. We've put a call into the British embassy to see if they're going to protect these guys. We should have a decision in a day or two."

"Did the cops find anything on them?"

"The gun is long gone. Best guess, at the bottom of the bay."

Chapter Twenty-Four

THE TRIAL STARTED ON a Wednesday because Judge Wilbur St. James was in a judicial conference Monday and Tuesday. I came in with my team a half hour early to give Josephine a chance to acclimate to the environment. She and I settled our bags at counsel table. Yolanda rolled the hand truck loaded with two boxes of files into a corner, then sat behind me in the first pew. Quinn sat next to her, where Eli would have been.

Throughout every trial I had had in private practice, Eli had sat in the front row. He observed the jurors and told me how they were reacting. He kept an eye on the other team, watching the defendant for tells. At break, he would pump me up with ringside encouragement as if he was a prizefighter's coach. When had he lost faith? I would never know. I had been too wrapped up in my clients and cases to notice.

Jury selection was brisk under the firm guidance of Judge St. James. I had asked for three days of *voir dire*, the process where we question prospective jurors, with another week for witnesses. Frank claimed he had a week of witnesses as well, an outright lie. An old defense trick was to ask for more time in order to manipulate the judge into curtailing the plaintiff's case. There was no way he had more than one or two witnesses—Cleville and someone else from Crown Productions, three if he called Cameron Aguilar, the guy Josephine had sent the selfies to.

It worked. The judge said we would have five days to try the case, including jury selection, opening, witnesses, and closing. That left two days for each of our cases and one day for jury selection. With fifty prospective jurors, we barely had enough time to find out their names and how irritated they were to have their lives disrupted by the court's summons.

The jury we ended up with included two college students; the female was premed, the male was majoring in education. Three were retirees, all male. We had one female executive secretary, a male engineer who wore horn rimmed glasses, two fidgety young men from the financial world, an unemployed male actor who was temporarily waiting tables, a male dog walker, and a female parking lot attendant. The two alternates included an accountant and a divorce attorney whom neither Frank nor I had met. Despite Frank's best efforts to skew the jury toward older, white males, we had a solid mixture of races: African-American, Hispanic, Asian, Native American, and three who identified themselves as mixed race.

Frank wanted jurors who liked the status quo—preferably white men and women who didn't see or acknowledge exploitation, who felt anyone could succeed and those who complained were demanding special treatment. He also wanted numbers-type people, accountants, engineers, statisticians, who trial attorneys believed to be less amenable to emotional arguments.

My approach was less knee-jerk than Frank's. I wanted people on my jury who had seen and experienced the inequities of American society. Numbers people could have feelings too. Mature white males mights be aware of bias. By the same token, a successful Black man could believe that he rose above his circumstance by virtue of hard work, and anyone who did not wasn't trying hard enough. Each person was an individual with unique experiences and beliefs.

Quinn and Yolanda sat in the front row behind me. Together with Josephine, who sat beside me, they observed the prospective jurors. When I was concentrating on one juror, another might react strongly to what was being said, so having another observer was invaluable. I heavily relied on Josephine's gut reactions to the people who would judge her. She had strong immediate impressions of those who would not listen to her story. I had learned after many trials that the client's instincts were accurate. Besides, this was her life, her story, her case. My job was to advise her, not to manage her. She had the final word as to who we rejected or accepted. We agreed on each decision.

Quinn's presence disturbed Frank. I had not introduced them, but he had to know who she was. She resembled me so much at that age. He showed it subtly. He glanced at her when he was facing in that direction. He was anxious, working his jaw muscle. Every time he stood or sat, he smoothed his jacket and tie with quick snapping motions. The knot of his tie was just the slightest bit tighter than he usually made it.

I wondered what it was like for a man who had gotten his own daughter with child to defend a rapist in full view of the person created by his abomination. Did any humanity still inside of him care whether Quinn knew how she had been conceived?

I hadn't told Quinn that he was her father, but she knew that he was her grandfather and that we were estranged. I was worried she would feel manipulated when she learned the truth. She was not there to harass Frank. She was there because I wanted her where I could see her and know that she was safe.

⬤

JAKE DISHED OUT PASTA onto the last plate, smothered it with a puttanesca sauce, and handed the plate to Quinn, who ferried it to the dining table. I sat at the breakfast bar watching them cook, too exhausted to wander safely around a kitchen full of fire and knives. Jake topped off my goblet of red wine and Quinn's. I brought them to the table, and the three of us settled into dinner.

"You've been pretty quiet all night," Jake said to me. "How's the trial going?"

I had torn off a chunk of garlic bread and bit into it. I was starving. I wiped the butter dripping down my chin. "Got jury selection done. Tomorrow is opening and I start my case."

"Any jurors you're worried about?"

"There's an engineer. I've never bought into the thing about numbers guys being unfeeling, but this guy is impassive. All I know is his name and that he wears horn-rimmed glasses. There are two young men, both financial industry guys, who can't sit still. They're both lost without their devices and a headset. I don't know if they'll be able to absorb our message in the old-fashioned way of watching and listening to real people. With the rest of them, it's too soon to tell."

"And what about you, Quinn? What do you think of all of this?"

Quinn had been watching us talk. "In a superficial way, it's just like on TV, you know, with the judge up there on the bench and the lawyers asking questions. But you don't get how hard this work is, how much goes into it. On TV, you don't see all the stuff the lawyers are doing, like giving emotional support to their client on top of thinking about the evidence and how a juror might react."

Jake gave me a wink. To Quinn, he asked, "Are you still thinking about law school?"

"It's so cool to see my mom in action. So, yeah, I might like it. Is there a law school around San Francisco?"

"A bunch of them," Jake said. "Stanford, where your granddad went. UC Berkeley, where you mom went. University of San Francisco is just down the street from here."

"Where did you go?"

"Golden Gate. That's in San Francisco, too. I was still on the force when I started, and they had a flex program that worked out. I didn't have the resources to quit work and go to school full-time. If you're interested, let's take a day trip, drive around to the different schools, see what you think."

"That would be totally awesome. Can we all go?"

"It'd have to be after the trial," I said.

"What about this weekend?" Quinn asked.

"Sorry, honey. A trial attorney is on the job twenty-four/seven from the first day of trial until the last. There's never enough time to do everything you need to do."

"Right after the trial?"

"You got a deal." I pulled a chunk of the garlic bread and passed the basket to Quinn. "Would it be a big deal to move your stuff out here?"

"There really isn't that much, just a few boxes. The house and everything in it was sold when my adopted dad passed away. All I really have is some pictures, clothes, and books. It's all in storage. I could have it shipped as soon as I find a place to stay."

"What? That's nonsense." Jake said. "You're staying here with us, young lady."

"Really?"

"Absolutely," he said.

She looked from Jake to me. "I won't get in the way?"

I took her hand and squeezed it. "You could never be in the way."

Jake lifted his glass. "Salut!"

Quinn and I raised our glasses in turn. "Salut!" We all took a drink.

After we put our glasses down, Jake topped them off again. "I don't like the idea of you being on your own until this whole Alpha Inc thing is settled. We don't know who put those guys onto you or if they got called off. For all we know, there's more of them. The two in jail still aren't talking."

"Any news on the diplomatic immunity?" I asked.

"What's that?" Quinn asked.

I was strangling down a forkful of pasta, so Jake explained. "A diplomat is immune from criminal prosecution. No way were these two jokers British diplomats, but it can extend to everyone on the embassy staff, not just the ambassadors. The feds are going to hold these two, Ajeti and Doda, until the Brits make a decision. If immunity isn't waived, they'll be set free and there's nothing we can do to touch them."

"Even for murder?" Quinn asked.

"Even for murder. So until we know what the situation is, I'd feel better if I knew you two ladies' were in good hands, either in court, with me, or with Gerry."

Chapter Twenty-Five

MICKEY WONG WAS SITTING in the last pew when we arrived for court. We exchanged polite nods when my team and I entered the courtroom.

Because I was plaintiff's counsel and this was a civil case, I made my opening statement first. I stood and took the lectern. As a general rule, I opened with a warm-up, but not today. I greeted each panelist, the twelve jurors and two alternates, in the eye, one by one, making sure I had their attention. After they coalesced into one organism, breathing in sync, I touched my pearl necklace for good luck and took my opening shot.

"Reginald Cleville is a rapist." Blunt and to the point. I still hadn't come up with the theme of my case, the storyline that would connect in a primal way with the jurors, so I decided to stick with the raw facts.

"Objection!" Frank was on his feet. Cleville half-stood with him.

"Approach!" Judge St. James was ordering us to a side-bar so we could argue our dispute without the jury listening in.

I threaded between the lectern and my table while Frank walked around. The Duke followed Frank.

"You may return to your seat, Mr. Cleville," the judge said. "Counsel only."

Cleville plucked at Frank's sleeve. Frank whispered something to him. Cleville gestured with an open hand at the judge. *Sotto voce*, he said, "He needs to understand." Frank gripped Cleville's shoulder, just as he had gripped mine that night at the cocktail party.

Cleville went back to the defense table while Frank and I met at the bench, with enough room between us to fit in a third person. Judge St. James motioned us closer. I stood on tiptoes. Frank stayed in his place. The judge gave us a frown and flipped on the white noise machine to keep the jury from overhearing our discussion.

"Ms. Gould," the judge said. "This is opening statement, the time when you set out the evidence you believe will be introduced. It is not the time for hyperbole." This was the first dispute of the case, and already he was making Frank's arguments for him.

"That is what I am doing. I'm aware of Your Honor's concern for the disruption to the jurors' lives and the time constraints presenting the case, so I am making my best effort to set out the evidence as concisely as possible. If the court prefers a detailed recitation of the facts, I'd be happy to do that, but it was my intent to highlight the salient events so as to provide more time for witness testimony."

Some attorneys drone on during argument when given the chance, afraid they forgot to say something important and wanting to make sure they leave nothing unsaid. Others won't stop talking because they are searching for some indication of agreement from the judge before they do. I had a two-punch strategy. The first punch was delivered in the sidebar. I could have stopped talking after my first sentence. But Frank needed to see early and often that every time he talked, I would prattle on for as long as possible, eating up more time that could be spent on evidence. To keep things moving along, the judge would eventually deny Frank's more dubious objections and Frank would get bored.

"Very well, counselor. See that you do." The judge motioned us to step back from the bench.

I resumed the lectern. Frank sat at his table, patting the air in Cleville's direction with a "no big deal" gesture.

Then I delivered the second punch. I repeated what I had just said so the jury could watch Frank's reaction as he was forced to sit through the words that had inflamed him.

"Reginald Cleville is a rapist."

I took a sip of water, letting my words sink in. Frank resettled in his chair. The jurors watched him, then focused on me.

"Good morning, ladies and gentlemen of the jury. My name is Maureen Gould, and I am privileged and honored to represent Josephine Navarre. Josephine, would you please stand up for the jury?"

She stood and gave them a shy smile. Some smiled back at her. A few—notably the older females, including Mrs. Beatrice Templeton, a White lady in a cardigan in the front row and Ms. Edith Chang, a Chinese lady in the second row—were stony-faced. These were the ones on alert for sneaky lawyer tricks. I had to earn their trust.

"Thank you, Josephine," I said, and she resumed her chair.

I turned back to the jury. "This is her story. From a young age, this remarkable young woman dreamt of becoming a movie producer. She worked hard in high school. She won a scholarship to the University of Southern California. There, she distinguished herself and won awards for a short film she had written, produced, and directed. Even before she graduated, she was hired as a production assistant at a small studio. Her dream was coming true. From there she envisioned working her way up through the industry until one day she would produce her own independent films.

"And then Reginald Cleville entered her life. He offered her a job. He recognized her ambition. And he took advantage of it. He personally took her under his wing. Because of her desire to impress him, he could manipulate her into tolerating his increasingly aberrant behavior. His plan culminated on a trip up here to San Francisco to scout locations for an upcoming film. One night in his hotel room, he forced her to perform oral sex on him."

Juror number nine, Norberto Bonifaz, the dog walker, covered his mouth with one hand. Juror number ten next to him, the horn-rimmed wearing engineer, pushed himself as far away from Bonifaz as he could get. Ms. Chang, on Bonifaz's other side, patted his arm.

I continued. "She broke free and ran out of the room. She returned to her hotel room and locked the door. That very night, even before the sun rose again, he sent hotel security to escort her from the premises. He fired her. She was left on the streets of San Francisco at dawn with nothing but her suitcase. He didn't even provide her with a ticket home. He just threw her out like garbage."

"Objection!" Frank again.

"Sustained," the judge said. "Move on, Ms. Gould."

Frank was right. The garbage remark was hyperbole. But no one won or lost an appeal because of an overly dramatic opening argument.

"And you will learn that this wasn't the first time Reginald Cleville preyed upon women in his orbit. You will hear from witnesses that long before Josephine Navarre was hired, this was a pattern, and that Crown Productions knew—"

"Objection!"

Judge St. James took in a deep breath. "Approach."

When we were gathered, the judge leaned into Frank. "Articulate your objection, Mr. Gould."

"There is no evidence whatsoever of prior acts."

The judge turned to me. "And your response?"

"As I set out in my brief, we have two witnesses who will testify to prior sexual assaults—"

"Objection!"

"Mr. Gould, you do not need to object during argument. This isn't evidence."

"Still, Your Honor, I wish to make it perfectly clear for the record that my client denies there were assaults, and we object to the use of that term in this proceeding."

I snorted. The party who picked the language won the battle. Clearly Frank's strategy was to force me to use words so neutral that the acts I described sounded clinical. This coming from a man who wanted to introduce erotic selfies. He was hoping to censor me and save all the drama for himself. I opened my mouth to respond when the judge held his hand up.

"Mr. Gould," the judge said. "Did you file a pretrial motion asking for specific language to be disallowed during these proceedings?"

"No, Your Honor, but the language is so inflammatory that it should not be permitted in any case."

"Your argument is deemed waived for having failed to assert it timely. Your request is denied."

The scoreboard read: Maureen 2, Frank 1.

"Exception," Frank said.

"You don't need to voice exception, Mr. Gould. This is not the nineteenth century. Your record has been made."

Frank said, "We request a stay in the proceedings so we can file an appeal of this ruling."

"Request denied. Step back." The judge flipped a switch and the roar from the white-noise machine died away.

I stood behind the lectern and waited for the jury to settle down. The constant interruptions had distracted them, the two young financial guys in particular. The one in the front row faced backwards, mouthing something to the one in the back. But I also noticed that some of the jurors leaned into me, anxious to hear what I had to say next.

"As I was saying."

The jury snapped to attention.

"Crown Productions knew about Reginald Cleville's pattern of sexually assaulting young women. They protected him. They defended him. Time and time again, they paid off his victims in exchange for nondisclosure agreements. They shielded him with the cloak of secrecy these agreements gave them and drove these young women from the movie business. In that way, they were complicit. If the truth was known, women would not have continued to seek employment with him. If the truth was known, he could not have accessed women at work. If the truth was known, talented young women, like my client Josephine Navarre, would not have been sacked for refusing to succumb to Reginald Cleville's sexual proclivities, and would have been allowed a fair chance of success.

"In a few moments, defense counsel will speak. It is up to you, the jurors, to decide whose story makes the most sense. I ask you to hold me to the promises I have just made you, that I will prove my case with the evidence that I just outlined. I also ask that you hold Mr. Cleville and Crown Productions to the same standard."

The judge stood. "We'll take our morning recess now. We shall resume in fifteen minutes."

I went back to my table and stood behind my chair. Everyone else stood. We waited in silence as the jury filed out and the door clicked closed behind them.

I looked at Frank, the monster who lived in my head. And then, like a miracle, a light bloomed inside my mind. That was the moment when I knew how I would explain the elemental nature of rape and rapists to the jury. I had my theme.

Cleville and Frank swept from the room. Mickey rolled out of the courtroom behind them, her notebook and pen in hand.

Josephine was weeping.

"Did I do okay?" I asked.

She shook her head. "You were great. It's just—it's just so hard to hear the whole thing told like that. You know, I try not to think about it, but I get these little flashes and I just hadn't put it all together like you did. How did you do that? It's like you know what happened better than I did." She wiped underneath her eyes, then examined her mascara-covered fingers. "I must look hideous. Do we have time for me to go to the ladies'?"

"We have twelve minutes," I said.

"No problem," Yolanda said as she picked up her purse. "I'll go with you."

When they were gone, I took a seat beside Quinn in the first pew. "So what do you think?"

"Your father, what's he like?"

Bile burned in my throat. "Complicated. We don't get along. After the trial is over, I'll tell you all about it. Why do you ask?"

"He keeps looking at me."

My stomach churned, but I didn't have time to get sick. I reached over the railing to grab a bottle of water out of my briefcase. I took a sip. "Ignore him. So what about my opening? Any thoughts?"

"You were awesome. I made some notes. I don't know if it matters, but I was watching the jury." She flipped open a file folder. On the left side was a map of the jury box with each chair numbered. Beneath that was a legend listing the numbered jurors, correlated to their seats. Each was identified by his or her gender, age, and race. To the left of the numbers were tiny photos of most of the jurors.

"Where did you get the pictures?"

"Facebook. Just about everyone has an account, or a friend or relative who does."

That explained the noise I had heard late last night coming from her room, the home office, where we had a small desktop printer. I had thought she was printing off law school applications.

Quinn had a legal pad of notes on her lap. "I noticed that juror number three, Mrs. Templeton, was shoved back on her chair. She's the one wearing the cardigan. She wore it the first day, too." Quinn pointed at a small picture of Mrs. Templeton in her file, smiling for the camera at a social gathering, wearing her cardigan. That had to be her trademark. "She made a face when you talked about what happened in the hotel room."

"What kind of face?"

Quinn scowled for me.

"She doesn't like hearing about it," I said. "But it's too soon to read into it. It could mean she's offended I would say something like that out loud, or that she's disgusted by what Cleville did. Can you keep an eye on her? And don't forget to watch the alternates. One of them could end up on our jury. Anything else?"

"Did you catch Number Nine, that's Norberto Bonifaz? He was upset."

"I did. Pretty sure he was horrified by what happened. But that doesn't mean he's sympathetic to us. If he thinks I'm twisting the facts and he feels manipulated, he could punish us."

The courtroom door opened. Josephine entered. Yolanda came in second but stopped, blocking Frank's and Cleville's entrance. Frank halted for a moment, Cleville crowded behind him. When Josephine walked through the gate and put her purse in her chair, Yolanda strutted forward as if she hadn't noticed Frank and Cleville.

The clerk entered from the side door and announced, "The jury is returning." The back door opened. While they were filing in, I leaned into Quinn. "Great job. Keep it up." Then I stepped through the gate and took my place standing beside Josephine.

"Are you okay?" I asked.

She took my hand and squeezed it.

"One last thing, before he starts talking. No matter what he says, do not react. Got me?"

"Gotcha." Josephine said and let go of my hand.

Chapter Twenty-Six

AFTER THE COURTROOM OCCUPANTS settled into their chairs, Frank took the lectern.

"Ladies and gentlemen of the jury, my name is Francis E. Gould and this is my client, Reginald Cleville." He swept an arm in the defendant's direction.

I rolled back so I could watch The Duke. He was pushed back in his chair with one hand against the armrest, locked in a stare down with Mrs. Templeton. The moment lingered while his color deepened to the purple of raw steak and a sheen broke out across his face.

Frank went on. "This is my opportunity to tell you what the evidence will show. Like you, I find these accusations distasteful. Some of the terms you will be forced to hear are not fit for polite company. Forgive me, I'm just an old-fashioned man. I was raised in a different era, so you will sometimes see me embarrassed by the things that will be said in this courtroom."

He was aiming his remarks at Mrs. Templeton, who I was now thinking of as "Cardigan Lady." She had been skeptical of me, but she wasn't warming to him, either. If anything, her expression hardened even more. She didn't like being pandered to.

"As awkward as this is for me to say, I must: Reginald Cleville is not a rapist."

The dogwalker Norberto Bonifaz stared at Cleville, whose color had lightened to medium rare. The others were trained on Frank.

"This case is about greed. It all boils down to money. Josephine Navarre wants to get something for nothing. You will learn that she obtained a job at Crown Productions in the same manner that anyone else does: she applied for it. She was interviewed by someone in the Human Relations department. Ultimately a person far beneath Mr. Cleville in the corporate structure decided to hire her. He had nothing to do with this. He was not even aware of her existence until she came to work on the *Golden Gate* project."

Here Mrs. Templeton examined Josephine, and I could feel Josephine's composure waver. Then the juror turned her attention to Frank. She was his canary in the coalmine.

He was speaking to her, using her as his gauge of what worked and how to pace his remarks. When he had her attention again, he resumed.

"At first, Ms. Navarre worked hard, as everyone else in Hollywood does. But as time rolled on, there were concerns about her reliability. She began coming into work late. There were gaps during the workday when she could not be found. She was spoken to on two different occasions and given warnings. The third event occurred on the night she was fired.

"There was a meeting of investors at the Mark Hopkins Hotel. That evening, Ms. Navarre appeared high-strung. Not long after it began, she excused herself to go to the restroom. Her coworkers had made remarks in the preceding months about her frequent visits to the ladies' room and there had been suspicions, but no one had ever seen Ms. Navarre using drugs. Regardless of what you may have heard about Hollywood, Crown Productions has a zero-tolerance policy regarding drug usage. If Ms. Navarre had made it known that she was using, make no mistake about it, she would have been terminated immediately."

The financial guys shifted in their chairs guiltily. Josephine slipped her hands under the table and began picking at her cuticles.

"From that day to this, she never gave a reason or excuse for failing to return to the Mark Hopkins meeting. She simply disappeared. This was her third offense. She was terminated the following day for unsatisfactory job performance. She was unreliable. It was as simple as that."

Now Juror Number Eight, Ms. Chang, a fiftyish executive secretary, looked from Frank to Josephine, then to Cleville. She was the same one who'd attempted to console Norberto Bonifaz when he was upset during my opening. My guess was that either Ms. Chang or Mrs. Templeton would be elected foreperson. Some juries see it as a clerical position, and will defer to an administrator like Ms. Chang. Others see it as a power position and will align themselves with the strongest personality, who I guessed was Mrs. Templeton.

Frank slipped one hand into his pants pocket. "Then the next thing you know, Josephine Navarre filed suit against my client, Reginald Cleville, claiming, of all things, that he accosted her. She has no witnesses whatsoever to confirm her story. If it was true, that would be a serious matter and a crime. Wouldn't she report him to the police? One would think so, but she did not. Because it wasn't justice she sought, it was money. Instead of calling the police, she ran to an attorney, made these wild accusations, and filed a multimillion dollar lawsuit.

"Reginald Cleville will not stand for this. He came to this country penniless. With little more than his own blood, sweat, and tears, he built an entertainment empire. Crown Productions is a multimillion dollar corporation that provides salaries to more than fifty full-time employees, plus casts and crews. His movies generate revenue throughout the industry. From publicists all the way down to the teenage girl who sells popcorn at the theater, workers depend upon the earnings his projects produce.

"Reginald Cleville will not see his good name disparaged. He will not see his enterprise destroyed. And he will not write a check to every young woman who tells a story. If word spread, it would open the floodgates to countless false claims."

Frank slapped his hand on the lectern, startling Norberto Bonifaz. "This extortion must stop. Here and now. With you." Frank gathered his notes and stepped to his table where he was greeted by a handshake from his client.

Judge St. James spoke. "Ms. Gould, are you prepared to call your first witness?"

"I need a few minutes to set up, Your Honor." I could have spent the first hour questioning Josephine without showing exhibits, but I wanted a chance to settle her before she went on the stand. The judge would call a short recess if I hinted at technical matters. Nothing bores the judge or jury quicker than watching someone fiddle with equipment.

"Very well." The judge stood. "We will take our second morning break now. Expect to be back in the courtroom in fifteen minutes."

FRANK AND CLEVILLE REMAINED at their table. Josephine, Quinn, and I left the court-room while Yolanda stayed behind to set up and test the computer and projector. Down the hall were a few conference rooms set aside for use during trial. I found a vacant one and ushered my team into it.

Josephine was trembling. "He's lying. He lied about all of it. Why did he say those things about hiring me?"

I said, "Workplace sexual harassment occurs when a supervisor who has the authority to hire, fire, or discipline a subordinate takes an employment action because of sex. We said he hired and fired you. Given his history, he probably hired you because he wanted to hit on you. Then he fired you when you refused. It's classic sexual harassment."

"What about this stuff about her disappearing at work?" Quinn asked. "That's new."

"Is there any truth to it?" I asked Josephine.

"There were times when someone couldn't find me, but that was always because I was with The Duke. He'd hunt me down when I was working on something and insist that I drop everything and follow him. He wanted me to take notes or do something stupid that he really didn't need me for. I kind of felt like he was just dragging me around to show off. So, yeah, I wasn't where I was supposed to be, but later on, I'd explain what happened and it was like no big deal because he's the boss."

"And the coke thing?"

"That's just fantasy," Josephine said. "I don't use drugs."

"Any drugs?"

She lifted her Versace bag for us to see. "Do you think I could afford this purse if I was using drugs?"

"No way," Quinn said. "But I have a question. Why didn't Frank talk about the selfies in his opening?"

I liked how Quinn dived in and wasn't afraid to ask questions. "Because he's saving them for dramatic impact. He expects us to paint a pure-as-driven-snow picture of Josephine, and then he will make her look like a promiscuous druggie."

"I don't get it," Quinn said. "If Mr. Cleville claims he didn't do anything to her and that there was nothing sexual in their relationship, who cares if she's an adult woman responsible for her own sexuality?"

That was my little girl talking. My heart was full.

"Good point," I said. "Two things. Frank's betting not everyone will see it that way. We do have some apparently conservative people on the jury."

"Like Mrs. Templeton," Quinn said.

"Who's that?" Josephine asked.

"Cardigan Lady in first row," I said.

"I'm not sure she likes me."

"She's suspicious of everyone and will be careful to come to a decision. Not to worry. I'm betting that when she does, she will be a powerful influencer on the jury. It's not about liking, so we can't charm her. It's about telling a story that makes sense and rings of truth."

"You mentioned there were two things," Quinn said. "What's the second?"

"Frank's working a fallback defense: if the jury believes The Duke came on to Josephine, then she welcomed it."

"Ew."

"Ew is right," Josephine said.

I reached for the door handle. "Okay, guys, we need to get back. Are we good?"

THE JURORS WERE IN their box, tensely waiting for the big show to begin. Mickey was in the back pew of the court. The bench was vacant.

The court clerk rose from her station, tissue box in her hand. She crossed the well, something she had not done before, and drew the jurors' rapt attention. She set the box on the small table in the witness stand next to the microphone. She produced a water pitcher that had been stashed behind the chair, half-filled a plastic cup, and set that on the table as well. Then she walked back across the well and took her seat behind a bank of computers. The entire ritual was performed and observed in silence.

The judge entered from the door behind the bench and eased himself into his chair. He surveyed the room, then said, "*J.N. v Cleville and Crown Productions* is now back in session. Counselor, please call your first witness."

"The plaintiff calls Josephine Navarre."

Josephine stood and crossed the room to the witness stand. She was wearing her court suit—black blazer and slacks, black heels, white silk blouse. Her braids were pulled into a chignon. She was sworn in, took her seat, and instructed to attach a small microphone to her blazer. I waited for her full attention before I began direct examination.

"Ms. Navarre, please state your full name for the record."

Josephine dipped her head toward the microphone on the desk. "Josephine Isabelle Navarre."

"And just to be clear, you are the plaintiff in this case."

"I am."

"Would you please tell the jury in your own words why you decided to file suit against Reginald Cleville and Crown Productions."

Josephine addressed the jury as we had practiced during trial preparation the week before. "I filed suit because he fired me."

"How did the sexual assault play into your decision to file suit?"

"Objection!"

Josephine didn't answer. When we had prepared for trial, we ran through her testimony. Seated around the conference table, Jake had played Frank's part while I was myself and Yolanda was the judge. Quinn played the role of a juror so that Josephine would become accustomed to someone watching her.

Judge St. James said to Frank, "State the nature of your objection."

"The question calls for facts not admitted into evidence."

"Sustained," the judge said. He bent toward Josephine. "That means you should not answer the question, ma'am."

"Yes, sir."

We had anticipated this particular objection, and that was fine by me. The jury's interest would be piqued. The question was still in the jurors' heads: Had he sexually assaulted her?

I resumed. "Let's back up, shall we? When you obtained employment at Crown Productions, what was your career goal?"

"I wanted to become an independent producer of films. I still do."

"Before obtaining the job at Crown Productions, what efforts had you taken to reach your goal?"

"It started back in junior high." She smiled. Her hands flittered in the air as she described her past. "I took videos of my friends, pretending I was interviewing them, and then downloaded them onto my laptop at home and edited them into little stories with some voiceover. Stuff like a day in the life of a twelve-year-old ballerina. I put them up on YouTube and they got a lot of likes. Then in high school, I took every elective I could find related to performing arts. I worked backstage in our theater productions. We had a film class. For my term project, I submitted a production with an all-female cast of the chess scene from *The Seventh Seal*. That's a Bergman film."

"Objection!"

"Grounds?"

"The witness is giving a narrative."

Judge St. James' gaze lingered on Frank longer than he needed to. Frank was right. I was supposed to break up her story into questions and answers, but it would go more quickly if he didn't interrupt. "Very well, sustained. Your next question, Ms. Gould?"

"After graduation, did you apply for film school?"

"Objection! Leading." Frank came from the school that a lawyer should object at every possible opportunity, breaking up the cohesiveness of the testimony. Another group believes that constant objections irritate the jury. The fact was, Mrs. Templeton had just sent Frank a disapproving frown in a schoolmarm kind of way. She wanted to hear the story without his interruptions.

"I'll rephrase, Your Honor. Ms. Navarre, following high school, what steps did you take toward your goal of becoming an independent film producer?"

Josephine remembered to face the jury. She connected first with Mrs. Templeton, then with each juror in turn as she spoke. "I received a scholarship to USC School of Cinema Arts. That was wonderful, because my family couldn't afford the tuition. Even with student loans, I was stretched. I had to work part-time to make ends meet."

"What kind of jobs did you work?"

"Theater, bookstore. Then I got a job waitressing—which paid better because of the tips, but it's hard work. At the same time, I did an internship with a small independent producer. I didn't get paid, I worked for credits. It was an incredible opportunity."

"How did your education at USC advance your career goals?"

"I learned everything there from the ground up. For my senior project, I wrote, produced, and directed a short film about the Great Recession of 2007-2009. That's when subprime mortgages led to a housing bubble that crashed. It had a huge impact on working families in Southern California. My focus was on how five different individuals recovered from losing their jobs and their homes and having their credit destroyed. There was tragedy and yet there were stories of resilience. I won a few awards for that."

"And after you graduated, did you obtain employment in the film industry?"

"My internship led to a job, but it was a small company and they were seriously strapped for cash. We didn't know from one day to the next if we were still in business. The producer invited Reginald Cleville to the office one day, trying to get him interested in signing on as executive producer on one of our projects so we could attract more investors, and that's when I met him."

"Did he hire you on the spot?"

Josephine shook her head. "He told me there were openings at Crown Productions and that I should contact his Human Relations Department to submit my application. I kind of felt disloyal, you know, because we hadn't invited him to the office for me, it was for the company. But my boss, she was wonderful. She said to go for it, it was a huge opportunity. So I did."

"Did they hire you?"

Her face brightened. "A few days later, I got the call."

Mrs. Templeton nodded, as did Ms. Chang. Mr. Bonifaz, who had been entranced in the story, shook his fists in victory and then clasped his hands down in his lap.

I needed to deal with two things before Josephine got off the stand. The first was the nondisclosure agreement.

"Exhibit one, please."

Yolanda tapped on the keyboard. The computer hummed to life and a document appeared on the screen facing the jury. Yolanda had placed paper copies of the exhibits on the witness stand while we were in recess.

"Marked for identification, this is exhibit one. Is this your employment agreement?"

Josephine thumbed through the paper exhibit. "Looks like it."

"On the last page, is that your signature?" Page four appeared on the screen.

"It is."

"There is some language bolded just above your signature. Would you read that aloud to the jury?"

Yolanda tapped on the keyboard again and the language on the screen was highlighted.

"The undersigned hereby agrees that—"

"Objection!"

"Grounds?"

"May we approach?" Frank asked.

The judge waved us forward. When we were standing before the bench, he activated the white noise machine. "What is the objection?"

"Judge Han previously issued a ruling regarding the nondisclosure agreement. She set it aside. It's null and void for the purposes of this case, and as such, it's irrelevant."

The judge raised his eyes to me. "Response?"

"The terms of Ms. Navarre's employment are very much relevant, Your Honor. We are showing that the conditions of the workplace environment encouraged secrecy and in turn sexual harassment. At the time she was employed, she was under the threat of a heavy fine, two million dollars, if she talked to anyone, co-employees included, about—"

"Your Honor! In her deposition, Ms. Navarre testified that she hadn't read the NDA before she filed suit. How could it possibly be relevant to her employment if she didn't know it existed?"

"I wasn't finished speaking. Because everyone in Crown Productions was subject to the same NDA clause. Our claim isn't just against Reginald Cleville, it is also against Crown Productions. Its culture gave Reginald Cleville *carte blanche* to exploit women in his employment. Crown Productions knew about his serial abuse. These NDAs were one of the devices that they used to protect him and to oppress his victims."

"Very well, you may proceed with your question, Ms. Gould."

While we had been arguing about the language, the contract was displayed on the screen, with the NDA clause highlighted for the jury to read. So if Frank didn't want them to know about it, he was too late. After I resumed my position at the lectern, I again asked Josephine to read the paragraph aloud.

"The undersigned hereby acknowledges that any and all matters relating to her employment, job duties, and business of Crown Productions are confidential and hereby agrees that s/he will not disclose said confidential information. In the event of disclosure, intentional or otherwise, s/he will pay the sum of two million dollars ($2,000,000) to Crown Productions."

Mrs. Templeton's mouth dropped open. Norberto Bonifaz swayed when the number was read. Mrs. Chang frowned. Other jurors wrote notes in the legal pads on their laps.

"Did you read the clause before signing it?"

Josephine's hand trembled as she lifted the half-filled cup. She managed to put it to her mouth without spilling, but appeared to have reconsidered trying to drink. Instead, she tilted it enough to moisten her lips and then, with both hands, set the cup back on the witness stand.

"To be honest, I didn't. Now I know I should have."

Mrs. Templeton and Ms. Chang seemed to stiffen.

"Why did you not read it?"

"Because I was told when the contract was handed to me that this was standard operating procedure and that if I wanted a job in the movies, I had to sign it."

Ms. Chang wrote a note on her pad.

"In your first job at the small company, were you required to sign a nondisclosure agreement?"

"No. There was nothing like it."

"Objection!"

The judge motioned for us to approach. "Quickly, Mr. Gould."

When we were lined up before the judge, Frank said, "The plaintiff's terms of employment at another company prior to Crown Productions has no relevance to this case."

"Response?"

"She was told that the contract was industry standard. The fact that she wasn't required to sign one at another movie studio is evidence that it was not."

"Hearsay."

"Mr. Gould," the judge said. "Any statements made by Crown Production employees are not hearsay. Evidence Rule 1222."

"Still, it's irrelevant."

"Overruled. After the lunch break, you may ask your question again, Ms. Gould. Step back."

As we walked to our tables, the judge informed the jury that we were taking a ninety-minute break for lunch and would resume at one thirty. Mickey picked up her satchel and left. When I talked to her later that day, she told me that she had asked Frank and Cleville for an interview during one of our breaks and they had both refused.

Chapter Twenty-Seven

JOSEPHINE WAS BACK ON the stand, microphone clipped to her blazer. The Crown Productions employment agreement was up on the screen, the nondisclosure agreement clause still highlighted.

"You may continue your examination, Ms. Gould," Judge St. James said. "Ms. Navarre, I remind you that you are still under oath."

Josephine nodded.

I cleared my throat for the jury's attention. "Ms. Navarre, after you went to work for Crown Productions, how did things go?"

"At first it was great! I mean, I liked the people. We had exciting projects. We were all enthusiastic and worked well together."

"What were your duties?"

"I did whatever anyone wanted me to. I followed around one producer and did what he asked—made calls, set up meetings, made sure things that needed to be done were getting done, stuff like that. Then the Duke noticed me. Mr. Cleville, I mean."

"You had met him before. Did he seemed surprised to see you?"

"Not at all. He congratulated me for getting the job. During the first few weeks I was at the studio, he was out of town, so I hadn't seen him. When he came into the office, it was like a tornado. Some people got out of his way. Others were sucked into his wake. One day, he pointed at me, and ordered me to follow him. The producer I was working with was like, whatever. We all worked for the Duke. He was the boss. We did what he said. That's what I had been told. So I followed him."

"What did he have you do?"

"At first, nothing. I just followed him around. Then when it was all over, I'd go back to work on the project he'd taken me away from."

"And then?"

"Objection!"

"Grounds?" Judge St. James asked.

Frank pushed himself halfway to a stand. "Was that a question? I didn't hear a question."

"Please restate your question for counsel's benefit," Judge St. James said.

"You were saying the first few times he asked you to follow him around, you weren't given anything to do. Did that change?"

"Little by little. I was told to carry around a clipboard and make notes of everything he said to everyone. Then before he left for the day, he'd have me come into his office and review everything that had occurred, who said what, and what he had told them to do. Seriously, I was a glorified secretary. Not even that, because I didn't do any typing or filing, I just took notes. But I was learning the business. It was an incredible opportunity. I felt so lucky."

"When he took you away from other projects, were there complaints?"

"After he left, I'd report back to the producer I was working for and he would ask me where I went. So after I told him, he always said, okay, cool. That was it. It wasn't like Mr. Gould said." She jerked her head to Frank. "I wasn't reprimanded or anything. Because the Duke was the boss. Everyone did what he told us to do."

"Was there a time when things changed?"

"Objection! The question is vague. Counsel is calling for another narrative."

"Please rephrase," Judge St. James said. The tide seemed to be turning. Judge St. James had sided with Frank on two objections in a row.

"Was there a time when your work duties with Reginald Cleville changed?"

"It's hard to point to a particular date. It was gradual. More and more, when Mr. Cleville came to the studio, I was expected to follow him around all day. We'd go over his schedule when he came in, and he'd give me a list of things he wanted to deal with and people he wanted to see. Most of the time, he didn't show up until after lunch. Then there was meeting after meeting until eight, most nights. By then everyone was gone, and we would meet again in his office. That's about the time he'd tell me to mix him a drink. He always kept alcohol in his office bar. At first, I'd just mix him a drink or two. Then he expected me to drink with him."

"Did you?"

"Just to be polite. What was I supposed to do? But I don't like hard liquor, so I'd only take a sip or two and that would be it."

"How did you feel about that?"

"I was thrilled. He's such a big name. He's made huge pictures. I was learning the business from one of the most successful contemporary moviemakers."

Cleville preened. His neck extended. His chin jutted up. He smoothed his tie with a languorous stroke, then eased the end inside his blazer.

"What about drugs?"

"No way. I don't do drugs. That's a dead-end street. I don't get where they get these ideas, accusing me of disappearing to use drugs. I worked every minute of the day when I was at the studio. Most of the time, if I got lunch at all, I ate an apple standing on my feet. But that was okay, you know, because that's the industry and I love it."

"Let's talk about your social life. Did you form any friendships at Crown Productions?"

"Sure, like anyone does. There were a bunch of us who used to go out for drinks on Friday night. Not late, because most of us had to work the next day."

"Was there someone special?"

"At the time, I thought so. His name was Cameron Aguilar."

"Were you exclusively involved with Mr. Aguilar?"

She nodded. "I thought it was going somewhere, so I wasn't seeing anyone else. But after a while, I quit hearing from him. I figured he was just busy. We all were. Maybe three weeks after the last time I saw him, he showed up one Friday night with another woman." She paused for a moment. "I guess he had moved on."

"You took some intimate photographs of yourself."

"He asked me to. Like I said, I thought we were in a relationship."

"Did you anticipate that he would share those photos?"

"No. I am so embarrassed. I guess that's what he does—meets girls, and gets them to take photos so he can show them off to his friends. It was right after I had sent them that he dropped out of sight."

"Would you say the photos are pretty graphic?"

"They are."

"Would you be embarrassed for anyone to see them?"

"Oh my God, yes. I was mortified when he"—she glanced at Frank—"threw them on the table at my deposition. It's bad enough that they exist, but to be in a room full of men drooling over them. I ran out." Her voice broke. "I'm not that way. It's just—it's just I thought we were in a relationship, and this was something special for us to share."

"And that is why I will not be showing these photos to the jury," I said. Anyone who showed those photos risked offending the jurors. Let Frank try his luck if he thought it was worth it.

I gave Josephine a moment to collect herself, then moved on to the next subject. "Did anything strike you as odd about Mr. Cleville's behavior?"

"There wasn't any one thing at first. Like I said, he had me mix his drinks at the end of the workday. Then he insisted I go with him to his hotel suite to work. We'd order room service for dinner. Sometimes a director or another producer would show up, and the meetings would last late into the night. That's why he hardly showed up to the studio before noon. But he was always working. At some point, I was expected to report regularly to his hotel by seven A.M. We would work in his suite, then take a limo to the studio."

"Pretty heady stuff—hotel suites, room service, limousines."

"Objection. Was that a question?" Frank didn't bother standing.

The judge leaned back in his chair, prepared to referee another fight.

It wasn't a question. I had been needling Frank, poking the lion to see if he was awake. "I'll move on. Did your relationship with Mr. Cleville change over time?"

"It became, I don't know—more personal? He'd ask me questions about who I was dating, if I ever dated white guys or older men."

"How did you respond?"

"I tried to be vague. I didn't think it was any of his business, and it made me uncomfortable that he was asking questions like that."

"Did you report his conduct to anyone?"

"No way. I didn't want to lose my job. This was my dream come true."

"Was there an event that sticks out in your mind when he acted differently toward you?"

"Like I said, I was expected to report to his hotel suite by seven A.M. every morning. By the time I got there, he was already on the phone to the east coast. Sometimes we'd go straight to the studio, but most of the time we ordered up breakfast and worked at the suite. At first, he would be dressed in a suit when I arrived. At some point—I don't remember when—when I showed up in the morning, he was wearing pajamas and a bathrobe. And then it was just a bathrobe."

"How did you know he wasn't wearing anything?"

"I could see his chest and legs. And then one day, he opened the robe, pulled it tighter, and retied his belt. I could see everything."

"Are you saying he exposed himself to you?"

I heard Frank stirring to stand.

Mrs. Templeton gave him a warning look.

"Yeah. I mean, yes. That's precisely what he did. He made a little joke out of it and apologized. 'Sorry, I forgot you were here.'"

"And what did you do?"

"Nothing! I couldn't move. I didn't know what to say. I mean, what do you say when someone does something like that? I was thinking, maybe it was an accident. I didn't want to make a big deal out of it if it was. Things were going so good. He said he was going to bring me to San Francisco to scout locations. And he kept making promises about how great my future was going to be."

"Did any particular phrase strike out in your memory?"

"He kept saying, stick with me, kid, and you'll be farting in silk shorts."

Mrs. Templeton pressed her lips into a thin line. Norberto Bonifaz snorted in disgust.

"I know. It was stupid. But when he said stuff like that, I thought it meant I would get a promotion. And he promised that when we got to San Francisco, I could tell him about the films I wanted to produce."

"Did he ever make time to talk about your ideas?"

She shook her head. "No. Never."

"What happened when you came to San Francisco?"

"I ran around during the day looking at locations, and brought him back pictures and video. Then one night we had an investors' meeting at the Mark Hopkins Hotel. That's where we were staying. We met in the bar."

"Who was there?"

"Mr. Cleville, two men I didn't know, and Mr. Gould, his attorney."

Judge St. James interrupted. "Ms. Navarre, do you mean the gentleman sitting at counsel table with Mr. Cleville here in court today?"

"Yes, sir. He was there."

The judge stood. "We stand in recess. Ladies and gentlemen of the jury, this break will be longer than usual. You may retire to the jury room."

THE JURY FILED OUT. When the door clicked shut, Judge St. James sat down. "You may be seated. Ms. Navarre, please remain in the witness stand. We're back on record."

The clerk pushed a button on her desk, observed her monitor for a moment, then gave the judge a nod.

"Before we go any further, I want Ms. Gould to outline for us the anticipated testimony from Ms. Navarre outside of the jury's presence. Ms. Gould, please enlighten the court."

I was still standing at the lectern. "Your Honor, my client identified Mr. Francis Gould as one of the attendees of this investors meeting. It was during this meeting that Mr. Cleville reached his hand beneath the table and groped her."

"I did no such thing!" Cleville said.

The judge raised his hand. "Mr. Cleville, this is a proffer. That means counsel is telling me what to expect. Her proffer is not evidence. It remains to be seen whether this testimony will be introduced."

I continued. "Because of the groping, she excused herself from the table claiming she had to go to the ladies' room."

Cleville slapped the table. "A lie! No one is listening to me. When do I get to tell my side of the story?"

The judge pointed at the defendant. "Sir, you have an experienced, capable attorney. I suggest you allow him to speak for you." To me, he said, "Go on."

"She locked herself in her hotel room. Later that night, she was summoned to Mr. Cleville's suite. He forced her to perform oral sex. She fought and freed herself. At some point, she heard laughter coming from the bedroom area, the doors to which were shut. That was when she left the suite. The next morning before dawn, hotel security escorted her from her room per Mr. Cleville's request. They informed her that her employment had been terminated."

A snorting sound came from Cleville. Frank whispered to him.

"According to Miss Navarre, how much of this did Mr. Gould witness?" Judge St. James asked.

"He was at the table sitting on her other side when she was groped. All Ms. Navarre can testify to is that he was at the meeting in the bar. She doesn't know if he saw Mr. Cleville's hand under the table, or whether he was in the hotel suite bedroom when Mr. Cleville propositioned her."

"Why wasn't this brought to the court's attention before the trial? Even if Mr. Gould didn't see Mr. Cleville 'do something,' as you say, he was a potential witness that something was not done. The rules are clear that an attorney who is a witness cannot represent a party."

"I felt that it was incumbent upon Mr. Gould to disclose the conflict. After all, he is the one who truly knows what he saw and did not see, and whether his testimony would be material."

The truth was, if I had filed a motion to disqualify Frank, it would have been interpreted that I was afraid of trying the case against him. When my motion was inevitably denied, Frank would have been even more emboldened and Judge St. James would have formed the opinion that my case was weak. Once the judge decided a party is wasting the court's time with an unsubstantiated claim, his treatment of the attorneys and parties would subtly convey his opinion to the jury. The air in the courtroom would feel dead. The jury would seem to fall asleep. It would be impossible to rouse the jurors after that.

"Very well. Mr. Gould, what do you have to say?"

Frank stood.

"Wait," Judge St. James said. "Madam Clerk, swear in Mr. Gould."

The clerk raised her hand and recited the oath.

Frank raised his own and said, "I do."

"Now, Mr. Gould," the judge said. "You are under oath. As an attorney, you are aware of the implications."

When Judge St. James put Frank under oath, a host of ethical rules had been invoked. If it later emerged that he had strayed from the truth, he risked disbarment.

"I understand."

The judge took up the questioning. "Mr. Gould, were you at this meeting described by Ms. Navarre?"

"I met with Mr. Cleville and two investors one night at the Mark Hopkins Hotel. Ms. Navarre was in attendance."

"What was your role in this meeting?"

"I represented an investment consortium."

"Did you witness Mr. Cleville reaching his hand underneath the table?"

"In good conscience, Your Honor, I cannot recollect that detail. It wasn't something I would have noticed."

"Did you witness Mr. Cleville touching Ms. Navarre in any way?"

"Not that I can recall, Your Honor."

"Do you remember Ms. Navarre leaving the meeting?"

"No, Your Honor. I was only vaguely aware of her presence. She could have left, as stated, and she could have made an excuse. But if she did, her departure did not make a significant enough impression upon me to remember."

"In your opening, you stated that she was nervous during this meeting. Where does this information come from?"

"Mr. Cleville will testify to that."

"Did you attend a gathering in Mr. Cleville's hotel suite later that evening?"

"No, Your Honor, I did not. At the time, my late wife was gravely ill. When our business was concluded, I went straight home."

"Very well." The judge stood. "We'll stand in recess. The parties shall assemble in thirty minutes when I render my decision. Meanwhile, Mr. Gould, I suggest you arrange for co-counsel."

After the judge swept from the room, Cleville spun on Frank. "What just happened?" Frank whipped his head around to see if we were nearby.

I led my team out, passing Mickey Wong on the way. She was writing notes furiously.

I gathered my team in a conference room down the hall.

"What's going on?" Josephine asked.

"If an attorney is a material witness to the events involved in a lawsuit, then it's unethical for him to represent a party. If another attorney finds out, then she or he is supposed to bring it to the court's attention. The judge wanted to know why I hadn't. What I told him was that I had left it up to Frank to decide if he was conflicted. Then Frank testified that he didn't see anything material, meaning anything important."

"But he lied," Josephine said. "When he said he was just representing an investment group. He wasn't just an attorney, he was one of the investors. That's why he gave the Duke that little painting."

The Diego Rivera.

"Are you going to tell the judge?" Quinn asked.

Good question. I realized I had been collecting secrets about Frank: that he had hired thugs to break into my office and steal my notes, the same thugs who had killed Sophia and Eli. That he had been behind that, too. That he stolen the Rivera.

If I made any accusation that couldn't be corroborated, no one would believe me, and my honesty would be questioned. When I told the biggest secret we shared—that he had raped me, and fathered my daughter—I needed to be taken seriously.

Chapter Twenty-Eight

WHEN WE ENTERED THE courtroom, Ian Napier, Frank's partner, was seated at counsel table with Cleville sandwiched between him and Frank. Mickey was at the back of the room.

The clerk stood. "All rise!"

The judge entered, carrying a file and a stack of books, as we scooted into place.

"You may be seated." Judge St. James said. "I've consulted the ethical rules and relevant case law. Mr. Gould, it is not apparent at this time that you have a conflict of interest because it has not been established that you are a material witness. Nonetheless I have concerns. Mr. Cleville, have you been advised of the nature of Mr. Gould's potential conflict of interest in that he cannot both be a witness and an advocate in these proceedings?"

Ian whispered in his client's ear.

Cleville said, "Yes, Your Honor."

"Do you waive this conflict of interest?"

Ian nodded for the Duke's benefit.

Cleville said, "Yes, Your Honor."

"Very well. Then I find that on behalf of Mr. Reginald Cleville, the conflict is waived. Now, as to Crown Productions, we have a problem."

Frank stood. "Your Honor, Mr. Cleville is the chief executive officer of Crown Productions and as such he is empowered to waive the conflict."

The judge tapped his pen on the desk. "I presume there is a board of directors."

"There is. Mr. Cleville is also the chairman of the board."

"Yet it is the alleged actions of Mr. Cleville that gives rise to the claims against Crown Productions, is that not correct, Mr. Gould?"

"It is."

"In that case, I find that although Mr. Cleville has the apparent authority to waive a conflict of interest, his actions may lead to a judgment against Crown Productions, thereby giving rise to a conflict of interest between himself and the company. His waiver on Crown Productions' behalf will not be accepted due to his own conflict of interest. Therefore, Mr. Gould, you may no longer represent Crown Productions in this trial. I see that your partner Mr. Napier is present. However, he too is unable to represent Crown Productions because the rule that applies to you applies to your firm as well.

"For this reason, we will stand adjourned until tomorrow morning—when I expect to see another attorney present in this courtroom to represent Crown Productions' interest. Are there any questions before I dismiss the jury for the day?"

A flurry of whispering took place at the defense table. The Duke's head was pressed together with Frank's. Ian Napier rolled his chair behind the two, so he could listen in. The clock on the wall ticked loudly as the judge watched the confab. The court clerk's head was down; she appeared to be writing notes.

After a few moments, Frank stood. "Your Honor, we are concerned that we would be unable to bring another attorney up to speed by tomorrow morning."

"Then do you request a continuance?"

"We do, Your Honor."

Josephine grabbed my arm.

"Very well. This is Thursday afternoon. We shall stand adjourned until Monday morning, at which time both parties shall be prepared to proceed."

"Three days!" Cleville shouted as he rose to his feet. "How the hell am I to get someone here that fast?"

Frank pushed his client down as he stood. "My client is anxious to proceed, but I am sure the court realizes that this is a complicated case. We don't know who would be available on such short notice, much less if they could be brought up to speed so quickly."

"Monday morning," Judge St. James said. "I suggest you make good use of your time. Madam Clerk, please bring in the jury."

* * *

I let Quinn drive Josephine back to her hotel after she dropped Yolanda and me off at the office. I needed to contact my witnesses and reschedule them. They were supposed to go on the stand Friday, but now they would testify Monday.

When we walked into the office, Yolanda asked, "do you want me to call Gerry?"

"We're fine. The bad guys are in jail. Besides, it's late. There's not much for either of us to do and we have all day tomorrow in the office. Let's close shop as soon as I finish these calls."

I reached into my bag and pulled out my cell phone. I had forgotten to turn it back on after we left court. I pressed the power button and the phone shivered to life. Within seconds, a clunking sound notified me of a text. It was from Jake.

"Call when you can."

Jake picked up on my second ring. "Got a minute? Remember those two guys, Ajeti and Doda?"

"How could I forget?"

"The British embassy denied their request for immunity. So they've asked for translators. Albanian."

I gave Yolanda a hopeful look. "Because?"

"They want to cut a deal. I'm flying down tonight, going straight to the airport from the office. Where are you?"

"We finished early for the day. The judge recessed until Monday."

"What happened?"

"Frank was conflicted from representing Crown Productions, so St. James gave him until Monday to have another attorney in the courtroom for the corporation."

"Where are you?" Panic was creeping into his voice.

"Yolanda and I are at the office. Quinn is dropping off Josephine then swinging back to pick me up. We're going home as soon as I reschedule my witnesses."

"I'm sending Gerry over."

"Please, don't. We'll stay home like good little girls all night. If you want to send him to the office on Friday, that's fine but I'm sure we'll be okay. There's only one way in and out, and we have security cameras all over the place. If they were going to try something at the loft, they would have done it by now. Besides, it'll be fun just to have a girls' night. Eat junk food, watch chick flicks. Having Gerry bunked out on the couch would cramp our style. And you got the bad guys, right? All locked up safe and sound."

"I don't know about this. First Sophia, then Eli. Whoever's pulling the strings has resources. The two in jail may just be the beginning."

"I haven't had any time alone with Quinn. At all." I needed to tell her about Frank, that he was her father.

There was a pause on his end.

"If you say so, but if I call, you answer the phone. And if you don't, I'll have someone busting down the door."

"Thanks, sweetie. I appreciate it."

It took a few minutes to telephone my witnesses and explain to them the new schedule. When I finished, Quinn was waiting for me in reception. Yolanda had already gone for the day. We ran by the grocery store to pick up cookies, ice cream, sundae fixings, potato chips, and frozen pizza.

That night, we flopped on my bed in our pajamas, surrounded by bowls and boxes containing a feast of salt and sugar in all their wonderous manifestations, and watched a series of meet-cute, live-happily-ever-after movies. We cried and laughed together. We recited our favorite lines to each other.

There was never a right time that evening to tell her the truth.

Jake called to wish us a good night. He had arrived in San Diego safely and was settled in his hotel room. They were still waiting for Albanian translators. Southern California had plenty of Albanian-speaking people, but finding someone certified for legal translation was proving difficult. Jake would hang around to see what came up. We promised to stay in the loft unless Gerry was with us.

Friday, we went into the office. Yolanda and Gerry were already there, she behind her desk, he at his post on the couch. As always happened during trial, a stack of telephone messages and emails had accumulated.

Quinn spent the day recombing through the evidence Frank had sent, just to make sure she hadn't missed anything. Jake called to report that they had found translators on the east coast, who were flying to San Diego. It would be Saturday, at the earliest, before the authorities were allowed to speak to Ajeti and Doda.

Late that afternoon I received a text from the Palace Hotel confirming my reservations for Mother's Day tea. I hadn't made the arrangements. My mother must have. I called Quinn into my office and told her about the text.

"Do you want to go?" I asked.

She seemed eager but tentative, waiting for a cue from me.

I went on. "Have you ever been to afternoon tea? Little sandwiches, tiny cakes, crumpets, clotted cream?"

"Sounds awesome."

"Brilliant," I said. "We have a table for three. I promised Jake we wouldn't go anywhere without Gerry. Is it okay with you if we bring him along?"

"Sure, why not? Yolanda too?"

"I could ask, but chances are she would want to spend the day with her kids."

▼

THAT SUNDAY, A BESUITED Gerry, the hulking mass of manhood, escorted Quinn and me to tea at the Palace Hotel. It wasn't the event my mother had planned, but it was a nice break from real life. She would have wanted to tell Quinn old family sagas, her favorite being Elizabeth Shaughnessy's life story.

Would she have said something about sending me away when she discovered I was pregnant? Would she have apologized to Quinn, to me? I would never know. I was grateful for the distraction when a waiter appeared and gave us charming explanations of the history of afternoon tea and a description of the offerings.

A string quartet played in the corner. The dainties were just what I had expected: a variety of crustless sandwiches, cucumber, smoked salmon, watercress; scones so tender they almost fell apart when clotted cream was dolloped on top; little cakes and cookies. As we ate, Gerry entertained us with stories of growing up in San Francisco—seeing the Giants play in the old Candlestick Park, flying kites in Crissy Field, going to the beach in Pacifica. By the end of the day, we had a long list of places Quinn would like to visit after the trial was over.

Jake called after Gerry dropped us off at the loft. The translators had arrived late Saturday, but interrogations hadn't begun. First, Ajeti and Doda had to speak with each of the attorneys separately. The defense lawyers had asked for immunity from prosecution in exchange for cooperation. The feds would let them stew until Monday morning, then counteroffer with a plea agreement. If that didn't blow the negotiations to hell, they would go back and forth most of Monday before agreeing to terms that would let questioning begin.

Jake had considered flying back to San Francisco but he would have to fly back down again. With the check-in time and highway travel, it was easier just to stay down there.

That night, we were too full to eat again. I was at the dining table on my laptop, tinkering with the script for my remaining questions for Josephine when Quinn came out of her bedroom.

"Mom, do you have a minute?"

It still sounded funny having her call me "Mom." In all those fantasies I nurtured of our life together, she hadn't spoken.

"Sure, honey, what's up?"

She had a bundle in her hand. "I don't know why I brought these with me. The thing is, today was supposed to be different. It was going to be you, me, and your mom. Don't get me wrong, I loved the tea—but the way your mom had planned, it was supposed to be different. I feel bad she wasn't there."

Regardless of what my mother had planned, talking about feelings was not something that had been encouraged in my family. I had never grown comfortable with it. My throat tightened but I managed to say, "I get it. Me too."

"So I thought you might like to read the letters she sent me."

"Are you sure?"

She placed them on the table.

"Up for a glass of wine?" I asked.

She went into the kitchen. "I'll pour. White or red?"

"White. I'll be right back." I moved Quinn's stack to the coffee table on my way to the hall closet. I opened the box containing those letters my mother had saved, still tied together with a pink ribbon. Now that I knew Quinn's handwriting, I recognized they had come from her. I came back to the great room, sat on the couch, and patted the spot next to me. Quinn came out of the kitchen with two goblets of wine, handed one to me, and sat down beside me.

"Let's get these organized, shall we? Date order, oldest on top."

She laughed. "You are such a lawyer."

I took a sip of wine, put the glass down, and handed her one packet while I sorted the other.

"Who has the oldest? I have one dated September 3."

"That's the first letter I wrote her. We had connected online and she had an email address, but she said she didn't like using the computer. She wanted me to write her the old-fashioned way instead."

I didn't know she could use the computer at all. Chances were she'd had Emily help her, and didn't want Emily reading the correspondence.

I opened the envelope. Three photographs fell out. I studied each photograph in turn, enjoying the history told there even though I hadn't been around to share in its making.

One was of Quinn as a little girl, about five years old. The second was a recent photograph of her with a group of girlfriends, clustered together for a selfie while they were hiking on a trail. A third was Quinn posed with a few other college-aged students, dressed in suits.

"Debate team," she said. "We won. Funny, I was thinking about law school even before I knew you were a lawyer."

"It's in the genes," I said. "You've got the mind for it."

"You think so?"

"Always questioning, examining, testing the evidence. If you don't mind having people tell you that you're wrong all day long, you'll be fine."

Her brow furrowed.

"But, hey, there's all kinds of law. You don't have to go into trial practice. You can make your career anything you want it to be."

"I want to help people."

Quinn picked up the letter and we read it together.

Dear Mrs. Gould,

Thank you for responding to my e-mail. I can't tell you how excited I am to meet my birth family. I have so many questions. According to the DNA, you are my maternal grandmother. Can you tell me about my mother? Is she still alive? Did she have more children? Is she happy? What about my birth father? Do you know anything about him?

I am enclosing photographs. I thought you might like to see what I looked like. Is there a family resemblance?

Yours truly,

Quinn Brennan

"Oh yeah, there's a family resemblance," I said. "You could have been my twin."

I felt warmth emanating from Quinn. "You think so?"

"For sure. Where's my mother's response?"

Quinn shuffled through the pile and handed me another envelope, this addressed in my mother's hand.

Dear Quinn,

What a delight it is to hear from you! I often wondered how you fared. I hoped that your adoptive family were nice people. We were told that they were well-to-do, a physician and a college professor. Please always know that we wanted what was best for you.

It was impossible for your mother to keep you. She was fifteen years old when you were born.

Your mother is well. She is an attorney and practices law here in San Francisco. She is quite successful. I am very proud of her. She has helped so many people.

She married a nice young man. He's a lawyer, too. They do not have children. She appears to derive happiness from her work.

As for your birth father, I have nothing I can tell you. We suspect it was a boy at her school.

Best,

Mrs. Francis E. Gould

I could feel Quinn staring at me. A boy at school. I had never said that, and nothing of the sort had happened. Before that night of the cocktail party, I had not so much as kissed a boy. "What do the other letters say?"

"We went back and forth about our lives. She told me about the Shaughnessy mining fortune and the mansion. I told her about my adopted family, school, stuff like that. I dropped some hints that I'd like to visit." She dug around in the pile again and pulled out another envelope addressed by my mother. "Here's the letter she wrote inviting me to come for Mother's Day."

Dear Quinn,

I am sorry for the delay in responding to your last letter. I would be delighted to meet you. I am certain Maureen would be as well. I haven't told her yet about our correspondence. I want to make it a surprise. Will your studies permit you to visit San Francisco for Mother's Day? You can stay with us at the mansion. Maureen's old bedroom is just as it was. May is a lovely time in the Bay Area. Please let me know at your earliest convenience.

Love,

Grandmother Gould

I laughed. Granny Gould. It had taken two decades, but she had eventually warmed to the role.

"How long was it before she answered your letter, the one she talks about?"

"A month. I was so scared that I had offended her, like maybe I was pushing too hard when I said I'd like to visit."

I patted her knee. "That wasn't it. That's when she started going to the doctor and they were doing tests. They were hoping it was just an ulcer, but it turned out to be stomach cancer. By the time she wrote you back, they had the diagnosis."

"You mean she knew she was dying already?"

I nodded. "But she didn't think it would end so soon." My mother had wanted to meet this remarkable young woman who had been my baby. The loss I felt still lingered, but the resentment toward my mother was fading. That happily-ever-after fantasy of raising the baby at the mansion was childish. My mother had been right to put Quinn up for adoption.

Quinn left the room. When she came back, she was carrying a box of tissues. She held it out before me. I pulled a hank and used it to wipe my eyes.

I pointed to a pink envelope. "What's this?"

"She sent me a birthday card."

The postmark was January 20th, sent in time for Quinn's birthday on January 27th. I didn't realize my mother knew her birthdate, much less had recorded it somewhere.

"May I look?" I asked.

She handed it to me.

The card was frilly. The cover said, "To Granddaughter, with Love." Inside were lines of poetry about the celebrant's birth "brightening our lives." In my mother's hand was a note, "Buy yourself something nice. Love, Grandmother Gould."

"She sent me a check for a thousand dollars."

"Wow." After I was sent away, my mother routinely sent me checks for my birthday and Christmas, or handed them to me after I moved back, but never that much.

"I returned it. I didn't feel right taking money from her. That's not why I had made contact, for money. Besides, I had money inherited from my parents. Not a lot. It was just enough to get through college even with student loans. I looked because I wanted to know you. And the family. She sent the airfare back to me a second time with a word that it make her happy if I accepted the money and said it was to make up for all the birthdays she had missed. So I used it to pay for my plane ticket."

My throat tightened. I was going to lose control completely if we didn't stop this conversation soon. "How late is it?" "Nine-thirty."

"I don't know about you, but I'm totally done for the day. Early morning is the best time for me to work anyway. Let's say we go to bed. I'll try not to wake you when I get up, but be ready to leave by seven-thirty, okay? I want to find a good parking spot since we're lugging around the files."

I had brought the two bankers boxes of case files home with me for the weekend. Boxes full of paper soothed my anxiety. Computers were great—when they worked right, which was never when I needed them—so I had assembled old fashioned trial binders.

"Sure thing," Quinn said.

I kissed her on the forehead, as had become my custom.

And, as had become hers, she said "Goodnight, Mom."

While I readied for bed, I pushed thoughts of my daughter and my mother out of my mind. Scenes of the next trial day replaced them: finishing Josephine's testimony, bringing on my witnesses, and the relentless nipping of opposing counsel, Francis E. Gould.

The final thought I had as I drifted off to sleep was that in my mother's letters to Quinn, she had never mentioned Frank. He was an unacknowledged presence looming over the correspondence. She had to have known the truth.

Chapter Twenty-Nine

JOSEPHINE WAS IN THE witness stand. Mickey was in the back pew by the door. The judge was on his bench, the jury in their box. Cleville was at the defense table, now flanked by three lawyers: Frank, Ian Napier, and Ken Vincent, who represented Crown Productions. I pitied the man who ended up sitting with my father and his wretched client.

I was at the lectern. "Ms. Navarre, when we last met, you testified about an investor meeting at the Mark Hopkins. Let's pick up there. Was any alcohol provided?"

"There was always alcohol, all day long. The Duke, I mean Mr. Cleville, drank Bloody Marys in the morning, wine with lunch and dinner, and mixed drinks from afternoon on. Whenever there were people around to entertain, like these investors, he ordered the most expensive champagne on the menu."

"Do you know if he had been drinking earlier that day?"

"He had. I went to his suite that afternoon to show him the photos and videos of different locations and by the time I arrived, he had a highball. He asked me to mix him another, and I did."

"Did he appear intoxicated?"

"He never did. Or maybe I never saw him sober. I don't know."

"Objection!" from Frank.

The judge: "Overruled."

"Did he tell you what to wear to the investor meeting?"

"He did. I have a short black halter dress he had seen me wear at one of the parties. Before we left LA, he said to bring it. That afternoon, he told me I should wear it."

"Did he make any other requests?"

"He told me not to wear pantyhose."

Mrs. Templeton made a tsking sound. Ms. Chang raised her head from her notes. She studied Josephine and then Cleville. While she was gazing at him, Cleville whispered something to Frank. Frank responded by flicking his hand as if he was batting away a fly.

"Did you do as he asked?"

Josephine's voice was quiet when she answered. "I did."

"How did you arrive at the meeting?"

"I went to Mr. Cleville's suite about ten minutes before we were to meet the investors in the bar. He had just opened a bottle of champagne and insisted we had to drink it or it would go flat. I had a glass. He had a few."

"Where were you during this time?"

"I was seated on the couch. He sat down beside me."

"Did you talk about anything?"

"He talked about how big this movie was going to be and asked me how I felt about having my name on the credits of a major motion picture for the first time."

"How did you feel?"

"I was thrilled. It was incredible. I thought all my dreams were coming true that night."

"Did he talk about anything else?"

"He said that where my name would be, how high on the credits, depended on what my job title was by the time we finished the movie. He said if I played my cards right, I might be listed as an assistant producer under his name. It's a huge leap. As an assistant producer, I would have a lot more responsibility and more pay. And from there, I would be in line to start producing my own projects."

"And he knew that you wanted to be a producer?"

"Oh, definitely. I mentioned it again that night. When I started to tell him about my ideas, he said it was time to go meet the investors."

"And so you went to the bar?"

"We did. Just as we walked up to the maître d's stand, he put his hand on my low back, like he was escorting me." Her shoulders tightened.

"Did that bother you?"

"It was a halter top, so the dress was backless. His hand was on my bare skin. Yes, it bothered me."

"Had he ever touched you like that before?"

"He had not."

"What did you do?"

"I tried to walk ahead of him as we were led to our table, but he kept up. I was afraid to say something or make a scene. I didn't want to embarrass him. If I did, I thought he might fire me. Everyone had to have seen his hand on me, like I belonged to him. The men we were meeting were already there and they all saw it."

"Were you seated at a table?"

"It was a booth. The men scooted over. Mr. Cleville said 'ladies first,' so I slid in. Then he sat on the end."

"So you were trapped in the booth with him?"

"Objection!" Frank again.

"Ms. Gould?" The judge.

My question was another needle at the old lion. "I'll rephrase. Ms. Navarre, how did you feel sitting in the booth, with investors to one side and Mr. Cleville seated on the end?"

"Trapped, just like you said." Now, because of Frank's objection, the jurors heard the phrase twice.

I took the opportunity to scan the jury. I saw some impassive faces, but the three that I had been watching—Mrs. Templeton with her cardigan, Norberto Bonifaz the dog walker, and Ms. Chang the executive secretary—all registered tension with stiff body language.

"And then what happened?"

"Mr. Cleville ordered more champagne. They drank and talked about the movie."

"Did you participate in the conversation?"

"No. Just before we walked into the bar, Mr. Cleville reminded me that I was just an assistant and I should keep my mouth shut."

"Then what happened?"

"He slipped his hand under the table. At first, he just rested his hand on top of my thigh."

"Did you say anything?"

"I didn't dare. Like I said, I didn't want to make a scene and get fired. Besides, he had just told me to keep my mouth shut."

"Did you try to move his hand?"

She shook her head.

"Then what happened?"

"Then his hand slid between my legs. He rested it there for a while. Then, he worked his way up my thigh. The side of his hand was resting against my, against – me."

Mrs. Templeton frowned. Ms. Chang set her mouth in a grim line. Mr. Bonifaz appeared baffled at first. When he realized what she meant, his mouth formed an "oh" and he grimaced. The two young financial guys were breathing shallowly.

"Go on," I said.

"And then he started digging his fingers into my leg."

"Marked for identification is plaintiff's exhibit two." Yolanda tapped on her keyboard and a photo materialized on the screen. "Ms. Navarre, is this a photo I took of your bruises?"

"Yes. You took that the day after I came to your office."

"So the photo was taken about a day and a half after Mr. Cleville groped you?"

"Your Honor!" Frank again.

The judge, "Overruled. Continue, Ms. Gould."

The photo showed Josephine's thigh with deep purple bruises, obviously the impressions of fingertips. The jury's collective spirit dampened. Their shock and outrage had progressed into sorrow. When both Mrs. Templeton and Ms. Chang finished examining the photo and gave me a nod, I asked my next question.

"So what did you do?"

"I told them I had to go to the ladies' room. That's the only thing I could think of to escape."

"What did you do after you left the party?"

Frank, "Objection to the term 'party.'"

The judge, "Overruled. You may answer the question, Ms. Navarre."

Frank's most recent objections were so petty the judge overruled them without asking me to respond, but I didn't feel vindicated. The judge was swinging from giving me a few wins to giving Frank some, then back to me in his effort to appear fair. I worried that when he swung back to Frank, his rulings would damage my case.

"I went straight back to my room and locked the door with both locks. I got out of that dress and pulled on an old sweatshirt and jeans, and I went to bed."

"Why did you go to bed wearing your clothes?"

"I was scared. Wearing clothes made me feel safer. What if he got into my hotel room and I was wearing a nightie? He'd think I was waiting for him, that I wanted to have sex. And that wasn't true."

"But he didn't come to your room."

"He didn't. He called around midnight. I must have drifted off. He told me we had to go over some new stuff that had come up in the investors' meeting and I needed to come to his suite right away."

"Did he say anything about your disappearance?"

"I figured if he did, I'd just tell him I had gotten sick. But he didn't."

"So you went back to his suite around midnight. What happened when you arrived?"

"The first thing he said was, 'where's that sexy dress you had on?' I told him that I spilled champagne on it and I had to rinse it out in the sink."

"Was that true?"

"No. I was just trying to find a way of getting out of this conversation without making him angry."

"How was he dressed when you arrived?"

"In the bathrobe."

"Please tell the jury what happened next."

"I went over to the dining table where we did our work. I had brought an e-notebook with me to take some notes. As soon as I sat down, he said, 'No, over there' and pointed me to the couch where we had been sitting earlier that evening. So I got up and moved over to the couch. Then he sat down beside me, really close. Like his leg was right up against mine. I scooted away to make room and when I did, he took the notebook out of my hand and put it on the coffee table. I was trying to avoid eye contact cause, you know, we were sitting so close. I was afraid he was going to kiss me, and I didn't want that to happen. Then he opened his bathrobe just as I felt his other hand on the back of my neck, pushing my head down."

I heard a gasp from the jury box, but I kept my eyes on Josephine. I wanted her to know that I was with her absolutely. As much as I could, I tried to share the memory with her to lessen her burden. She wasn't alone anymore.

She lifted her chin and was blinking rapidly to stem back tears, but it was no use. She found the tissue box on the witness stand and plucked one out, then dabbed at her eyes.

"Counsel," Judge St. James said. "Does your client need a moment before we continue?"

Josephine smiled up at him. "No, sir, I'm fine. Thank you." She took a deep shuddering breath, then waited for the next question.

"Was he aroused?"

A sob broke from Josephine. She grabbed a wad of tissues from the box, covered her face, and began to cry uncontrollably.

The judge stood. "We'll stand in recess. Fifteen minutes."

As the jury shuffled past Josephine, the ladies and Mr. Bonifaz sent her consoling looks. The financial guys craned their heads, trying to see who in front of them was holding up the line. These two would vote with the crowd when the jury eventually deliberated, just so they could leave quickly. The engineer alternate juror scrutinized the room, first making eye contact with me, then over at the defense table, then at Josephine, his expression blank. He was weighing the evidence. The others focused on the door on their way out. It could be an effort to appear unbiased, I told myself.

CLEVILLE, FRANK, AND THE other defense lawyers left the courtroom, Mickey in their wake. They had turned her down for an interview before, but she would continue to ask. Whatever they said would be important to her story. Their repeated refusals to speak would be important as well.

Yolanda, Quinn, and I circled the witness box. Yolanda filled the plastic water cup and handed it to Josephine, who took a sip, both hands shaking, then put it down. Quinn handed Josephine her purse. She pulled out a make-up mirror and consulted it as she wiped under her eyes with her little finger, then reapplied lip gloss. The tallest of us three, I stood in the center between them, blocking the view so as to give my client a sense of privacy.

The clerk returned to the courtroom and said, "The judge is on his way."

I gave Josephine's hand a squeeze and she squeezed back. I resumed the lectern. By then, Frank, Cleville, and their entourage were in place, as was Mickey Wong. The judge came in. Still standing, he signaled the clerk who pushed a button. A few minutes later, the jury filed back into the room.

When everyone was seated, the judge announced, "We're back on record. Ms. Gould, you may resume your direct examination."

"Ms. Navarre, before the break we were discussing what happened that night when you were in Mr. Cleville's suite. You testified that he had pushed your head into his lap."

"Yes."

"What did you do next?"

She pulled herself upright. It was then I noticed how much weight she had lost, how gaunt she appeared. "I did what he wanted me to do."

"And that was?"

"I performed oral sex on him."

"Did you try to refuse?'

"He was too strong. I was scared. I thought maybe if I did this one thing for him, then he would leave me alone and I could get away."

"Then what happened?"

"He was pushing my head down so hard, I gagged. He got mad. He said I wasn't doing it right. He threw me on the floor and I thought he was going to rape me. I don't know what happened, I just lost it. I started kicking. I think I might have screamed. He grabbed my foot and he was coming at me. So I kicked and caught him somewhere, I don't know where. He yelled "You bitch," and let go. I got up and ran out of the room. That's the last time I saw him until the deposition."

She took in another deep breath and let it out slowly.

"What about that e-book you had brought? Do you know what happened to that?"

She shook her head. "I forgot it. I never saw it again."

There was a stirring in the jury box. It could have been anything. Someone taking off her sweater or someone reacting to the lost e-book.

"You testified at your deposition that you heard laughter coming from the bedroom."

"I didn't know anyone else was there. I thought we were alone. But apparently there was some kind of orgy going on in the bedroom. I heard girls laughing. They sounded young."

I waited for an objection from Frank, but it didn't come.

"Were you aware that Mr. Cleville had planned to host a party after the investor meeting?"

"I was not."

"Do you know who attended the party?"

"I couldn't tell you. I never saw any of them."

"After you ran out of the suite, what did you do?"

"I locked myself in my room again. I was trying to figure out what to do next. He had been drinking. Maybe he wouldn't remember what happened. I was thinking about whether I should quit my job and if I did, how would I explain it when I looked for work. I worried about what he would tell potential employers about me."

"Did you come to a decision?"

"I didn't have time. Around five A.M., two hotel security guys knocked on my door and said they were instructed to escort me from the hotel, and I was no longer employed by Crown Productions. They stayed in the room while I packed. They went with me down the elevator and out of the hotel. Then they left me standing there on the sidewalk."

"No further questions. Thank you, Ms. Navarre." I took my time as I collected my trial book, stickies, highlighters, pens, and moved them over to counsel table, to give Josephine a breather before cross-examination started.

As I turned toward my table, I caught Mickey's eye. She blinked at me slowly, an acknowledgment. Josephine's testimony would be the bones of her story.

Chapter Thirty

FRANK TOOK MY PLACE at the lectern with legal pad and pen. I pushed my chair back from counsel table—ostensibly to cross my legs, but in truth, to keep an eye on Cleville.

"Ms. Navarre, let's be clear about this, shall we? What you described here is a criminal act, yet you never called the police. Why didn't you?"

"I was confused. I mean, I didn't realize at the time it was a crime because it wasn't a 'rape' rape. It's not like he dragged me off the street."

Cleville lifted a hand as if to say "See? It wasn't rape." A number of jurors tilted their heads in his direction. Cleville was effectively testifying through gestures and snorts. I could do little to keep him from acting out, so I focused on Josephine, hoping to guide their attention to her. He would have his chance to tell his side of the story when he was on the stand under oath.

"You mean it wasn't a stranger attack?" Frank asked.

"That's right."

"And, in fact, you were never raped, were you?"

"If you mean sexual intercourse, no, but—"

"You had known Mr. Cleville for several months before this night?"

I could have objected. She should have been allowed to finish her answer. But if I protected her, the jury might conclude I was shielding her from telling the truth. Josephine was a strong woman. I had to give her a chance to prove it.

She faced the ceiling while she appeared to calculate how long she had known Cleville. "I had started working for Crown about six months before."

"You had been in his hotel suite numerous times before that night, is that correct?"

"Yes."

"In fact, too many times to count?"

She hesitated. "That's where he worked. I was his assistant. I had to be there."

Frank pointed at Ian Napier, who tapped on a keyboard. A photograph lit up the screen: a picture of Josephine in her little black dress, standing next to Cleville with his arm around her waist.

"Defendant's Exhibit A. Can you identify this photograph for us, Ms. Navarre?"

"It's a picture of Mr. Cleville and me taken at some event. I can't tell you when or where."

"Perhaps we can winnow down that time frame. Do you recall when you purchased that dress?"

"In August."

"Why did you buy it?"

"Mr. Cleville said I needed something to wear for an event. He gave me his credit card and told me to go down to Rodeo Drive."

"He paid for the dress."

"That's right. I had just graduated and couldn't afford to buy anything that would be appropriate."

"So it's your testimony that a backless minidress was appropriate?"

"You should have seen what the actresses were wearing. My dress was pretty tame by comparison."

Trial lawyers call Frank's strategy "death by a thousand cuts." He would pick apart Josephine's story bit by bit, challenging each morsel in isolation, so that when he finished, the disassembled puzzle would flummox the jury. My job would be to put the story back together again before the trial was over.

"Do you allow all of your employers to purchase minidresses for you?"

"It was for work. He wanted me to go with him and I had nothing to wear. So the answer is 'no,' because I had never been to one of these events before."

"That was a pretty big deal for you, wasn't it? Big Hollywood producer takes you out for a night on the town."

Josephine's voice was level. "Like I said, it was an industry event. That's how business is conducted in Hollywood. You have to be seen so you can remain relevant."

"Was that what you were doing? Remaining relevant?"

"I don't understand the question."

"Never mind. I'll withdraw. Take another look at the exhibit, Ms. Navarre. Is that Mr. Cleville's arm around you?"

"It is."

"Before the night in question, had he put his arm around you or touched you in anyway?"

"You have to understand this is Hollywood. Complete strangers will put their arm around you for a photograph. It doesn't mean anything."

"But we can agree that the night in question was not the first night Mr. Cleville touched you, is that right?"

"If you say so."

"Let's turn back to the night in question. You testified that you met Mr. Cleville in his suite, wearing this dress, and drank champagne."

"Right."

"Did you often drink alcohol with Mr. Cleville?"

"Not often, but there were times it was expected. I couldn't say no. I was afraid of losing my job."

"So in order to stay in Mr. Cleville's good graces, in hopes for a promotion within his production company, and in the hopes that he would advance your movie career, you agreed to meet him, alone, in his hotel suite, wearing this dress, for champagne?"

"That's not what happened. You make it sound like I was trying to seduce him. I was just doing my job. He told me to come to the suite first and then we would go meet his investors."

"You testified that Mr. Cleville put his hand on you as you entered the bar, but you didn't object."

"Like I said, I couldn't. We were in public. I didn't dare embarrass him. I was afraid of losing my job."

"And you testified that when he put his arm on your thigh, you didn't remove it."

"I was afraid that someone would see."

"But if no one saw Mr. Cleville put his hand on your thigh, why would anyone notice you removing it?"

Josephine's eyes widened. Cleville gave a small victory punch. Ian Napier guided Cleville's arm back down to the table.

I wasn't worried. In practice, we had anticipated Frank would make this point.

"I didn't know if anyone did or didn't see it. But I was afraid if they saw me move his hand, he would get mad at me."

"And you'd lose your job."

"That's right."

"And you claim that he gave you bruises?"

"He *did* put those bruises on my leg." Josephine's voice was strident. The cross-examination was beginning to unnerve her. But I had to let her defend herself for as long as she could.

"But those pictures were taken, what—one day, two days, after the meeting?"

"So what?"

"Do you have anyone who will testify those bruises were not on your leg before the meeting?"

"No." She drew the word out in her southern California drawl.

"Do you have anyone who will testify they saw the bruises forming immediately after you left the meeting?"

Her face was deadpan. "No. I was alone in my hotel room. No one saw my leg until they took pictures in my attorney's office."

"So you have no one who can corroborate that you did not cause those bruises yourself?"

At this, Cleville's head whipped from Napier to Ken Vincent as if to say "Aha!"

"You're just going to have to trust me."

"Because you're telling the truth."

"That's right."

"Like you were telling the truth when you excused yourself from the table that night, saying you had to go to the ladies' room?"

"I wanted to get away from him. That's why I said that."

"It wasn't true, was it?"

When she answered, her voice sounded small. "No."

I scooted forward in my chair, ready to stand up and make an objection.

"And like you were telling the truth when you told him that you had spilled champagne on your dress?"

"Like I said, I didn't want him to be mad at me."

"So you can agree we have established that you are not always truthful, correct?"

"If that's how you see it."

"And we can agree that you are at times untruthful when it suits you."

"I was trying to save my job."

"And now that you have been fired from your job, you expect the jury to believe that now you're telling the truth to them?"

Josephine's face became stony. I imagined she was groping for a pithy comeback but was forced to edit out swear words in deference to the judge and jury.

I stood. "Objection. Counsel is badgering the witness."

The judge scowled at me. "Badgering the witness" was not a proper objection. Some TV writer had made it up. I wanted to give Josephine a moment to breathe.

To my surprise, the judge said, "Move on, Mr. Gould. Ask another question."

Frank tapped his pen on the lectern. "Which brings me back to the question, if you're telling the truth, why didn't you call the police?"

Josephine leaned into the microphone. "Because I didn't understand that it was a crime."

Frank scowled. "But you do now, is that correct?"

"Yes."

"And at some point before you took the stand in this trial, you came to understand that the events you claimed occurred might be criminal."

"I don't see what you're getting at."

"Yet you never, not from that day to this, reported these events to the police."

Josephine looked at me with doubt in her eyes. Frank had gotten to her. She was wondering why I hadn't reported her assault to the police, and whether I had made a serious mistake that would cost her this case.

"It never occurred to me to call the police."

"But it occurred to you to hire an attorney."

"The thing was, there was this story on the evening news just the night before about this big court case. When I was standing there on the sidewalk in front of the hotel, I didn't know what to do. I remembered seeing that story, so I thought I should call the reporter and see if she could help me."

"That reporter is Mickey Wong, who is sitting in the back of this courtroom. Is that right?"

"Yes."

"Is she doing a story on this trial?"

"I don't know, you'd have to ask her." I hadn't talked to Josephine about Mickey.

"Objection!" I was on my feet.

The judge was curious. "Grounds?"

"The press has a constitutional right to attend public proceedings, Your Honor. If Mr. Gould believes that there is something illegal with Ms. Wong's attendance, then he should make his concerns known and we can have her employer's attorney appear and respond."

Every trial attorney is afraid of lawyers who represent the press. They don't negotiate and they are only happy to take the case up to the US Supreme Court where, more likely than not, they will win.

Cleville was plucking at Frank's sleeve again. Frank said, "I withdraw the question."

"Objection sustained," the judge said. "Go on to your next question, Mr. Gould."

"So let me get this straight. You saw a news story about a sensational sexual harassment trial. Then you put on your little black dress, went to Mr. Cleville's suite, drank champagne with him, went to a bar with him and drank some more, lied about where you were going next, disappeared, and the very next day, you hired Ms. Gould to file a multimillion dollar sexual harassment suit against your employer."

"It wasn't like that! He fired me. He fired me because I wouldn't have sex with him."

"But, according to your testimony, you did have sex with him. The act you described is sexual, is that right?"

"You're making it sound like I made this all up! I am telling the truth. This is precisely what happened. He forced me to do that thing and then he tried to rape me. So I ran away. And the next morning he fired me."

I caught the judge's eye and let him see me glance at the clock on the wall.

"I see it's time for a morning recess," the judge said as he stood. "We shall reconvene in fifteen minutes."

THE BREAK WAS JUST long enough for everyone to go to the restroom. Mickey followed us out to the hallway, notepad in hand. I shook my head. Now wasn't the time for a quote. I needed a moment alone with my client.

We went to the ladies' room, where I stood with Josephine at the sink while she repaired her make-up.

"I shouldn't have worn mascara," she said.

"Sorry. I didn't warn you. I wear waterproof."

Looking at me in the mirror's reflection, she gave me a wan smile.

"You're doing great. He's almost finished."

"And then I'm done?"

"And then Ken Vincent gets to cross-examine you."

She paused her efforts, holding up the tube of lip gloss she was about to apply. "Why?"

"Because he represents Crown Productions."

"Christ, will this never end?"

"Soon," I said. "I promise. Remember, don't let them push you. If you need a moment to collect your answer, just breathe."

"What's this thing about calling the police? Why didn't you tell me?"

"It wouldn't have mattered if you had, Josephine. I used to prosecute these cases and I know. They wouldn't have charged Cleville because you didn't have any corroboration. By the time you got to my office, you had brushed your teeth and taken a shower, destroying any DNA they could have gotten off you. There were no witnesses. There was alcohol involved. Believe me, the case wouldn't have gone anywhere. What's worse is that Cleville would have claimed you were using the police to leverage a big payoff."

"He made it sound like I did something wrong."

"That's his job. He's getting paid to attack your case. We talked about this when we prepared. Don't worry: you're holding your own. And that's because truth is on your side."

Back in the courtroom, Josephine stepped into the stand. After the judge and jury arrived and we went back on record, Frank delivered his *coup de grâce*.

He dropped his voice and in a slow cadence said, "The truth is, Ms. Navarre, this is all about money, isn't it?"

"It's about justice."

Frank scowled again. "You didn't ask for justice. You asked for money. Lots of it. Millions, in fact. You think the jury should give you millions of dollars after you voluntarily performed a sex act for Reginald Cleville."

I knew she was ready for this question. Josephine took a deep inhale, faced Frank full-on, then exhaled. "I filed this suit because Reginald Cleville exploited me for his own personal gratification and then tried to destroy my career when I wouldn't satisfy him. I want him stopped. I want to make sure that he never abuses another young woman again. That's why I filed suit. So all the young women who come after would be warned. The world needs to know that Reginald Cleville is a rapist."

Cleville was stunned by her answer. He spun around to Frank, palms upward as if to say, "What are you going to do to fix this?"

"Objection," Frank said. "Nonresponsive."

"On the contrary," Judge St. James said. "You asked the question. You must now live with the answer. Are there any more questions for Ms. Navarre?"

"Not at this time, Your Honor."

Frank sank into his chair while Cleville chattered into his ear.

"Mr. Vincent, does Crown Productions care to cross-examine the witness?"

I did not dare look at the jury, but I sensed energy swell from them, wrapping itself around Josephine and me. Even if I had the jury, that didn't mean I had the judge. He could still destroy my case. And if I had the jury now, that didn't mean I would have them when they deliberated. We were a long way from a verdict. Anything could happen.

Ken Vincent took the lectern. "Ms. Navarre, my name is Kenneth Vincent and I represent Crown Productions. I have a few questions for you."

Josephine waited.

"On the evening in question, when you attended the investor meeting at the Mark Hopkins hotel, was there any other employee from Crown Productions at that meeting?"

"No."

"And just to be clear, there were no other Crown employees in attendance during any of the events that you described on that day besides yourself and Mr. Cleville."

"That's right."

"And did you inform any other employee at Crown Productions about Mr. Cleville giving you his credit card to purchase a dress?"

"No. I didn't think I had to."

"Was anyone else from Crown Productions with you when you worked in the hotel suite?"

"No one. I don't see what that has to do with anything."

"Thank you, Ms. Navarre. I have no further questions."

The judge's head jerked up from his notetaking. He surveyed the room. "Counsel, approach."

It took a minute for me, Frank, Ian Napier, and Ken Vincent to line up. We barely had enough room to stand shoulder-to-shoulder, and I was grateful when Ken stepped between Frank and me. The judge engaged the white noise machine.

"The pictures," the judge said. "I was anticipating the introduction of the so-called 'selfies.'"

"If I may, Your Honor," Ken said. "After deliberation, we concluded that the testimony regarding the selfie photographs was sufficient and we did not wish to offend the jury by introducing this salacious evidence. Although material, we were concerned the jury would wrongly punish the defense for showing these exhibits."

"We've heard from Crown Productions' attorney. Is Mr. Cleville in agreement?"

Frank spoke. "Yes, Your Honor."

"Ms. Gould, do you have any redirect?"

Anything I did after Josephine's last answer would suck energy from the room. "None, Your Honor."

"Very well, then. I will excuse the jury for their noon recess. You may step back."

Chapter Thirty-One

I WAS SLOTTING MY notes into my briefcase when Ken Vincent appeared at my elbow. "Do you have a moment?"

"Just you and me?"

He blinked in assent. He was leaving Frank out of the conversation.

I could imagine only one reason Ken would want to talk to me alone. He intended to make a settlement offer. I wanted Josephine stashed away so I could speak to her privately about it before we had to respond.

"Hey, Yolanda," I said, "why don't you guys pick up lunch and I'll meet you back at the office."

"Let's go somewhere quiet," Ken said, touching my elbow.

As he escorted me from the courtroom, Mickey Wong raised her eyebrows at us. She knew the signs of negotiations.

"Later," I mouthed.

Ken and I went down the hall to the small conference room. I leaned a hip against the table, tired of sitting and tired of standing. "What's up?"

"First, I want to extend my condolences about your mother. She was a fine lady and was very kind to me when I was an associate."

"Thanks. You were at the funeral, weren't you? I saw you at the church."

"I was in town. I visit from time to time to see friends." He took a deep breath. "So let's get down to business. I have been authorized to extend a settlement offer. Before we talk numbers, I think you should know where my client, Crown Productions, is coming from. There's no evidence tying Cleville's actions to the corporation."

"You're joking, right? He's the chief executive officer. He's the largest stockholder. He is Crown Productions."

"Not quite. If you take a look at our corporate structure, you'll see that Crown is a separate entity, governed by an independent board of directors. While Mr. Cleville is on the board, he is just one director. And while he owns more stock than anyone else, he does not have the majority of shares. He only owns forty per cent of the company. The other directors can outvote him."

My research had turned up that Crispin, his brother, owned twenty per cent of the stock. By combining the Clevilles' shares, they were able to dominate Crown Productions. But without his brother's support, Reginald had no power.

"Crispin would need to join the other directors if they were to stage a coup."

"As I said, the Board held a vote and authorized me to make this settlement offer. There's another point that needs to be made. As Chief Executive Officer, Reginald Cleville is just another employee. Crown has a strict sexual harassment policy. There is a protocol for filing these claims, of which Ms. Navarre never availed herself. There was no way for the Board to know what was going on."

"A sexual harassment policy that no one knows about and no one is trained on."

"It's in the employee handbook."

"So what? Who reads that stuff? Can you even show that she was given a copy of this handbook?"

"Crown's procedure is to give every employee a copy of the handbook when they're hired."

"So that would be 'no.' You have no one who can definitely state that she or he gave Josephine Navarre a copy of the handbook, or that she or he informed my client about this secret sexual harassment policy. What good does it do if it's just a piece of paper stuck in a drawer?"

Vincent sighed deeply. "What matters is that you can't tie Crown to this case. You don't have the evidence. Regardless, my client is sensitive to the possibility of a runaway jury and cognizant that it is the deep pocket in this case. It would like to bring its participation to an end. So I'm authorized to offer your client the sum of one hundred thousand dollars in full settlement for her claims against Crown Productions."

"And just to be clear, this doesn't include Reginald Cleville."

"Mr. Cleville would not be included. Your claims would go forward against him."

"Thanks, Ken. I'll inform my client and let you know what she says."

As I pushed myself off the table, he said, "But."

"But?"

"We need an answer before court resumes this afternoon. The offer expires at that time."

"That's not enough time to digest it and come to a decision."

"Sorry, Maureen. It's the best I can do. Take it or leave it. Here's something you need to understand. At the conclusion of your case, I'm going to argue a motion to dismiss Crown Productions, and my client is confident that Judge St. James will let us go. After that happens, we have no incentive to come to the table."

▼

WHEN I ARRIVED AT the office, lunch was spread out on the conference table, but no one was eating. They were waiting for me.

Without speaking I sat down at the head of the table and took a giant, very unladylike, bite out of my turkey croissant. The others dived into their food. When I had enough food inside me to kill my hunger pangs, I said, "Okay, now I can talk."

"What did Ken Vincent want?" Yolanda asked.

"He has a settlement offer. One hundred thousand dollars."

"Is that all?" Josephine asked.

"He wants to see how little you'll take," I said. "The thing is, we don't know what's going to happen. Ken thinks the judge is going to let Crown Productions out of the case because we can't show that anyone other than Cleville knew or should have known that he was harassing you. He's going to ask for the dismissal this afternoon. If he's right, and the judge lets his client out, we won't see any money from Crown."

"What if he's wrong?"

"If the judge denies his motion, and if the jury is riled up enough, we could end up with a multimillion dollar verdict against Crown."

"Or a better settlement offer if the judge keeps his client in, right?" Quinn asked.

"Exactly," I said.

"I don't get why it matters who the judgment is against, as long as we win," Josephine said.

"It matters because Cleville sank all his money into the production company. He lives extravagantly, but he actually doesn't own anything. All he gets is a salary. We could win a zillion dollars against him and see very little money. It also matters because if we let Crown out now, Amber and Valerie won't go on the stand. Valerie's story, especially, is identical to yours. If they testify, it shows that Cleville was a serial predator and because Crown Productions settled with them, the Board of Directors knew it. But Amber and

Valerie's testimony is only relevant to prove that Crown knew what was going on. The judge would never allow their evidence if Crown was dismissed because as to Cleville, it is character evidence and inadmissible."

"But it's true. He is a serial predator."

"I can't change the evidentiary rules. I can only work around them as best I can."

Josephine put her fork down. "So they only want to give me a hundred thousand. That's all I'm worth to them. It's like he's getting away with it."

"I get it. It's a nuisance offer. They figure that is how much it would cost them to finish the trial, even if they win, and then defend an appeal. The thing is, that's how the law works. The only way you're going to get a lot of money is if we win huge against Crown Productions."

"And now you're saying we can't. After all this time, violation, loss of my job, my career, I walk away with nothing."

"Okay, first off, a hundred grand is not nothing. Before you reject this offer, you need to understand that this may be your last chance to get any money. The trial could go sideways on us at any minute. Second, I'm telling you what Ken said because I have an ethical obligation to explain it to you."

Josephine put the lid back on her salad and pushed it away. "But the other girls, Valerie and Amber. They're testifying today, right? Shouldn't that matter to him?"

I swallowed the food that was in my mouth and washed it down with coffee. "That's why he wants us to take or leave his settlement before we resume court this afternoon." I was starting to wonder if Ken Vincent knew something I didn't. If Valerie and Amber testified to what they had told me, Crown Productions would not be dismissed.

My phone chirped from the depths of my purse. The caller ID said it was Jake. "Sorry, I have to take this."

I answered the call. "Hey, Jake, give me a minute." I took the last bite of my croissant and walked down to my office as I ate. I closed the door behind me and flopped across the couch. "Okay, I can talk now."

"Ajeti and Doda are cooperating."

"Anything good?"

"They know Crispin Cleville from his time in MI-6."

"I thought he was a diplomat."

He laughed. "Right, no. He was a spy. Diplomacy was his cover. He hired them for the movie company, security for events mostly. They admitted that they were in London, and in San Francisco when Eli was killed. We tied them to the rental car that the shooters drove."

"Have they admitted to either of the murders?"

"Not yet. They admitted they knew Eli. They said he was giving them information. In fact, he's the one who gave them the selfies. He took them from Josephine's phone."

I was stunned, even though I had considered the possibility. He had betrayed me. I had always thought I was a shrewd judge of character, but I was wrong. And I still missed him.

Jake interrupted my reverie. "How's the trial going?"

"Josephine was fierce. She's done testifying. This afternoon I'll put Amber and Valerie on the stand. Ken Vincent made a low-ball offer on behalf of Crown, take it or leave it. He's betting the judge will dismiss the studio because I didn't show that it knew or should have known what Cleville was doing. If I let him out, Amber and Valerie won't testify. Here's the clincher: I have to accept the offer before they go on the stand."

We were silent for a few moments.

Thinking aloud, I said, "If Ajeti and Doda testify, I could link them to Crown Productions, right? Crispin hired them to stop my case. It's an admission of guilt."

"Or the judge might conclude Crispin was acting alone when he hired them, so their evidence is irrelevant to show what Crown Productions knew."

"Dammit. You're right."

The timer that I had set on my phone buzzed. "Got to go. Love you."

"Love you too."

Back in the conference room, I gave Josephine and my team the news.

The color drained from Yolanda's face. "I knew it. They were following us. Maureen. How do you even know they were shooting at Eli that day? Did you ever stop to think you were the target?"

Quinn spoke for the first time. "But they're locked up now so everything's okay, right?"

I frowned at Yolanda. There was no reason to frighten my daughter.

Josephine dabbed her mouth with a paper napkin. "If I understand correctly, they killed two people to stop my case and, when that didn't work, they want to throw a hundred thousand dollars at me to go away? How cheap is life to these bastards?"

I had been so caught up in the whirlwind of the trial, the offer, and Jake's news that I hadn't thought about it that way. If I was right and Crown Productions, not just Crispin, knew about Ajeti and Doda, that meant Ken Vincent's client was willing to murder two people before it made a nuisance settlement offer. How cheap was life to them, indeed.

Josephine folded her napkin, placed it neatly by her plate, then reached for her purse and stood. "Fuck them."

▼

WHEN WE ARRIVED AT court, I expected to see Valerie Vann and Amber LeRoux in the hallway. I had originally planned to start them mid-morning but when Josephine's testimony ran long, I passed a note to Yolanda asking her to call them and let them know to be in court by one P.M.

When we stepped off the elevator, they weren't sitting on the benches. Before I had a chance to ask, Yolanda said, "I called them. Neither answered, so I left messages."

I peeked into the courtroom. It was empty.

Quinn checked the ladies' room. She returned, shaking her head.

Mickey came out of the courtroom looking for us, and I asked whether she'd seen two young women wandering around the halls. She had not.

I pulled Josephine aside. "If these two don't show up to testify, the judge or the jury might let Crown Productions off the hook. Maybe you should rethink the settlement offer."

"No way."

The defense team stepped off the elevator. While Cleville, Frank, and Ian strode into the office, Ken Vincent hung behind. I walked down the hall and he followed. "Sorry, Ken, no deal."

He patted my shoulder like a kind uncle. "Is your client sure about this? We won't come to the table again."

"I know my job. She's been advised, and has made her decision."

"I didn't mean to offend."

"Don't mind me. I'm kind of wound up. Trial does that to me."

"I understand. Sorry we couldn't work it out."

I was too. I had a bad feeling. I had spoken to both Amber and Valerie a few days before, and they were still both enthusiastic about going public. For both of them to disappear could not be a coincidence.

When court resumed, I was at the lectern. I had already handed Frank the new witness list Yolanda had typed up during the lunch break, and given one to the court clerk. Frank remained standing after the judge sat down behind the bench. The jury had not yet been called in.

"Is there something you wish to bring to my attention, Mr. Gould?"

"Your Honor, not a few moments ago, plaintiff's counsel served me with an amended witness list identifying two individuals heretofore undisclosed in this case. Obviously, her strategy is to sandbag the defense with surprise witnesses mid-trial. I strenuously object to this trial by ambush."

"Ms. Gould, any response?"

"Roman Ajeti and Aleksander Doda are newly discovered witnesses. They are employees of Alpha Inc, a security contractor used by Crown Productions. They were arrested as they tried to cross the border into Mexico following the drive-by shooting of my investigator, Eli Conroy. We have evidence that they were in London when a potential witness was murdered as well."

Frank threw his arms in the air. "Your Honor! Plaintiff's counsel cannot possibly be accusing my client of murder. This it outlandish!"

The judge held up a staying hand. "Take a seat, Mr. Gould. We shall examine this issue in an orderly procedure."

Frank threw himself in his chair. Cleville, face red and bloated, stared at him. Ian Napier took notes furiously while Ken Vincent leaned on one elbow at counsel table, a look of deep concern on his face.

"Ms. Gould, please enlighten the court. What is the anticipated testimony from these two newly discovered witnesses?"

"They will admit that they worked for Crown Productions, that they were in London at the time the witness was murdered, that they rented the car that was used in the drive-by shooting of my investigator who was leaking information to the defense—"

"Your Honor!" Frank.

"This is your last warning, Mr. Gould. Another outburst from you will see you sanctioned. Do I make myself clear?"

Frank sat back down.

"As I was saying, they will testify that my investigator leaked information about my case to the defense."

"Can these individuals testify to this from their personal knowledge?"

The judge wanted to know if they had seen or heard Eli talking to the defense. Jake hadn't said.

"I'm not sure if they had personal knowledge, or if they were told that by someone at Crown Productions."

"For what purposes do you intend to introduce this testimony?"

"The fact that these individuals were hired to spy on my team. Also we have a witness, Ms. Valerie Vann, who will testify that these individuals were parked outside her house, an intimidation tactic. We believe the circumstantial evidence will establish that they killed Sophia Lamar to keep her from testifying and that they also murdered my investigator to keep him from confessing to me about his espionage. We believe the evidence shows that Crown Productions anticipated a large judgment against it as a result of this case, and that its actions in trying to stop this litigation constituted an implied admission of liability."

"When are Ms. Vann and Ms. Leroux expected to testify?"

"I had planned to put them on this afternoon, but there seems to be a scheduling problem. They should be available tomorrow morning." I had no idea where they were or why they hadn't shown up. I needed time to find them.

"Is there any other testimony you expect from these two men?"

"No, Your Honor."

"When you say they worked for Crown Productions, whom did they report to?"

"Crispin Cleville, the chief financial officer."

"Will they testify that they had any contact with Reginald Cleville?"

"I'm not sure, to be honest."

"Very well. When would they testify?"

"With the court's permission, I would have to arrange for a video link. They are currently incarcerated in San Diego."

"When at the earliest?"

"Tomorrow morning, if the court makes a ruling this afternoon."

"You are aware, Ms. Gould, that you were allowed two days for testimony and this is the second half of your second day. You were expected to have your witnesses ready to testify. There is one thing this court abhors, and that is wasting the jury's time. Explain to the court, if you please, why I should not deem your evidence has concluded and allow the defense to begin its case."

While I had been speaking, Yolanda left the courtroom to check the halls for our witnesses. She came back and shook her head.

I had no choice but to move on. If I could buy time putting someone on the stand, then I could put Amber and Valerie on tomorrow morning—if I could find them tonight.

"The plaintiff will call Reginald Cleville."

"You can't do that!" Cleville shouted.

The judge pointed at Frank. "Advise your client."

Frank and Ian closed in around Cleville, both whispering furiously. He argued with them. "She can't do that. I refuse. I've got nothing to say. I thought you said—"

Frank stood. "May we have a moment alone?"

"Five minutes," the judge said.

Cleville and his attorneys strode from the room. When they returned, Frank remained on his feet. "Your Honor, we had no warning that Mr. Cleville would be called by the plaintiff."

The judge rocked thoughtfully in his chair. "He is listed on the plaintiff's witness list."

"Be that as it may, we have not prepared him for hostile questioning."

Ken Vincent stood. "Your Honor, may I make a suggestion that would save the court's time? Both Crown Productions and Mr. Cleville would stipulate to extending the plaintiff an extra day to finish her case. We suggest this afternoon could be used to allow both parties to brief the surprise witness issue before the court rules as to whether it will permit testimony of Roman Ajeti and Aleksander Doda."

Ken was politely warning that if the judge allowed me to introduce these two witnesses before he had the chance to stuff the file with two inches of briefing, the case might be mistried or overturned on appeal.

The judge buckled under Ken's threat. "Given the late notice of the plaintiff's amended witness list, fairness dictates the defense has adequate time to respond. Have your briefs filed no later than three P.M. The jury will be sent home. We stand in recess."

Chapter Thirty-Two

YOLANDA FAXED MY BRIEF precisely at three P.M. to court and to Ken Vincent and Frank's offices.

A few minutes later, we received the defense filing. No surprises. All parties had cited the same cases, arguing that they supported our opposing positions. I argued fairness dictated the testimony should be heard. The defense argued I was on a fishing expedition, hoping to find incriminating evidence without any reason to believe it was there; that I had pushed this case to trial on a shortened timeline; and that I had told the court I was prepared to go to trial, so I shouldn't be allowed to add witnesses in the middle of the proceeding.

While I had worked on the brief, both Yolanda and Quinn called Valerie and Amber repeatedly. Both of their phones seemed to have been turned off. They left messages, but no one returned the calls.

I dropped Quinn off at the loft. Although we had spent most of our time in the company of other people, we had been together constantly since she first appeared in my office. I thought a break might do us both some good. I was poor company during trial, distracted and short-tempered when my train of thought was interrupted. She graciously suggested she could do with a nap.

As I drove across the Bay Bridge to Amber's friend's apartment, Yolanda drove down to Saratoga to find Valerie. Rush hour traffic clogged the bridge, so it was early evening by the time I found the apartment. I buzzed the bell four times before a young woman opened the door a crack, a chain crossing the gap. She was sweaty from exercise.

"May I speak with Amber? I'm Maureen Gould."

"She doesn't want to talk to you."

"Can you tell me what happened today? I was expecting her to come to court."

"She left."

"When?" I was starting to feel sick.

"Last night, right after that guy came."

"What guy?"

"Some old guy. I thought he might have been some actor friend of hers from the old days, he was that handsome for someone his age. He came in. She talked to him for a while and then he left. Next thing I know, she packs up her bag and wants me to take her to the airport."

"Did you catch a name?"

"I don't remember a name, but she said he was a lawyer working for that guy you're suing."

"Older, like old enough to be my father?"

"No way. Your age, maybe forty at the most."

Ken Vincent. He had found Amber. She had just shown up in San Francisco a few days ago and I hadn't disclosed where she was staying. Someone must have followed her from my office—someone who wasn't Ajeti or Doda, because they had already skipped town.

Back behind Sunny's wheel, I called Yolanda. She was heading home from Saratoga. "Did you talk to Valerie?"

"She wouldn't come to the door. Talked to her husband, though. He told me to get off his property. He said two new thugs were sitting outside his kids' daycare when he went to pick them up yesterday. They followed him all the way home and then kept on driving after he pulled into the house. He'd never seen them before. Then last night, there was a call. You'll never guess from who."

"Ken Vincent?"

"How'd you know?"

"Because he showed up at Amber's friend's apartment. Right after he left, she went to the airport."

"What are you going to do now?"

"If Amber and Valerie testified, that would have proven Crown Productions knew about Cleville's history and had reason to be worried about a big judgment against it. Without them, all I have is Cleville and maybe Ajeti and Doda if the judge lets me put them on."

Jake called right after I disconnected from Yolanda. I was stuck in traffic on the freeway on the Oakland side of the bridge. There must have been an accident a few miles up.

His first words were, "They confessed."

"Did I hear you right?"

"They confessed to everything. To killing Sophia. To shooting Eli. To shadowing you and Yolanda in London. To breaking into your office. We got some more out of them about the work they did for Crown Productions and Crispin Cleville. Crispin was their connection. Everything went through him. The feds picked up Crispin at his apartment in LA."

"Did they give up The Duke?"

"Ajeti and Dodaclaim they never talked to him. They won't say who authorized the hits, but they admitted that Crispin hired them."

"If they want a good deal, why wouldn't they give up whoever hired them to do the murders?"

"Because they're afraid of whoever it was. And you should be too. Where are you?"

"I'm on the freeway, trying to cross back to San Francisco." I told him about Amber and Valerie not showing up to testify, my visit to Amber's friend, and Yolanda's visit to Valerie. "So when Ken Vincent made that settlement offer today at the noon break, he knew my witnesses weren't coming because he had already scared them off."

"I don't like this. Where's Quinn right now?"

"I dropped her off at home." The lane to my left was starting to move.

"Have you talked to her?"

"She said she needed a nap, so I haven't called." I was starting to get worried. "I'll ring her and call you back."

I called Quinn's number. It rolled over to voicemail. I called Jake and told him.

He said, "I'm calling Gerry."

Thirty minutes went by. I managed to squeeze my way into the fast lane just before it came to a sudden halt. The car ahead of me had stopped so quickly, I had to slam on my brakes. Barely a foot separated us. The same happened with the truck behind me. I didn't have enough room to pull into the commuter lane on the left or the slower lane on either side.

My cell rang. It was Gerry. "Hey, Maureen, I'm at your place. Quinn isn't here. There's a phone on the charger, looks like she forgot it. And there's a note that says she went out to dinner with her grandfather."

The car ahead of me moved a little, giving me enough room to jut into the commuter lane. I gunned Sunny and rushed up on one motorist after another, apologizing to each of the drivers in my head. The first and second cars pulled to the right, letting me by. Sunny flattened herself to the ground as I flew up on the next car, a red Mustang. He didn't move out of my way. I rode his bumper for a few seconds. If anything, he slowed down a fraction. He had to have known I was there.

A spot opened on my right. I took it and floored the gas pedal. The Mustang sped up, trying to block me from pulling in ahead of him. We were side by side when a Ford Fiesta ahead of me suddenly slowed. I pulled into the right lane, downshifted, and crossed ahead of the Fiesta and the Mustang, pulling away from him as if he was a scooter. On the bridge, traffic opened up enough that I could zigzag from lane to lane.

When I pulled up to the mansion, my father's Jaguar was parked in front.

I THREW OPEN THE door and ran inside. I stopped in the darkened foyer, trying to calm my breathing so I could hear. Voices floated to me. I jogged down the hall toward my father's den. The voices faded. I backtracked, then strode down the main entry to the parlor.

There was my father, drink in hand, ensconced in the wingback chair nearest the fireplace that had always been designated as his. Quinn was perched on the edge of the matching chair, my mother's. Between them was an antique drum top table with one crystal high ball glass, filled with two fingers of whiskey, and a half-empty decanter. The only illumination came from the dining room where the chandelier had been dialed low.

Frank was speaking in a quiet tone when I walked in. He leaned across his chair, his free hand was extended, and rhythmically tapped her armrest in emphasis to his words. He was feeling no pain. The folds of his reddened face, demarking jowls and bags, were softened by sedation. His right lid was almost closed. What I could see of his eyes glittered black in the half-light. The glass in his right hand tilted precariously and would have spilled if it wasn't nearly empty.

Quinn's hands were pressed together between tightly-clamped knees. Her face looked down, but as he spoke, she followed him from the side of her eye, smiling politely.

I flicked the wall switch on, flooding the room with yellow light.

"Mom!" Quinn stood and came to my side. I put my arm around her and kissed her on the forehead.

"I was worried," I said.

"I left a note, did you find it?"

"I tried calling your phone."

"It was dead, so I left it on the charger. I had no way to call you."

Frank noticed his drink was empty. He studiously removed the decanter's stopper, fumbled and dropped it on the carpet, then gave a little shrug as if to say, "someone will pick it up." As he poured, most of the whiskey fell outside the glass, forming a pool that crept across the tabletop to the edge, its shiny surface undulating.

"You're home," he said. "Good of you to visit after such a long time. I was just filling our little girl in on the rich and storied past of the Gould clan."

"And the Shaughnessys," Quinn said.

He threw an arm in the air. "I stand corrected. Maureen, you never told our little girl that my father was a justice. Not just a judge, but a justice on the California Supreme Court."

"The courthouse is named after him. I told her."

"That's right. A pillar of the community." Frank pushed himself into the depths of his chair.

"We have a long day tomorrow," I said to Quinn. "Time to go home."

Frank stood. "We need to talk about that, Maureen. I'm told you rejected Ken's offer. Not very bright of you, my dear. You don't know who you're dealing with. You don't know what they are capable of."

"Oh, I think I do. Sophia is dead. Eli is dead. Your two thugs are cooperating. Crispin Cleville was arrested."

He staggered toward us. I pulled Quinn in more tightly.

"You don't get it," he said. "You just don't get it. These are dangerous people I'm talking about. They aren't done yet. People have invested their life savings. If the movie doesn't get made, they won't get their money back."

"What people?"

Frank struck an indignant pose, swaying as he did so. "I'm not at liberty to discuss that with you."

"We're out of here." I reached into my pocket and pulled out my remote starter.

A millisecond after I pushed the button, a burst of light filled the house. I was looking at Frank when it happened. His eyes cut toward the street, then his face seemed to dissolve into whiteness as I was temporarily blinded.

My arm was still around Quinn. I felt her turning around in the direction of the blast. A boom thundered and I felt the first shockwave rolling through the house toward us. Glass shattered all around us.

I pulled Quinn onto the floor and covered her with my body. She was curled up tightly like an egg, so I knew she was alive. But I didn't know whether she was injured. Her back was warm. It felt dry. No blood. I felt her ribcage expand as she drew in a breath.

We were huddled like that for what seemed like a long time. Behind my clenched eyes, I saw red threads swirling in darkness. When I could hear again, the sound that came through to me was muffled at first, then sharpened. Car alarms up and down the street were screaming.

I sat up with one hand on top of Quinn, holding her down to keep her safe. I opened my eyes. When my vision cleared, I saw the walls were bathed in a flickering red light.

A car bomb.

▼

WE WERE BACK IN the loft. Outside the window, the sky was turning to the pearl gray of a San Francisco dawn. Gerry, wearing a shoulder holster, stirred a pot of hot chocolate on the stove. Jake was on his way home.

Quinn and I sat side by side on the couch, wrapped in blankets. The blast had shaken us, but we weren't injured. It had blown Frank back into his chair. He had some minor cuts from flying glass, but refused to go to the hospital.

The police said the car bomb had been installed after I went inside the mansion.

"What happened last night?" I asked Quinn. "Why did you go with him?"

"He showed up—without calling, but then he doesn't have my number. Someone buzzed the door, and I saw on the camera it was him. I let him in. He asked where you were, and I told him that you were working. He said he came by to see me and would like to take me out to dinner. I figured nothing was wrong with that. So we went."

"Where did he take you?"

"We never had dinner. He wanted to show me the mansion first. When we got there, he started drinking. He told me about being sent off to seminary when he was thirteen years old. His parents wanted him to become a priest because they didn't think he had what it took to be a lawyer. I felt so bad for him."

I used to feel sorry for him, too.

"Did he show you my room?"

"He never got around to it. He just kept talking about himself. Stuff I'm sure you heard before."

"Like?"

"Like when he proposed to your mother. How her grandmother, Elizabeth Shaughnessy, was against the marriage. She didn't think he was good enough, even though his father was sitting on the Supreme Court already and the Shaughnessy money came from mining. He said there hadn't been an educated person in the Shaughnessy family before he came along."

"To be fair, my mother went to Stanford, but she was the first woman in her family to go to college. They had no sons, and they didn't send their daughters to school until her. She had wanted to study engineering but the school said because she was a girl, she should major in mathematics. That's where they met. He was in law school at the time."

Elizabeth Shaughnessy had not liked my father, but she would not have held his profession against him. I wondered, not for the first time, if she had sensed something wrong with him. "Did he say anything else?"

"He promised to tell me about my father. But he never did."

Chapter Thirty-Three

I MUST HAVE FALLEN asleep on the couch. I startled when the door opened. As I oriented myself to the day, the last words of the trial I had been dreaming about were still in my ears. It was my own voice saying, "A secret is a prison." I knew what my closing argument would be.

The sky outside the window was pink. Quinn was cocooned in her blanket beside me. Gerry was watching us from the chair, arms crossed. He stood when Jake entered the room. "Look, man, I am so sorry. I should have been here."

Jake gripped Gerry's arm. "No apologies necessary, bro. You had no idea."

Jake knelt down in front of me.

"They killed Sunny." That was all I could get out before I started sobbing. It was a stupid thing to say. It was just a car. Quinn and I could have been killed. Innocent passersby, too. But the image incised in my brain was the black husk of what had been my car, still smoking. I had been stoic throughout the crisis, but once the emergency had passed and I knew my daughter was safe, emotions overwhelmed me.

Jake held me and we rocked for a long time. I could feel Quinn stirring beside me. She stroked my back.

It wasn't the car, I knew that. It was Frank abducting Quinn. He had been alone with Quinn. When he was drunk. During the entire drive to the house, I had prayed that he wouldn't do to her what he had done to me.

I also had a nagging feeling that Frank had lured me to the mansion with her.

"Maybe we should give the judge a call," Jake said. "Tell him what happened. You could use a day off."

I shook my head. "We have to end this. Frank said there were investors who were afraid our case will shut down the movie and they'd lose their money. He hinted they were behind everything, Sophia, Eli. He must have told them I would be there at the mansion last night."

He sat on his heels. "You're saying your father set you up to be murdered?"

I didn't want to believe it. "He could have told them he was going to get me there and have a talk with me. He tried to settle the case again. Maybe the bomb wasn't meant to kill me, but to scare me."

"It makes sense. Roman Ajeti and Aleksander Doda Demyan won't give up who hired them to kill Sophia and Eli. If professional hitmen are afraid of whoever hired them, these guys must be ruthless. Their investors have to be identified in the discovery Frank gave you, somewhere."

"We didn't get the financial stuff, remember? The judge bifurcated punitive damages from the main case. We aren't entitled to it until we win the first trial. Valerie isn't cooperating, and Amber disappeared. All I have left is Cleville, Ajeti and Doda. Then I'm done."

"Ah, forgot to mention something. Here's the thing about Reginald Cleville. The boys caught him trying to fly out last night. He must have heard about his brother's arrest. He's down at the station now."

"He's in custody?"

"He agreed to go in voluntarily."

"Right." Two detectives, and maybe a few uniformed police officers, looming over the suspect suggesting that all he had to do was come in to answer a few questions, clear up some things. He knew that if he refused, he would look guilty. Not really voluntary, but for this case, I didn't care. "If I don't put someone on the stand today, my case is over. They'll let him go in time for court?"

"I'm sure the judge will give you another day, given someone blew your car up."

"What about Ajeti and Doda? Will they testify?"

Jake shrugged. "You know how snitches are. The teleconference link is set up. Their lawyers and interpreters will be available. They won't tell you who hired them for the hits, but you could get some background out of them."

"They could flip any time and tell us everything we need to know."

"They could."

"They would if they hear about my car."

"Or that might be enough to scare them into silence."

"I can't risk it. We have to go today."

Jake pushed to a stand. "I'll make the coffee."

"One more thing," I asked. "Did the cops talk to Frank? What did he say?"

"Saw nothing. Knows nothing."

Right.

WHEN WE ARRIVED AT court, Mickey appeared at my elbow. She had heard about the explosion and wanted to know more. I told her we would talk about it later. I was focused on questioning Cleville, Ajeti and Doda, and didn't want to be distracted.

Court started late. After being released, Cleville had insisted on going back to his hotel for a shower and a fresh suit. He sat at counsel table, tired but dapper. Frank was erect as ever in one of his black suits, but the bags under his eyes were dark and his flesh loose at the jawline. Long, thin scabs crossed his face from the flying glass. Ian Napier was business as usual, as was Ken Vincent.

The jury was not in the room when the judge signaled the court clerk to begin recording.

Ken stood. "Your Honor, you may have heard there was a terrible accident last night at the home of Mr. Gould during a family gathering. Ms. Gould and her daughter were visiting when someone attached a bomb to Ms. Gould's vehicle and detonated it. As you can see, Mr. Gould sustained a number of facial injuries. No doubt, the attack has unsettled everyone involved in this case. We believe that it would be in the best interests of the parties to recess the trial for the remainder of the week."

"Is that the position of Mr. Cleville as well?"

Frank said, "Yes, Your Honor."

"Ms. Gould, what is your client's position?"

I stood. "Absolutely not, Your Honor. We're prepared to go forward and finish our case today."

"Are you sure about that? Frankly, Ms. Gould, you look exhausted. I don't know how you are still on your feet."

I felt unsteady. Little sleep, coffee, and the donuts Gerry had gone out for were not the healthiest start to the day. I gripped the edges of the lectern with both hands. "We insist."

"Very well. The clerk will bring the jury back in."

I tore off a bite of beef jerky while we waited for the jury. When I took the lectern again, I felt more stable. "The plaintiff calls Reginald Cleville."

The Duke shuffled across the well and was sworn in.

"Mr. Cleville, are you the chief executive officer of Crown Productions?"

Cleville pulled an index card from his pocket and held it with both hands as he read. "Upon the advice of counsel, I hereby invoke my right to remain silent under the constitutions of the United States and the State of California."

What? The Fifth Amendment allowed witnesses to refrain from answering questions that would incriminate them. How Cleville's job at Crown might be criminal, I didn't know. "Your Honor, would the court order the witness to answer the question?"

The judge shook his head. "Move on, Ms. Gould."

"Mr. Cleville, were you in San Francisco earlier this year?"

"Upon the advice of counsel, I hereby invoke my right to remain silent under the constitutions of the United States and the state of California."

"Mr. Cleville, do you know Josephine Navarre?"

He read the card aloud again. Cleville wasn't going to budge.

"Your Honor, may we approach?" I asked.

"Ladies and gentlemen of the jury, I realize we got a late start, but it appears that we need to take up a matter outside your presence. I would ask you to retire to the jury room until called."

Mrs. Templeton gave the judge a disapproving look. The two financial guys shuffled excitedly toward the door, cramping the space of the people before them, anxious to return to their phones. Norberto Bonifaz cast me a conciliatory glance.

The door drifted close behind the jurors, slowed by the hydraulic mechanism. After the knob snicked into place, the judge spoke. "Do I hear an application?"

"Your Honor," I said. "I request that the court compel the witness to answer my questions. At this point, we are trying to establish for the record that Mr. Cleville is the chief executive officer of Crown Productions and that he was here in San Francisco with Ms. Navarre scouting locations. This is all background information. There should be nothing remotely incriminating about his responses."

"Mr. Gould?"

Frank stood. "It came to our attention yesterday that Mr. Cleville's brother, Crispin, the chief financial officer of Crown Productions, was arrested for conspiracy to commit murder in relation to the deaths of Sophia Lamar and Eli Conroy. There appears to be some kind of allegation that these deaths are linked to this trial. Criminal law is not my specialty, and because of Ms. Gould's insistence upon going forward today, we were unable to consult with a qualified defense attorney. However, it is conceivable that if these allegations taint Crown Productions, Reginald Cleville could be vulnerable to prosecution as well. In an abundance of caution, I have advised and my client has decided to take the Fifth Amendment to every question posed."

"Ms. Gould, is it true that Crispin Cleville was arrested?'

"That is my information."

"And is it true that the allegations concerning him involve this trial?"

"That is what I've been told."

"Very well. Your request is denied, Ms. Gould. Mr. Cleville, you may stand down. Ms. Gould, do you have any additional witnesses?"

"We are prepared to call Roman Ajeti and Aleksander Doda."

"Those are the two individuals currently incarcerated in San Diego, your newly discovered witnesses, am I correct?'

"Yes, Your Honor."

The judge opened a file on his desk and pulled out a sheaf of papers. "I've reviewed the parties' briefing. There is a dearth of evidence to suggest the accusations against Mr. Ajeti and Mr. Doda can be linked to Reginald Cleville. Further, the plaintiff has been unable to show the likelihood of winning her case against Crown Productions. Therefore Crown Productions has no incentive to abort these proceedings, as the plaintiff argued, as it has little reason to be concerned about an adverse judgment. Accordingly, I find that the plaintiff's theory that these two individuals were actors in a conspiracy to intimidate the plaintiff, her witnesses, or her attorney, is not supported."

"Your Honor," I said. "The federal government disagrees. That is the reason these two are being held and the reason Crispin Cleville was arrested and why Reginald Cleville tried to abscond from the jurisdiction last night."

"Objection!" Frank was on his feet. "Mr. Cleville—"

The judge shook his head. "Let's stay on track, shall we? Why the federal government is investigating these individuals and the evidence upon which it relies have not been provided to this court. All the plaintiff has argued is supposition. Her theories are insufficient to justify setting aside the rules of court and procedure. I remind the plaintiff that she insisted on trying this case at the first opportunity and had ample notice of this trial date. She cannot now claim she is unprepared. For these reasons, I deny the plaintiff's request to take testimony from the new witnesses. Do you have any other witnesses, Ms. Gould?"

"No, Your Honor."

"Then I take it the plaintiff rests her case?"

The last thing in the juror's memories about our case would be Cleville's Fifth Amendment assertion. It was not the dramatic finish I had planned. I had scripted questions for Cleville, confronting him with Josephine's testimony, bit by bit. His entitlement and his outrage when challenged should have been the momentum that carried the jurors to their deliberations. Instead, his taking the Fifth Amendment felt like a punctured balloon sputtering to the ground. But I had nothing more.

"Yes, Your Honor."

"Very well, is the defense prepared to call their first witness?"

Still sitting, Frank said, "On behalf of Reginald Cleville, the defense rests its case."

Judge St. James' face registered shock. "Mr. Vincent?"

"On behalf of Crown Productions, the defense rests its case."

The judge leaned back in his chair. "Are the parties prepared to go to closing arguments?"

Ken stood. "Crown Productions has an application, Your Honor." It was standard protocol at this juncture of the case for the defense to make an argument that there was no proof and the case should be dismissed. Ninety-nine times out of one hundred, it would be denied.

"Proceed."

Ken took the lectern. "As the Court wisely observed when ruling upon the plaintiff's newly discovered witnesses, the plaintiff has failed to produce sufficient evidence establishing that Crown Productions knew or should have known that Mr. Cleville's acts, if true, constituted sexual harassment. There is no evidence that prior to Ms. Navarre's interaction with him that night, that she, any other witness or any other person lodged a complaint with Crown Productions, the Human Relations department, or any other employee. In fact, Ms. Navarre emphatically denied that she had made any complaints."

"Very well. Is there an application on behalf of Mr. Cleville?"

Cleville leaned in front of Frank, pointing to the lectern.

Frank gingerly pushed himself up from the chair. "On behalf of Reginald Cleville, we ask the court to dismiss the plaintiff's complaint." When Frank lowered himself into his chair, Cleville wiped sweat from his face, then said something into the ear of Ian Napier, who fixed his attention at the state of California emblem over the judge's bench.

"Very well. The court denies the motion by Reginald Cleville and grants the motion by Crown Productions. We will take a short recess, then bring back the jury for closing arguments."

Everyone stood. As soon as the judge left, Ken began packing up his briefcase.

"You're leaving me!" Cleville said. "How dare you! I'm your biggest client, you two-bit hustler. Who do you think paid for that fancy suit on your back? You know what? That's fine. You're fired."

Ken didn't respond.

Cleville continued to sputter insults as Ken skirted into the well, briefcase in hand, and came around to my table. "I'm sorry we couldn't work it out, Maureen. Good luck to you."

I needed luck. The judge had gutted my case when he dismissed Crown Productions. Valerie and Amber, my two collaborating witnesses, had disappeared. His Honor wouldn't allow me to present Olstop and Demyan.

It all boiled down to whether the jury believed Josephine.

Chapter Thirty-Four

I STOOD IN THE well facing the jury. Mrs. Templeton watched me, her hands folded in her lap. Ms. Chang, too. Norberto Bonifaz clutched the arms of his chair. I waited for the two financial dudes to settle down. They exchanged looks, then posed themselves with eyes on me.

"Secrets bind the shamed to the guilty."

Mr. Bonifaz's fingers dug into the armrest.

Having their attention, I began my closing, walking slowly back and forth, making eye contact with each juror, not lingering on one in particular.

"A secret is a prison. The parties to the secret, both the shamed and the guilty, are locked in a cell together. The fact of their shared secret creates an intimacy that only they share." I paused, letting my words soak in.

"The cell walls are built of fear. The guilty uses fear to trap the shamed with him forever more. Because the guilty know that if the shamed one spoke, her word would be doubted. And she knows it too.

"How many of us have heard the phrase 'and then she cried rape'? Everyone, I can see by the nods of your heads. 'To cry rape' is synonymous with lying. It means that a woman has resorted to, in the opinion of men, the foulest, most devious accusation. Within those few words is the implication that a good man's honor is being impugned, and he cannot respond lest he be accused of unchivalrous behavior. So because of his gallantry, he is the one who is trapped, he argues. He claims his virtue is his castle, but it's nothing more than those same prison walls where he keeps his captive.

"This lie has been so deeply woven into our culture that the phrase 'and then she cried rape' is part of our lexicon. The damage this myth has wrought was played out for you in this courtroom. When our society accepts 'and then she cried rape' as a truism, it cloaks a rapist in a fortress of impunity. Without so much as saying one word, he will be believed.

"When a woman reports sexual abuse, she is scrutinized. Her word is suspect. She is accused of lying, trickery. Her accusers seek a hidden agenda. Every woman knows this. And that is how his castle walls become her prison walls. They are not built upon the presumed virtue of man. They are built upon the fear of women.

"Rapists know this. They know that their presumed virtue will protect them. They don't expect to be exposed and when they are, they are outraged.

"As you have seen.

"They are outraged because she told. She challenged not his virtue—because he has none, he is a rapist—but she tarnished his honor, his appearance of virtuosity. The truth is an inconvenient matter to the rapist. What is important to him is how he appears.

"So when a woman as heroic as Josephine Navarre breaks out of the prison of secrets, when she tells the truth, she is attacked. You saw it here for yourselves. They accused of her of being a gold digger and an extortionist.

"Josephine Navarre was vulnerable because she had a dream. She needed to work her way up the Hollywood infrastructure to build her career. Reginald Cleville used this dream against her. Everyone she worked with and for at Crown Productions confirmed that it was her duty to do just as Reginald Cleville dictated, no questions asked. That was the expectation, the norm, and he pretended to take her under his wing, as a professional would mentor a protégé.

"Instead, Reginald Cleville used Josephine Navarre's ambition to lure her into his hotel suite. He spent months grooming her, educating her that his behavior in Hollywood was the norm—with the long hours, the alcohol, working from a hotel suite instead of an office, in his bathrobe. Every little act of his was designed to normalize intimacy even though, as she told us, she did what she was told because he was her boss. But that evening in the Mark Hopkins bar, when he groped her leg, he had crossed the line. She was afraid and she ran away.

"Later that same night, he lured her to his suite with the claim that there was work to be done. She went, as she had done so many times before, when his whim commanded. We know that there was no work. As soon as she arrived, he forced her to perform oral sex. He would have raped her if she had not run away. And he fired her. To him, her job was to please him sexually. Her job had nothing to do with making movies. And when she fought back, he threw her away."

I stopped pacing.

"The law is a clumsy instrument for obtaining justice. At the end of the day, there is only one way a jury can say 'we believe you,' and that is to award a money verdict. When Josephine Navarre came forward and testified to you about the heinous treatment she received, she broke out of that prison of secrets. Her reason was to make sure Reginald Cleville never traps another woman again. Our hope and prayer are that you, the jury, agree that my client told the truth. It has been my honor and privilege to represent this courageous young woman, Josephine Navarre. On her behalf, I thank you for your time and attention."

I took one step back, easing myself from the jury's sphere. As I walked to our table, I saw Josephine wiping her eyes. The judge had pulled himself close to his desk and leaned on his elbows. Ian Napier gave me an apologetic smile. Cleville's face was as bloated and reddened as I had ever seen it. Frank was slumped in his chair.

When our eyes met, Quinn's lips were parted. She glanced at Frank, then back at me. A frown formed on her face as her mind churned. She brought a hand up to cover her mouth, her expression begging me to deny her suspicion. I could not. In that moment, the secret that had shackled me to Frank infected my perfect baby girl.

I wished she had never found me. I wished she had never learned the truth.

Quinn stood and walked toward the door. A man sitting in the back of the room rose to open it for her. It was Jake. If he heard the closing, he must have come to the same conclusion Quinn had. But I had to tell him in person. He deserved to hear it from me.

I walked back to counsel table, passing behind Josephine, and gave her upstretched hand a squeeze. I gestured to Yolanda to go after Quinn. I had to stay and finish the trial.

Frank pulled himself to a stand to give his closing.

▼

"LADIES AND GENTLEMEN OF the jury, learned counsel is an engaging speaker. There is no denying that. But please do not allow yourself to be dazzled with rhetoric, for rhetoric is all the plaintiff has.

"Let's look at the evidence, instead. The plaintiff claims that she was subjected to a pattern of grooming, but she told no one. She did not object to my client. She did not report his behavior to anyone at Crown Productions. She stayed in her job. She continued to work for Reginald Cleville.

"The plaintiff claims that she was at a tableful of investors when Mr. Cleville slipped his hand between her legs and groped her so violently, she suffered bruising. But no witnesses came forth. No one saw the alleged assault. She didn't tell him to stop. If we are to believe it occurred at all, she admitted she didn't try to move his hand. When she went to her room, she didn't call anyone to complain.

"Then, she claimed that she was called to his hotel suite in the middle of the night for work. Again, no witnesses.

"And despite claiming she had been assaulted, she did not go to the hospital to be examined. She did not call the police."

Frank slammed the lectern. "It was not until after she was fired that she did anything. And what was that thing she did? She called a lawyer. She filed a lawsuit. And here her attorney stands before you and dares to equivalize justice with money. She argues the only way to stop *this monster* is to give her an award. How would enriching Josephine Navarre save the women of the world?"

He paused, then shrugged casually. "It wouldn't. You know that. No, what it would give her is a windfall. A wholly unjust result because if everything she said was true, Josephine Navarre went to that hotel room in the middle of the night for one purpose and one purpose only, and it was not work. If we are to believe Josephine Navarre, the only reasonable explanation is that she went to that hotel suite for the purpose of engaging in sexual activity with Reginald Cleville so that she could later extort money from him.

"Think about it! After months of working long hours, often well into the night, going to parties, drinking every evening together after work, visiting him in his hotel room, dressing provocatively—allegedly at his request—if this progression of events took place as she said, how could she not know, expect, consent to, and desire sexual intimacy from Reginald Cleville?

"And when she was fired the following morning, as the old saying goes, hell hath no fury like a woman scorned. Just as her attorney told you, Josephine Navarre cried rape. Now it is up to you to decide if her story makes sense. Is it reasonable? Is it logical? Is she telling the truth?"

The jurors studied him as closely as they had me. The two financial guys were sitting upright, riveted for the first time, as he spoke. Not a good sign. If they were against us, but three were for us—Mrs. Templeton, Ms. Chang, and Norberto Bonifaz—that left seven undecided. Nine jurors had to agree for me to win the case. It could go either way.

▼

THE JUDGE GAVE THE jurors their instructions and sent them out to deliberate, then he left. The court clerk tidied her desk. Frank snapped up his briefcase and stalked out of the courtroom, Cleville and Ian Napier in tow. Mickey Wong followed them out.

Jake opened the gate, stepped through, and put an arm around my shoulder. "You were brilliant."

I smiled gratefully.

"He's right," Josephine said. "You don't know what it's like to see someone fight like that for you. I didn't know what to expect, you know, we've had our ups and downs. But in the end, you believed in me. I can't thank you enough."

I was too tired to argue that I had never lost faith in Josephine's case. It was my job to test it from all angles, to find the weaknesses before they were exposed. I wouldn't have invested the time if I doubted her.

"You're welcome."

"What's next?"

"We go back to the office and wait for the court's call. You should come with us. When the jury comes in, we're expected to be back in court in twenty minutes."

"A word?" Jake asked.

Josephine took the hint. "I need to go to the ladies'." She picked up her purse and left.

"Frank and Cleville won't be waiting at Frank's office. They were picked up on their way out of court. They're going downtown to answer a few questions. Crispin Cleville talked all night long. They couldn't shut him up if they wanted to. Ken Vincent was snagged as he left court, too."

"Ken?"

He took my hand and led me to one of the pews in the center of the courtroom.

"Crispin named the secret investor that everyone is afraid of. Proteus LLC. It's a corporation formed recently in California for the purpose of making investments. Frank is the attorney who put it together, and is one of the members."

"Frank didn't have any money."

"We can't tell from the state filings how much interest in Proteus he has, or what his donation was, but he was definitely one of the investors and expected to see a handsome return when this movie was released."

"He could have embezzled from a client to get the money and he needed it back before someone found out. He stole the Rivera. I wouldn't have suspected him of theft before this all happened, but you're always hearing about some lawyer who borrowed money from his trust and couldn't pay it back."

"We don't think that's what happened. This will be difficult for you, but you need to know. The other Proteus LLC investors are several individuals known to the federal authorities as human traffickers."

My head felt wrapped in gauze. I couldn't connect what Jake was saying. "You mean like pimps? Where on earth would Frank meet people like that?" All of his friends had been bankers, investment advisors, hedge fund managers, business tycoons. If he was visiting the dark corners of San Francisco, surely someone on the police force would have spotted him. Word would have reached Jake.

"They abduct children in Asia and sell them to pedophiles."

"I don't get it. Where is Frank going to hook up with child traffickers? How would he meet them? His office is on the Embarcadero. He lives in Pacific Heights."

"Someone must have made an introduction," Jake said.

"Someone, like who?"

"Ken Vincent."

"What? You have got to be joking. He's the nicest one of the bunch. If anyone was a kiddie diddler, it had to be Cleville."

Jake shook his head. He waited for me to connect the facts.

Ken Vincent, with the movie star looks, was my father's former associate. He flew back and forth from LA to San Francisco, and would have had easy access to Frank. He had intimidated Amber and Valerie into not testifying so that the judge would dismiss Crown Productions. He kept trying to settle the case before I got Crown Productions' financial records. If I had gotten those records, I would have found Proteus LLC's investments in the movie.

Ken, all charm, but elusive about his personal life. Thailand, a place infamous for the abduction of children for the sex slave industry, was one of his favorite destinations.

"Frank's going to say he didn't know where the money came from."

"He can say what he likes, but he knew. He had to have known."

My breakfast was in my throat. I covered my mouth and doubled over, trying to hold it down. Jake jogged up to counsel table and grabbed a wastebasket. He put it at my feet and rubbed my back as I heaved.

Frank was fronting for pedophiles.

What had happened to me wasn't an isolated incident. It was who he was. He didn't travel internationally, so he must have met these people in San Francisco. They were his friends. When I was small, when he claimed he was working nights and weekends but didn't answer the office phone, when my mother suspected he had a mistress, he must have been with them. Abusing children.

I wasn't the only one. All this time, I had thought that Frank raped me because of our unique relationship, because when I had embarrassed him that night at the cocktail party, he needed in his own twisted way to dominate me. That could have been true. But the more fundamental truth was that I was convenient, just someone who was available at the moment. He ruined my life to satisfy an urge.

I told Jake the truth. While I spoke, I felt like I was floating. I had no sense of my body or where I was. I was not in the courtroom, nor was I in my bedroom. The story spilled out from me as if I was narrating scenes projected on a movie screen.

Afterwards, we were quiet for what felt like a long time. It struck me, sitting in a middle pew of the gallery, how much the courtroom resembled a church. The air felt heavy with the things I had said.

A door squeaked. Yolanda stuck her head in. "I've got Quinn and Josephine with me. We'll wait in the hall." The door drifted closed behind her.

Rapist, pedophile. What else could Frank do? Had he authorized my murder to stop this case from going forward?

"Whoever gave the orders had Sophia and Eli murdered. That bomb that was planted in my car. It was done at the mansion. There was only one person who knew I would come there that night. Frank had abducted Quinn to lure me."

"We don't think it was Frank," Jake said. "But we believe he knew who it was."

"Then who?

"Ken Vincent, again."

I snorted. The man my mother tried to set me up with was not only a pedophile, but had tried to murder me. It all fit somehow.

Chapter Thirty-Five

THE JURY WAS OUT for three days. During that time, Reginald Cleville was charged, made bail, and skipped town. We later learned that he landed in Qatar, which had no extradition treaty with the United States, and was once again living the high life trading on his title. Meanwhile, his brother, Crispin, couldn't afford bail. Reginald had taken any cash they had. Crown Productions' board of directors held an emergency meeting, terminated both Clevilles' services, and hired a new attorney to guide it through bankruptcy.

Ken Vincent posted bail. He was allowed to return to LA, and continued to practice law with an ankle monitor hidden under his tailored suits.

Frank was arrested and remanded. He couldn't make bail. I thought about visiting him jail, but what for?

Quinn was distant the first twenty-four hours. She spent her evenings in her room. I came home from the office, after waiting for a verdict all day, to find her sitting on the couch, absorbed in her tablet, playing games. I dropped my briefcase on dining table and went into the kitchen.

"Would you like a cup of tea?" I called as I put the kettle on the stove.

"Yeah, sure." She didn't sound enthusiastic.

I rummaged through the cabinet. "Cookies? I think we still have some chocolate chip left."

"Okay." This time her voice was closer. She had moved to the breakfast bar. "Any news from court?"

"The jury is still out."

"How long, do you think?"

"You never know."

We ran out of small talk. I set a plate of cookies on the counter. After the teabags had steeped, I put her cup in front of her and one in front of the stool next to hers, for me.

After I sat down beside her, I said, "I owe you an explanation." I kept talking until the whole story was told. She listened without interrupting.

"You should have told me."

"You're right. I should have. And I am so, so very sorry. I was afraid. I was holding onto that juvenile fantasy of playing on the nursery room floor with my baby girl. And when you appeared, I lived it out for as long as I could. But it wasn't fair to you. I was being selfish. I was afraid that when you knew the truth, you would hate me. And I'd never see you again."

"You were just a kid," she said. "It wasn't your fault. I could never hate you. You're my mom."

After judge's chambers called to say a verdict had been reached, my team gathered at the courthouse steps before going inside. Josephine in her black court suit, dreads pulled into a bun at the nape of her neck. Yolanda with the new purple tote she had ordered online. Quinn was wearing one of my suits.

Mickey Wong passed us, giving me an upward nod on her way inside.

"What do you think it is?" Josephine asked.

I honestly had no idea. In the end, there wasn't a lot of evidence. It all hung on whether the jury believed Josephine.

"I can't tell you," I said. "Either way, we did our best. I hope you know that."

When we entered the courtroom, I was struck by how lonely Ian Napier looked, sitting alone at counsel table. His client and the two attorneys he'd tried the case with were in jail. This would be a watershed moment in his life as well. Without Frank, his rainmaker, he wasn't going to attract new clients. And with his own reputation damaged—how could he possibly not have known what was going on?—he was unlikely to find new partners.

The court clerk was standing at her station as we walked up the aisle. She gave us a kind smile. She would have no way of knowing what the verdict was. But she would appreciate that our lives, especially that of Josephine's, would change forever in the next few minutes, and how anxious we must be.

I held the gate door for Josephine and followed her to our table. Yolanda and Quinn sat directly behind us, where Eli once had sat. We shared one last round of squeezing each other's hands, then took our seats.

Judge St. James entered. He stood behind the bench, arranged his robe, then said, "Madam Clerk, please call in the jury."

Everyone in the courtroom stood. Several minutes passed as we waited. The judge glanced at the clock. I turned around to see if Mickey was at her station. She was, device in hand, prepared to thumb the news to the nation.

The jury door opened and Josephine gripped my hand. Her fingers were cold.

Mrs. Templeton was the first juror to look at me. Her face was solemn. Her eyes scanned the room. When they fell on Ian Napier sitting alone at his table, they widened. She was surprised. The jury, if they had obeyed the rules, had not watched the news while in deliberations and had no way of knowing that Cleville, Frank, and Ken Vincent had been arrested. She quickly recovered and took her place, standing in front of her chair as the remaining jurors filed in behind her.

Norberto Bonifaz stole a look at me. It could have been conciliatory, I told myself. He would have been a hold-out and if he had failed to convince other jurors, he would have felt guilty.

Don't get your hopes up.

Mrs. Chang was right behind him. She looked tired.

"You may be seated," Judge St. James said. Clothes rustled and chair squeaked as each person settled.

"Would the foreperson please rise."

Mrs. Templeton stood.

"I understand that the jury has reached a verdict in this case."

Josephine's grip was crushing my hand.

"We have, Your Honor."

"Will the parties please rise?"

Josephine and I both stood again. She was clutching my hand. Out of the corner of my eye, I could see Ian Napier on his feet, staring numbly into space.

The judge spoke again. "Madam Foreperson, please read the verdict."

Mrs. Templeton slipped on a pair of readers that were dangling on a chain around her neck and held a page in front of her. "We, the jury in the case of *J.N. versus Reginald Cleville*, find by a preponderance of evidence that the defendant, Reginald Cleville, sexually assaulted J.N. on the date specified in the complaint."

"Was this verdict reached by a consensus of at least nine jurors?"

"Yes, Your Honor."

"Were you able to agree upon a judgment for damages?"

"Yes, Your Honor."

My hand didn't hurt anymore from Josephine's grip; it had gone numb.

"And what figure have you found Reginald Cleville is liable to Ms. Navarre?"

Ms. Templeton held the paper up so she could read aloud. "We the jury in the case of *J.N. versus Reginald Cleville*, find the defendant Reginald Cleville is liable to the plaintiff J.N. on all counts.

Norberto Bonifaz's face broke into a smile. Mrs. Chang looked over at my client.

"What did they say?" Josephine whispered in my ear.

"We won."

Her head was close to mine. She frowned in confusion, then mouthed, "Seriously?"

"Seriously," I whispered. "We won."

She fell away from me as she dropped into her chair.

I bent over her. "Are you okay?"

"We won," she said. She tried to pull herself back onto her feet until Judge St. James said, "You may be seated."

I don't remember much of what happened after that. The judge went through the usual motions of thanking the jury, then sending them home.

After the judge left, Ian Napier came up to me, hand extended, and said, "Congratulations. You earned it." He shook Josephine's hand. "Good luck to you, Ms. Navarre."

Immediately after the jury was dismissed, Mickey caught Norberto Bonifaz on the courthouse steps. He told her the thing that had swayed the jury was the e-book that Josephine had brought to the Duke's suite that night. If she had gone there for sex, she wouldn't have brought an e-book. It was obvious to Mrs. Templeton and Ms. Chang that she had gone there for work, and they had convinced enough of the other jurors as much.

A few weeks later, we had a one-day trial to decide on the amount of the judgment. Crown Productions had been dismissed so it wasn't required to produce its financial documents. Cleville had skipped the country. Frank was in jail. Ian Napier appeared on Cleville's behalf, submitting his client's tax records. Lots of money coming in. Lots more going out, if accounting could be believed.

The jury awarded Josephine twenty five million dollars. But the judgment was worthless. Cleville had spent all his money and had been living on credit. We could have appealed the dismissal of Crown Productions, but it was bankrupt. The bankruptcy trustee offered Josephine two million dollars to settle her claim, and she took it.

The real justice came via an interview.

▼

MICKEY HAD SOLD HER bosses on a series of stories about sexual harassment, focusing on three stories.

Josephine told her story while sitting in my conference room, as did Amber and Valerie. And I told mine.

I told the story of how, when I was fourteen years old, a man, a trusted member of the family, crept into my bedroom during a cocktail party and raped me. I sat on the bed in my bedroom in the mansion while I told the story. The camera panned to the door, to the billowing curtains, to my hands as I spoke, and to close-ups of my face as I explained about the emptiness I felt, the betrayal because my parents had not protected me, and the shame. At the time, I knew that something unspeakably bad had happened. Somewhere deep down inside me, I'd believed that it was my fault because I had wanted love.

As I told my story more often, the shame dissipated. It comes back again in waves, but not like it was. Less frequent, too, are the nights when I wake up struggling for breath, covered in cold sweat.

▼

THE NIGHT THE FIRST segment aired, we had a watch party at the loft. Everyone was there: Mickey, Dr. Howard, Josephine, Amber, Valerie, Yolanda, Jake, Gerry, Quinn.

Frank never made bail. He was convicted of a conspiracy relating to money laundering and disbarred. I packed all of his things, his clothes, his books, and put them into storage for him, for when he was released decades from now. Bank records revealed that he had blown all the Shaughnessy money years earlier, beginning when he bought his first Jaguar. The state bar discovered he had been leeching money from his trust account to support his lifestyle. After Frank's conviction, Jake made sure the Rivera, which the authorities had found in Cleville's suite, was returned to me.

Quinn lives with us permanently, sharing her room with Germaine Greer, the cat, who follows her devotedly. She finished her college degree online, took the law school entrance exam, earned an outstanding score, and was accepted to every school to which she applied—Stanford, Berkeley, University of San Francisco, and Golden Gate. In a few weeks, she will have to decide. My fingers are crossed for my alma mater, but any place Quinn chooses, I will support.

Yolanda, Quinn, and I scrubbed the mansion from top to bottom. Jake and Gerry did handyman things. I sold the Rivera painting to pay for a new roof, boiler, and electrical system.

On January 27, Quinn's birthday, we opened the doors of the Elizabeth Shaughnessy Foundation for Abused Women and Children, where we offer counseling, resettlement, and vocational training and placement. The space that I had once dreamt of converting into a nursery for Quinn became the daycare.

THE SUN, CENTERED IN what looked like an orange blanket, hovered at the ocean's horizon while the cloudless indigo sky darkened. One star after another began to sparkle. The flames of tiki lanterns lining the path flickered in a soft breeze. The gentle surf of the outgoing tide whispered in the distance.

I followed Quinn from the hotel. We each had a wreath of baby's breath in our hair and carried pink tulips, my mother's favorite flower. I wore Elizabeth Shaughnessy's pearls. She looked like an angel in the full-length white gauzy dress she wore, which matched mine. For the first time in my life, I didn't want to hide my scars, and chose billowy elbow-length sleeves. The scars were pink, instead of red, and receding because I no longer had the urge to scrub them.

Jake and Gerry waited for us in the pergola, each wearing linen pants and Hawaiian shirts. Yolanda, who was officiating the renewal of our vows, was in a purple caftan. Mickey Wong was there too, wearing a linen sleeveless shift. I did a second take when I saw her in a dress and she flipped me off.

By the time Jake and I kissed, the sun had disappeared. For the briefest moment, a green light flashed across the sky and was gone. The night was perfect, on the beach with my closest friends, my husband, and my daughter, drinking champagne beneath the stars.

As much as I love the law, my family is now my life.

The End

Hope You Enjoyed Implied Consent!

HELP READERS FIND THEIR next great read! Post a quick review here:
https://www.amazon.com/Implied-Consent-Maureen-Gould-Thriller/dp/B0BSWK
KG64

Author's Note

This story came to me during a Lit Reactor "The Big Idea" workshop. It was July, 2020, when we were in lockdown. I was suffering from wanderlust and had a lot of time to think about where I'd go if I could travel. The one place I ached to visit was San Francisco. I had just read Ronan Farrow's *Catch and Kill*.

Somewhere in the convergence of the events, my protagonist, Maureen Gould, was born. She's a San Francisco lawyer who lives in a condominium converted from an old warehouse not far from where I worked when I was in college. Her office is in Jackson Square Historic District through which I passed as I walked from Chinatown to Fisherman's Wharf on my last visit to The City. From her office window, she has a view of the iconic Coit Tower.

She zips around in a bright yellow BMW M-5. Yellow because that was the color of the Rolls Royce that belonged to the bigger-than-life lawyer Melvin Belli. He drove the Rolls to Sacramento when he gave a talk at my law school. We were as enchanted with the car as we were with him.

The title "Implied Consent" was inspired by the legal concept of consent. It's an issue that comes up consistently in assault cases: the accused claims that he did not force himself on the victim because she agreed to his actions.

Consent can take two forms: express or implied. Express consent would be words or writing, such as when a person signs an agreement allowing a doctor to perform a procedure upon her. Or a woman saying "yes."

Implied consent is not so clear. Often the accused will claim that the victim didn't fight back or say "no," so effectively gave her consent.

I have feelings, strong feelings.

The right to bodily autonomy cannot be neatly piecemealed, as if it is subject to an algebraic equation. There are a myriad of valid reasons why a victim might not voice an objection or fight back. Her minds, her hearts, her own history and her history with the accused, the reasons she finds herself in that situation, the pressures upon her, and just plain old fear bear upon her as she finds herself backed into that corner where, if she doesn't come up with a strategy quickly enough, it can well be too late.

For convenience sake, I use the pronoun "her" for the victim. But a "he" or "they" be victimized.

Secrets bind the shamed to the guilty. She knows that if she tells afterwards, the inevitable questions will be: Why didn't you say "no"? Why didn't you fight back? She feels like she is the one who will go on trial. Abusers count on her shame to keep their dirty secret. The very injury the abuser inflicts becomes the shield that protects him.

The only way out is the truth. This is the story I hoped to tell in this book.

Keenan Powell
Anchorage, Alaska
12 October 2022

About the author

Keenan Powell is the Agatha, Lefty, and Silver Falchion nominated author of the Maeve Malloy Mystery series.

Despite being one of original Dungeons and Dragons illustrators, art seemed an impractical pursuit – not an heiress, wouldn't marry well, hated teaching – so she went to law school. The day after graduation, she moved to Alaska.

She is the author of the Maureen Gould Legal Thrillers, Maeve Malloy Legal Thrillers, the Liam Barrett Gilded Age Novels, and numerous short stories.

When not writing or practicing law, Keenan can be found embroidering or studying the Irish language.

Follow her at:

Amazon: https://www.amazon.com/stores/Keenan-Powell/author/B0788TKBJW

Facebook: https://www.facebook.com/keenanwrites

Goodreads: https://www.goodreads.com/author/show/17008872.Keenan_Powell

Bookbub: https://www.bookbub.com/authors/keenan-powell

Acknowledgements

Bringing this book forth was at times painful and joyful, tedious and invigorating. It could not have been done without the kind and gentle support of my cherished friends Ellen Byron, Tracy Clark, Bruce Robert Coffin, Cynthia Kuhn, Jenni Legate, Catriona McPherson, Kelly Oliver, Hank Philippi Ryan, Janel Wright, and James Ziskin. Thank you.

A huge thanks is due to my daughter, Rory Bryant, who suffers with compassion and grace through my prattling when I'm lost in the pages.

To Ellen Clair Lamb, editor extraordinaire, thank you for saving me from myself.

And what a cool cover designed for me by Mila Book Covers! I love it.

Also by

Sneak Preview: The Millionaire, A Maureen Gould Legal Thriller

Prologue

The second hand crawled across the wall clock, then everything happened at once.

A door concealed in the courtroom's wood paneling swung open. A security officer pushed my client in on a wheelchair. As he was rolled in from the dark hallway, Tony blinked rapidly under the bright overhead lights. Handcuffs that secured him to the frame dangled from his bony wrists as he leaned forward to knuckle hornrims back up his nose. When he searched for me, he whipped his head around as if to shift his bangs out of his eyes, but his hair had been shorn. It was barely long enough now to cover the scar from the jailhouse beating.

I gave Tony a nod, then touched Granny O'Shaughnessy's string of pearls at my throat, my good luck talisman. "You're as smart as any of them," she used to say, "and smarter than most."

The guard locked the chair wheels, unlocked Tony's cuffs, and helped him to stand. Tony braced his hands against the counsel table as he shuffled into position before his chair. The guard stashed the wheelchair in a closet hidden in the paneling, then struck a stance a few feet away, easily within reaching distance, as if Tony, in his present condition, was any kind of threat.

I held the chair steady as Tony lowered himself and noticed the scar beneath his eye looked inflamed. When he reached for water, he miscalculated the distance, upsetting the half-filled glass. I caught it just in time and offered it to him. He grasped it with both hands and took a sip. The liquid rippled in his trembling grasp. He carefully set the glass down.

I squeezed his hand. "Breathe. You'll pass out if you don't."

In the next few minutes, the world would shift on its axis for all those involved in the case. Tony would spend his life in prison or go free. The victim's widow, who had sobbed through most of the trial, would see justice done – as she believed it to be – or feel twice cheated, first by the murder, then again by the system. The assistant district attorney's win/loss record tilted in the balance.

An old glory hound once told me that if you want to own the wins, you got to own the losses too. It's the difference between being attached to the outcome and doing the next right thing, he said. I wasn't so Zen – I wanted to win this case – badly. Not just for me, but because I was certain my client was innocent. If I lost, he would most likely die in prison sooner, rather than later.

The clerk strode in. "All rise!"

When I reached out to help Tony to stand, he waved me off. "I can do this myself."

We stood in sync, like well-rehearsed ballerinas rising for the grand finale. I shifted my weight closer in case I needed to catch him. Another door opened and Judge Han flowed onto the bench. She spun her chair into position and gazed into its depths for a long moment before she gathered her robes to sit. Once settled, she scanned the room, her face a mask of dread, only pausing for a slight moment when she made eye contact with me. "Madam Clerk, I understand the jury delivered a verdict."

"It has, Your Honor."

"Then please bring the jurors in."

As the jury filed in, the air behind me, filled with the anxiety of the onlookers, was so dense it pressed against my back. Behind the prosecutor, a paralegal comforted the widow now scraping at her reddened eyes with a tissue. Beside the widow stood her adolescent son and daughter.

Behind me was my husband, Jake, and my daughter, Quinn. They had a vested interest in the outcome. This was my first murder trial and, as befell lawyer's families, it had been the hub of our lives for months. To be more accurate, it had been the hub of my life. If I was physically present in the condo, I was mentally living in the case. I wouldn't hear Jake or Quinn talking to me. I had forgotten my night to cook or bring home take-out. I had fallen asleep on the couch still wearing my suit, my laptop charge dribbling away, surrounded by files. At one point, Jake thought it was funny to leave me messages written on stickies, stating things like "brush your teeth."

My most enthusiastic cheerleader, paralegal, and office mom, Yolanda Martinez, was in the first pew as well. The only person missing was my investigator, Eli Conroy. He should have been here. He had been with me when this case first started.

"You may be seated," the judge said. I held Tony's chair still as he lowered himself, then I glanced at the assistant district attorney. Before the trial started, she had gotten a court order that there should be no "indicia of disability displayed" to the jury lest its verdict was swayed by sympathy. Ergo, Tony was brought into court by wheelchair out of the jury's view and the wheelchair was then hidden. I was admonished not to be over solicitous. There was an entire hearing about whether Tony should remain seated when the judge and jury entered and exited, thus hiding his frailty, during which I argued the jury may dislike him if he was seen to disrespect the court. It was then agreed that he could stand and sit again but only if unassisted while the jury was in the room.

With my look, I dared opposing counsel to object to my holding his chair. She gave me a slow blink instead, then faced the judge. The verdict was in. Nothing I could do would sway them now. She knew it.

Now settled, the jurors stole looks at the widow, who now sobbed uncontrollably as she grasped at the hands of her frightened children for support.

"Madam Foreperson," the judge said. "Please pass the verdict to Madam Clerk."

The clerk walked across the room, took a document from the foreperson, then carried it to the bench. The judge read the verdict silently.

"Very well," she said. "Mr. Paredes, please stand."

Learn more: https://www.amazon.com/gp/product/B0CS9R5BFS